DARK
HORIZON

Also by James Swallow

Airside

THE MARC DANE SERIES:

Nomad
Exile
Ghost
Shadow
Rogue
Outlaw

DARK HORIZON

JAMES SWALLOW

WELBECK

First published in 2023 by Welbeck Fiction Limited,
an imprint of Welbeck Publishing Group
Offices in: London – 20 Mortimer Street, London W1T 3JW &
Sydney – Level 17, 207 Kent St, Sydney NSW 2000 Australia
www.welbeckpublishing.com

A CIP catalogue record for this book is available from the British Library.

Hardback ISBN: 978-1-80279-318-5
Trade paperback ISBN: 978-1-80279-319-2
Ebook ISBN: 978-1-80279-320-8

Printed and bound by CPI Group (UK) Ltd., Croydon, CR0 4YY

10 9 8 7 6 5 4 3 2 1

For Mark Smith, with gratitude.

PROLOGUE

How would it feel if the air itself picked you up by the scruff of your neck and shook you bloody, like a dog with its teeth in the throat of a rat?

Sergeant Colin Brady wasn't usually a man given to introspection, to think with that kind of depth. His line of work didn't offer much leeway for that sort of thing. Most days, Colin was nothing but business; busy being boss of his small piece of British turf in a foreign land – in this case, the security checkpoint on the road to an RAF base on the coast of Cyprus.

But the chaos unfolding around him had knocked something loose in his normally well-disciplined head; made his mind go wandering as his pulse thudded wildly and sound-shock rang in his ears. He had been gathered up by an invisible giant and thrown aside as easily as he tossed the end of a spent cigarette into a bin.

He had no memory of the transition, just the bone-shaking impact of *nothing*, and then . . .

Then he was lying flat on the ground, his bare hands and his face pressed into a layer of grit and brick fragments, with pain coursing up and down his body. He had no idea how he got there, a good six metres away from where he had been standing.

One moment he was outside the gatehouse, stepping after Lance Corporal Grey as the other man called out to him.

'Something's up, boss,' Grey said.

There was a car, he remembered, a rundown little Fiat, the image of the grubby orange vehicle coming back to him. *But it didn't slow down. They're supposed to stop.*

Colin tried to stand, and the pain punished him severely for his audacity. The front of his duty uniform was lacerated from top to bottom, the camouflage pattern of his MTPs scarred with dozens of shallow cuts that were steadily oozing blood. Splinters of metal and glass were lodged in his chest, his neck, his face. He looked as if he'd picked a fight with a threshing machine and come off the worse.

He sat up slowly, his head swimming, and gave a racking cough that brought up thick, black spittle. A settling cloud of dust and smoke surrounded him, a roiling, stinking haze that reeked of petrol and some kind of acrid chemical. The smell collected in the back of his throat, and he swallowed a retch.

Reaching up, Colin rubbed a hand over his cheek, and it came away sticky and red. His regulation short brown hair was matted, and he belatedly realised he'd lost his regiment beret. *And my weapon too.* He peered around, blinking, but couldn't find his rifle. *I had it on my shoulder*, he told himself, his thoughts slow and ponderous. *When Grey called out.*

No cover and no gun. He would be deep in the shit when his commanding officer heard about that.

Colin looked toward the gatehouse and the drop-down barrier across the base entrance, but neither of them were there any more. The barricades had been replaced with a mess of broken metal and concrete, and the gatehouse was a slumping heap of rubble. There was no sign of Lance Corporal Grey or the other two men who had been on guard duty that morning.

He tried to call out, but his voice didn't work properly, the sound of it weird in his ears. The smack of compacted air that had hit him had done something nasty to his senses, but some of his hearing was coming back. Below the ringing in his ears, he heard the sizzle of super-heated metal as it cooled, the crackle of flames. And sirens too, warbling on the wind. It was hard for him to get his thoughts in a line. They slipped away from him, coming in and out of focus.

With effort, Colin finally rose to a standing position, hissing at the jagged pokes of agony down his front. His sense of balance was all over the place and, when he tried to walk forward, he listed like a drunkard. He stepped slowly, one foot in front of the other.

Where the road out of the nearby town met the route into the RAF base, there was now a shallow crater of hot, blackened debris. Pieces of broken Jersey barriers and bits of the orange Fiat littered the ground.

The car. It didn't stop, he remembered. It raced straight into the barriers at full tilt, and that was when the mental replay in Colin's head abruptly ended. He'd blotted it out, hadn't he? Like how it happened to people in films.

The explosion. He could only remember it by the evidence it left behind, the experience of being in it mercifully wiped from his memory.

The lad Grey had been right there, yelling at the driver to stop. Where was he now? Was anything left of him? Colin cast around, straining to listen for anyone calling for help, but the rising-falling sound of the sirens smothered everything.

Vision fogging, dots dancing in front of his eyes, he limped on, fighting down another hacking cough. As he came closer to the crater, he could see shapes at the edges of it, objects that looked like clumps of wet rags. Bits of shredded uniform and butcher's block remnants.

Colin shuddered and his gorge rose. But he had to look. He had to be sure.

Who did this? The sad reality of it was that the base could have been the target of any one of a hundred different threats, as payback for offences both real and imagined.

Colin dredged up his fractional memory of the orange Fiat. He hadn't seen the driver, just a dark shadow behind the windscreen. He recalled briefings about the brutal potential of what the military called VBIEDs – vehicle-borne improvised explosive devices, or car bombs to the likes of the general population. Even a small car like the one that had rocked up today could pack in a few drums of a lethal, destructive homebrew. Common ammonium nitrate fertiliser, diesel fuel and a cocktail of chemicals, wired to a trigger switch in the hand of some nutcase 'true believer' aching to go out in a blaze of glory.

In a flash of destruction lasting less than a second, three of Colin's men had been torn apart. And for what? If he had no idea who was responsible for this, if he couldn't look them in the eye and know the reason for it, what was the bloody point of it?

He heard vehicles coming and took a look over his shoulder. A pair of soft-sided Land Rovers had rolled up behind him and men were climbing out, scrambling toward the ruins of the gatehouse to search for survivors. Other uniformed figures were sprinting down the track from the base proper, some with rifles, some of them in white coats carrying medical kits.

On the far side of the road, a group of locals were gathering around the front of a nearby café, which had been kicked in by the blast wave, intent on offering their help.

Then, down from the road to the town came a civilian ambulance roaring along at full clip, the light bar over the cab flashing madly. Tyres screeching, it skidded to a halt near where Colin stood swaying.

He stared at the canary-yellow vehicle and refocused. How had it got here so fast?

Despite his injuries and the concussion dragging on him, part of Colin's brain was still working as usual, the suspicious and observant part that made him so good at his job on the gate.

He stared at the vehicle and something about its livery looked off to him. From a distance it would have passed muster, but not from this close.

It was the letters spelling out the word 'Ambulance'. They had been hastily painted on. It wasn't right.

It wasn't a real ambulance.

Colin twisted about, sucking a breath to shout out a warning, but his ruined throat let out a wheeze instead of a bellow, and the effort of doing that was enough to make him collapse.

He stumbled and fell in a dizzy heap as the driver of the fake emergency vehicle climbed out and walked slowly towards him. It was a woman, small-framed with short black hair. Her face hidden behind a paper surgical mask, she was lost in a paramedic's uniform clearly sizes too large for her.

Colin kept trying to call out, but the hollow rasps that escaped his mouth were lost amid the constant keening of the sirens.

The woman's shadow fell across him and he looked up. Colin shook his head, reaching up to try and grab her, but he had no more strength left. She deflected him easily, and it was then he saw the cluster of wires going from the cuff of her sleeve to a slim metal tube gripped in her hand.

When Colin had been briefed about the VBIED tactics used by some terror groups, the one that had stuck with him was the 'second tier' method. In these scenarios, attackers would explode a vehicle bomb in a location where local first responders would be able to quickly arrive on site. And then, when enough medics, firefighters or helpful civilians were in place, they would detonate a second device to do as much damage as possible to anyone who had come to assist.

He felt giddy as he realised what was going to happen. The fake ambulance was twice the size of the destroyed Fiat that preceded it, and it could easily hold a half-dozen more oil drums packed with improvised explosives.

'No,' Colin forced out the gasp as tears of pain misted his vision. 'Don't.'

He couldn't see her face, but he heard the sneer in her voice when she looked down and answered. 'Hamid is right about you,' she said, acidic contempt dripping from every word. 'You are all weaklings.'

The name she spoke meant nothing to him; then he heard the click of a switch closing, and Colin Brady's world turned into a storm of searing white fire.

TWO MONTHS LATER

ONE

If John Price had known he would be dead in ten minutes, he might have spent his last moments differently.

Instead of swallowing down his burning anxiety and following the directions he had been forced into obeying, he might have acted on some wild impulse to fight back. He might have risked everything in an instant of desperation.

But Price had no clue how close he was to his end, and so the fear drove him, controlled him and stifled him.

He held on to the steering wheel of his Porsche Cayman in a grim rigor as it sped along shadowed roads, the English countryside a black blur flashing by. He stared blankly out of the windscreen, past the swishing wipers and the rash of rainfall speckling the glass. Driving on automatic, Price didn't look at the man sitting next to him in the passenger seat, with his one gloved hand wrapped around the silenced, nickel-plated semi-automatic resting in his lap. He didn't dare to.

It was early evening but the dull clouds overhead made it seem later. A pool of illumination thrown from the sports car's headlights lit the dark ribbon of the narrow lane beneath the Porsche's tyres as it bent right and left with little warning, thick border hedges crowding in from either side and heavy, stooped trees lofting overhead to meet above like leafy archways.

Price drove too fast, like he always did. Faster than his wife and daughter liked, and well over the speed limit. Once upon a time he had done it just to be contrarian, to do it his own way for once and buck the rules, but now it was second nature to him. A bad, ingrained habit he never thought to correct. And he had no need to, he reasoned. He drove these roads week in and week out, off from their home in rural Kent out to the small commercial airport at Ridley Hill, and he knew them like the proverbial back of his hand.

When he couldn't sleep, Price took his Porsche out in the dead of night while everyone else in the house slumbered in dreamland, and he belted down these gloomy, narrow roads as fast as he dared with the car's lights turned off. It was a foolish, juvenile risk for a grown man to take and, in this moment, with a killer sitting beside him, he realised how thoughtless he'd been on those dark nights.

Thinking about his wife Sylvie and his daughter Janine brought a faint sound out of him, halfway between a gasp and a sob. He did love his family, after a fashion, even if that was something he'd never learned how to adequately express. In his mind he played out the absolute worst scenarios his imagination could create about what might be happening to them.

The car's wing mirror clipped some overhanging branches with a *rat-a-tat* snarl as Price's attention drifted, as did the Porsche's driving line. The man in the passenger seat immediately reached forward and slapped his hand on the top of the dashboard.

'Pay attention,' he warned, each word like a whip crack, and Price flinched at the command.

The man holding the silenced pistol had a low snarl of a voice and an Eastern European accent that Price didn't have the experience to place. Densely set and broad across his shoulders, he had the build of a rugby fullback and a head of short, ash-grey hair thinning too early for someone of his age. His face appeared drawn and gaunt in the half-light of the car's interior. Cast against Price's slumped manner, a man who had once been a trim figure but now gone to seed, there was no question as to which of them was in the dominant role here, gun or no gun.

'Get your head straight,' added the passenger, shifting in his seat so he could glare directly at the driver. 'You know what will happen if you make mistakes. You know who will suffer the consequences.'

Price managed a wooden nod, staring at the road but not really seeing it. The last sight of his family was burned into his mind's eye. Sylvie holding Janine close to her in a terrified embrace. Panic and confusion writ across the pair's faces, accusation and dread radiating off his wife as the door closed on them. He could hear her asking the unvoiced question: *What did you do to bring this to our house?*

But Price didn't have an answer. He didn't know the gunman and his thuggish cohorts. And, at first, he hadn't understood what they wanted from him.

At first.

'Look, I can't take you inside,' said Price, at length, but his words came out in a dry croak and he had to repeat himself. 'Through the gates, I mean. You realise that?' He nodded at a laminated RFID card resting on the dash. 'The security pass is only for me . . .'

'You will stop by the perimeter fence. At the end of the runway. I will get out, and you will do as you have been told.'

Price took that in with a blink, and a brief thought rose. Don, the ageing gate guard at Ridley Hill, might be on duty. If Price could warn him somehow, raise the alarm . . .

'I know you are thinking of testing our resolve.' The man with the gun spoke carefully, cutting off Price's train of thought. 'Do I strike you as someone who does not keep his word?' He raised his other hand and drew a thumb across his neck in a slow, throat-cutting motion. 'If you disobey, I assure you it will not go well for the women.' Then he looked away, as if the conversation was starting to bore him. 'Follow directions and in a few hours this will be over.'

'H-how do I know you won't kill us afterwards?' Price stuttered, and his voice sounded high and reedy as he forced out the question.

'Obey and there will be no need for bloodshed,' the man replied. 'You will be the guilty one. You will take the blame. That will be enough.'

Price's panic surged and the words burst out of him in a cry as he shot a fearful look in the other man's direction. 'I don't believe you!'

His fractional moment of distraction from the road ahead came at exactly the wrong instant.

Exiting a blind curve, the Porsche emerged into a straight where a branching drive led off to a nearby farmhouse. Parked over the mouth of that drive sat the angular bulk of an ageing Ford 7810 tractor, half of the tall rear wheels extending out into the lane, adorned with the bright crimson triangle of a road safety reflector blazing from the car's headlights.

Price stamped hard on the brakes but it was already too late, his inattention and the wet surface of the road amplifying his mistake tenfold. The speeding car slammed into the tractor with enough force to lift the rear wheels, and the raw, punishing physics of the impact transferred the Porsche's forward velocity into a shock of motion that flung it sideways across the narrow road.

The car half-rolled and collided with the trunk of an oak tree, punching in the roof and destroying the windscreen in a torrent of glass. Branches as thick as girders invaded the car's interior, and John Price's end came quickly and completely as his chest was crushed in an instant.

The Porsche lurched and finally came to rest on its side, the engine roaring helplessly, the wheels spinning at empty air.

There was a moment of darkness and loss in the seconds after the impact, and when Matvey rose slowly from it, his first reaction was disgust. Warm liquid trickled down on to him, and he batted it away, his hand coming back wet.

The Porsche's anti-collision airbags had deployed, salting the air inside the car with powdery residue, and he clawed at the white mass in front of him, ripping it away so he could move. The harness on the vehicle's faux racing-car seats had kept him in place as it spun through the crash, saving his life.

But the driver had not fared as well. An ugly mass of damp, moss-sheathed wood pinned the Englishman in place above Matvey, and blood dripped in drools from his mouth and nostrils.

There was no point in checking on him. His eyes wide open, his expression one of frozen shock, Price was quite dead.

Matvey's annoyance came to a head. He swore under his breath, cursing the idiot for his carelessness in a string of gutter oaths, muttering every last virulent swearword in the Russian language as he worked the seatbelt fastener to release himself.

The latch let go and Matvey dropped against the passenger-side door, now pressed to the muddy ditch at the foot of the oak tree. He smelled rain-damp, hot oil and the raw musk of newly splintered wood. Could the car catch fire? He had no idea, but he wasn't going to wait around to find out.

Ignoring the pounding ache in his head and the shock of pain from his joints, Matvey felt around in the footwell until he found his silenced pistol where it had fallen, relieved that the gun hadn't been thrown out and lost on the road. He scrambled out of the gaping void where the Porsche's windscreen had been and into a gulley of ankle-deep water that sucked at his boots.

There were voices in the air, coming from behind him. He turned back towards the road, finding the shape of the damaged tractor and a barn beyond it. People were heading his way from that direction. He saw the glow of the flashlights they carried bobbing among the hedgerows as they came closer, drawn by the sound of the collision.

Matvey ducked low and moved off as quickly as he could, careful to stay out of sight, sticking to the cover of the ditch. If he was discovered, there would be too many questions and not enough answers.

He gripped the pistol tightly. Back in the old country, he might have chosen to kill whoever came looking and take his chances after the fact, but it was different here in Britain. The nation was tiny – too small for the brutal acts of violence his work often employed to go unnoticed. The local *musor* – the police – were not so easily bribed or cowed as those he tangled with back in the land of his birth. He couldn't just stride away from this with a swagger and a threat. There were going to be consequences; repercussions that would cost him real money unless the situation could be salvaged.

As he paced through the drizzle, he took stock and coldly dissected the problem at hand. Matvey had always been good at being dispassionate and clinical when situations became intense. It was how he had managed to stay alive this long, when men of lesser character – the hot-headed and the short-sighted – had ended up in the ground.

He retrieved a blocky satellite phone from the zip pocket of his black leather jacket and scowled at it. The antenna was bent and the screen had fractured into a web of cracks, but the touch-sensitive surface still worked. Pulling off one glove with his teeth, he prodded at the device, checking the clock.

We still have time. He didn't want to entertain the other possibility – that one fool's mistake might ruin the job that Matvey and his crew had spent the past week preparing for.

He had a certain reputation to maintain. It was the reason people paid him as well as they did. If word got out that Matvey could not deliver, it would not only be his bank account that would suffer. It would make him look *weak*. It would make him appear *fallible*. And that was a death sentence. There was no room for errors in a business populated by killers, thugs and predators.

When he was sure he had put enough distance between himself and the crash, Matvey left the gulley and cut across fields in the direction of a nearby village, using the steeple of a darkened church to orient himself. As he walked, he worked the phone and dialled one of the handful of numbers in the memory.

Stepan answered on the fourth ring. His tone was wary, his English slow and over-enunciated. '*Yes? Who is calling, please?*'

Matvey replied in their native language, quick and clipped. 'We have a problem. There will have to be a change in plan.' He described the situation and, to his credit, Stepan didn't say a word until he was finished.

'*That fucks everything*,' the other man said bluntly. '*The stupid bastard! We have no leverage over a corpse!*'

'Indeed.'

Stepan made a spitting sound. '*What the hell do we do now?*'

'The responsibility is mine,' replied Matvey. He came to a halt in the middle of the cold, damp field, standing amid rows of tilled earth and the beginnings of a potato crop. 'I will call up the line to the client. I will explain it to them. It will be their decision to proceed or to pull the contract.'

Stepan was quiet for a moment, and Matvey knew what he was thinking. '*What about the women? Whatever comes next, they have seen our faces.*'

'They are there with you?'

'*No. I am in the kitchen. Luka is watching them in the living room.*'

Matvey pictured Price's wife and daughter, sitting side by side on their expensive sofa, in the over-decorated sanctum of the dead man's home. Despite what he had promised, they would never have been allowed to live through the night. This simply meant that the timetable for their disposal would have to be brought forward.

'The kitchen,' he repeated. He had intended to do the work himself, but now there wasn't time. 'There will be knives there, for cooking. Use one of those. Do it swiftly.'

Matvey heard the rattle of a drawer being opened. '*All right.*' Stepan's tenor changed, becoming oddly calm. He knew that tone of old; the other man looked forward to what would come next. It was part of the reason he employed him. Stepan was a slave to certain base needs and, when correctly controlled, that made him both loyal and effective.

'Call me back after you are done,' he added, tapping at his own device as he started walking again. 'I will send you my location. Come pick me up.'

'*All right*,' Stepan repeated, and the ambience of the call shifted as he left Price's kitchen and walked back into the living room.

Matvey heard the first fractional note of a woman's scream, but the line suddenly went dead, and the only sound was the whisper of the fading rain.

TWO

'We're going to see it,' insisted George, and to add emphasis to his statement, the 13-year-old bounced up and down on his heels, tilting his head right back to look up at the early evening sky. Almost painfully skinny, the boy's lanky beanpole figure gave him an uncoordinated manner, but he made up for it with his winning smile and a boundless energy that could be endearing, if sometimes a little tiring.

'Yeah,' offered Alex. The boy's father tried to sound like he meant it, but the sideways look he threw at Kate said something different. Burly and bearded, Alex's rangy build showed clearly that the kid had not been gifted with any of his dad's genes. He carried a heavy box in his thick arms like he was a human forklift.

Auburn haired and not quite as slim as she'd like, Kate was a little taller than Alex, a detail that some men she had known considered a shortcoming, but it had never bothered him. He'd once joked that she had the figure of a showjumper, and while Alex had clearly meant that as a compliment, Kate didn't like the comparison. It made her sound haughty and a bit too posh and, despite her middle-class upbringing, that wasn't her at all.

She returned his questioning glance by holding her hand out flat and giving it a 'maybe' wiggle. George might not get his wish, but she hoped she was wrong.

Following the boy's line of sight, Kate scanned the horizon with a professional's eye, automatically estimating the wind speed and sky conditions. The rain clouds were blowing away, she had to admit, and in among the growing gaps between them she could already see a handful of the brightest stars. The howl of a passing police siren several streets away briefly hooked her attention, drawing her gaze away.

'Right here.' George stopped at a point in the middle of the end-terrace house's oddly spade-shaped garden and snapped out the legs of the tripod over his shoulder, fiddling with the screw fitting at the top. 'This is it.'

'Hold this, will you?' Alex passed Kate his smartphone and she flicked it to life as he deposited the box and set to work assembling the contents. The cylinder of the reflector telescope inside came together in quick motions, and father and son soon had it mounted and aiming upwards.

They had doused every lamp in the house and Kate picked her way around the plant beds, taking extra care in the semi-darkness not to put a foot wrong and crush something. If she did – and she had before now – Alex wouldn't make a big deal about it, but George's mother would, even though the woman hadn't lived in the house for over three years.

Kate covered the phone with one cupped hand so the glow from the display wouldn't ruin everyone's vision. On the screen, a live stream of the BBC's Six O'Clock news summed up the headline of the day, the faint voice of the newsreader burbling out of the phone's speaker.

'*The government's stance on the recent terrorist incident at Akrotiri remains unchanged,*' said the well-dressed woman on the little screen. As she spoke, video footage rolled, showing the aftermath of the attack that had taken place two months ago in Cyprus. '*In a joint statement from the Security Services and the Ministry of Defence, read in Parliament today, the Prime Minister reiterated their intention to act against these threats to the United Kingdom and its allies by using, quote, the strongest possible measures, unquote.*'

Kate's jaw hardened as she watched the replay, the viewpoint panning over the ruined checkpoint at the RAF airbase and the rifle-toting men from the regiment running past to secure the area. She pictured herself walking through that same gate, on more than one occasion. She knew it well.

Like a snapshot pulled out from another existence, an unwelcome flash of memory from her time in service rose up from the past she kept boxed up and silent. She remembered herself and Wardy laughing like drains over some idiotic joke he'd made as they wandered off base and into town, intent on having a pint down at a local bar called the Hamlet.

Kate knew if she let the recollection take on weight and shape, next would come the directionless anger and sadness, and she wasn't going to allow that. She stamped on the moment, snuffing it out, forcing herself to stay rooted in the present.

George was talking to her, and she realised she'd missed it. 'What?'

'I said,' the boy repeated, 'how much longer now, Kate?' He dropped into a crouch and fiddled with the telescope's eyepiece and finder scope, leaning on the optical tube to aim it at the right patch of sky.

'Almost time.' She forced a smile. Exactly on cue, the newsreader on the screen segued into an *'and finally'* story, talking about the British astronaut currently up in orbit aboard the International Space Station. *'Viewers in the south east looking toward the northern sky will be able to observe the orbit of the International Space Station in just a few minutes, so do be sure to wave!'*

George made a face. 'That's stupid. They have good telescopes up there, but he wouldn't be able to see us.'

'Well, we'll wave anyway,' said Alex. His voice had a roughened quality that, if Kate was honest, was one of the first things that had attracted her to the affable divorcee. Alex liked to describe his tone as 'smoky', which was tellingly accurate when you realised it was actually because of some smoke inhalation damage. A side-effect of his career as a firefighter for the local authority, he wore it with typically self-deprecating humour.

Kate looked up again. With impeccable timing, the rain clouds rolled away to present them with a cold, clear evening sky.

She listened to George as he called out some of the visible constellations and their component stars. 'What's that bright one again?' Kate indicated a particularly brilliant point above them, encouraging him to go on.

The boy gave her a dubious look. 'I know you already know what it is,' he said, with an eye roll. 'That's Polaris, the pole star. Everyone knows that.'

'Quite right,' she allowed, 'I forgot.' George's interest in astronomy was the only thing he and Kate had connected over, and she was determined to build on that foundation as best she could.

Alex was a lovely guy, and after they had moved in together earlier in the year, Kate was ready to admit to herself that he might be the one she'd spend the rest of her life with. But to get there, she would need to get his son on side, and that was still a work in progress. The boy was clever but moody with it, and that was hard for Kate to navigate. She'd grown up as an only child and, even in her youth, other kids had been a puzzle she had trouble solving.

'Okay, any second now.' She darkened Alex's phone and peered into the heavens.

Alex pointed at a pair of blinking dots moving from east to west. 'That's not it?'

She shook her head. 'That's the AeroNordic flight out of Gatwick.' She didn't add that it was an Airbus A320 on its way to Oslo, even though the details came to her automatically.

Like George and his stargazing, Kate Hood had caught the flying bug in her pre-teens and had grown up absorbing everything she could about things with wings. Now it was what she did for a living, and that bit of her aviation-geek mind had never switched off.

'There, there, there!' George cried out, his voice going up an octave, and he stabbed a skinny finger into the sky. Its light as sharp as a diamond, a speck of brilliant white followed a perfect line across the evening from the north, on course to pass directly over their heads. Reflected sunlight captured by the Space Station's massive solar panels made it impossible to miss, and the boy clamped himself to the telescope's eyepiece to get a better look. 'It's like a big metal butterfly! Dad, quick, check it out!'

Alex did as he was told and gave an appreciative whistle. He beckoned Kate to him as the Station's orbit raced by. 'Your turn!'

'Wow.' To Kate's amazement, the reflector scope captured enough to render the ISS not as some ill-defined blob of light, but as a hazy cluster of angles, as a definite physical object. She was struck by the elegance of the thing, and still trying to take it all in when, just as quickly as it appeared, it vanished behind the roof of the house.

'That. Was. *Incredible.*' George punctuated each word with a nod, grinning from ear to ear.

'I forgot to wave.' Alex smiled. His son's enthusiasm was infectious. He gave Kate an imperceptible nod, and she took her cue.

'So, do you want to go up there one day, George? Be an astronaut?' She pitched the question at the boy, and he studied her with great seriousness.

'It's very hard to do. It's not as simple as flying a plane,' he said, with enough dismissiveness that Kate felt faintly insulted. 'And I'm not that good at maths, and you have to be *really* good at maths to be an astronaut,' he said, thinking on it. 'But I do like space stuff.'

'Well, I have something that could help with that.' Kate reached into the box and pulled out the book she'd hidden in there earlier. 'I know your birthday isn't for a while yet, but I saw this and I thought you might like it.'

'*Stars and Sky: An Illustrated Guide.*' George read the title aloud.

'What do you say?' Alex asked, as George took the book from her and flipped it open.

'Thanks, Kate,' said George, without looking up. He pored over pages displaying glow-in-the-dark images of constellations and the planets of the solar system, instantly becoming lost in them, and she smiled.

Alex flashed a thumbs-up. *Good choice.*

'Dad, can we stay out and look at some other stars?'

'I suppose so . . .'

'Dad, can I take this book with me when I go to Mum's? Can I show it to her?'

'Sure.' Alex gave Kate a wan look. His ex-wife had wanted to take their son this weekend but, after much negotiation, Alex had convinced her to change her days on the proviso she got an extended visit from George later that week.

'Does Laura actually read books?' Kate couldn't stop herself from making an off-hand comment, and she regretted the cheap shot the moment she said it. George didn't seem to notice, however. From what Kate understood of Alex's ex, she had more interest in vapid gossip weeklies than hardbacks.

Alex made a face, but before he could add anything, a trilling tone sounded from Kate's jacket pocket.

'Is that mine or yours?'

'Mine,' she said with a frown, drawing her smartphone and handing back Alex's. The flare of light from the screen instantly glared in her dark-adapted eyes, and she squinted at it. The caller ID did nothing to improve her mood. *Teller,* read the display.

'Let me guess,' said Alex, raising an eyebrow. 'It's Brian?'

'It's Brian,' she confirmed.

'He does know you're off for the weekend, right?' It was a sore point between them how the harried owner-operator of Teller Aviation Solutions had a very elastic idea of the boundaries between the work time and free time of his contracted employees.

'He's my boss,' said Kate, as the phone rang on. 'He'd bloody well better.' She sighed, knowing that to let the call go to voicemail would not be the end of it. 'I should answer, or he'll keep on ringing.'

'Right.' Alex turned away and crouched down beside George at the telescope. Kate knew that if she got one-word answers from him, he was not happy.

She stalked away toward the house, raising the phone to her ear, and gave a terse response to the call. 'What?'

'*Kate Hood.*' Brian Teller said her name as if he was summoning the server at a restaurant. '*Where are you? Are you at home?*' As usual, he didn't waste time on any of the social niceties, always sounding distracted, as if he was doing five different jobs at once and speaking to you was the least significant of them.

'I'm busy,' she retorted. 'I'm out.' She was in the garden, so that was technically correct.

'*Oh, with your bloke? So you won't be far off, then ... How quickly can you come in?*'

Her lip curled. 'Monday,' she said firmly. 'I'm in on Monday morning. After the weekend.'

'*No, no, no,*' said Teller, as if that reply was contrary to the rule of law. '*I'm sorry about this, but I need you to drive the bus right now, Kate. We have an all-hands-on-deck situation.*'

'I'm not on the schedule,' she said firmly. 'You know that. Price is.'

'*He was,*' Teller corrected. '*Now you are.*'

'Price does your night flights, not me.' Kate's tone turned flinty.

Why were they having this conversation again? She had gone through this more than once with him, and each time she had made it clear in no uncertain terms exactly what she was prepared to offer Teller's company in terms of commitment.

But he didn't seem to remember any of that. '*You have to come in,*' he insisted. '*John was supposed to be here an hour ago and he's ... well, he's vanished. His phone's switched off and no one answers when I ring his house. Meanwhile, I have a plane spooling up to go and no bugger to fly it.*'

'That is a thorny issue,' she noted, without sympathy. 'And also not my problem. I'm not the only pilot you employ, Brian, there's other people you can ask—'

'*Not for this job,*' he snapped, cutting her off. '*This one needs someone I can rely on, someone discreet. That's you or John Price, and no John means ...*' He let the sentence hang.

She stared at the lawn grass beneath her feet. Anyone listening in on this conversation might have thought that Teller was pushing his luck. But they wouldn't have picked up on what was floating under the surface of the man's words. Not quite a threat just yet, but it soon would be.

'This is the first time in months I've been able to set up a whole weekend to spend with Alex and George,' she told him. 'It's not easy, with the shifts he works, and the boy's mother.'

'*I sympathise, I honestly do,*' said Teller, rushing out the platitude with more speed than compassion. '*But this isn't a big ask, not really. A short hop, no stops, no overnight, you'll be back before dawn. Please don't make me beg. I promise, I will make it up to you.*'

'What, by giving me a raise?'

'*Well, obviously I'll pay you for tonight. Rate plus fifteen per cent.*'

'Still not interested.' She shot a look back down the garden at Alex and George. 'I'm ringing off now. I'll see you on Monday.'

'*No, Kate, no.*' Like a switch flipping, Teller's manner turned icy. '*If you drop me in it here, then I will be forced to reconsider your position with Teller Aviation Solutions moving forward. I don't need to remind you that I went against considerable advice when I brought you on to my team.'*

'Here it comes,' she muttered, but he didn't hear her.

'I've gone the extra mile for you,' he carried on, the words coming machine-gun fast. *'I mean, I thought we had an understanding. I've been willing to overlook certain facts in order to keep you flying when others wouldn't, and I would hope that meant you'd give me some latitude in return.'*

Kate stiffened, waiting for the inevitable threat to land. She didn't have wait long.

'If that's no longer true, then you're welcome to look for employment somewhere else but, frankly, if the black mark on your record comes to light, you'll be lucky to get a gig folding paper planes.'

'Fuck you, Brian.' She wanted the retort to sound furious, but it came out tired. He had barely bothered to sugarcoat it. The cruel calculation of Teller's warning was right there, clear as day. *Do the job or you'll regret it.*

And the hateful, searing reality of it was that she didn't have a choice. There were truths that Kate kept to herself that she didn't want aired for everyone to hear, especially Alex and his son.

'Yeah, yeah, fuck me.' He heard the defeat in her tone. *'Half an hour, all right? We'll sort out the details when you get here. Don't be late, the client is very fussy.'* Teller cut the call and left her staring at nothing.

'You're going.' Alex stood right behind her, and Kate hadn't heard him approach. He didn't make it a question or an accusation, just a plain statement of fact, and somehow that was worse.

'I'm going,' she replied, and she saw how unhappy he was about it. But Alex understood, and reading the tone of her voice, he drew her into a hug. 'I really don't want to,' she added.

'Tell him to stick his plane up his arse,' Alex said quietly, so his voice wouldn't carry. 'He's a prick. You don't have to work for a bloke like that.'

I do. She held back the words. *Because no one else will fly with a pariah.*

'Never liked him,' continued Alex. And as always happened when he got annoyed, his native north London drawl grew thicker. 'All mouth and trousers, that one. Always has some sort of angle. Some shady shit going on.'

'He pays me on time.' It was the best thing Kate could think of to say in the moment. 'And I need to keep my job, and we need the money.'

She could tell he wanted to argue the point, but they both knew that would only make everyone feel worse and solve nothing. Alex accepted the inevitable, letting it go for now, and released her. 'It's still bollocks, though.'

'It is,' she agreed. Kate leaned in and kissed him deeply. 'I'll be back by tomorrow morning. We can bring out the telescope another night, right?'

'Sure.' He forced a smile and squeezed her hand. 'Come home safe, love.'

'Always do.' The exchange had become a ritual for them, something she told Alex when he went on duty at the fire station, and that he told her when she set off to fly somewhere. She paused, hesitating over saying goodbye to George, then decided against it.

Kate rushed back through the house, picking up the flight bag with all her gear ready to go like always, and in five minutes she was in the Mini and on the road.

Her last sight of their home was a glimpse in the Hatch's rear-view mirror. The next time she saw it would be from a few thousand feet up, as she passed over on the flight path out of Ridley Hill, and deep into the night sky.

THREE

'This is it,' said Miles, as he swung the steering wheel of the Ford Focus to thread the car down a narrow side street. Away from the main road through Deptford and down toward Surrey Quays at the edge of London's Docklands, the city crowded closer, the buildings dark shapes in the evening's murk.

Miles was a bit too aggressive on the turn, causing Ray in the back seat to swear out loud as he lurched against the door, the digital pad on his lap almost slipping out of his fingers. 'Give us some warning first, will you?'

'Yeah, nah.' That off-hand reply was the closest to an apology the driver was capable of giving, his concentration on getting the car through the narrow lines of black iron bollards on either side of them.

In the front passenger seat, Thomas Finn shot Miles a weary look, but the other man didn't notice, gunning the engine as they passed under a railway arch. The nasal snarl of the Ford echoed off the bricks.

The three Security Service officers in the car had little in common on the surface. Finn was the well-presented one, his smooth physique the result of an expensive regimen of male grooming products, a careful diet and a lot of time spent in the gym. Accented by his shaven head, he had a beard so carefully maintained it looked more like something carved out of teak than facial hair, and beneath the deliberately nondescript black jeans, black T-shirt, black trainers and black jacket he wore, he was trim and poised.

Miles didn't go in for any of that. He deliberately cultivated a look that one of Finn's colleagues had scornfully described as 'council flat chic', mostly track wear and hoodies that accented his pale complexion. Usually, he was impossible to lever out from behind the wheel of whatever operational car they were using, but the man was smarter than he looked. He knew how to blend into the urban landscape better than anybody and, most importantly, he took orders and didn't moan about them.

Ray was dressed similarly to Finn, his dark features given to a studious look thanks to the rimless spectacles perched on his pug nose. A specialist pulled in at short notice that morning from an off-shore posting at one of MI6's European stations, the guy was quiet, but he'd already made it clear that he didn't approve of how this whole operation was being assembled on the fly.

Ahead of the car, a tall chain-link gate parted at the last moment and they slowed, rolling through and past a tall Sikh man in similarly unremarkable clothing. The man did little to conceal the suppressor-muzzled MP5 submachine gun hanging from a strap over his shoulder.

He waved them by with an impassive, stony expression. Finn knew the type: foreign private military contractors, possibly ex-army or law enforcement, and certainly not legally permitted to carry firearms in the heart of the British capital. He spotted more of them as the Ford turned around the edge of a blacked-out warehouse, and Miles brought the car up behind a pair of vehicles that were already waiting. The contractors had all the approaches covered, watching every possible angle.

The larger of the two vehicles was an Iveco Daily truck, dirty white with slit windows along the sides, a familiar sight to anyone who had ever seen the police shipping criminals to and from their court dates. Inside would be a set of secure compartments with restraints, the whole thing set up to make sure whatever passengers it carried would not go walkabout. The other vehicle was a giant American sports utility vehicle, a GMC Yukon with a front grille bigger than a widescreen television, opaque windows, diplomatic plates and a wheel stance that told Finn it carried far more weight than a stock model. He assumed it would have run-flat tyres, armour plating and bulletproof glass, and from the glimpse of the interior he got through a half-open door, he could see banks of electronics that were likely to be connected to the odd bulges and antennae fitted to the roof. Similar units were deployed by the United States Secret Service on presidential motorcades, so seeing one here was hugely out of place.

'Park there.' Finn indicated a spot off to one side and Miles gave a nod, his head panning around the end of his skinny neck to take everything in.

'Does it bother you that the Yanks can roll around our town with shit like that?' Miles offered the question to the air, indicating the great black hulk of the SUV, 'no questions asked?'

'Where do they even get those rigs from?' Ray looked up from his tablet and nodded his agreement. 'It's not like they can ship it over piece-by-piece in diplomatic pouches.'

'They have permission,' said Finn, less convincingly than he'd hoped.

'Yeah, nah.' Miles snorted. 'Letting the CIA do what they want in our backyard isn't the same as giving them permission.'

'Semantics.' Finn straightened his jacket. 'You two wait in the motor. I'll handle the introductions.'

'Don't forget to curtsey,' muttered Ray.

Finn ignored the comment and rose out of the Ford, to be instantly met by two of the Sikh mercenary's associates. One had another silenced SMG, the other a metal detector wand that he brandished like a short sword.

'Really?' Finn's lip curled and he offered up his Security Service identity card, refusing to accede to a pat down. 'Do you want to cup my balls and ask me to cough as well?'

'Maybe later, but not without dinner and a movie first.' A portly woman with shoulder-length auburn curls and an acerbic East Coast American accent approached, waving off the gunmen. She was shorter than Finn, and her moon face looked him up and down, making no attempt to hide a brisk evaluation that bordered on leering. 'So, King Charlie sent you, huh?'

'In a manner of speaking.' Finn couldn't be sure if the woman was making a joke. He didn't really get the American sense of humour.

Sarcasm dripped off her reply. 'To be honest, I hoped for someone a little more James Bond-y.' She mimed a beard-stroking motion. 'Not like my fucking barista.'

It had already been a long and problematic day for him, so Finn decided to push back on her attitude. 'Well, *I* didn't expect someone who looks like they should be doing a comedy set on the Upper East Side, but here we are.' He offered his hand. 'I'm Thomas Finn. Field officer, Section K, MI6. I'm your liaison.'

The woman smirked and shook her head, ignoring the gesture. 'They already told you who I am, right?'

'Your name is Lillian Breeze, you're from the Central Intelligence Agency,' said Finn, and he let his hand drop. 'I understand you're a senior case officer at—'

She cut across him. 'Don't say *senior*. Makes me sound like I should be in a nursing home.'

'What would you prefer?' Finn stiffened at her tone. 'Veteran? Experienced?'

'The second one,' Breeze snapped. 'That at least suggests I know what the hell I'm doing.' She walked away, beckoning like she was grabbing at a handful of air. 'C'mon, liaison. Liaise with me. The guest of honour is gonna be here soon.'

Finn trailed after her. Back at MI6's headquarters in Vauxhall Cross, he'd been warned that Breeze was an abrasive sort, tempered by two decades of working on the Middle East desk at the CIA's centre of operations in Langley. The woman could be capable and ruthless when she needed to be, but she lacked the ability to temper her opinions and play politics, so his briefing went. So, while others of lesser calibre had been promoted up the line, Breeze was treading water, stuck in the same role. She should have had a pleasant corner office somewhere; instead, she was here, on a chilly, damp dockside on chaperone duty.

That would give anyone a chip on their shoulder. Finn kept this in mind as he let her talk. She didn't like being quiet.

'Here's how this is going to work,' Breeze told him. 'We've got point, you follow. I don't want to be dealing with any dick-measuring while the asset is present – it doesn't help with the process. We need focus here. MI6 is helping us, and in return you people will get some of the product at the end of the day when this little bird sings. I don't want you sneaking off to call your bosses when my back is turned. You should already know this.'

He nodded. 'The dynamics of Six's responsibilities in this operation were made clear to me, ma'am.'

'Uh-huh.' Breeze sounded dubious. 'You fucking *ma'am* me again, I'll drown you like a bag of kittens.' As they passed the SUV, she pointed at a man climbing out of the vehicle, and Finn stole a better look inside at the high-tech hardware lining the rear compartment. 'That scruffy mutt is Marty Chester,' she said, 'running my tech and comms tonight. Say hello, Marty.'

'Uh, how are you?' Chester was caught off-guard but recovered quickly. Around Finn's age, he had an unkempt mop of curly black hair framing a thoughtful face, and not an iota of poise about him. Finn's first impression was of a geek-squad type more than a field agent, but before he could build on that, Breeze was dismissing the other man.

'And say goodbye, Marty. Didn't I tell you to stay in the vehicle?'

'I, uh . . .' Chester wilted under Breeze's gaze, then silently drew back into the SUV and closed the door behind him.

'Impressive kit in there.' Finn indicated the SUV. 'What does it do?' He already had an idea – localised wireless jamming, cellular network intrusion, radio monitoring and probably more – but he played dumb, to see what she would admit to.

'Don't be nosy,' Breeze warned, as they walked on. She inclined her head in the direction of a third person, a man drawing on a vape pen as he stood in the lee of a half-demolished wall. 'That's Knox. Don't talk to him, he bites strangers.'

Knox gave Finn a shallow nod of greeting. Wiry and watchful, the man's aspect screamed ex-operator, from the cut of the field jacket he wore down to the military-spec boots on his feet. He had a threadbare baseball cap pulled down tight over his head, and a rough patina of heavy stubble on his chin that was the polar opposite of Finn's well-maintained beard. Knox was most likely former Tier One Special Forces, either from the US Army's Delta Force or US Navy's SEAL Team, seconded into the CIA's clandestine action group known as Ground Branch. The man was obviously the door-kicking, trigger-pulling type, with a predatory intensity that made Finn instinctively give him a wide berth.

MI6 and the British Security Services didn't have anything like Ground Branch, or at least nothing that would be publicly admitted to, preferring to pull in the police's SCO19 tactical unit or the lads with black balaclavas from Hereford when someone needed shooting. The American approach of loading up the site with gunmen and stone killers made Finn step carefully, and Miles's comments in the car came back to him. This operation was supposed to be a low-key, minimal footprint thing, but Breeze hadn't got that memo.

'Something wrong?' She picked up on his discomfort.

He nodded at two of the PMCs and their weapons. 'In my experience, the more guns you have around, the more trouble they cause.'

'Don't be such a pussy . . .' She was going to add another dash to the insult but the insistent shrilling of a ringtone interrupted, and Breeze pulled the thick rectangle of a smartphone from her pocket. Finn recognised it as a 'blackphone', an encrypted, satellite-enabled device. Breeze had to let it capture a shot of her face before she could use it, passing through a security layer before she jammed it to her ear. 'Yeah, what?'

Finn couldn't hear the voice on the other end of the call, but by the way the expression on Breeze's face changed, he could guess at what was being said. The woman's manner turned serious, and he wondered if the foul-mouthed attitude she'd put to him was purely for show. Now the CIA agent was all business.

She cut the call and gave him a nod. 'He's coming.' Breeze raised her voice and repeated the words so everyone heard her. 'Asset is incoming! Look alive, ladies!'

Ahead of them, a crumbling, disused quay extended out into the greenish churn of the Thames, lit by the reflected glow from the buildings on the north bank. Finn watched the PMCs take up firing positions, and he shifted nervously, feeling exposed. There were tower blocks off behind them, and if this rendezvous had been leaked to the wrong people, there were ample places for a sniper to be waiting.

He rubbed the back of his neck as the sound of a high-powered outboard motor reached them. On the river, a sleek speedboat running fast and low to the water shot past the hulks of moored barges, its running lights off. Finn picked out figures in the boat, other men with other guns, and a black shape that could have been a duffel-bag on the deck between them.

With a throb of acceleration, the speedboat raced toward the dock, cutting its outboard to coast in silently at the last moment. Knox and a couple of the PMCs were ready for it as the boat bumped up against the quay, and with quick motions they grabbed the duffel-bag shape. It moved suddenly, the shadow growing arms and legs.

The bag was a person, dressed in dark clothes, their head lost under a sagging cloth sack. Incongruously, the person had no shoes or socks, and their bare feet slapped on the cold concrete of the dock.

Breeze saw that and made a tutting sound, pointing a finger. 'What's this shit?'

'He kicked off,' said one of the men on the boat, barely hiding a smirk. 'Struggled. Lost his gear in the drink.'

'So fucking professional.' Breeze scowled, then signalled Knox to walk the captive to them. She glanced at Finn. 'You wanna meet the star of the show?'

He shook his head. 'That's not protocol.'

'Oh, did I not make it clear that this is my gig, my rules? I'm pretty sure I implied all of that.' She gestured at the black hood. 'Off, off. Let's get a look at him.'

'Right.' Knox pulled the bag from the captive's head and the man beneath it flinched in fear.

Under the hood he was gagged, with a set of sound-deadening headphones over his ears and blacked-out goggles across his eyes, rendering the man blind and deaf to everything going on around him. Knox peeled them off without being gentle about it, finally revealing an Arab face with a broad brow, deep-set eyes and a trembling mouth. Finn had been told he was in his mid-forties, but he had an undernourished cast that aged him another ten years. The captive was, quite clearly, utterly terrified.

'Yusuf ibn Saleh ibn Kalb al-Amal.' Breeze reeled off the man's full name like a mantra. 'Hello there. *As-salamu alaikum.*'

Offering the traditional Arabic greeting of '*peace be upon you*' seemed to Finn like a cruel joke, given Yusuf's obvious circumstances and his clear physical distress, and yet the man automatically attempted to respond in kind, stuttering through the words.

'Don't speak.' Breeze silenced him before he could get too far. 'There's gonna be time for that later.' She leaned in and looked him over, giving Yusuf the same piece-of-meat appraisal she'd shown Finn minutes earlier, putting him in mind of a farmer considering a pig to send to slaughter.

'Please.' Yusuf brought up his hands, the wrists held together with clear plastic cable ties. 'Who is in charge here? I-I keep telling people there has been a terrible mistake . . .' His eyes were wide and wet.

'We don't make mistakes.' Finn felt compelled to speak to justify his presence and opted for something threatening and vague. Yusuf's head jerked up in a birdlike motion and he looked him right in the eyes.

'I don't know who you think I am or what you think I have done . . .' The words fell out of the prisoner's mouth in a rush, his Saudi accent muddying them. 'I am not a criminal!'

'I told you not to speak.' Breeze nodded at Knox, who pulled Yusuf back by the scruff of his neck, the gag going into his mouth once again. He struggled half-heartedly, but in a moment the headphones, goggles and hood were back in place. The man's body language became the picture of defeat.

'In the truck?' asked Knox, nodding toward the white van.

'Yeah, time to go.' Breeze blew out a breath. 'Like they say in the movies, we're Oscar Mike.'

Finn took his cue and turned back to the Ford, catching sight of Miles. He made a winding-up motion and the driver nodded back, starting the car. 'We'll take the lead,' he said. 'Just stick to us like glue and we'll be at the change-over soon enough.'

'How long's it gonna take?' Breeze checked her watch.

'Weeknight, traffic's thin,' he replied. 'Forty minutes, an hour tops.' Finn saw Knox directing two of the PMCs, the pair of them indelicately shoving Yusuf aboard the transport van.

'Oh, fun. Plenty of time for us to get to know one another better.' Breeze called out toward Chester, who stood in the SUV's half-open door, anticipating their departure. 'Marty! Clear up your gear, the hipster's riding with us in the MOU.'

'I am? The what?' Breeze said the name like '*moo*', and Finn guessed it was another of the abbreviations the clandestine services were so fond of.

'Mobile. Operations. Unit.' Breeze spelt it out as if talking to a dim toddler. 'You wanted to take a look inside, right? And I'm guessing it'll be a better ride than that piece-of-shit pool car you came in.'

Finn couldn't argue with that. Compared to the close confines of the Ford Focus, the big Yukon was like a mobile home. And his curiosity was getting the better of him. 'Okay, fine.' He glanced around, finding the rest of the PMC operators as they stood their posts. 'Are you bringing the goon squad?'

'Gee, should I?' Breeze saw the serious look that answer drew, and gave a snort of laughter. 'Lighten up. This is an escort operation, it's not like we're invading.'

'Oh?' Finn eyed her, his tone cooling. 'Because with the firepower you brought to cover one sickly-looking bloke with bare feet, I wasn't really sure.'

She laughed again. 'I like you, hipster. I like that British sarcasm. You keep doing what I tell you and we're gonna get on fine.'

In the next minute, the convoy hit the road – the Ford, the van and the SUV in a loose line following the course of the River Ravensbourne toward the suburbs of south London, and the Kent countryside beyond.

FOUR

'I think we're here,' said Grace, bringing the police car up through the narrow lane, craning her neck to look out over the steering wheel. 'This is the spot,' she added, with more certainty, slowing the Volvo to a stop well short of the incident area. Another unit was already there, the blue flicker of the other car's light bar blinking in the gloom.

Small-framed, enough that her stab vest swamped her, Constable Isla Grace was dark-skinned with wide observant eyes and a fuzz of hair cut tighter than an army squaddie's. Her stature made a lot of people underestimate her; civilians, offenders and other coppers alike, but generally they learned their mistake when their assumptions came back to bite them in the arse.

Her colleague in the Volvo's other seat, Constable Jacob Harris, had seen it happen on more than one occasion. When the need came, when Grace went off like a bomb, swinging her baton like a ninja, men twice her size would go down fast, crying for their mums. Harris tried never to piss her off, even if he often did, as he was doing now while cramming the last chunks of a double cheeseburger into his mouth, along with the last few fries cooling at the bottom of a McDonald's take-out bag.

'Jake.' Grace raised an eyebrow at his dining habits. 'Can you not do that?'

'Not wasting it,' Harris replied thickly, around a mouthful. Compared to his colleague, he was a long stick of a man, wiry like a basketball player, pale like a mortician. 'I imagine the victim of this particular RTC would like me to be fully nourished in order to apply my complete policing skills to the situation.' *RTC* meant *road traffic collision*, a terse and bloodless abbreviation that covered a multitude of unpleasantness, all part of the process so that officers like Grace and Harris could keep a professional distance from the daily traumas that formed their work.

Case in point; on the road lay the crumpled remnants of what had once been the sleek frame of a Porsche sports car, now caved in and ruined. Harris swallowed the last of his fast-food meal and took a breath, getting his 'work face' on while Grace climbed out.

Harry Peake, a sergeant from their shift, approached the car with a bright Lumos flashlight in hand. 'All right, Isla?' Peake usually had an affable way about him and, as one of the most experienced officers at the station, he was considered the old man of the team despite the fact he was barely five years older than the next youngest copper. His good-natured manner was muted tonight, replaced by a frown.

'You need some back-up, Sarge? Is it a bad one?' Grace looked off at the ruined Porsche. In the course of their duties, they had all seen the horrors that a cruel twist of fate could inflict on a person, by accident or by criminal intention, but still she felt compelled to ask the question.

'One fatality,' Peake confirmed. 'Killed instantly. Probably didn't feel a thing, for what it's worth.'

Harris walked up, using his own torch to scan around the area. 'Skid marks there, but close to the point of impact, see?'

He aimed at a section of the road. 'Doesn't look like the driver tried to slow down, at least not until the last second.'

'No,' Peake said gravely, putting some light on the rear of the damaged tractor parked near the mouth of a side road. A mess of glass, metal and plastic fragments glittered in the spill of the beam. 'He must have missed this thing as he was coming up the road, and by the time he realised he was going to hit it, it was too late. Distracted, probably. On his phone, or mucking about with the radio . . .' He trailed off.

Peake walked them toward the wreck, the three officers taking care to follow the exact same line of approach to the spot so that no evidence would be disturbed.

Grace sniffed the air, smelling oil, stale petrol and fire retardant. 'Any witnesses?' She nodded in the direction of the house off the driveway.

Peake shook his head, explaining that the residents had only heard the moment of the car crash, not seen it. 'The homeowner was first on scene,' he added. 'Young bloke, nice lad. Didn't handle it well.'

'Puked up, did he?' Harris nodded sagely. 'That happens.'

'Do we have an ID on the driver?' Grace indicated the car.

Peake flipped open his notebook, his thick fingers leafing to the relevant page. 'DVLA says the motor's registered to a Mr John Price. Lives in Wethill, down near the cricket club. Same name as we found on the body, in his wallet.'

'I know that place,' offered Harris. 'Leafy little village. Well off. Very *Daily Telegraph*.'

'Oh right?' Grace's reply was dour. 'That fits with a Porsche in the garage then.'

Harris gave a sigh. 'Tragic to see a nice ride like that in such a state.'

'I'm sure Mr Price isn't too happy about it either.' Peake's frown deepened. 'Poor sod's still in there. We'll need an angle-grinder to cut him out.'

Grace and Harris exchanged looks, and she made the inevitable offer. 'Sarge, do you want another set of eyes on it, just for safety?'

'I might have missed something,' he allowed. 'Yeah, go ahead. Tread lightly, though. CIU will have my nuts if you touch anything.'

Harris looked around again. 'Where are they, anyway?'

'Running behind,' said Peake. 'Tanker lorry turned over up on the bypass; they were busy with that.'

The Collison Investigation Unit was a mobile scene-of-crime team deployed to incidents like this one, equipped to deal with roadside scenarios where it wasn't possible to close off an area for days, as one might if this was a private property or some other building. Once deployed, the CIU would sweep the area quickly and effectively, but there was always the chance something might get overlooked. Having Grace and Harris take a peek lessened the chances of that.

The policewoman shot her colleague a look as they closed in on the wreck. 'How's that cheeseburger sitting now?'

'Fine.' Harris coughed, getting a greasy back-taste on his tongue. 'I'll manage.'

Grace produced her own flashlight to probe the Porsche's crumpled, debris-choked interior. Pinned to his seat, the late Mr Price was a grisly sight, the dead man's eyes wide open and staring right through her. She avoided looking directly at him, instead concentrating on the material that had been hurled out of the car by the force of the collision.

She spotted a bulky shoulder bag lying on its side, the contents burst out from within. Papers, maps and what resembled a log book of some sort fluttered in the breeze, the pages soaking in the rain puddles on the road. The closer she looked, the more Grace thought she saw marks on the paper. 'Jake. See that?'

Harris was closer to the bag, on the far side of the wreck, and he approached surefooted and careful, dropping into a crouch. 'Maps,' he confirmed, then looked closer. 'Good spot, Gracey. There might be a partial here.'

He was talking about a shoe mark, the imprint of someone who had walked over the papers without realising it.

'Harry!' Grace shouted back down the lane. 'The bloke from the farmhouse – did he come up the driver's side or the passenger side?'

'Driver's side,' Peake called back. 'Because he upchucked into the bushes right there.' The older officer pointed past her to the undergrowth at the base of a nearby tree.

'This looks like a boot print,' said Harris. 'Come see.'

Grace was glad to remove herself from close proximity of Price's corpse, circling round to join her colleague. Illuminated by both torches, it was clear that Harris was correct. The chunky, tell-tale tread of a military boot was visible in the middle of a crumpled map sheet, pressed in place against the road.

'The victim's wearing brogues,' she noted.

'Not likely to have got out of the car, what with him being speared by an oak tree,' said Harris, with calm sarcasm. He pointed at the Porsche's passenger seat, where the seatbelt hung loosely. 'You thinking what I'm thinking?'

'Price might have had company,' said Grace. Immediately, the two officers rose as one and began directing their torch beams into the shadows and scrub along the side of the road. If there *had* been a passenger, if that person had stumbled away after the crash, they might be injured, possibly lying unconscious in a ditch somewhere.

But there was no trail of blood and no immediate signs that anyone in distress had gone wandering off into the gloom. In fact, aside from the boot print, there was nothing close at hand to suggest that John Price had been anything but alone. The only way to know for certain would be to let the forensics team scour every inch of the wreck, and it might be days before they would have a definitive answer.

Peake walked over, gesturing with his Airwave radio. 'CIU's close by; be here any minute,' he explained, then halted as he caught the urgency in the air. 'What now?'

'He may not have been the only one in the car,' said Grace, jerking a thumb at the wreck.

Peake's eyes widened. 'Oh, great. If we have a lost lamb, that complicates it. As if we don't have enough to be dealing with already.'

Harris nodded, looking up at the black, moonless sky. 'It's fields and woods for miles around here, dark as anything.'

'Better ring for the dog section,' said Grace, then she caught up with what Peake had said. 'What, is something else going on?'

'Added complication, could be nothing . . .' Peake replied, the latter half of his sentence unconvincing. More blue lights flashed off the trees around them as the CIU van came into view, a bulky silver Transit with a checkerboard livery of blue and neon yellow. 'Support officer back at base called in,' he went on. 'She tried the numbers listed for the Price household. No joy. No one's picking up there – phone rings and rings.'

Grace took that on board. The first creeping sense that something might be amiss began clawing at the back of her neck. 'He had family?'

'Wife and a daughter,' added Peake. 'We'll need to send someone over to check on them.'

Harris gave Grace a look. Having been teamed up together for some time, the two officers had grown into a working relationship where a lot could be communicated with just a glance. Like hers, the other copper's instinct for trouble pulled at him. The circumstances of the crash were ringing a wrong note for both of them.

Nearby, the CIU team was already decamping in swift order, sliding open the side of the van to remove their gear for going over the site. Grace watched them, then shot a look at her colleague. 'Wethill, where Price lived. You said you know it?'

'A bit,' Harris hedged. 'I can find it.'

Grace looked back at Peake. 'Sarge, me and Jake can go to the house, do the check.'

At length, the older policeman gave a nod. 'All right, then. On the hurry-up. Quicker we get this done, quicker we get the road clear and knock off for a cuppa.'

'Don't hit anyone,' said Breeze, aiming the comment at the SUV's driver, as they accelerated along the A-road. 'Remember that these limeys drive on the wrong side of the highway.'

Behind the wheel, Knox didn't appear to register the comment, maintaining the same blank, laser-eyed focus he exhibited whenever he did anything. Breeze searched her memory, trying to recall if she'd ever seen the dour asshole even crack a smile over dozens of different operations. Nothing came to mind, and she dismissed the thought with a sniff.

In the back of the Yukon's commodious interior, Marty showed the guy from Six the inner workings of the satellite communications module bolted to the roof of the SUV, getting animated by technical details that to her ears were dull as anything. Marty acted like a first-time dad going on about their newborn, and Breeze raised an eyebrow.

Is it something about the male psyche, she wondered, *that predisposes men towards being nerds?* All men were geeks in some way or another, she decided, even tough, humourless dicks like Knox. When they were little boys, they learned batting averages and species of dinosaur off by heart, and when they were grown men, it was bullet weights and hardware specifications.

Breeze had a keen memory for dry facts too, but in her case each one had a connection to something messy, something emotional. She had an encyclopaedic knowledge of human weak points, of how much and which kind of pressure one needed to exert to get a desired result. It was a talent she applied so effortlessly, so often, that these days it came to her as easy as breathing.

She decided to turn it on Finn, as a warm-up exercise. 'Marty, how do you make this stuff sound more boring than it already is?' She eyed the other man across her seat-back. 'I'm over my jet lag. Don't put me to sleep again.'

'It's interesting,' said Finn, taking the bait.

Breeze kept looking at Marty. 'He's saying that cos the British are polite.' Her gaze slipped to the MI6 officer and she threw out a leading question. 'So. The asset. Not quite what you expected, huh?'

'I was briefed,' Finn noted. 'Briefly.'

'Betcha your bosses told you the guy could be some badass Bin Laden motherfucker, right? A real *haji* tiger.'

Finn's lip curled, and Breeze knew she was right. 'First impressions can be deceiving.'

'That's the first non-idiot thing you've said. Good, glad to hear it.'

He frowned, unconsciously tracing the line of his well-trimmed beard. 'Whitehall gave us information that was ... patchy. Actually, I hoped you might be good enough to fill in some of the gaps? Special relationship, and all that?'

'*Special* is right,' Breeze replied, with a snort. 'Maybe you missed that you Brits aren't exactly our favourite people right now? I mean, your boss and my boss don't get on, know what I mean?' It wasn't any secret that the current President and the UK's Prime Minister didn't see eye to eye, each one quietly – and sometimes not so quietly – considering the other to be divisive and ineffectual.

'You don't give a toss about that,' said Finn, proving that he was at least a little bit perceptive. 'Elected leaders come and go – on your side of the pond and mine. But our work doesn't alter, does it?'

'True enough,' she allowed. 'Who knows, some collaboration here might end up with us singing *kumbaya* round the goddamn campfire.' She let that hang, and Finn filled the silence that followed.

'Yusuf's role in the group is unclear,' he noted. 'From what we've been able to determine, he has a fair bit of freedom of movement around the organisation, but probably not any actual influence. The prevailing opinion is that he's a glorified go-between, at best.'

That chimed with one of the CIA's estimates on the guy, but not all of them. 'There's a voice inside the agency who thinks he's more than some messenger boy,' said Breeze. 'There are details that don't match up about Yusuf. Some photos of him look like two different guys. Some data connects him directly to terror attacks, other info says it wasn't him. Some of the intelligence we got puts our boy in conflicting locations at the same time.' She sucked in a breath. 'We need to nail shit down, one way or the other. Is this prick really a low-level mook, or some kinda player?'

'A voice in the agency,' echoed Finn. 'That would be yours, I imagine?'

'You *are* sharper than you look,' Breeze noted.

'And you're out on a limb.' Finn nodded in the direction of the transport vehicle riding up ahead of them. 'It doesn't take a genius to see it's a tough sell, convincing anyone that man is a hardened terrorist.' He sniffed. 'When you took that hood off him, I thought he might wet himself.'

She shrugged. 'There's zero chance this guy here is innocent, or near as makes no odds. The whole point of this thing is to find out for certain.'

'Whichever way it pans out ...' began Marty, confident enough to float a comment of his own, 'it's not going to be a lot of fun for Yusuf.'

'I know there are people who didn't want this to happen.' Finn took in everything with a sweep of the hand. 'On your side and mine. There's a case to be made that this asset would be of more use if he could be turned. Even a ... what did you call him? A "low-level mook" inside the al-Sakakin organisation would be a valuable source.'

It was the first time any one of them had said the name out loud – *al-Sakakin*, loosely translated from Arabic, meant *the knives*, and that was how the members of that terrorist group saw themselves. They were the sharp blades cutting open the belly of the monstrous, lumbering West, plunging daggers of fire into the hearts of infidels. These were cunning, violent men and women who had splintered away from jihadist groups like al-Qaeda and al-Shabaab because they considered them too lenient towards their enemies.

'We're talking about the people that AQ and ISIS call *extremists*,' said Breeze. 'And that's a pretty fuckin' high bar.'

'I don't disagree.' Finn looked away, glancing out at the streets flashing past them. 'We've seen how adept they are at suborning assets of their own, and striking high-value targets with showy attacks.'

'Yeah, that hit in Cyprus was hardcore.' Breeze had an enemy's clinical respect for the cold-eyed precision of al-Sakakin's operations. At the RAF airbase, their staged vehicular explosive attacks on the perimeter had effectively doubled the number of fatalities.

It was their signature tactic. Cyprus was the latest hit in a concerted terror campaign, following strikes against a German hospital, a military base in the Philippines and a holiday resort in Croatia. They liked to make a statement, drop a lot of bodies, and they made sure the world's media got it in widescreen and full colour.

'Quite,' agreed Finn, then he sighed. 'But if this man isn't who you think he is; if he isn't Yusuf, we're pissing into the wind.'

Breeze eyed him, her tone hardening to a challenge. 'So what's your read on him? Go ahead, be honest. I got no interest in you soft-pedalling it.'

Finn took a long moment to answer, the road rumbling under the SUV's wheels, and Breeze could sense Chester and Knox listening intently to what the Brit would say next.

'If the asset *is* Yusuf,' began Finn, 'if he can move around the group with impunity, then he's the closest we've come to Nasir and Hamid since we started chasing those bloodthirsty bastards.'

Nasir and *Hamid*: two more names that sent a cold charge through the air. The brothers were in the cohort at the apex of al-Sakakin's structure, their chief tactician and enforcer respectively, both from a handful of extremists who had been behind the original formation of the splinter faction. Veterans of proxy wars and brutal bombings, their dirty fingerprints were on every kill the group had ever made.

The notion of putting them in the ground kept Breeze up at night. It wouldn't only make the world a safer place, nailing either one of them would be a career-maker, and it would make every indignity she'd weathered at the Agency worth the agitation.

It would prove her *right*.

'But if the asset is nobody,' continued Finn, 'then everyone will be looking the wrong way when the next attack comes.'

'And we'll take the blame,' Breeze said, with a tight, false smile. 'Don't forget *that* detail.'

FIVE

Kate left the Mini in the car park and hauled her flight bag's strap over her shoulder, marching grimly toward Teller Aviation's office and hangar block. A fresh breeze came out of the clear evening sky across Ridley Hill's runway. It carried to pull at her hair, and she paused to put her reddish-brown tresses up into a tight, business-like ponytail.

Situated, as the name suggested, atop a flat hill of greenery and low trees, the airfield was the modern incarnation of what had started life as a grassy strip for rich hobbyist pilots in the interwar decades. The Second World War made it a possession of the Royal Air Force, a base for some of the Spitfires and Hurricanes of the Battle of Britain's 'Few', and that legacy still lingered in a list of names on a stone memorial down by the gate. But, eighty years later, the fighter boys who had hurled themselves into the air to duel with enemy Messerschmitts wouldn't have recognised Ridley Hill at all. Demobbed and sold off to civilian interests after the conflict, it had gone through good times and bad before blooming in the eighties, becoming a compact private airport for moneyed City traders and yuppies leasing their Learjets and Gulfstreams, shoulder to shoulder with a handful of general aviation types.

That was well before Kate's time, of course, but there was a formative memory of this place that lingered in her. An image burned into her mind when she was still a teenager, from a school trip to an air display held over Ridley Hill's field: a Tornado F3 interceptor hurtling by in a low-level pass, the roar of its turbofan engines chasing a split-second later, the jet outrunning its own sound.

Younger Kate had been entranced by the plane, and when a boy in her class sneeringly told her that *girls aren't allowed to drive those*, it crystalised a dream she spent years of her life struggling to make real.

And she *did it*. Years later, after making the grade in one of the most arduous military training programmes in the world, she'd strapped herself into the cockpit of a GR4 variant of the very same aircraft. It had felt like the biggest victory of her life. In a world that was good and right and fair, that would have been the peak of it.

But fate was mocking. It liked to give you what you wanted and then twist it. Twist and twist, until everything broke apart.

That Kate's path shook her out here, back to the same place, felt like some crass moment of grand irony. Every time she turned up to work, the sharp edges of what she had lost jabbed at her, the wound of her failure never quite allowed to scab over and fade.

Ridley Hill's glory days of well-heeled passengers fuelled by cocaine, cash and Champagne were a distant memory, and the current iteration of the airport served three types of client: learner pilots and instructors on single- and twin-engine props, a hangar where a privately owned flight of vintage warbirds roosted in between air-show appearances, and a couple of executive jet companies, of which Teller Aviation Solutions was one.

It was almost but not quite a backwater, overshadowed by other, better-appointed airports throughout Kent and south-east England. But that semi-obscurity suited Kate Hood fine. Here, she was out of the way, overlooked and uncommented upon. She could continue to do the one thing she was good at, and no one would bother her.

That was how it was *supposed* to be. But more and more, Kate wondered if that was a lie she told herself.

She changed in the locker room beside the pilot's lounge, noting the absence of anyone in that part of the building. Usually there was somebody about, and the fact that there wasn't added another ringing alarm bell to the clangour in her thoughts. If Brian Teller had given everyone the evening off, there had to be a reason.

On went her working uniform, the crisp white cotton shirt and black captain's boards on her epaulettes, plus a clip-on tie embroidered with the TAS logo and then a flight jacket over the top. Had it been daytime, she would have leaned into the look and worn a pair of aviator sunglasses to give it a little *Top Gun* flair. Teller liked his crews to play the part for the clients, be they noisy posh kids jetting down to the Balearics or dour oligarchs off to Europe. Like most commercial pilots, Kate had a love-hate relationship with the popular stereotypes associated with her job, but it was hard to deny that a fair few of the flyers she knew lived the epitome of them.

Paperwork came next, but when she looked for what she needed in the office, it wasn't there. Kate's temper was thinning when Teller suddenly entered the room from the hangar-side door and stared her down.

'Good. You're here.' He gave her a frantic 'follow me' wave. 'Come on!' Before she could respond, he was gone again, the door banging shut behind him.

'Twat.' Kate threw the sotto insult after her boss, then pulled her bag with her and trailed after him.

Teller didn't slow down as he strode across the hangar's gleaming white floor, forcing Kate to jog to catch up. He had ten years on Kate, but you would have thought it was more than that, his lined face and pinched expression ageing him before his time. He tried to leaven things by dressing like a younger man, all cargo trousers and tight-fitting polo shirts, but that made it more obvious. Teller had a fidgety, distracted quality to him that Kate found hard to deal with for extended periods. He was one of those people you met at a party who were constantly looking for someone more important to talk to, and he didn't care to hide it.

He curved around the ice-white wing of the company's primary aircraft, one of a pair of well-appointed Embraer Phenom executive jets, as she caught up and fell in step.

'There better be a bloody good reason for dragging me in like this,' she said.

'Like I said on the phone,' he replied quickly, 'rush job. John's nowhere to be found. You've got to take over.'

Her tone sharpened. 'Are you at least going to fill in some of the useful details, like where I'm flying to and who I'm taking there? Or do you want me to wing it and kite around in circles?'

'I *want* you to do your job,' he retorted. 'I *need* to know you won't get pissy about this, all right?' Teller made the request but didn't actually wait to see if Kate would agree to it. He ploughed on, out through the hangar doors and on to the flight apron. 'It's a night hop down to North Africa. A small airfield in Morocco. Handful of passengers. The client's supplying their own co-pilot. There and back, nothing fancy.'

She stiffened. Morocco wasn't on the usual list of itineraries, and the notion of crewing the aircraft with a complete stranger led her toward an unpleasant possibility, one that Kate immediately didn't want to give voice to.

But then Teller came to a halt a few feet away from the company's number three aircraft, the bird that *never* had the job of ferrying the idle wealthy or the corporate bigwigs.

The jet's registration code was G-LTTP, and one of the wits in the maintenance team had suggested that stood for *Late To The Party*. With a bullet-shaped fuselage, and a pair of engine nacelles either side of its high tail, the British-built Hawker 800 had a stocky look to it. Slightly smaller and heavier than the Phenom, it was an older aircraft now out of production and not as sleek or Instagram-worthy as its Brazilian-made stablemate. On the Teller Aviation Services flight line, the Hawker sat at the back of the pack – the one that got the assignments that were less showy, less glamourous . . .

Less legal, thought Kate.

Modified internally, a lot of the luxurious bells and whistles the company's usual clientele demanded had been stripped out of the Hawker, turning it into an aircraft better suited for light cargo runs, ambulance flights or the repatriation of remains.

But no one who worked for Brian Teller could ignore the flying elephant in the room: the fact that the Hawker was always going out or coming back in the hours of darkness, and that its cargoes and flight plans weren't discussed among the staff. Teller liked to bang on about 'discretion' and 'sensitivity' when it came to his company's operations, but as Kate's partner Alex had so eloquently put it, you couldn't escape the suspicion that there was *some shady shit going on*.

Teller was smart about his business. It wasn't as if they were trucking suitcases full of cocaine up from Colombia. It was more like slipping the possessions of some tax-dodging Russian billionaire out of the country ahead of his debtors coming knocking, or scooping up some drunken wild-child pop star from Cannes before the paparazzi tracked them down – done discreetly and sensitively so that no one got a whiff of it.

Teller made sure the people working for him, the waifs and strays of the aviation world, were grateful – or, as in Kate's case, *desperate* – for the work. Because people in that position didn't tend to make a fuss when their boss bent the rules.

That might have been something that could be overlooked, if Brian Teller's desire to earn and the rising costs of running millions of pounds' worth of jet planes hadn't driven him to seek other patrons. Kate realised that the rumours she had been hearing around the place about the jobs John Price had been flying were more than the product of some overactive imaginations.

'What's the load?' She looked Teller in the eye, daring him to lie about it.

'I'll pay you what Price was getting,' he said. 'And in return you don't ask that question again, right?' It was a typical Teller reply. His first instinct was always to throw money at a problem.

The offer was not enough to silence Kate's concerns. 'I'll say this once, so you understand it clearly, Brian. I will not do anything illegal.'

Teller rocked back, looking her up and down. 'Listen to you! Laying down the law. What's the weather like up there on your high horse?'

'Don't patronise me.' Her temper flared like cold fire. 'I have more than enough black marks of my own to deal with. I don't need any more.'

'Yes, quite,' Teller said airily. 'Remind me how long you were out of work after the whole . . . unpleasantness?' Again, he didn't wait for her to reply. 'How many job offers did you have? Oh, it was bugger all, wasn't it? At least until I came along and stuck my neck out to get you flying again.'

She let the bag drop off her shoulder, feeling the moment coming to a head as a flush of heat rose in her cheeks. 'You're threatening me?' If Kate Hood had a character trait she loathed the most, it was her temper. When the right buttons were pushed, her cool reserve could dissolve in an instant, and that always ended up with her saying or doing something she couldn't take back. She was close to it now.

'Don't be so dramatic,' he replied. 'I'm telling you it like it is, Kate. I'm a realist.'

Her jaw hardened. 'In my experience, people who make that claim just want carte blanche to be an arsehole.'

'I don't—' Whatever Teller was going to say next, the rest of the sentence died in his throat as a convoy of vehicles rolled up to sudden halt outside the open doors of the hangar.

Kate saw a nondescript car, a big American 4x4, and between them a panel truck. But no, not a truck. A prisoner transport. The second the convoy stopped rolling, men with serious, hawkish demeanours decamped from the vehicles, looking around in all directions like they were expecting trouble.

'Balls.' Teller looked at his watch. 'They're early.'

The surge of annoyance building in Kate turned icy cold and the truth they were dancing around could not be ignored any more. The presence of the truck could only mean one thing.

'No.' She prodded Teller in the chest. 'No. I'm not doing this.'

'Why do you have to be so bloody difficult?' Teller hissed back at her. 'Why can't you hold your nose and do a shitty job for once without complaining about it? You're not too good for this work, Kate!'

A hard-faced man disappeared into the back of the transport truck, and Kate saw movement behind its reinforced glass windows. His comrades stood around, their hands close to bulges under their jackets. She knew military types when she saw them, the trained-in, action-ready stances, and the feral alertness in their eyes.

'So it is true. You're running dark flights,' she said, finally saying it out loud. 'Renditions.'

Teller winced. 'We don't use the "r" word.'

'Bloody hell, Brian!' The gauge of her temper flicked back to the other side of the dial again, from cold shock to hot anger. 'I knew you were capable of dubious crap, but I never seriously thought you could . . .' She trailed off, then shook her head. 'How deep are you in to this?'

Kate knew for a fact that John Price had been on 'special' call for night-time trips for a least a year, and she thought about the flights the Hawker had made that no one talked about. *How long had this been happening right under her nose?* It galled Kate that she knew something was off but that she had never bothered to look too hard at it. *Too afraid to rock the boat*, she thought.

It could be dressed up in any kind of obfuscating language, excused through whatever loopholes or justifications might exist, but the work of a rendition operation was and always would be dirty and sordid. It was an exercise in the systematic abuse of a person's legal rights, plain and simple.

At the centre there would be a prisoner. A suspect held by a government, always in a nation that liked to style itself as democratic and righteous, a suspect believed to have information vital to national security or to pose some other sort of threat. By law, that person could not be forcibly compelled to comply with investigators, not in countries where nasty euphemisms like 'enhanced interrogation' were prohibited.

But there were plenty of other places where those types of laws didn't exist. So-called black sites, inside the borders of nations with a much more permissive relationship with institutionalised torture. And all it took to get there was one short plane flight.

Teller let out a sigh. 'Do you know how much it costs to keep this company going?' He shook his head. 'Of course you don't. But it can't have escaped your notice that we're barely running half the flights we did two years ago! COVID, Brexit, climate change ... you can blame whatever cause you want, the result's the same. Incoming is way down and outgoings continue to rise. Some brainless influencer posts on social media that a private jet is bad for the environment and all of a sudden I have fifty cancellations to deal with. Meanwhile, I'm trying to keep the wolf from the door.'

'And you're doing that by illegally ferrying prisoners to countries with no human rights treaties?'

'It's not illegal,' Teller said firmly.

'But it *is* immoral.' Kate glared at him.

'Well, sadly noble ethics can't pay for aviation fuel, servicing, ground fees, your wages and a hundred other bills.' He shot a nervous look in the direction of the parked vehicles. Some of the men were casting questioning glances in Teller and Kate's direction. He leaned in and his voice turned low and urgent. 'Do you want to keep flying, Kate? Keep working?' Teller gestured at the truck. 'You think I like being part of this? Of course I bloody don't! But I don't have a choice! It's not like I'm doing this to make myself millions – I'm doing it to stay afloat. It's not just my neck or your neck on the line, Kate. It's John and his family, it's our crews and techs, all the way down to Maggie on the front desk. I don't take these jobs, we go bust and it means everyone is out on the street, as simple as that.'

Kate blinked as she thought about the plump, efficient, fifty-something woman who ran the phones in the front office. Maggie was a ray of sunshine, the sort of person who always had a smile, always remembered people's birthdays, who soldiered on despite having an elderly mum with dementia, paying for a care home whose costs ate into most of what the receptionist earned. Without work, her life would collapse. And Maggie was only one of a dozen people in Teller's employ.

But the alternative was nauseating. She wasn't naive, and as former military herself, she understood full well that sometimes an aggressive approach was the only solution to a threat. But there was a world of difference between going up against an enemy in combat and torturing someone to within an inch of their life.

Teller was silent for a moment, and then his manner shifted. He drew himself up, becoming formal and distant. 'I don't have to justify myself to you. I won't lose what I have worked for years to achieve, do you understand me? This is the situation: you are going to fly the Hawker. You are going to do as you are told. And that will be the end of it. If you refuse, if you step out of line . . . If you make me do this, I will sack you on the spot and your career really will be over. For good this time.' He didn't blink as the threat unveiled itself in all its potency.

'If *I* make you do it?' Kate echoed his words. 'You nasty little prick.' She wanted her reply to be cutting, but she heard the fight fading from her own voice as the weariness set in. For a moment, she thought about threatening to go to the press, and dragging this into the daylight. But if she did, it would be Maggie and the other staff who would ultimately suffer the consequences.

It didn't matter if Teller's claims he had no choice were true or not, he had taken away Kate's agency and left her with nothing but an escalating series of worsening options.

She couldn't look at him any more. Feeling sick inside, Kate snatched up her flight bag and stalked away, marching back towards the waiting Hawker.

SIX

'This is him,' said Finn, from the corner of his mouth, as a man approached them. 'Teller, the owner.'

'Right.' Breeze took a breath and stepped up to meet him beside the hangar's open doors. 'Mr Teller. We ready to go?'

Teller paused, fingering the folder in his hand. He looked between Breeze and Finn, having clearly expected the MI6 agent to be the person in charge. He recovered quickly and offered a thin, perfunctory smile. 'You're a bit early.'

'Does that present a problem?' Breeze gave him a solid, unswerving look.

'Not a problem. Just ... we have to re-calibrate the timetable.' His smile widened, but it didn't meet his eyes. 'There are procedures we have to follow. We can't take off whenever we like.'

'Yeah, I know how it works.'

She read the man, taking the measure of him. It was a skill Breeze had honed through her years of experience as a case officer; the ability to take a mental snapshot of a person and judge in moments as to whether they would make a useful asset. She equated it to having a radar in her head that could pick up the blips of human frailties so they could be exploited.

This guy exhibited a few tells that Breeze knew she could take advantage of. He had a way about him that suggested a core of arrogance that would respond to flattery, and a needy streak that could be controlled through greed. But better than that, he seemed desperate, as much as he tried to hide it. That was the button she'd push to get what she wanted from him.

Breeze nodded at the Hawker jet. 'That's our ride?'

'Pre-flighting as we speak,' said Teller. 'If I can ask you to be patient . . .'

'Then who the fuck is she?' Breeze indicated the woman moving around inside the Hawker's cockpit, visible through the canopy windows. She had the white shirt and shoulder boards of a pilot, and she was definitely *not* the man that the Brits had vetted to handle the flight. 'Where the hell is . . .' Breeze had forgotten the pilot's name, and shot a look in Finn's direction for a cue.

'John Price,' said the MI6 officer.

'Price,' repeated Breeze.

Teller's colour faded. 'John is . . . currently unavailable. I made the decision to substitute him with one of my other personnel. Katherine Hood.' He offered her the folder. 'A good pilot, also former military, although she was Royal Air Force whereas John was a naval aviator. I assure you, she's highly competent, very professional.'

Breeze smelled a lie in there somewhere and filed that away for later consideration. '*You* made a decision? Without informing us, *you* did that?' She closed the distance between them, and Teller retreated a step. 'It was obviously not communicated to you that you do not have the authority to make last-second crew changes.' She plucked the folder from his hand, giving Hood's personnel file the briefest of glances before handing it off to Finn, who leafed through the pages, scanning the text intently.

'Where is Mr Price now?' Finn's question was terse. If anything, he sounded more annoyed about it than Breeze. 'He should be here.'

Teller equivocated, and she knew he was trying to dig himself out of the hole. 'I'm afraid he didn't come in today. I haven't been able to reach him, and I was aware of the urgency of your needs. *That* was clearly communicated to me. So I brought in a replacement.'

Breeze turned and strode over to the SUV, where Chester sat waiting. 'Marty! Look alive.'

As she reached the vehicle, Finn stepped closer to speak so his voice would not carry. 'This is highly irregular. Price's undergone a full evaluation. Whenever Six has used Teller's company, he's been the pilot. The man's a known quantity. We can't swap in someone else at the last second.'

'I know that!' Breeze shot back. 'Damn it, this is the last thing we need tonight.'

'So, what gives?' Marty stepped up, his brow furrowing. 'Do we scrub the whole flight?'

'Of course we fucking don't,' Breeze retorted, and bit down on her next thought before it slipped out.

Teller was more right than he knew – there was a real urgency to this whole operation. Only Breeze and Knox were aware of it, but there was an additional piece of time-critical intelligence that the CIA had chosen not to share with the British.

Intercepted cell phone chatter gathered through the agency's PRISM listening network had isolated an uptick in communications between known al-Sakakin affiliates. There were plans in motion among the extremists' network for a new terror strike that would go beyond their recent targets in Europe and Asia, and into the United States.

The prediction was for a chemical attack, or possibly another truck bomb. Hard details were thin on the ground. The weight of a lot of expectation rested on Breeze's shoulders, and she had pulled in many favours to be the one to take charge of Yusuf's interrogation. She had to get results, and get them *quickly*. But Price's sudden disappearing act was ringing a lot of alarm bells.

'The asset can't stay here,' she said firmly. 'We already booked him a suite with a view of the beach.'

Marty glanced at Finn. 'What about your guy? You brought a co-pilot, right? Can't he fly the plane solo?'

'Ray?' Finn shook his head. 'No. That's a . . . bad idea. Not to mention against aviation law.'

The other man looked around, surveying Ridley Hill's runway. 'OK, then can't we get someone else up here who *is* cleared? Or swing a, I dunno, a military flight?'

'That would take too long, and too many questions would have to be answered,' said Finn, before Breeze could reply. 'And it widens the circle of information.'

'What he said,' she added. 'And don't say fly commercial, that's about as dumb as putting the asset in a box and shipping him by FedEx.'

'So it's this or nothing.' Marty folded his arms. 'OK, I can run the replacement's name through the agency grid, see if anything pops. What did that guy say her name was?'

'Katherine Hood,' said Finn, watching the female pilot through the canopy. He handed the file to the other man. 'Take this. I'll talk to her and make an assessment.'

The by-the-book option was clear. If they were going to follow that, the next step was for Breeze to contact Langley and call off the whole transfer. That would most likely end up with some black helicopter wheeling in to scoop up the asset and re-disappear him, and she'd never get a hand on Yusuf again.

Breeze's shot at cracking al-Sakakin's weak link would be gone forever. She'd be back in Washington DC by day's end, doubtless to be called on the carpet as to why some minor snafu had derailed the entire operation.

And God help her if, in the meantime, Nasir and Hamid set off something horrific on US soil. The blame for that would fit nicely round her neck, and there was no shortage of people in the agency who would line up to put it there. In the intelligence community, one either became a hero or lived long enough to be the scapegoat, and Breeze had plenty of enemies inside the Beltway.

'*Fuuuuuck.*' She pinched the bridge of her nose and drew out the swearword into a long, exasperated exhalation. 'I do not need this shit today.' Without looking, she waved her hand at the two men and nodded. 'OK, yeah. Both of you, get to work.'

Finn strode quickly across the apron, sparing Miles a sideways look as the other agent got out of the car. He could see Ray in the back seat, poring over a map of the proposed flight plan.

'There's a problem.' Miles was perceptive when he needed to be, and it didn't take a genius to guess from Finn's tight expression that the evening was not going smoothly.

'Stay there,' Finn told him. 'I'm sorting it.'

'You want me to call in to Control?'

Finn shook his head. 'This operation is under a blind. No contact once active.' He sounded more confident than he felt. The whole plan for tonight revolved around certain factors being in the right place at the right time, and one of those was

John Price's backside in the captain's seat. Without him, the night's work could fall to bits before it even started.

Finn hesitated at the foot of the steps leading into the Hawker's cabin and looked away, in the direction of the service road leading down to the airfield's main entrance. All would be well if Price's Porsche suddenly appeared – as if it was just a matter of the man turning up late, delayed by traffic or something else trivial – but all Finn saw was a police car zipping past on the main road.

He felt a vibration in his breast pocket. He had an encrypted sat phone hidden there, and not the standard Ministry-issue device used by his colleagues from Six. Careful to conceal the action from any observers, Finn walked behind the plane, putting the fuselage between him and everyone else, before removing it to check the message.

What he read there made the blood drain from his face. Finn considered his situation for a long moment and sighed.

Adapt and advance, he told himself. *It's that, or nothing*. He typed out a quick text message in reply and sent it, before secreting the phone again.

The MI6 officer boarded the plane and studied the interior. The main cabin was stripped down, lacking the opulent leather-clad and wood-inlaid detail of a typical executive jet. There were four seats arranged club style – two facing two – an open area behind them for cargo, along with a simple enclosed toilet and a basic galley. At the head of the aircraft, the vestibule leading into the flight deck had been retrofitted with a security door, the same as one might find on any airliner. Typically, jets of the Hawker's tonnage didn't even have a curtain to partition off the two areas, but the jet's modifications spoke to an understanding about what the aircraft could be used for.

Finn entered the cockpit without asking permission, and that earned him a severe look from the auburn-haired woman in the captain's seat. 'Mind if I join you?'

'You're not my co-pilot,' she replied, evaluating him in a single glance. In the middle of running a sequence of pre-flight checks, she deftly ran her fingers over levers on the central console, then worked at the battery switches on the panel above her head.

'I am not.' Still, he moved toward the other crewman's position. 'You're Katherine, I believe?'

'Cargo goes in the back,' she said, in a commanding tone that he ignored.

'I don't doubt it.' Finn clambered awkwardly over the console between the seats, grabbing at bits of the dashboard panel to steady himself.

'Watch where you put your hands,' said the pilot. 'Don't touch any of the switches.' Even as she said the words, Finn inadvertently did precisely that, setting off a trilling alarm that the woman reset with a low grunt of annoyance.

'Sorry,' he offered.

'This isn't a rental car,' she said testily. 'Whatever you're paying doesn't allow you to sit up front.'

'Your plane, your rules – is that it?'

'Yes, exactly.' She made a dismissive motion. 'Please go away, I have to concentrate.' The pilot moved from button to button, muttering the names of their functions under her breath like a quiet litany.

'I will, in a moment,' said Finn. 'This won't take long. We need to ask you some questions.'

'*We?*' She leaned back to toggle a switch on a panel behind her and a warning bell rang, quickly followed by the low whine of the jet's auxiliary power unit starting up. 'Who is *we*? Whatever private mercenary contractor you run with?'

Finn raised an eyebrow. 'I'm afraid you're mistaken. I'm employed by His Majesty's Government, Ms Hood. As I understand you once were.'

She looked away, and he saw the scar of an old wound there. 'Not for quite some time.' The pilot returned to the main panel, her hands continuing to move from point to point as she went through the series of start-up procedures.

Finn noted she didn't once glance down at the checklist crib sheet taped to the side panel. *She knows her stuff*, he thought. 'I've always liked working with former military, I have to say,' noted Finn, keeping his tone conversational. 'They understand the need-to-know. They get the job done.'

'And they don't ask questions.' She plucked the rest of the statement out of the air. 'That must save you a lot of trouble.'

'It does, rather.' Finn absently stroked his beard.

At first he thought the pilot's spiky manner stemmed from his uninvited imposition on her space, but there was more beneath that. *She doesn't want to be here. She's doing this under duress.* He looked out of the canopy, finding her boss in conversation with one of the ground crew. Something had seemed off to Finn about Teller's insistent assurances regarding Hood, and now he wondered what strings the man had pulled to get her to be here tonight. *That could be useful to know.*

She flicked the switch to test the cockpit's alert systems and enunciators, giving Finn an unexpected jolt as the yoke in front of him gave off a quick, loud vibration. The pilot took a little amusement from his surprise. 'Don't piss yourself. It's a stall warning, it's supposed to do that.'

He refocused his attention and took a gamble, going for the direct approach. 'What kind of aircraft did you fly? For the RAF, I mean?'

The reply took a moment to come, and when it did it was sullen. 'Fast ones.'

'Then you've been combat deployed, of course.' He considered Hood's age and the possible postings she might have been a part of. 'Operation Shader, in the Levant?'

The pilot gripped the flight yoke a little tighter but didn't answer directly. 'Need to know,' she replied, throwing his words back at him.

'I can find out,' he said, off-handed. The fact that she didn't confirm it was another indicator. In Finn's experience, military pilots made a point of having been in the thick of it, and Hood's reticence spoke volumes. 'I imagine Mr Teller hasn't fully briefed you,' he continued, 'so let me fill in the pertinent details.'

'Feel free,' she said dryly.

'This will be a low-profile flight. You will follow the route we have for you exactly. Keep radio communications to the absolute minimum requirements. You are not to engage in conversation with anyone who boards this aircraft for the duration of the outbound leg, unless directly spoken to. You will remain on the flight deck at all times with the security door partly open unless otherwise ordered, and when we reach our destination, you will not deplane.'

She gave a sarcastic snort. 'What if I need to pee?'

'Hold it.'

'Is that everything? Where exactly am I going to land?'

'Your co-pilot has the relevant charts and paperwork. And if he gives you a command, you're to follow it.'

'So I'm not even in charge of my own aircraft?' Hood bristled at that. 'Why am I even here? Why don't you get your own people to fly this trip? I imagine there's no shortage of you spooks. That's what you are, isn't it?'

'Plausible deniability,' he replied. 'I don't think you're an idiot, Ms Hood. You understand what is being done here.'

'Oh, I understand, all right.' Her reply was hard and judgmental. The pilot didn't need to add that she thought it repugnant. That was laced into every syllable she spoke.

Finn studied her. Hood was nothing like Price, who had made a virtue out of his incuriousness, and he had to consider that she might become a problem if he didn't tackle her head-on.

'Does it offend your sense of fair play?' When she didn't reply, he carried on. 'How is what the Security Services does any different from what you did from the cockpit of a fighter jet? Each job has an objective, a target. In order to neutralise it, you do what is required. It's not always neat and clean.'

'Whatever you say.' She tried to be dismissive, but Finn could sense the woman was conflicted. Then she looked up, inclining her head toward the transport truck outside. 'Who's the guest of honour?'

Despite her misgivings, and whatever moral code Katherine Hood adhered to, there was enough restraint still there to make her follow the orders she'd been given – even if she disliked them. Finn assumed that, as former military, she was used to the black-and-white binaries of *ally* and *enemy*. Presented in those terms, it might be possible to keep her on-mission when the time came.

'You know I can't tell you that,' he said, rising back out of the seat. 'But if you want a hint . . . well, you only have to watch the news.'

SEVEN

The truck rocked as Breeze climbed aboard, and she found a narrow gangway inside that led to a line of tiny holding cells. Knox stood sentinel in front of one cell's door, those either side of it vacant.

With a flick of her eyes, Breeze dismissed the big man, and Knox gave their prisoner one last warning look before stalking away. He pushed past her, hesitating by the door. 'Be right outside.'

Breeze waved him off with a nod. She didn't anticipate any problems from the asset that would need a stone-hard son of a bitch like Knox at her shoulder, but one could not be too careful. She flipped open a fold-down seat opposite the occupied cell and settled carefully on to it.

On the other side of the plastic door, Yusuf peered back through the scuffed transparent barrier. His eyes were wide as saucers and he had the sheen of a flop sweat over his dark brow where his hair receded. 'Wh-where are you taking me? Will you please give me an answer?'

'Oh, you'll like it there,' she told him. 'Warm climate. Friendly people.'

'You are American,' he said, blinking nervously.

'What gave it away?' Breeze sniffed.

'The men who kidnapped me, they were British.'

'You haven't been *kidnapped*,' she corrected, with a terse chuckle. 'You're, ah, helping us with our investigations.'

'Please.' He put a lifetime of pain and fear into that one word. 'I am begging you. Have mercy. I am not a bad person!' He shook his head, wiping tears from his eyes with the heels of his hands, the wrists still fastened together with thick plastic strips. 'Why is this happening to me?' The question wasn't for her, but an entreaty to cruel fate. 'What have I done to deserve this?' He bowed his head, switching to Arabic, making a plea to his God.

Breeze leaned forward and tapped hard on the plastic. 'Hey. *Hey!*' She pointed at her face. 'Look at me. Don't go asking for divine intervention, that's a waste of everyone's time. Allah can't hear you. And he sure as shit isn't going to see you where you're going.'

Yusuf's jaw worked, but no words came out. He shrank back from her as far as he could go, until his back was pressed up to the far wall of the tiny cell.

'I'm talking about a hole so dark, so deep ... even the fucking ghosts are afraid to haunt it.' Breeze shook her head, warming to her performance. 'A man goes in there ... he drops off the face of the world.' She paused, making a show of listening. 'You hear that sound?' In the quiet, over Yusuf's gasping breaths, the murmur of an idling jet engine reached them. 'That's your ride warming up, buddy boy. And it's gonna be a one-way trip, unless you level with me.'

'No.' The word was a sob. 'I do not know why this is happening! I do not know what you want me to say, I cannot tell you what I do not know! You think I am someone who does terrible things, is that it? But you are wrong!' He stared at her with his wide, watery eyes. 'Can you not be mistaken?' Is it not possible that you have arrested the wrong man?'

'Oh, we screw up all the time,' Breeze said airily. She let out a bleak snort of gallows humour. 'Like you wouldn't believe! Finely oiled machine, my tits! This line of work is like running over a bridge that's collapsing in slow motion – you gotta be able to stay one step ahead of it.' She folded her arms across her chest. 'But there are the good days. Like when your file came across my desk. I knew we had something important.'

'I-I am *nobody*,' said the prisoner, suddenly spent. 'I am nothing. I *know* nothing.' He gave a brittle laugh. 'Just ask my wife.'

'I don't think you have a wife.' Breeze shook her head again. 'And you must know *something*, Yusuf. Everyone knows something, even if they don't know they know it.'

He blinked at her. 'You speak in riddles.'

'The place we're taking you to,' she said, 'it doesn't have an official name, just a military identification number. Location One-One. But the guys back at home have a nickname; they call it *Snake Eyes*.' She made a casting motion with her hand. 'Like with the dice in a craps game, right?' Yusuf shook his head, not understanding the reference, and she went on. 'Two ones, lowest score. Bad luck for you.'

The captive stared at the floor and made a valiant attempt to push down his panic and find a manner approximating calmness. 'My name is Yusuf al-Amal. I am a businessman from Jeddah. I work for a small company that exports sidr honey from Yemen.'

'It's a good cover,' Breeze noted, and she meant it. The team of diggers the CIA had tasked with systematically dismantling the man's life story had said so. *Airtight*, they had reported, *perfect*. 'Very believable. Gives you good freedom of movement; covers up a multitude of sins. We might have missed you if we hadn't been looking close enough.'

Yusuf took in a breath, forcing himself not to be distracted. 'We . . . *I* have no connection to the extremists you Americans are searching for.'

Breeze spoke, as if she was having an entirely different conversation. 'You know, some people . . . we both know the kind, right, bleeding hearts with their goddamn avocado toast and chai fucking lattes? Those people like to say, "Oh, enhanced interrogation, it doesn't work, it's not reliable." And they're right. Most of the time it is flaky as hell. Do it wrong and the asset will tell you anything just to make you stop hurting them. They'll admit to everything, even if it isn't even close to being accurate.' She held up a hand. 'But, see, that's where the talent comes in. The skill of it. It's about being able to apply exactly the right amount of pressure to a person – not too little, not too much – and finding the sweet spot.' Breeze closed her fingers, like a snake's jaws snapping shut. 'That's where the good content is, when you peel back the lie.'

'You are going t-to torture me.' Yusuf's brief, careful calm began to fracture again.

Breeze shook her head. 'No. I'm going to watch someone else do that.' The folding chair creaked as she sat back. 'You ever get in trouble in the water, like nearly drown? Ever had an electric shock off something? Ever been so thirsty or so tired you thought your head would split? You know how that feels? Because you will.'

Yusuf rocked back and forth, each breath coming faster than the last. 'I . . . I have answered the questions the British asked me.' He was working himself into an anxiety attack.

'I promise you! I did not lie! If I could help, I would do that, but I swear to you on my life, I am not a criminal!' His voice cracked and shuddered. 'I am—'

'Were you gonna say *innocent?*' Breeze interrupted him. 'We'll find out for sure soon enough.'

The door at the far end of the compartment clattered open and she shifted to see Marty Chester standing on the threshold, his ubiquitous tablet in one pale-fingered hand. He never put the device down, as if it was surgically attached to him. Marty's expression was sheepish.

'What?'

'The, ah, the check on the Hood woman?' He jerked a thumb in the direction of the plane outside. 'Acceptable, given the circumstances.'

'Any red flags?' Breeze stood up and turned her back on Yusuf, who had started to cry into his palms.

Marty hesitated, reluctant to speak in front of the prisoner. At length, he held up his thumb and forefinger a short distance apart – the universal gesture for 'a little bit'.

Breeze sucked her teeth. 'Figures.' She marched down the truck, leaving Yusuf to his weeping, and climbed out. She slammed the door shut behind her and put a heavy hand on Marty's shoulder. 'Explain it to me,' she demanded, 'and you better not tell me she's a card-carrying Communist.'

'Blimey, you weren't wrong about this place.' Grace surveyed the homes passing by the police car on either side of the road. 'Bit posh, innit?'

'Yeah,' noted Harris, driving them by a flower-adorned sign reading *Welcome to Wethill*. 'Twinned with *LeSnob Du Mer* in the South of France, or some such bollocks.'

'That's not a real town,' she replied, with a snort. 'You're making that up.'

'The preservation society will be well miffed to hear you say that.'

They drove past a perfectly manicured green and neighbouring duck pond, both swathes of shadow in the evening gloom. Soft amber light spilled out of a thatch-roofed pub called the Hen & Horseshoe, but there were few other signs of life aside from the odd twitching curtain as they drove through the village proper, away from the core of old fifteenth-century homes and out toward the sprawl of newer, post-war builds. The houses put up in the last hundred years were spread further apart; a mix of identical retiree bungalows alongside three-storey red-brick properties behind gates and low walls.

One of the latter was listed as John Price's residence, and Harris took the car up the short gravel drive to park in front of the place. 'Lights are on,' he noted, indicating an exterior lamp by the door and a glow through the windows. Their casual banter faded away, both of them becoming serious and watchful.

He followed Grace, stepping carefully, trying to take in everything at once. From here, it didn't seem like anything was awry. The evening was quiet, nothing more than a mutter of wind shifting the branches of nearby trees.

'I'll try them again.' Grace dialled Price's landline from her cell phone, and they both heard the jangle of the phone ringing inside the house. When no one picked up, she cut the call and sighed.

Harris glanced in his colleague's direction. He quietly hoped that the house was completely empty, and that it wasn't just a matter of someone being in the bath with the radio on and missing the sound of the phone. Because if there was a resident here, it would be Price's wife or his daughter; and then Harris and Grace would be in the unenviable position of having to give notification of a tragic death to a loved one.

They had training for that sort of thing, of course, but it didn't come easily to the policeman. No one liked doing notifications. It made Harris feel sad and useless, and he never really knew what to say when confronted with somebody bursting into tears. Angry people, those he could handle, but he found the other end of the emotional spectrum tough to parse.

Grace was adept at it, though. She embodied the quality of her name whenever they had to deal with a MOP – *member of the public* – rendered distraught by some unpleasant news.

'Knock, knock?' she said, nodding at the door.

'Look around first?' Harris countered.

Off a nod from Grace, he wandered to the detached garage and examined the sheet-metal door. An up-and-over affair, it had been made to be secured with a handle at the bottom, but there was a thick bar of shadow down there and the door wasn't fully shut.

Harris nudged it with the tip of his patrol boot and it moved freely with a metallic creaking. He imagined Price leaving in his car, coming back to close the door but not securing it. *Who would do that?* he thought. Not that Wethill was exactly a hotbed of crime, but it wasn't smart to leave anything open, especially if it gave a potential offender open access into your property.

'Jake.' His train of thought pulled up sharply when Grace called out his name. He found her by the house's bay window, up on tiptoe, her nose pressed to the glass. The tone of her voice said *trouble*. She leaned back and met his gaze. Her face had a stony cast to it, an expression he rarely saw on her and always dreaded.

Grace didn't have to say any more. Harris came up as she stepped away, and he peered in through a fractional gap between the closed curtains.

'Tell me what you see in there,' she said.

'Living room,' he began. 'Sofa. Armchair. Coffee table.' He turned his head, changing the angle, assembling a mental image of the space on the other side of the window through the thin vertical slices of it visible through the gap. The interior of the Price household was softly lit by a table lamp, mostly dark-coloured woods and faux Victorian in style, with bookshelves and pictures on the wall. 'Don't see anyone.'

'You sure?'

Harris was going to reply in the affirmative when his eye caught on something and he blinked, refocusing his attention. There was a door at the far end of the room, a grid of frosted glass squares, and beyond it probably a dining room or a kitchen. Close to the bottom of the door was a mark on the glass, streaks that looked fresh.

That looked *wet*.

As his gaze snapped to that spot, he saw something else. Visible through the gap between the edge of frame and the half-open door, on the floor of the other room there was a pale, curved object. It looked like a vase lying on its side, white like porcelain.

Harris pulled his torch from the pouch on his belt and put a powerful beam of LED light into the room. His gut tightened. The streaks on the glass were rust red, and the shape on the floor wasn't porcelain at all, but the pale pink of flesh.

'Body?' Grace asked gravely.

'Body,' he replied.

'Going in, then.' Grace snapped on a pair of blue nitrile gloves and tossed another set to Harris, who mirrored her actions. 'There's a side gate here – use the kitchen door?'

'Yeah, sure.' Harris's heart beat faster as he gave the smaller woman a hand up and she rolled over the metal gate and into the back garden. Grace pulled the bolt from the other side to open it, and then they both circled up and around the house.

'Police officers!' She called out a warning as they approached. 'We're going to make a forcible entry! Anyone in the house, make yourself known!'

'Back door's already open.' Harris pointed with a jut of his chin. As with the garage, the plastic-framed door had been left in a hurry without being secured.

With a flick of her wrist, Grace snapped open her collapsible baton to its full length and used the tip to push the door open. Harris swung up his flashlight and bathed the kitchen in clinical white light.

The beam caught on something and he froze.

There were two of them. The bodies lay stacked on top of one another in a corner. Black patches of blood on the tiled floor glistened in pools, spatters and trails, making it clear that after the savage attacks that had killed them, the middle-aged woman and the teenage girl had been moved, in an attempt to hide them from sight.

Instinctively, Grace reached up and made the sign of the cross over her forehead and chest, whispering a few words of soft prayer as she did so.

Harris's response was baser, but no less heartfelt. 'Bugger me.'

'Single line,' she reminded him, warning her colleague to follow exactly the same path into the kitchen as she did, as they had at the site of the car crash, in order to minimise any possible contamination of what was now a major crime scene.

Harris pulled his Airwave and called in to the station while Grace stooped and checked the motionless bodies, in the vain hope that they might still be alive. But after a moment, she looked back up at her colleague and shook her head.

The radio call raced invisibly away, awakening the first responses from the wider system. People would be alerted, messages would be sent. An ambulance, a scene-of-crime unit, and the Murder Investigation Team would all be on the way in short order. The whole mechanism activated, a wave of motion and intention radiating out from the site of this grisly discovery.

'It's the wife and the daughter.' Grace's tone became flat and emotionless. She stood up and backed off, careful not to touch anything.

'You sure?'

She pointed to a framed photo hanging beside a corkboard festooned with shopping lists, memos and other papers. The face of the dead man in the Porsche was there, smiling alongside those of the woman and the girl in happier times.

Harris surveyed the room, holding his radio away as the voice of the dispatcher crackled. On the walls there were more bloody streaks, smears that looked like handprints and the debris of items that had been broken or knocked into disarray. 'There's been a struggle,' he added, and then his gaze fell upon an object sitting on the draining board.

An expensive chef's knife, with an eight-inch blade. Whoever had used it in the act of brutality hadn't bothered to clean it off, leaving the murder weapon discarded, the bright metal coated with a film of congealing blood.

That detail alone suggested multiple possibilities – everything from a killer who had fled in shock at their crime, to one who had prepared well enough to leave no physical evidence behind them.

'Out, out,' said Grace, waving him away, and Harris obeyed, backing on to the garden patio. He caught sight of her face as she came after him. She covered it well, but the viciousness of the stabbing had caught her off guard.

'You all right, Isla?' When she didn't respond, he sighed in sympathy. 'Yeah, me neither. What have we walked into here?'

Grace took a breath. 'Murder-suicide?'

'Price kills his family and then deliberately drives his car into the back of a tractor.' Saying it out loud made it seem unreal, but they had both seen worse caused by less comprehensible reasons. A disturbingly large number of murders could be traced back to someone the victim knew personally, and when a woman was killed, the high likelihood of her partner being the culprit was a bleak, sobering statistic that Harris had seen play out again and again.

In the moment of silence, he knew they were both considering the same question: *why?* What motive, what reasoning would there be to unpick behind this horrible event? If John Price had murdered two members of his own family and then left the scene, what had compelled him to do such violence in the first instance? And had he taken his own life out of remorse after the fact?

'The passenger.' Grace spoke quietly, and Harris almost missed what she said, until she repeated the words. 'The passenger in his car. If Price really wasn't on his own when it went off the road . . . if there was someone else *there* . . .'

She trailed off and a chilly trickle travelled down the policeman's spine. 'There might have been someone else *here.*'

EIGHT

The Hawker was alive and ready to go, the low note of the jet's twin Garrett turbofans resonating up into the cockpit as the engines idled.

Kate lost herself in the rote motions of the pre-flight preparation, the actions coming to her as automatically as breathing, but the routine stalled when her fingers dithered over the keypad of the flight computer. The spook with the beard hadn't given her any more detail than Teller had, so for the moment, the aircraft remained set on *Destination Unknown*.

It was one more item on top of the pile of things she hated about this situation – that they wouldn't even trust the pilot with her exact end point. Without it, she couldn't make precise fuel calculations or flight duration estimates, she couldn't prepare a route that took into account the locations of airports for diversion or emergencies. It was a load of cloak and dagger rubbish, and Kate hated every second of it.

She looked out of the canopy, watching two of the people from the convoy of arrivals standing in close conversation. The taller of them was a late-twenties gangly sort with the pale monitor-screen tan Kate associated with techies and desk wonks. His slump-shouldered manner and his constant bobbing nods suggested to her that the man was used to being told what to do. A stocky woman with dark hair and constantly moving hands was grilling him, and Kate immediately identified her as an American. The distinctive cues in their body language set them apart from the less animated manners of Brits. That and the way the woman dressed – in a trouser suit two seasons behind the current European style – sealed the estimation for Kate. This person was the one in charge, moving through the space like she owned it, and the pilot felt a stab of resentment toward her.

Are you the reason I'm here, she wondered? *Are you the one who gave the order?*

The pale man looked up and caught Kate staring at them. He said something to the woman and she glanced in her direction. Kate reflexively broke line of sight, suddenly certain of the fact that they had been talking about her. She chewed her lip and glanced away, instead catching a glimpse of the man with the beard, the soft-spoken Englishman who had invaded the flight deck.

From her vantage point, she found him in the shadows of the Hawker's starboard wing, standing against the fuselage where the others wouldn't be able to see him. The bright slab of a sat phone illuminated his face as he worked away with his thumbs, typing out a message she was too far away to read.

Watching him send his text made Kate think of Alex, and she pulled out her own phone, flicking to a chat app that used images of bright cartoon animals as its user icons. Stabbing out letters with her index finger, she wrote a quick missive more for her peace of mind than for Alex's. She wanted to make sure he knew he was in her thoughts, and she wanted to reconnect before it was time to depart. There was no way to know when she would have the chance again.

HEADING OUT SOON, she wrote. DON'T WAIT UP. I'LL BE BACK TOMORROW MORNING. Kate punctuated the message with a heart emoji, then the little caricature sparrow that represented her trilled the words into the ether.

Alex and George were what was best in Kate Hood's life right now, and every moment she was denied the chance to be with them frustrated her.

After a moment, the phone gave off a pulse of vibration and Alex's cartoon bear grinned, emitting two more hearts and a thumb's up. FLY SAFE, it said.

'What is that?' A prim voice spoke up from the vestibule and Kate turned in her seat to see a dark-skinned man with a rounded nose looking down at her through a pair of rimless glasses. He indicated the phone. 'Finn should have told you – no personal electronics for the duration of the flight.' He opened his hand. 'Let me have it.'

'Who are you?' Kate looked the guy up and down, ignoring the demand.

'You can call me Ray,' he explained, still holding out his hand. 'I'm the co-pilot. Can I have your phone, please?'

'No, piss off,' Kate said, without heat, and she slipped the device back into her jacket pocket. The little act of defiance made her feel slightly better.

'We have procedures,' began Ray.

'So do I,' she shot back, silencing him. 'One of them is not getting dicked about by clients.' Kate pointed at the empty seat next to her. 'Why don't you see if you can impress me by sitting down and coding in the flight plan? Because I don't want to be doing this a single minute longer than I have to.'

He hesitated, and she could see him thinking about pushing back. But no matter what his bearded mate had said, Kate was damned if she would let some right-seater boss her about on her own aircraft. *Better to set out my stall first thing*, she thought, *than let these people try to walk all over me.*

Frowning at his wristwatch, Ray gave a sigh and took his position, flipping open the cover of a tablet computer that displayed the reference data required for the flight. He navigated around the Hawker's cockpit with the assurance of someone familiar with the aircraft type, punching in the relevant codes on the flight computer with quick, jabbing motions.

At least he seems competent, she thought, watching him work. *That's better than nothing.*

'You served?' She sensed the lingering stamp of military training on the man and decided to see if her instincts were right. If he was ex-RAF like her, Ray might have been a year or two behind her in the forces.

'Voyager flight crew.' The admission came reluctantly, stiffly, as if he had to prise it out of himself with a needle. '101 Squadron.'

Kate accepted that without comment. The Voyagers were the Royal Air Force's tankers, derived from the same airframe as civilian A330 airliners. It was altogether possible she might have taken fuel from his aircraft when flying a Tornado, but she stopped herself before saying that out loud. This man wasn't her comrade in arms, and he was not someone she was going to trade war stories with. It wouldn't pay to get too chummy.

Her attention returned to the screens in front of her. With Morocco as their destination, Kate expected to see the most likely landing site come up as Mohammed V International near Casablanca, or maybe Menara Airport outside of Marrakesh. But Ray's input brought up a location that she didn't immediately recognise, the airfield's four-letter ICAO code unfamiliar to her.

'What's your experience dealing with rougher strips?' He said. 'The less well-maintained runways, I mean.'

'If it's flat, I can land on it.' Kate answered the challenge with reflexive pilot's bravado. She indicated the screen. 'Where is that?'

'Sidi Ifni.' The name meant nothing, but she knew there were a dozen disused and mothballed airfields along the western coast of the North African country. 'It's not important,' continued Ray. 'We'll barely be on the ground five minutes for the transfer, then we'll transit north to Ben Slimane to tank up, then home.'

'Transfer?' She echoed the word, but Ray didn't elaborate.

Despite his assurances, Kate was not mollified, and in silence she studied the datum, elevation and runway length for their destination. A creeping, nagging disquiet crawled along her spine, pulling her back toward home as if there were invisible cords trying to tether her to the ground. Nothing about this flight sat well with Kate, and with each passing moment, she wanted more and more to tear away her headset and walk off the flight deck.

To hell with Teller and his thinly veiled threats. So what if he bad-mouthed her to everyone who listened, what would that alter? *Nothing*. Kate would still be a pariah to those in the know.

Except, if she walked out, she would be a pariah without a job and no real chance of ever having a career in aviation again. *Wings well and truly clipped.*

'Hold your nose,' she said, under her breath, recalling Teller's earlier comment. 'Just hold your nose, Kate, and fly the bloody plane.'

'What's that?' Ray looked up from his tablet.

She didn't reply. Movement outside the Hawker caught her attention as the dark-haired American woman and the guy with the beard – the one Ray had called Finn – climbed the steps to board the jet. Ignoring a censorious look from her co-pilot, Kate shifted in her seat to watch them enter the cabin.

'Oh, this is delightful,' said the American, turning up her nose at the Hawker's austere, stripped-down interior. 'So I'm guessing no caviar and cognac service, huh?' She found a seat and settled into it like she was planting a flag of conquest. 'Well, I've flown TWA, so I have seen worse.'

'Creature comforts aren't really in the budget for this sort of thing,' said Finn, noting Kate's attention. 'We're more of an economy class operation these days.' He stepped into the vestibule. 'Good to go?'

Finn addressed the question to Ray, but Kate took it from him, nodding at the cabin. 'All set. Take your seat, please.'

'There's still one more passenger to come.' Finn looked past her, and Kate followed his line of sight.

A figure in baggy black overalls was led out from the transport truck by their bound-together hands, their head lost under a dark sackcloth cowl. Grim-faced and muscular, the hard eyes of the man dragging the captive darted left and right as they walked the short distance to the Hawker.

He was the type that immediately set alarm bells ringing in Kate's head. *Not someone I want on my plane*, she told herself. But she couldn't stop herself from wondering who his charge might be. Ordinary criminals didn't warrant this kind of thing. Only the highest level of dangerous individuals deserved the black-bag treatment.

Kate had glimpsed the edges of activities like tonight's operation when she had been on deployment, catching it out of the corner of her eye as unmarked aircraft came and went from airstrips in the sandbox.

CIA, people would say. *MI6* or *PMC.* Whatever convenient three-letter acronym covered it best, they ultimately sounded the same warnings.

Don't ask questions. Mind your own business. Or you'll regret it.

The thuggish man pushed the hooded prisoner up the stairs and into the cabin, and Kate could see the captive's shoulders trembling with fright. Finn took control, guiding the prisoner to the seat opposite the American. He clipped the bound wrists to a metal bar on the inside of the cabin wall that Kate hadn't noticed before. She heard a weak moan as the hooded figure slumped, shrinking like a plastic doll exposed to a high heat.

The man with the hard eyes stood on the cabin threshold, watching Finn work with an expression of unfiltered dissatisfaction. When Finn was done, the other man leaned in and growled something in his ear. Kate didn't catch all of what he said, just the last part of an accusatory question.

'. . . handle this?'

'Get off the fucking plane, Knox.' The American snapped out the order at him before Finn could frame a reply. 'You're not coming with us. Not after last time.' She made a 'tut tut' noise and waggled her finger. 'Langley hasn't forgotten how you kicked the hell out of the last guy cos he looked at you funny.'

'Not what happened,' said Knox, grinding out the words. 'Still bullshit.' He gave Finn a last, razor-edged glare and stepped off the Hawker before closing up the hatch behind him.

'Jeez, I thought he would never leave,' said the American woman, each word fast and sharp. 'Can we *please* get this bird in the air if it is not too much trouble?' The last she directed straight down the line of the cabin toward the flight deck.

Kate took a long breath and let her hands settle on to the controls, scanning the panel and finding nothing but green lights and ready indicators. Adjusting her headset mike in front of her lips, she pressed the button that gave her control of the intercom speaker back in the cabin.

'This is your pilot speaking,' said Kate, as she eased the throttle forward and the Hawker began to roll. 'Flight time to our destination will be ...' she scanned the numbers on the screen, '...approximately three hours and twenty seven minutes. So, if everyone will kindly belt up, we'll be on our way.'

The numbers rolled around her head as she guided the jet on to the runway and lined up for departure, half-listening to Ray communicating tersely with Ridley Hill's control tower.

Just keep your eyes front, hands on the yoke, brain engaged. That had been the mantra recited by her flying instructor at RAF College Cranwell, a lifetime ago when training evolutions had been the only thing she had to worry about. *Fly the plane. That's your first and last job.*

'Not my last, if I can help it,' she muttered.

Kate poured on the power and the Hawker accelerated away, its nose rising off the ground, its wings biting into the night air.

'So, it's kind of like time travel,' said George, waving a hand at the ink-black sky overhead. He indicated the pole star high above them, the words spilling out of him. 'The light we're seeing isn't from right now, it's from hundreds of years ago, that's how long it takes to get here. We're looking into the past!'

Alex showed a lopsided grin. 'It amazes me how you remember all this. So how old is it, then?'

'Three hundred and twenty three years.' George answered without hesitation. 'Because it's three hundred and twenty three *light years* away. So that means, uh . . .' The boy trailed off, the numbers escaping him.

'That's what it looked like at the end of the seventeenth century,' offered his father. 'Well. Who needs a time machine, eh? You can just look up.'

'Yeah.' George recovered his momentum and flipped to a page in the book that Kate had given him. 'See, it says here that Polaris is actually three stars not one. It only looks like one from very far away. And because it's the brightest, if you can see it, you can always find your way home.'

Alex nodded along, not wanting to derail his son's enthusiasm. George came across like a bright kid when you got him talking about what he was interested in, but unfortunately that interest didn't extend to a lot of the subjects he studied in school. Listening to him expound, it was hard to believe this was the same boy whose teachers complained about his poor marks and inattention at every parent's evening.

We see this quite often in families where a divorce has taken place, the headmaster had told him, making little effort not to sound judgmental. *Or where a parent is absent. The child is easily distracted and lacks focus.*

Alex couldn't escape the sense that was a dig at him, but his shifts with the fire brigade were not always negotiable, and that meant sometimes George had to be a latchkey kid. It wasn't ideal, he knew that, but there were precious little options available, and he wasn't about to cede full responsibility for his son to his ex-wife Laura and whichever boyfriend she currently had.

We'll make it work. A few nights ago, Kate had squeezed Alex's hand and said those words, making it a promise – and for the first time in a long while, he'd felt like everything might get better.

If only outside influences didn't keep on pulling them off the course they wanted to follow. He sighed and refocused his attention on George. 'It's getting chilly. We should go indoors.' He walked over to the telescope and put a hand on it.

George made a face. 'Can we wait a bit?'

'Is there something else you want to look at?'

The boy stared at the ground. 'I wanted to wait until Kate flew over.'

'Oh. Right.' Alex thought about her message. He hadn't told George what she wrote, but the boy knew that the text had been from her.

Alex still wasn't a hundred per cent sure what his son thought of the woman in his life, and he'd elected to let the boy make his mind up on his own. Alex and Kate had been together for some time now, and it was likely they'd stay that way. Recently, he had been wondering if he hadn't made that clear enough, but this was a good sign – George had finally formed his own connection with Kate.

He looked at his watch. 'Should be soon.' They both turned to look in the direction of Ridley Hill, and presently the sound of aircraft engines came to them through the cold night air.

'Is that her?' George pointed at a cluster of blinking running lights around the angular shadow of an executive jet as it climbed high over the roof of the house, gaining altitude as it passed.

'I reckon.' Alex waved at the plane, but George just watched it go, his hands by his sides, his head turning to follow the jet until it vanished out of sight beyond a stand of trees. His son looked glum and distant. 'What's up, kiddo?'

George began the work of dismantling the telescope, finding his way to a reply. 'If Kate doesn't come home, does that meant we'll have to go live somewhere else?'

Alex frowned, looking up again as the sound of the jet's engines faded away. 'What makes you think that Kate won't come back?'

'Mum didn't,' said George, in a voice that broke his dad's heart, just a little.

'Find a place to park,' said Matvey, peering out through the side window of the BMW. 'Away from the streetlights.'

'OK.' Luka licked his lips and guided the black car over to the kerb beneath a heavy-canopied oak tree growing out of the pavement. He killed the engine and the interior of the vehicle darkened, the only weak illumination spilling from the satellite phone in Matvey's hand.

'Which one?' Stepan spoke up from the back seat, and he sounded vacant, indifferent to the whole thing.

'Twenty six.' Matvey read the details off the phone's tiny screen, and jutted his chin at the house across the street. 'The one with the blue door.'

Stepan leaned forward. 'Looks empty. Nobody home.'

Matvey had to agree with that initial impression. The house was an ordinary two-storey affair, a semi-detached construction with a garden behind and a cracked, crazy-paved driveway at the front. A cobalt-coloured Vauxhall Corsa sat on one side of the drive, a dormant shape in the gloom.

No lights were visible through the windows of the ground floor, or the bedrooms above, and no windows were open. It wouldn't be difficult to gain entry, if they needed to – they had the tools in the car to deal with the locks on the retrofitted double-glazed front door – but there would be little point breaking in if what they required was not present inside.

'If we have to go searching . . .' Luka was clearly thinking along the same lines. 'That will eat up time we do not have. We are already well behind schedule.'

'I am aware,' Matvey growled, rubbing a hand over his face. His headache had not abated. An after-effect of the car crash, that and the fresh cuts on his forehead and cheek nagged at him, fouling his mood. He found a pack of painkillers in his jacket and dry-swallowed two more of the chalky tablets.

'Are you certain this is the right place?' Stepan glanced around, his nose wrinkling in disdain. 'Not like the other house. This one is small.'

'You grew up in a shit-box apartment in Saratov, what do you know?' Luka looked back at the other man, taking the opportunity to goad him.

'I will bury you in a shit-box,' Stepan replied, with a mix of malice and studied disinterest.

'Both of you, shut your mouths.' Matvey had seen the two men on this trajectory before, and he stamped on it before it went too far. Stepan and Luka were like dogs, they were manageable when there was meat in the dish for them, but without that they became bored and turned on one another. 'This is where they told us to go.' He aimed a finger at the house with the blue door. 'Look.'

A faint glow had appeared in one of the lower windows, as if someone had turned on a light in a back room that had now filtered through. The glow wavered as a shadow passed in front of it; the house was occupied after all.

Luka grunted. 'We do it the same way as the other one?'

'It is not women this time,' noted Matvey, glancing at his phone before putting it away. The information he had been given mentioned a man and a young boy. 'We will try a different approach.'

'Pity.' Stepan worked at his knuckle, where dried blood had gotten into the folds of his skin.

'This is how we will proceed,' said Matvey, his tone hardening. The other two men listened intently as he outlined the way they would take control of the house and its occupants.

NINE

In a wide, slow turn, the Hawker banked around from its departure point and settled into a southerly flight path, taking it over the countryside of the High Weald and East Sussex, on course to go 'feet wet' over the English Channel along the shore somewhere between the seaside towns of Pevensey Bay and Bexhill.

From there, the jet would be over water for most of the duration, first following the French coastline, then skimming the edges of Spanish and Portuguese airspace, before finally crossing the mouth of the Mediterranean toward North Africa. Weather conditions were decent all the way down, with nothing but a few brooding rain cells over the Bay of Biscay, lurking there like surly teenagers on a corner looking for trouble.

Kate made a mental note to give the storm complex a wide berth and thought again about her computations. It wouldn't be a problem with the available weight of 'Jet A' fuel the Hawker carried in her wing tanks. The jet's duration margins were good – providing Kate's passengers didn't decide to do something stupid like change their destination at the last moment.

Now they were airborne, the pilot could at least lose herself in the work of flying the aircraft, maintaining her focus on the practical, manageable business of the job instead of dwelling on the reasons behind the flight.

Or so she would have liked.

'Get out of there,' said a voice at her back, and Kate saw the American woman reflected in the canopy window, standing in the flight deck vestibule with her hands on her hips. She was talking to the co-pilot. 'Go take a cigarette break or something.'

'There's no smoking on board this aircraft . . .' Ray blinked, uncertain if he should obey, but then he gave in and removed his headset, climbing out to venture back past the American.

Kate pointedly ignored her as she came forward to take his place. She made a meal of squeezing herself into the co-pilot's position, adjusting the seat and fiddling with it – but Kate noted she was careful not to touch anything vital, not like Finn had been. The pilot immediately had the sense that the woman was putting on a show for her, making more of a fuss than she really needed to.

When she finally put on the headset, Kate kept her eyes on the horizon and addressed her with chilly insolence. 'Does this look like a theme park ride to you? Whatever you're paying Teller, you don't all get to come up here and have a turn.'

'Oh, bless your heart for thinking you have a say in it.' The woman smiled sweetly. 'But you're right. Don't worry, Katherine, I'm not as impressed by the pretty lights as the usual rubes you must jet around.' She took in the view outside with a sigh. 'You get that a lot, I bet. Supermodels and their beefcake boyfriends posting shots for the 'Gram.' She made a mocking duck-face pout.

Kate shot her a look, her patience fading fast. 'Who the hell *are* you?'

The woman cocked her head. 'Lillian Breeze, US State Department. Pleased ta meetcha. I'm the momma bear of this little group of cubs. I wanted to introduce myself; explain a few details.'

'State Department,' echoed Kate, in a dour tone. 'I've heard that one before.'

'I'll bet you have. It does cover a multitude of sins.' Breeze made a face as she shifted her position, trying to get comfortable. 'Why don't they ever make these seats for the ample-assed? It's a fucking micro-aggression.' She blew out a breath. 'Look, can I level with you?'

'Please don't try me with the, "it's just us girls here" speech,' Kate shot back. 'I don't appreciate having my intelligence insulted.'

'You clearly do not.' Breeze paused, reframing her approach. 'I'm sorry about this.' She gestured at the air, and for the first time Kate felt like she actually meant what she was saying.

Or has she just found the right way to talk to me?

'I know Teller pulled you into this job with zero notice,' the other woman went on, brushing a stray curl of dark hair from her face. 'Something about cancelling your whole weekend, huh? Yeah, I'd be pissed too if I were you. But we are, collectively, shit out of luck right now, what with your colleague Mr Price having upped and vanished.'

Kate said nothing, aware of Breeze watching her closely.

'You know anything about that?' The American offered a prompt. 'You friends with him?'

'No, and no,' she replied. 'John's rather old-fashioned in his attitude towards women.'

'Meaning he's a stuffed shirt? Like Teller? Some flyboys really don't take kindly to skirts in the clubhouse.'

She knew Breeze was fishing, but Kate couldn't stop herself from answering. 'One can't always choose who one works with.'

'Oh, I heard *that.*' Breeze gave an emphatic nod. 'But this is the life we chose, right?'

Kate took a breath. Breeze was working her, trying to make her engage so she could establish a rapport. Tellingly, the other woman had yet to divulge anything about herself, while she had already gotten Kate to impart more than she wanted to.

Kate met her gaze. 'And what life is that, Lillian?'

Breeze's open expression closed down, becoming serious. A shutter descended, and the pilot wondered if *now* she was seeing the real person, or another mask. 'Katherine. Or is it Kate, Kathy, Katie? What do you prefer?'

'Directness,' she replied.

'Fair enough.' Breeze nodded again. 'I know you're former military, so you probably have a good idea what the fuck this is about.' She waved her hand in the air. 'I don't want to have a problem with you.' She pointed back at the cabin. 'I have plenty to be dealing with already. So, I want to be one hundred per cent certain that you are not going to be more trouble for me to reckon with. Now, I took a look at your jacket, the Ministry of Defence gave my people access.'

'Did they?' Kate's reply was cold. 'How generous of them.'

'You seem like a straight shooter,' continued Breeze. 'Am I right about that?'

'I'll do my job.' Kate broke eye contact, scanning the screens in front of her for somewhere else to look. *She's read my military file,* she thought. *Which means she knows the reasons why I left.*

'Look, I understand what it's like, doing this kind of work,' said Breeze. 'Of course I fuckin' do. We gotta grind through twice as hard as them, just to keep the same pace.' She inclined her head toward the men in the cabin. 'If you're clinical and tough, then you're a cold-ass bitch. If you're forthright and direct, that makes you aggressive, belligerent.' Breeze paused. 'In case you're wondering, I picked Team Belligerent – it was a good fit for me. So I get it, I really do. I empathise.'

'That's nice.' Kate kept her tone neutral. She knew something more was coming. 'You want to hold hands now? Maybe we can synch up our moon cycles.'

Breeze allowed herself an amused chuckle, and the expected intimidation came following on behind. 'I like your attitude. But know this – if you jerk me around, Katie, I will not hesitate one second before absolutely destroying you and all you hold dear. Am I clear?'

Even though Kate saw it coming, the pressure of the threat landed hard, like a ball of lead in her chest. 'You've given that speech a fair few times, haven't you?'

'Sure thing,' said Breeze. 'Does it show?' She shifted in the seat again and spared her a wan smile. 'It's nothing personal. It's just the job.'

'Right,' Kate retorted coldly. 'I understand completely.' She returned to the controls, turning away from the American woman. 'So now you can sod off my flight deck.'

At first, Alex thought he had misheard the knock at the front door. It was hesitant, wary, and it wasn't until it sounded a second time that he was sure of it.

'Door,' called George, by way of confirmation, his voice echoing from the kitchen.

'Yeah, I've got it.' Alex walked up the short hallway, his brow furrowing. *Who would be out there at this time of night?*

Most people would be at home in front of the television, not up and about bothering their neighbours. He wondered idly if it might be Patricia, the elderly lady who lived alone across the road. Sometimes she randomly appeared to borrow something or make an excuse for a chat. But not usually after sunset. And when she called on them, she always used the electronic bell that lit up and triggered its built-in camera.

Alex saw a shadow through the fan of frosted glass at the top of the door and didn't recognise the pensioner's thin profile. He automatically put the heel of his right hand on the back of the door and opened it enough to peer out.

A man in a black leather jacket, with thin, ashen hair and a broad build stood on the step. His gloved hands knitting together, he affected a slump-shouldered, apologetic posture. 'Hello. Thank you! So sorry to bother you.'

His accent reminded Alex of one of the development firefighters who had come on to his crew a few months ago; a Polish-born trainee by the name of Marek. But unlike Marek's warm manner and easy grin, the man on the doorstep had a plastic smile that didn't reach his eyes, and scratches on his face that looked recent.

Something about him immediately put Alex on alert, and he pressed his foot to the door, annoyed at himself for not having secured the chain-lock before opening it to a stranger.

'Can I help you?' Alex kept his tone brisk and deliberately unwelcoming.

'I am very sorry . . . you were going out?' The man pointed with one hand, the other disappearing into the pocket of his jacket. Alex was still in his coat and shoes from having been stargazing in the garden with his son. 'Sorry to interrupt! I am pleased I caught you!'

'Listen, if you're selling something, whatever it is, we're not interested.' Alex began to close the door.

'No, no!' The man held up a hand and shook his head. 'Please! I hope you can help me! I am quite lost. My car, you see . . .' He pointed at a black shape parked up the road, lost in shadow. 'The computer voice with the map? She does not work any more!'

'You mean the sat nav?'

'Sat nav. Yes.' The man nodded vigorously, glancing up and down the empty path. 'But I should say no. And so I am not sure where I am.'

'This street is Luna Road,' explained Alex. 'Is that where you were looking for, mate?'

'Oh yes.'

As the other man replied, Alex noticed for the first time that the house's digital bell was missing from the doorframe. The whole wireless unit had been physically removed from its mounting. His face fell.

'Is there something wrong?'

'My doorbell—'

Alex started to answer, but the sound of splintering wood carried down the hallway from beyond the kitchen, and he heard George call out a worried 'Dad?'

For a fraction of a second, Alex's attention split between the stranger on the doorstep and the fearful tone of his son's voice. He did what any good parent would do and glanced towards his son.

The man in the jacket had been waiting for exactly that moment, having been prepared to act on the distraction from the second he approached the house. The long, nickel-plated pistol he had concealed came out of his pocket as he shoulder-charged into the half-open door, slamming it back on its hinges.

The door cracked against Alex's leg and he stumbled, briefly caught off-guard, long enough for the stranger to club him across the face with the butt of the gun. The brutal impact lit sparks of light and sent a harsh bolt of pain through his skull.

Alex fell against the wall, knocking down a framed picture of a lighthouse that had been a gift from his sister. The man in the black jacket was already over the threshold and inside the house as Alex recovered, adrenaline burning through his brief moment of inattention.

He pushed back with a growl on his lips, his big hands rising, forming into fists, ready to fight – but then he stopped dead.

Alex hadn't quite grasped what the man in the jacket had used to strike him with, but now he saw it. The shape of the shiny, long-nosed semi-automatic pressed into his sternum, and the stranger's faux-hapless act had evaporated.

'Make the wrong choice and you will die,' he said carefully. 'Then the boy. That is what she will see when she comes home. Is that what you want?'

Stiff and wooden, Alex shook his head, the fight in him suddenly stalled.

This wasn't the first time someone had threatened him with a gun. A few months back, he'd been called in on a shout at a rough estate where a house had been turned into a makeshift cannabis farm. The resident had come after the firefighters with a sawn-off shotgun after Alex had told him they couldn't save the place – and his crop of dope plants – from the electrical fire consuming it. But that bloke had been high as a kite, and in his dumb fury he hadn't remembered to load any cartridges.

One look at the iron-hard eyes of the stranger with the pistol told Alex this man was in a totally different league. He had a predatory coldness about him, and there was zero doubt in Alex's mind that he could kill without a second's hesitation. That, however, was not the greatest of the fears that gripped him.

George.

Alex wanted to shout out his son's name as loud as he could, tell him to run and run and not look back.

The man with the silenced gun cocked his head, and as if he plucked the terrified thought from Alex's mind, he raised a gloved hand and waggled an admonishing finger at him.

'Think, Mr Walker,' he said, and the fact the gunman knew his name made the chill in Alex's blood grow ever colder. 'Think about your son.'

A wave of fatigue came over him, and his cheeks became hot as his colour rose. Alex felt ashamed and defeated. He tasted a trickle of blood on his lip, oozing from a fresh cut on his face. At length, he let his hands drop.

'Good decision.' The man stepped back, gesturing with the pistol. 'Stand up slowly.'

As he did so, the man reached for the hallway light switch, flicked it off, then on, then off again. Out on the road, Alex saw an answering flash from the headlights of the parked car.

'Dad?' He turned toward the sound of George's voice and the unfolding panic of the night's terrible turn racked up another few notches.

Another stranger stood at the far end of the hallway, one gloved hand on George's shoulder. Alex's son still held the kettle he'd been filling to make some tea, and it shook in his grip. The man holding George shared the Slavic look of the man in the black jacket, and he had the bored, malicious eyes of a brute.

'He . . . he came in over the back,' said George, blinking as he tried to hold back tears. 'Broke our fence.'

'Far worse can happen,' said the man with the gun.

Alex took a shaky breath and tried to exert some tiny measure of control over the situation. 'What do you want? If you're looking for money, you've come to the wrong place.'

'We are not looking for money,' said the thug. 'We are looking for you.'

Then, when Alex thought it couldn't get any worse, a third man strolled into sight, crossing the driveway. *Three of them. Or are there more?*

The gunman's expression soured and he said something severe to the new arrival before he could enter the house. It sounded like Polish or Russian to Alex and, while he didn't know what was said, the gist of it was clear enough. *Go wait in the car.*

The third man gave a disappointed sigh and sloped off back the way he had come.

Then the gunman closed the door and from a different pocket he produced the wireless doorbell unit. He let it drop to the floor before crushing it beneath the heel of his boot. The device gave off a strangled electronic bleat and then nothing.

The man's attention returned to his captives. 'The boy will make tea for us,' he said, gesturing at the kettle in George's hand. 'And afterwards, we will have a conversation about what comes next.'

TEN

Breeze settled into the seat across the narrow table from the asset, helping herself to a bottled water as she studied the prisoner.

He rocked gently back and forth in his chair, and over the ambient background rumble of the Hawker's engines, she could pick out the rhythm of what he was mumbling through his gag, beneath the cowl covering his head. Breeze couldn't hear the individual words, but she knew a prayer when she heard it. He was reaching out to his god for deliverance, but the poor bastard had already been forsaken.

'You spoke to Hood, then?' Finn hovered nearby, nodding in the direction of the flight deck as Ray returned to his position. 'What's your read on her?'

Breeze shrugged. 'Short fuse. Very few fucks to give. My kind of gal.'

The British agent didn't appear pleased with her off-hand evaluation. 'I don't like being forced into using someone we haven't had time to vet properly. Price was reliable, a known quantity. This woman . . .' He trailed off.

'I'm not giddy about it either,' she admitted. 'But we're gonna play the hand we're dealt.' Breeze shifted and briefly focused on him. 'Shouldn't your people in London be looking into whatever the hell happened to Price? I mean, your pilot disappears on the very night he's needed – that smells like shit to me.'

'I've informed Vauxhall Cross,' he said, referring to the MI6 headquarters in London. Finn fingered his beard. 'It may be a coincidence.'

'No such thing, so find out for certain,' she retorted. Then Breeze turned back to the asset. 'Do we need to keep him like this? Take off the cover.'

'That is not protocol.'

'Same excuse again? Ask me if I care. Go on, do it.'

'Fine.' Finn leaned over and the prisoner flinched as he removed the hood, then the headphones, gag and finally the blacked-out glasses.

She wondered what had been going through Yusuf's mind. With his senses of sight and sound stolen from him, her captive would have nothing but the motion, the vibrations through the floor and the changes in pressure to tell him what was going on.

The man jerked in his chair, trying to look in every direction at once. When he saw the cabin window next to him, he leaned closer to it, blinking as he peered out into the night.

'Nervous flyer?' Breeze offered him a bottle of water. 'Thirsty?'

He looked back at her, his dark eyes partly illuminated by the steady pulse of the running light on the jet's wing. He studied the plastic bottle like it was a venomous snake and made no move to take it.

'I'm not gonna poison you with a goddamn bottle of mineral water, Yusuf.' She put it down on the table in front of him, within his grasp. 'Drink up. It may be a long time before you get another opportunity.'

Warily, he reached out with his bound hands and worked off the cap, before finally taking a deep draught. As he drank, Breeze shot Finn a look that clearly meant *get lost*, and he took the hint, retreating to the other end of the cabin.

The prisoner guzzled down half the bottle before coming to a panting halt. At length, he looked up at her. 'Where are you taking me?'

'Already told you,' she replied. 'A deep, dark, dusty hole.'

'A p-prison?' He stiffened at the thought.

'No.' She spoke slowly, plucking at his fears like a harpist working the strings of her instrument. 'Something much worse. You know the kind of place. I'll bet your friends in al-Sakakin have told you horror stories about them. Let me assure you, it's a nightmare.'

He stared at the table. 'Why are you doing this to me? What have I done to wrong you?'

'I don't want you to think I'm a bad person, Yusuf,' she went on, paying no attention to his entreaties. 'I have a code of ethics. I believe in second chances. I'm gonna offer you one right now.' Breeze tapped on the oval window. 'All I have to do is give an order.' She made a looping motion with her finger. 'I just need to say the word, and this plane will turn around and go right back to where we started. We can leave that dark hole far behind.'

'If . . . if I give you what you want from me. Yes?' He gripped the water bottle so tightly that the thin plastic crackled.

'See, I knew you were a smart man.' Breeze nodded to herself. 'That's what your surveillance file suggests. A smart man, caught up in dangerous company.' She paused, stacking up conversational gambits in her mind like they were cue cards at a debate. 'Your file doesn't say you're a killer, Yusuf. But

111

your friends certainly are. They've hurt a lot of people. Maybe you've known that all along, maybe you've tried to pretend it isn't as terrible as that. I don't care what lies you tell yourself so you can sleep at night.'

The captive looked down at the table, unable to hold her gaze any longer. When he didn't respond, she pressed on.

'You can stop more needless deaths from happening. If you talk to me, if you tell me the truth, I will keep you safe. We can do the right thing, you and I.' Breeze pointed upward. 'If Allah is watching, my friend, what do you want him to see?'

A muscle in his jaw twitched, and Breeze thought he might shout something angry back at her, but then Yusuf sagged and wiped a hand over his mouth and unkempt beard. 'I swear to you that I would tell you anything and everything you want to know, *if* I knew these men you speak of. I told the British, again and again, I know nothing of these people. I am a businessman! I am not a criminal! You are holding an innocent man against his will and you are breaking the law!' By the end of his retort, the prisoner was sobbing.

Irritation flared in her, and Breeze reached out, snatching away the half-empty water bottle, tossing it across the cabin and far from his reach. 'Innocent, huh?' She growled the words. 'We'll see about that.'

They were passing over the coast when a ringtone played a repeating snatch of synth-heavy music, the intro to a Europop tune from the mid-eighties that had been a favourite of Kate's mother.

The notes chimed around the flight deck as she fished her phone from a pocket, earning Kate another censorious look from Ray.

He flicked the mike pick-up away from his mouth and shook his head. 'You still have it switched on? I told you before, you can't use that device, let alone keep it activated.'

'And I told you before, sod off.' Kate's eyes narrowed as she saw the name on the caller ID: ALEX WALKER.

He knew better than to call her at the office, so to speak. Alex understood that he should only ring her if there was something that absolutely couldn't wait, and so the needle on Kate's anxiety gauge immediately spiked.

'You need to turn that off,' Ray insisted.

'You need to mind your own business,' she shot back.

Despite what airlines liked to imply, using a cellular telephone on board an aircraft would not immediately cause it to plummet out of the sky. One lone cell phone signal was unlikely to mess with a jet's avionics; it was only when a few hundred passengers were using them at once that it could become a problem. But Kate knew that Ray worried more about matters of security than electronic interference.

'I signed the Official Secrets Act when I was in the Forces,' she added, in an off-hand attempt to mollify him. 'Don't worry, I'm not going to blab about your precious cargo over an unsecured line.' He was still complaining when she slipped back one cup of her headset and pressed the phone to her ear, leaning into it to take the call. 'Alex?'

'*Kate.*' That single word was enough to make her stomach drop. Alex's roughened voice was heavy with desperation, and she knew immediately that something was wrong. '*I'm . . . I'm so sorry . . .*'

Before she could ask him what he meant, there was a clicking, scuffling sound as the phone on the other end changed hands, and the next voice she heard belonged to a stranger.

113

'*I am speaking to Katherine Hood?*' The man's accent was distinctive but careful, each word clear as a bell. '*The pilot of aircraft Golf Lima Tango Tango Papa?*'

'Yes. Who is—?'

'*You will restrict your replies to one-word answers,*' he broke in. '*We have Alex and his son as our captives. They will be harmed if you do not do exactly as I tell you. Do you understand this, Ms Hood?*'

Kate felt ill, her gut twisting into knots. She stared at the canopy glass, seeing a distorted reflection of her own face. The woman looking back at her had gone ashen.

'*Do you understand?*' The voice repeated the question firmly.

'Yes.' Kate could see Ray from the corner of her eye, flicking glances at her in between scanning readouts on the Hawker's control panel.

'*If you attempt to raise the alarm or inform anyone else aboard the aircraft of this conversation, we will know,*' he continued. '*If you refuse to comply, there will be consequences for disobedience. The boy and his father will suffer.*'

'No . . .' The denial died in her throat, turning to dry ash.

'*By now, you will be aware of the nature of the operation you are involved in. You are going to change the destination of that flight. Comply, and Alex and George will be permitted to live. Refuse, and it will not go well for them.*'

Kate said nothing. The confining walls of the flight deck drifted away from her, becoming untethered, and the constant rumble of the engines rose to a howl. She stared at her own reflection, feeling a stifling surge of hot fear – and impotent anger – open up inside her.

'*In a few moments, you will receive a message providing map coordinates. You are to take control of the aircraft and divert it to a landing strip at that location.*'

'How?' Her mind raced with the myriad terrible possibilities.

'*You are resourceful,*' said the man on the phone. '*You will find a way. You have thirty minutes. We are watching. If we see no evidence of a change in heading within that time, it will be considered non-compliance. Is this understood?*'

'Yes.' Kate forced out the word. She was rigid with tension, unable to move.

'*Once you have command of the aircraft, drop below the radar threshold.*' The voice paused. '*You may think of testing my resolve. Be assured, I am a man who keeps his word. You do not wish to suffer the same fate as your colleague, Mr Price, and his loved ones.*'

The line went silent, and Kate's body suddenly let out the breath she had been holding in. At her side, the co-pilot gave her another questioning glance.

She turned away from him, rubbing her fingers at the corner of her eyes, holding the phone out of Ray's line of sight. Kate's heart hammered in her chest, cords of terror and near-panic tightening around it. Had the co-pilot heard any of that? Did he suspect something was wrong?

If he did, what would come next? She couldn't afford to let anything happen to put Alex and George's lives at risk. Kate gulped in a breath of air, tasting bile in her throat. The man on the phone had mentioned John Price, and the other pilot's unexplained disappearance suddenly took on a horrible, sinister cast.

She thought about the trembling man under the cowl that Breeze's team had marched aboard the Hawker. This was about *him*, whoever he was. Someone wanted that man badly enough to make these dire threats; perhaps even to commit murder.

'Are you finished?' Ray asked the question with a prim sigh. 'If Finn sees you with that phone, he'll go mad. At least put it away!' He looked back over his shoulder through the half-closed door to the cabin beyond, afraid the bearded man might come in at any second.

Kate's phone let off a pulse of vibration as a message arrived, and she turned it so only she would be able to see the screen.

The message was a photo of Alex and George, the father holding his son close to him in a protective embrace. Kate swallowed a gasp at the sight of Alex's hangdog face lined with streaks of blood, and a hollow distance in his eyes.

The 13-year-old boy was small and fragile. In his hands, he held a sheet of paper with a set of navigational coordinates that Kate's trained pilot instincts automatically retained. The numbers burned themselves into her mind and she hesitated with her thumb over the 'erase' key.

The photo made the nightmare real. The callous voice on the call had been ghostly and disconnected, but seeing Alex and George's obvious distress brought the bleak threat into sharp, undeniable focus.

They were what mattered to Kate most. More than her job, her uncertain future or her tainted past. If she lost them, the world would crumble around her and she knew she would never survive going over that edge for a second time in her life.

The roaring of the engines grew, building in her head like harsh overpressure. But it wasn't the jets – it was the thunder of the blood in her veins, the hammering of her racing heartbeat. Kate took a shaky breath, the memory of acrid seared plastic and burning fuel in her nostrils.

The box of old, pain-marbled recollections she kept buried deep inside her opened a crack, in danger of letting out the phantoms Kate hid from the world. She held on tightly to the Hawker's yoke, making it the anchor to keep her in the here and now, mentally slamming closed the lid on yesterday's trauma before it could return to engulf her.

After a moment, Kate carefully slipped the phone into a pocket and took a long, metered breath to steady herself.

'All done, then?' prompted Ray, unwilling to let the matter drop. 'No more interruptions?'

'All done,' she echoed tonelessly. Kate's gaze slipped to the clock on the control panel, noting the time.

Thirty minutes and counting.

The Scene of Crime officers had come in like the blazes, racing out to the Price household with all due haste, and when Grace had wondered out loud how they had arrived so quickly, Harris noted that the daughter and son-in-law of a certain chief superintendent had a house just a quarter mile away down the leafy lanes.

The locals had woken up to something unpleasant happening in their sleepy Little England hamlet, shaken by the strobing of passing blue lights and the growing number of coppers milling around. Blue and white tape shot through with POLICE LINE DO NOT CROSS warnings now hung across the entrance to the Prices' driveway in bleak garlands, and behind it the SOCOs were pulling on disposable paper overalls, shoe covers and gloves. Grace watched them work, each one rendered into a genderless, near-identical figure, like something out of a child's toy box.

At her side, Harris moved from foot to foot, a new, nervous energy rolling through him with no place to discharge itself. She felt the same way. Neither of them were strangers to the nastier parts of human nature. You couldn't be an ordinary plod without running into that kind of thing sooner or later, but the callous brutality of the murder scene in the house had left both of them struggling to process it.

The killings didn't look like acts of madness or passion. They were brutal and efficient.

'Head's up, Gracey.' Harris jutted his chin as a man in a heavy greatcoat and thunderous mood came marching up the gravel drive toward them.

Detective Inspector Mohan Khan wasn't a man whose company regular coppers like Grace and Harris ever wanted to find themselves in. A hard-eyed, unsmiling officer with a face like weathered teak, he was known to work as a hatchet man for the higher-ups, and his appearance at any crime scene usually meant that someone, somewhere, was in for a serious bollocking. The lower ranks had a nickname for him – they called him 'The Wrath', a play on words from the title of an old 1980s *Star Trek* movie. But no one laughed when they said it. If Khan had ever possessed a sense of humour, it had been surgically removed upon joining the police service.

To Grace's silent dismay, she watched Khan demand an answer from one of the SOCOs that sent him coming their way, homing in on the pair of constables like a heat-seeking missile.

'You two.' He aimed a thick finger at them. 'First on site?'

'Yes, boss,' Harris answered. 'We were following up on an RTC with a single fatality. This is the unfortunate gentlemen's home, and, uh . . .' He ran out of breath, stumbling over his next words.

Grace took over, earning a grateful glance from her colleague. 'Bodies of the wife and daughter in the kitchen, sir. Multiple stab wounds. Not a pretty sight.'

'Husband did it?' Khan glanced in the direction of the house. Grace wasn't clear if he was genuinely asking them to venture an opinion, and they both elected to remain silent. 'I have already spoken to Sergeant Peake,' he said. 'I've been briefed. The house: any sign of forced entry?'

'No, sir,' said Grace.

'The garage door and the back door were both unsecured,' added Harris.

'Murder-suicide.' Khan let the words drop where they fell, as if he was testing out the notion. 'Husband killed them, he went for a drive, put his car into the back of a tractor,' he said, parcelling out the events in swift order. 'Or not.' The senior officer turned his searchlight glare on Grace. 'Sergeant Peake informed me that you found possible evidence of a passenger in the car. He gestured at the air. 'Correct?'

'I believe so, sir.' Grace gave a nod. 'Obviously, the forensics bods will know for certain—'

'Obviously,' Khan replied, cutting her off. 'But that potentiality does shake up this bag of shit quite a bit, doesn't it?'

'Sir.' She nodded again, and Harris mirrored her.

'A lot of wealthy people around here.' Khan held up a finger. 'Town council members, a judge, so on and so on, all within earshot of this house. You can be sure concerned telephone calls will be flying about.' He fixed them both with a steady gaze. 'And here we are tonight, spread thin and dealing with it on the back foot.'

'Don't follow, boss,' said Harris, his brow furrowing.

'Accident on the motorway.' The senior officer's reply was clipped. 'Tanker lorry. It has proven to be a far more thorny issue than first assumed. For now, this incident has much less manpower on it than we would like.'

'We' being the upper ranks, thought Grace. *Why do I get the feeling this will be a long night?*

Khan folded his arms across his barrel chest and made the two of them walk him through everything that had happened, step-by-step from the moment they arrived at the car crash, to the radio call going out about the bloody scene in the kitchen.

He listened intently, probing for more detail here and there, absorbing every word that came out of their mouths. Grace stuck to the plain facts of the matter, leafing back through the scribble in the pages of her notebook where she had jotted down everything that appeared relevant.

When they were done, Khan gave a slow, approving nod. 'Assuming your conclusion is viable,' he said, 'assuming Price was not alone in the car, we must entertain the possibility his family was also not alone in the house.' He nodded toward the street. 'A neighbour mentioned seeing another car in the drive tonight. If we have an unknown person connected to both incidents, identifying and locating them is the highest priority.'

Once again, Grace didn't know if he wanted her to agree or if he was thinking aloud, so she said nothing, waiting for whatever came next.

'On the way here, I spoke to the senior CIU officer at site of the crash.' Khan glanced back at the house. 'The car's satellite navigation system is intact. It appears Price followed a route that he drove on a regular basis. To Ridley Hill airport.'

'He's a pilot?' Grace recalled seeing framed photos on the walls of the house, including one particular one of Price himself leaning against a single-engine light aircraft.

Khan snapped his fingers. 'You two are doing nothing more than being doorstops here. Get out to that airfield, canvas the site for anyone who knows Price. If he was on his way there, he probably had a reason.'

Grace and Harris exchanged glances. There was a conversation they both wanted to have about how close they were to the end of their shift, but one look at the steely glare from the DI told them that there was overtime in their immediate future, whether they wanted it or not.

'Yes, sir,' Grace and Harris answered in unison, accepting the order.

With her colleague trailing behind her, Grace headed back to their patrol car.

ELEVEN

The co-pilot interpreted Kate's sullen silence as rudeness on her part, and she was content to leave him with that. The last thing she wanted was to deal with Ray's continual enquiries, not while her mind churned with fear and anxiety as she tried to make sense of her next move.

The digital clock on the Hawker's control panel continued its inexorable march toward the top of the hour, closing the gap on the thirty-minute deadline.

A thousand bleak possibilities had gone through her thoughts – everything from the prospect that this whole thing had been falsified with deepfakes and simulated voices, to the horrible notion that Alex and George might already be lying dead, and that Kate Hood would be next.

The consequences of the grim choice weighing her down were heavy like lead. Suppose she obeyed the faceless voice on the phone; suppose she gave him exactly what he wanted. *What then?* There was no guarantee that Alex and George would be safe and no way to know if the man holding them hostage would keep his word.

And what would happen to her? The landing coordinates in the message were within the Hawker's flight range, up along the Mediterranean coast of Algeria, probably the site of some dusty and disused airstrip co-opted for exactly this situation.

What would happen when she touched down there, if the prisoner in the hood was turned over to his liberators? Did they want to save him or kill him?

She glanced at Ray, thinking of him, of Breeze and Finn. And of herself.

They won't let us live, Kate told herself. *They get what they want and we're dead.*

Was that a trade she was willing to risk? Her life and that of three strangers to save the man she loved, and his son?

Yes. She felt a little ashamed when her answer came quickly.

Kate thought about coming clean to Breeze, wondering if the acerbic American would take her seriously. But if she did, what would that mean for Alex and George? The voice on the phone had warned her he'd know if she talked. It was possible they might have surveillance on board the Hawker. She glanced around the cockpit. There were hundreds of places someone could hide a listening device if they had a mind to.

Or did they have another way to know? Her gaze settled on Ray for a moment. What if there was someone on board working *with* them?

Kate sighed and straightened in her seat, struggling to find a way to get her hands around the problem. There were so many variables, so many different ways it could go horribly wrong, but right now she knew only one thing for certain – when the thirty-minute deadline expired, if she had not obeyed, the man on the phone would hurt Alex and George in order to punish her.

I can't allow that. Her jaw hardened. *And as long as I'm still flying this plane, I still have some measure of control.* She thought about Breeze's prisoner. *Whoever he is, they want him. I can stop them getting him, so that gives me something of value.*

But before she could consider what could be done with that leverage, the problem in front of her – or, more accurately, the problem sitting in the co-pilot's seat – had to be dealt with.

She checked the control screens. A few moments ago, the city of Lisbon had passed under the port wing, its faraway lights a smudge of glowing amber in the darkness, glimpsed through the clumps of dogged rain cloud that had followed them down the Algarve coastline. Next, they would pass around Cabo de São Vicente at the southernmost tip of Portugal, and then it would be a run across open water until they came in sight of land again, approaching the shores of Morocco.

If she was to take the Hawker where the kidnapper wanted it to go, Kate would need to course-correct soon, shifting to a heading due east over the Strait of Gibraltar, across the Alboran Sea and into the Med. Of course, Ray and the others would not agree to that. The co-pilot had to be deleted from the equation.

Kate had flown the Hawker 800 on a couple of occasions before tonight's events, but that had been more than a year ago. Still, she remembered that this particular jet had a few mechanical quirks that Brian Teller had gamely suggested his pilots 'work around', rather than having to commit to a costly full tear-down and repair. Every individual aircraft had its idiosyncrasies and G-LTTP was no exception.

Now she had to gamble on one of them to get her what she needed.

When the moment was right, with Ray's attention briefly elsewhere, Kate surreptitiously adjusted the settings on the Hawker's portside engine. After a few seconds, the turbofan gave a warning grumble like a faraway thunderhead and a status light popped up on the dashboard.

Ray's head came around in a bird-like jerk as he saw the alert. 'What's that?'

Kate faked a weary grimace. 'This crap again. I'm sick of asking Teller to sort it out.' She leaned forward, peering at the engine readouts. 'It's probably nothing, don't worry about it.'

'Doesn't feel like nothing,' snapped Ray, as a faint shudder made its way up the length of the fuselage. He reached out toward the panel that would correct the tiny mismatch that Kate had deliberately created, and in that moment she put pressure on the Hawker's starboard rudder, deliberately making the shudder worsen. Ray's hand dropped to the arm of his seat automatically to steady himself.

'Yeah, maybe you're right.' Kate shot him a look and did everything she could to hide the lie she uttered next. She reached for her seat belt fastener. 'Do me a favour? Take the aircraft. I'll go back and make a visual inspection of the intake. There's been an intermittent issue with a panel working loose in the past . . .'

Ray's eyes widened at the idea of a piece of the ducting coming off in mid-air, perhaps to get sucked into the turbine blades. The pilot didn't need to say more. In the worst-case scenario, something like that could severely damage the engine and force the Hawker to make an unscheduled emergency landing – or worse.

'No.' Before she could unbelt, Ray had already released his safety restraint. 'You have to stay up here. I'll check it.' But before he left his seat, he hesitated. 'You said this is a reported problem with this aircraft? Well, that should have been brought to my attention before take-off!'

Kate shrugged. 'If you know Brian Teller, you know he likes to play his cards close to his chest. I'm sure he didn't want to risk scrubbing the flight and losing whatever you people are paying him.' When Ray didn't respond, she pushed her point. 'Look, if you're that worried about it, I can contact air traffic control and tell them we need to divert to Faro. We can check it out on the ground.'

'Absolutely not.' Ray's reply was firm. 'Stay off the radio. I'll have a look, make an evaluation. Any decision to change course will not be yours to make.'

'Whatever you say,' she allowed.

Ray left his radio headset hanging over the back of the seat and worked his way through the cockpit vestibule and down the length of the passenger cabin. Kate watched him exchange a terse comment with Finn, then head for a window on the portside of the plane. Anyone looking through it would have a clear view of the number one engine's intake maw, and any visible issues with it.

But there was nothing wrong with the engine, and the whole story about the loose panel was a complete fabrication, something that sounded just problematic enough that it couldn't be ignored.

Activating the automatic pilot to maintain the Hawker's straight and level flight, Kate took a deep breath and threw off her headset and safety restraints before vaulting out of her seat in a quick, agile motion.

Finn was the only person looking in her direction. He saw the sudden, unexpected movement and his eyes widened in surprise, but she caught him off-guard and he didn't move, not until well after she was already at the cockpit's security door.

Kate slammed her shoulder into the door across the vestibule and slid it shut, her hands falling to the case-hardened steel locking bolts, closing them tightly one after another. The bolts thudded home and she turned the latches that would double-secure them, completely isolating the flight deck from the rest of the aircraft.

Her hands trembled as she backed away from the door, the rapid spike of adrenaline that had carried her through her actions fading as fast as it had arisen. Someone banged a fist on the other side of the door and Kate heard a muffled voice as Breeze called out her name.

She stood looking at the door for what felt like a long time, the consequences of her illegal act pressing down on her. Then, with finality, Kate tore herself away and returned to her seat.

Her hands shook as she brought up the flight computer, and she had to force herself to remain calm. She wasn't a stranger to stress – she'd flown fighter planes in active war zones after all – but that was very different to what she was doing now. Kate set to work re-calculating the Hawker's route and fuel figures, losing herself in the numbers, blotting out the noises from the door.

When that was done, she switched off the autopilot and resumed control of the Hawker. With steady, gentle pressure, she tilted the wings to put the jet into a slow, steady bank, to aim it eastward.

There would be no turning back now; the pilot had hijacked her own aircraft.

One moment Ray was leaning on the curved wall of the Hawker's cabin, his nose pressed up against the oval window, and the next there was noise and shouting, and the sudden sinking realisation that he had been played for a mug.

There didn't appear to be any obvious problem with the portside engine and no sign of any loose panels visible in the glow cast from the interior. There was only the crash of the security door shutting firmly, and the woman from the CIA swearing as she hauled herself up out of her seat.

She spun to aim a finger in the asset's face and the man recoiled from her angry expression before she'd even said a word. 'You. Don't move,' snarled Breeze. Then she turned her glare on Ray. 'And you, you goddamn moron, you left Hood in the cockpit *on her own?*'

'I didn't . . .' *I didn't think*, he was about to say, and he clamped down on the reply before he voiced it. The pilot's blithe mention of a potentially lethal engine problem had briefly overridden Ray's normal caution, and now they would pay for it. His cheeks turned hot with humiliation. Hood had known *exactly* what buttons to push to send him off the flight deck, exploiting the same instincts for safety that were hard-wired into every serving pilot.

'Katherine Hood, can you hear me? You need to open this immediately, do you understand?' At the other end of the passenger cabin, Finn worked the door's handle, pushing at the panel to no avail. He raised his voice so the pilot would hear him, not that it seemed to matter. Silence returned from the other side of the door, and he gave an audible grunt. 'She's bolted herself in,' he confirmed.

'No shit, Sherlock.' Breeze's retort was acidic. Her gaze dropped to the asset, eyeing the man in the prison fatigues. 'Mask this prick up. I don't want him talking.'

'No! No!' Yusuf held up his hands, as much as he could from where they were secured to the wall, his face ashy with panic. 'Please, oh please don't put that on me again! I won't speak, I promise. I beg you!'

'He's the least of our concerns,' said Finn. He turned to Ray. 'Let me guess. She sent you back here on a fool's errand?'

'Hood said there was an engine issue,' he confirmed. 'Except there isn't.'

'I refer you to my previous answer – *no shit*.' The American moved to the security door and banged hard on it, calling out to the pilot. When there was no response, she turned to Finn and prodded the bearded man hard in the chest. 'You. *Fucking*. Assured. Me. You said this woman wasn't going to be a problem!'

Ray watched a change drop over Finn's face, a bland and neutral veneer that gave nothing away. 'With all due respect, I'd like to remind you that *your* man Chester also gave her the green light.'

'Someone is fucking with me,' growled Breeze, shaking her head. 'The first pilot vanishes, second one gets foisted on us with zero prep time . . .' Exasperated, she pressed the heel of her hand into the bridge of her nose. 'Damn it! This is deliberate! Should have scrubbed it and gone home . . .'

'Except you made it clear that wasn't an option,' said Finn, flicking a look at Ray.

The co-pilot couldn't read Finn. Ray had only met him and the driver Miles that morning at a sketchy briefing in a windowless office at Vauxhall Cross. MI6 had pulled him abruptly from his last assignment with virtually no warning, forcing Ray to make an apologetic call to cry off from the family dinner he was supposed to be attending right now. Instead of sitting down to his maiden aunt's delicious roasted chicken at her flat in Peckham, he was thirty thousand feet up over the Atlantic, in the middle of what was looking more and more like a life-threatening situation.

He thought of the lurid, disturbing stories he'd heard about pilots who locked out their crews and the horrible aftermath – the angry and the suicidal flying an aircraft into the side of a mountain. But that wasn't the play here.

Ray looked across at the asset, the man rocking back and forth in his seat and muttering prayers under his breath. This was about *him*.

'Get it open,' demanded Breeze. 'There's gotta be an emergency release, or something—'

'There isn't,' said Finn, cutting her off. 'Unless you have a blowtorch in your pocket, we're not getting in there if Hood doesn't want us to.'

'That's the whole point of the thing,' said Ray. 'It's not a security door if a hijacker can get through it at will.'

'*She's* doing the hijacking, not *us!*' Breeze retorted, fixing Ray with a murderous stare. 'You know what, this is on you, so unless you got something useful to add, shut the fuck up.' The woman went back to Finn. 'Hipster, you have a weapon? I know you do.'

Finn straightened his jacket, unconsciously smoothing the line of it down over the bulge where he carried a holstered pistol. 'You're asking me to discharge a firearm inside a pressurised cabin?'

'That would be a very bad idea,' added Ray. Visions of a ricocheting bullet punching through the Hawker's thin metal fuselage, and the resultant catastrophic loss of pressure made his stomach tighten with sickly fear.

'Yeah, I've seen the movies,' Breeze said dismissively, 'I know what happens. So if not that, give me another solution!'

Finn sighed and glanced at Ray again. 'Look around, see what you can find in the cabin. There might be something we can use.'

'Right.' He moved to the nearest storage bin and cracked it open. Inside was a waterproof sack coloured bright international orange, full of gear for use in an emergency landing.

As Ray sifted through the contents, Breeze took a deep breath and drew herself up. 'Step aside,' she told Finn, moving back to the security door. 'If our girl Katie won't let us into the cockpit, maybe I can get into her head instead.'

'I . . . do not want to die.' The asset's soft, fearful words were almost lost, his hands cupping his face as he leaned forward against the table in front of him.

'Yeah, me neither,' managed Ray, concentrating on the items in the bag.

Once the Hawker was on the new heading, Kate broke a whole other set of rules by deactivating both of the jet's onboard transponders, pulling the circuit breakers to render them useless. Normally, the devices would 'ping' out the aircraft's identification code to any local air traffic control or nearby planes in the same airspace, helping them to track it along its course, but now the Hawker was on its first step to becoming a ghost in the complex web of intersecting flight paths over the Strait.

Switching off a transponder wasn't technically illegal, but it was suspicious, and within a few minutes a radio call crackled through Kate's headphones as a query came in from Gibraltar International. Some attentive ATC operator in the tower there must have seen the code string fade from their screen and opted to contact the aircraft.

'*Hawker Lima Tango Tango Papa, Gibraltar ATC. Do you copy, over?*'

Kate hesitated with her thumb over the button on the yoke that would key her mike and decided to remain silent.

The next call was more urgent. *'Hawker Lima Tango Tango Papa, Gibraltar ATC. We show no transponder code from your aircraft at this time. Please respond.'*

'Typical,' she said aloud. 'Who rattled your cage, eh?' Kate had vainly hoped she might slip by unremarked, getting lost among dozens of other planes flying there and back through this particular patch of sky, but it wasn't to be. She was unlucky enough to be under the gaze of someone at Gibraltar both competent and observant.

She sucked in a breath and pressed the button. 'Gibraltar ATC, this is Hawker Lima Tango Tango Papa. We have a minor electrical issue. Stand by – should be resolved soonest.' The controller began to respond but Kate cut him off by silencing the channel and switching off the radio entirely. Hopefully her reply would buy some time, and the ATC's attention would move on.

On the control panel, the clock read six minutes shy of the top of the hour and Kate's deadline.

She took a deep breath and recovered her smartphone from her jacket. Careful not to make any mistakes that might be misinterpreted, Kate prodded out a message with her index finger and sent it to Alex's phone.

I DID WHAT YOU WANTED. AIRCRAFT HAS BEEN DIVERTED.

It seemed like an eternity before the phone vibrated in her palm and a reply appeared in a bubble of text.

CONTINUE ON COURSE TO THE LOCATION PROVIDED. AVOID RADAR DETECTION. WAIT TO BE CONTACTED.

She waited for more to come. When it didn't, Kate tapped out another sentence.

I WANT TO KNOW THEY ARE SAFE, she demanded, seeing Alex and George's faces in her mind's eye. I WANT TO TALK TO THEM.

There was another long pause, and Kate's panic threatened to crest. If she antagonised these people, there was no telling what they might do. But she couldn't afford to appear weak; she had to push back.

The phone buzzed again. YOU DO NOT GIVE THE ORDERS.

'Oh please, no . . .' The threatening tone of the reply made her feel ill.

Then a photo message appeared in the chat queue, and she was afraid to open it in case it revealed something horrible.

Kate reluctantly pressed the on-screen tab and was rewarded with another picture of George and Alex. In this image, they were both sitting on the living room sofa, across from the television. They appeared haggard and glum, staring into the camera with real fear in their eyes.

On the wall behind them she could see the clock, clearly showing that the image had been captured less than a minute ago. They were alive and whole, at least for the moment.

Another text message followed swiftly. DO AS YOU ARE TOLD AND THEY WILL NOT BE HARMED. DISOBEDIENCE WILL NOT BE TOLERATED.

UNDERSTOOD. Kate sent the reply before slipping the phone back into her pocket. The grim weight of what she had done came down on her, pressing her into the seat like the force of a high-G turn.

She tightened her grip on the flight yoke, briefly closing her eyes. From behind her, the banging on the cockpit door became more strident and forceful.

TWELVE

The rain had returned, sounding a monotonous rhythm across the roof of the car, the ticking of an off-kilter metronome. Through the rivulets running down the windscreen, Miles kept a wary eye on the Americans, watching their big black SUV beside the Teller Aviation hangar. The prisoner transport that ferried the asset to the airstrip had departed, but the CIA's vehicle resolutely remained in place. As long as it was there, Miles's orders remained to keep watch.

A drinks machine inside the hangar's back office had exuded the cup of watery, unpleasant coffee that Miles held in one hand. He sipped at it more from the need to have something to do rather than anything else. None of Breeze's people had spoken to him since the jet took off – not her tech guy or her pet shooter, not the armed private contractors that escorted them – and he had the distinct impression they regarded him as some kind of obstacle rather than a colleague.

The arrogance of the CIA team made him scowl. They were on British soil, on *his* turf, but they acted like they were the ones in charge.

He could see the big-framed shooter stalking a circuit along the spill of light thrown from the hangar. Periodically, puffs of grey would wreath his head and coil around the bill of his baseball cap as he pulled on a vape pen, and he peered into the rainy night, looking for threats that didn't materialise.

Bloody Yanks, Miles thought sourly, glaring at the guy as he prowled. *Wherever they go, they act like they own the place.*

The CIA's hulking four-by-four leaked a faint electronic glow through one fractionally lowered window, and Miles could tell from the stubs of different antennae on the vehicle's flat roof that it carried a load of counter-surveillance, monitoring and tactical gear. Dark flights like tonight's little escapade had, in the past, attracted the interest of crusading reporters and other nosy types; an occupational hazard for operations such as this that hid in plain sight. Miles imagined that scanners inside the mobile ops unit were watching for any red flags that might indicate someone out on the airfield perimeter taking too much interest in this evening's departure. Had they detected anybody, that person would likely have found themselves being mobbed by grim-faced PMC men and dragged off into the darkness.

All that gear inside the SUV had another function, though. Everything about this operation was being streamed in real-time around the world to CIA headquarters in Langley, Virginia – and if MI6 had asked nicely, they might be getting a slice of that feed secondhand.

Miles's scowl deepened. By contrast, all he had was a plastic cup of ditch-water coffee and a motor that even the car-thief scallies back on his old estate wouldn't have bothered nicking.

He pulled back the sleeve of his hoodie and checked his wristwatch. In the next half hour the team on the flight would officially make contact with their opposite numbers from the DST, the General Directorate for Territorial Surveillance in Morocco. Those men would be waiting for the jet when it arrived at the airstrip at Sidi Ifni, ready to take custody of the asset for 'processing' in one of their off-grid holding facilities.

Miles had never seen a real black site but he'd gone through the rigorous preparation demanded by the Security Intelligence Services at No. 1 Military Training Establishment, the SIS's 'school for spies' at Fort Monkton in leafy Hampshire. Inside a bland concrete blockhouse, Miles and the rest of his trainee class had been put into a convincing facsimile of a secret prison so they would have some experience of what it was like to be interrogated by the enemy. For days, bellowing instructors and hard men seconded from the SAS physically and mentally abused him, pushing him to find out where his limits were.

He'd made it through, drawing on the reservoir of inner strength his tough upbringing had gifted him, but it had been a close-run thing. Miles never told anyone how close he'd come to cracking under the pressure. He thought again about Yusuf al-Amal, and the abject panic he saw in the man's eyes back on the dockside. Someone as soft as that would crumble like wet sand when the Moroccans got their hands on him. He almost pitied the bloke.

The Security Services and the Central Intelligence Agency weren't exactly troupes of choirboys, but the DST was in another category entirely. They excelled at the callous arts of rendition and covert incarceration, allowing the governments of other powers to keep their hands clean and maintain plausible deniability, while they acted as jailers and interrogators for the most dangerous men and women on the planet.

Miles had made his peace with this grubby reality. In his mind, it was a clear binary choice – if a bad actor had information that could shut down terrorist networks and ultimately save lives – using any means necessary to get that information was justified. Rights and morals didn't enter into it. This was about stopping mass-murders, plain and simple. He thought about the recent incidents in Germany and Cyprus, the brutal deaths and blood on the streets. If Yusuf al-Amal was knowingly connected to the people behind those atrocities, in Miles's consideration he'd already renounced his chance for a fair trial.

If. Miles hung on that word, frowning. The asset didn't come off like some stone killer jihadi fanatic. He reminded Miles of his dentist.

Maybe Breeze and the Yanks had made a mistake. Maybe they had black-bagged the wrong man. But that was for other people to decide, not Miles.

A flurry of movement drew his attention back to the SUV. The tech bloke, Chester, almost ran into one of the contractors in his haste to get out of the vehicle. Miles clocked him carrying the chunky form of a satellite phone, and through the vehicle's open door he saw a grid of screens and consoles.

'Knox!' Chester shouted the shooter's name at the top of his lungs, and the other man snapped around like a cat hearing a bird. 'Get over here!'

The tech couldn't conceal the alarm in his voice, and the contractors in earshot heard it too. They reacted as Knox did, getting ready for trouble.

Miles leapt out of the Ford, tossing away the rest of the unpalatable coffee, and strode across to the SUV. Something was evidently kicking off, and he wasn't going to watch from the sidelines.

'Trouble?' He made it to Chester first, fixing the other man with a hard look.

'It's, ah . . .' The technician hesitated on the cusp of telling him, then drew back as Knox came sprinting across the apron toward them. 'We're handling it.'

'Oh, right?' Miles made it clear he was unconvinced. 'Handling what, exactly?'

'Step back.' Knox walked into the conversation, imposing himself between the MI6 agent and the technician.

Chester paled a little and held up the sat phone, its glowing screen showing it was active. Knox snatched it out of his hand, studied the screen, and grimaced.

Miles heard Breeze's faint but unmistakable voice issue out of the device. *'Don't keep me hanging, Marty, we have a serious situation up here!'*

Miles stiffened. If there was a problem on the flight, his first order of business would be to keep Vauxhall Cross in the loop. 'Let's put that on speaker, yeah?'

Knox eyed him. 'I'm not doing that.' He nodded at the Ford. 'Be smart. Go wait in the car.'

'Fuck off, mate,' said Miles, without heat. He was half the body mass of the American, and he didn't doubt the guy knew a dozen ways to kill him. But he hadn't backed down when those SAS bruisers had been at him in training, and he wasn't about to do it now. 'You're here by the grace of the Crown, innit? And as far as you're concerned, right now I'm the one wearing it.' He pointed at the phone. 'If there's a problem, we're all on.'

Knox clearly saw that further argument wasn't going to wash, and indicated the SUV. 'Get in.'

The vehicle was roomy and surprisingly comfortable, with a row of seats rigged up opposite the console fixed to one side of the interior. Miles's gaze swept over screens and panels, catching sight of the feed from a flight tracking display.

The big American sat heavily and held the sat phone in one hand, aiming it like a weapon. 'Go for Knox,' he said into the microphone. 'Be advised, we have one of the Brits with us.'

'*Uh huh.*' Breeze's voice came back instantly. '*Marty, you there?*'

'Affirmative.' Chester gave Miles a wary glance, before moving over to put himself in front of the monitor screens, attempting to block the other man's view.

'*Okay, here's the thing. Hood, the pilot? She's locked us out of the cockpit and she won't respond.*' The woman wasted no time hedging. '*She faked out Six's guy, got him off the flight deck. You following?*'

Knox glared at Miles as if this sudden, worrisome turn of events was his fault. 'Copy that,' he growled.

Miles heard Finn in the background say something he couldn't quite catch, and Breeze relayed it. '*We've changed course. Heading east now.*'

'You tracking them?' Knox prodded Chester and nodded toward the screens.

'Last known location is here.' Chester clicked a mousepad and manipulated the flight display, zooming in on an area of the map. 'There's a time delay on positional reporting from the jet, but it looks like the transponders have been nixed. That can't be a coincidence.'

'Going dark,' said Miles. 'Pilot's been compromised.'

'*You think?*' retorted Breeze.

'Can you forcibly access the cockpit?' Knox stared into the middle distance and Miles had the sense he was playing out that tactical scenario in his mind's eye.

'*Nobody brought a can opener,*' said the woman. '*And we can't exactly climb out and bang on the windshield.*'

Knox gave a curt nod. 'All right. I'll kick this up the line. If you figure out a way to get in, call back. Otherwise, sit tight. Copy?'

The immediate shift in Knox's manner didn't escape notice. Suddenly he was talking like *he* was the one in charge, giving Breeze orders when all along Miles had been under the impression the acerbic woman was the boss.

'*Sit tight?*' Breeze's reply was flat. '*I know the protocol, man. Don't bullshit me on this.*'

'We'll do what we can from here,' said Knox. 'Mobile out.' He cut the call and tossed the phone back to Chester, who caught it awkwardly.

'What's the protocol?' Miles met his gaze.

'Not your concern,' began Knox, but Chester shook his head.

'In the event of a hostile takeover of an aircraft under Agency control,' he said, as if reciting the words from a manual, 'if the situation cannot be resolved, lethal force options are to be deployed.'

'Shoot down a civilian jet?' Miles blinked at the thought. 'We didn't agree to that! You won't get permission ...'

'We don't *need* permission.' Knox glared at Chester for his lack of silence. 'We already have it. Had it the second this op was green-lit.'

'And Breeze knows that,' added Chester.

Miles scowled. Things were starting to run away from him, but as the only MI6 officer on site, he still had a job to do. 'I have to call this in.'

Knox fixed him with a pitiless glare. 'You're not gonna do that. This operation is strictly radio-silent, you get me?'

He snorted. 'I reckon a hijacking puts the mockers on that, don't you?'

'Step out,' Knox went on, nodding toward the door. 'And keep your mouth shut.' And then, very deliberately, the American let his jacket fall open to reveal the butt of a pistol protruding from a hip holster.

Miles wasn't a fool; the implication was crystal clear. 'Right,' he said, at length, opening the SUV's door.

'Smart choice,' offered Knox, pulling the door closed as Miles stepped back out into the drizzle.

He stood there in the wet, forcing down the churn of worry building in his gut. A simple escort and hand-off had just become something far more complex, far more dangerous.

When the Brit in the hoodie was out of earshot, Knox cursed with enough force and blasphemy that his long-dead pastor father might have been compelled to rise from the grave and give him a beating.

Chester recoiled from the snarling tirade and, when it settled, he ventured a question of his own. 'You're not seriously going to drop the hammer on them?'

Knox pulled off his hat and ran a thick-fingered hand through his dark, close-cropped hair. 'You just said it. Breeze knows how things work.'

'The whole point of this was to secure the asset for interrogation, not blow him to bits!' Chester shook his head. 'Dead, he's worthless!'

'I am aware,' Knox shot back, gripping the hat tightly. 'Shit-fire! I fuckin' warned her; I told Breeze this operation was half-assed and ready to fall apart, but she never damn well listens. She pushed this thing to go active against my advice, and now look at it . . .'

'She wanted the asset for herself,' said Chester. He glanced around, as if checking to see that no one was listening. 'I mean, come on, you have to know about what people are saying back at Langley, right? *Breeze has lost her edge. Breeze doesn't bring in good intel product any more.* There are people who want her hung out to dry. Is it any wonder she's going at this so hard?'

'Reasons don't matter now,' said Knox. 'Now we gotta deal with the fallout.' He replaced his hat and took a breath. 'Get me a secured sat-com line to Operations and spin up our local tactical options for an armed intercept of the plane.'

Chester's colour drained as the reality of what he was being told to do finally hit home. 'I can tell you right now, friendly military aircraft in that area belong to NATO allied forces, not ours . . . Only non-American pilots and planes.'

'That's a negative.' Knox made a throat-cutting gesture. 'Too many people in the loop for a "shoot down". We bring in outsiders, too many questions get asked. Bad enough the Brits are in on this; we don't need more complications. Find me something we have full control over. And do it fast.'

The situation looked fishy from the moment the police car drew up to the barrier at Ridley Hill.

Harris rolled down the window, peering out at the dark and empty security hut. He glanced in Grace's direction. 'No one about? Have they knocked off for the night?'

'It's lit up over there,' she said, indicating a cluster of hangars along the line of the runway. 'Someone's home.' His colleague straightened her stab vest and exited the car, moving to the hut. Harris watched her look inside, then give a shrug.

There was a manual release for the barrier, and she pulled it, clearing the way for them to continue. Harris started rolling forward and Grace climbed back in.

'Go on,' she told him.

He got the car under the barrier before it dropped back down of its own accord, fingers drumming on the steering wheel with a nervous energy that wouldn't dissipate. Harris had the distinct, unpleasant sense of something bad on the horizon; a gut feeling he couldn't shake. It had been getting worse all night.

'Teller Aviation,' said Grace, reading off a sign by the pathway. 'That's where Price worked. Up there.' She pointed at the hangars lined up along the slip road. Harris couldn't see any aircraft but there were a couple of vehicles parked near the front of the lit-up buildings.

'I'm not liking this,' noted Harris. 'Feels off to me.'

'Cheer up,' said Grace, in a decidedly unhappy voice. 'We're on overtime now, you knob. Lucky us.'

'I should be on my way home by now,' he retorted.

'To do what? Feed your cat and watch some Scandi drama on Netflix? We're doing proper policing, aren't we?'

'Are we?' Harris guided the car slowly toward the hangars. 'More like we're getting the jobs no one else wants.'

Grace clapped her hands together and answered with a sing-song lilt. 'Welcome to the modern police service!' She gave a dry chuckle. 'How long have you been out of Hendon, and you're only now figuring that out?'

'Well, I don't—' He didn't finish the thought. Without warning, two figures in black came out of the rainy shadows, stepping out in front of the police car. Harris stamped on the brakes and the vehicle lurched to a sudden stop, both he and Grace rocking forward against their seatbelts.

Harris thought he'd been mistaken by what he saw through the rain-dashed windscreen, but he was dead right. The men in black jackets were armed with short-frame MP5 submachine guns, similar to the type he'd seen used by the Metropolitan Police's elite Special Firearms Command. But these guys didn't look like the men from SCO19. They looked like soldiers.

'Back up, back up!' Grace shouted at him to put the car in reverse, but as his hand dropped the gearstick, Harris saw a third man reflected in the wing mirror. He too had a gun, aiming down it at the rear of the police car.

'Hands!' One of the gunmen, a Sikh guy with a tight-bound turban, roared the order at them. 'Show me your hands!'

It was a surreal moment. The two police officers were accustomed to being the ones who did the shouting, and this abrupt and terrifying role-reversal left them with nowhere to go but to obey.

'Get out,' said the gunman. He moved closer, leading with his weapon. 'Slowly. Driver first.'

'Jake . . .' Grace shot him a worried look.

'Just do what they say, Isla,' he told her, trying not to show fear. 'We'll be OK.' Harris's mind raced as he carefully opened the car door and climbed out into the drizzle.

Heavily armed SAS types at a dull little airstrip in the middle of Kent? On the surface that didn't add up but, then again, he'd been on the edges of enough special operations during his career to know that stranger things happened.

'We're police officers,' he announced.

The gunman standing behind him actually sniggered. 'Yeah, the motor's a dead giveaway.'

'Quiet!' The Sikh man admonished his colleague and came forward, looking Harris over. With his free hand, he pointed at the taser holstered on the policeman's belt. 'You reach for that, I will put you down. Clear?'

Harris caught sight of Grace as she followed him out into the rain. 'Who the hell are you people?'

Grace's question went unanswered and Harris saw the other gunman press a hand to an earpiece he wore, speaking quietly into it.

'Why are you here?' The Sikh glanced between them. 'Someone call you?'

'We're conducting an investigation,' said Harris. 'Do you know how many laws you're breaking right now?'

For the first time, the man's expressionless manner dropped, and he showed a sneer. 'Yeah, see, that's not what's going on here.'

The man with the earpiece nodded at a voice only he could hear. 'Knox wants us to bring them up to the hangar,' he told the others.

'Now you'll find out,' said the Sikh, and he held out a hand to point the way.

With little other choice, they left the car and walked to the brightly lit aircraft hangar, Grace and Harris side by side and the three armed men arranged around them.

Inside, out of the rain, two gleaming executive jets stood under fluorescent lights, and a man with a rough-hewn beard and a baseball cap waited angrily for their arrival.

He gave the Sikh a severe look, gesturing at the two police officers. 'What the hell is this? Didn't you have someone at the gate?' He had a gruff American accent that crunched his vowels and made everything he said sound like a threat.

'You told us to watch the perimeter—'

'Forget it.' The American held out his hand to Harris and Grace. 'You two, give me your IDs.'

Harris stood his ground, unwilling to turn his warrant card over to a stranger. 'And you are?'

'Let me handle this?' Another man emerged from behind one of the jets before the American could respond. A skinny bloke in a hoodie, with a London drawl, he could have been the cousin of the shoplifter Grace had rugby-tackled in a supermarket car park earlier that evening. But his manner wasn't that of a street criminal, it was all business. He produced an identity wallet of his own and Grace released an audible groan when she saw it. 'I'm with the Security Services,' he explained. 'You've walked right into the middle of something you shouldn't have. Can I see your warrant cards, please?'

Most people wouldn't have known what an authentic SIS identity card looked like, but Grace did. She'd had the mis-fortune of crossing paths with the spook brigade back when she was pushing papers at the case progression unit and, following her nod, Harris reluctantly provided his own ID for show.

'They're just regular coppers,' said the hoodie guy after examining their cards. He waved off the gunmen, who backed away, their weapons disappearing back under their jackets.

Despite the situation, Harris chafed at the man's dismissive description of them. 'Is the owner of this place around? Because he's got a lot of explaining to do, believe me.'

'We sent Mr Teller home. He agreed to let us handle things tonight,' said the American, with an implied threat buried in the statement.

'What things?' said Harris.

The American ignored the question. 'What do you want?'

'We're looking for information about a man named John Price,' Grace cut in. 'Know him?' The moment she said the name, the chill air of the hangar turned even colder.

'The other pilot?' The American asked the question and the man in the hoodie nodded.

'Teller said he didn't turn up for work,' said the SIS agent.

'I regret to inform you that's because he's dead. Car crash, a couple of hours ago, a few miles from here.' Matter of fact, Harris let that drop, and he took a tiny bit of pleasure in momentarily wrong-footing these people. They clearly had no idea of what had happened to the pilot.

But then the American strode up to him and looked Harris square in the eye. 'All right, officer. Let me tell you what's going to happen next.' Every word he spoke was like a nail being driven into wood. 'My people are going to have someone very senior call your chief and tell him to roll over like a good little doggie. And then you and your partner here will tell us every fuckin' detail you know about John Price.'

THIRTEEN

Finally, the moment came when the man with the greying hair left Alex alone with his son, moving out of earshot to stand in the corridor.

Alex listened to be sure that the man was talking to his companion and then he leaned closer to his son, lowering his voice to a hushed whisper. 'You all right?'

'Yeah.' George's plaintive reply told the lie of that. The boy sat rigidly on the living room's sofa next to his father, staring at the bay window that looked out toward the street. He had his hands folded in his lap, knuckles white where they gripped each other tightly, so as not to tremble.

The house was full of shadows, with all but a couple of table lamps switched off, throwing the place into gloom. Their home always had a welcoming glow to it after sunset, but the presence of the invaders had ripped that away. The familiar and friendly turned grim and forbidding.

'It's all right to be scared,' Alex told his son. 'But don't let *them* see it, right?'

'Right.' George nodded, sparing his father a glance. 'I won't.' The boy stiffened, putting on the bravest face he could manage.

Alex's heart caught in his chest. He wanted to pull George into a hug, but he hesitated. The man with the gun would see any sudden movement, and Alex had the horrible sense that their captors would take any gesture like that and turn it against them.

'Dad, what do they want?' George looked up at him. 'Are they here because of Kate?'

'I don't know.' But he did. There was no other explanation. These men had broken into the house and taken them hostage because they needed to lean on Kate, and Alex and George were the leverage.

He felt sick with dread, trying to guess what they were forcing her to do. Alex was angry and afraid in equal measure, but he knew he had to keep his racing emotions in check, not just for his son, but for Kate as well. His mind screamed at him to *do something*, but the vivid image of that long silver pistol dominated everything. He couldn't let them hurt his boy.

If the two of them were going to get out of this in once piece, Alex needed to *think*, not *react*.

He looked across the room at the end table where the house's landline phone had sat. The device lay in pieces on the carpet, the cable ripped out of the wall by the gunman's grimacing friend. The other man had taken Alex's cell phone, forcing him to unlock it at gunpoint, and he hadn't seen it since.

We can't expect help to come to us, he thought. *We'll have to go and get it.*

Alex took a long breath and put himself in the same mental space he always went to on a call-out; in that last instant before he climbed out of the fire engine's cab to storm into some burning building.

He cleared his mind of everything but the problem right in front of him. *The flames blocking the path inside. The thugs blocking the way to safety.* They were the same thing, just different kinds of hazards.

He spoke into George's ear. 'You remember what we practised to do, if the smoke alarm goes off in the house? If there's a fire?'

The boy nodded. 'I remember. Get out. Stay out. Call 9-9-9.'

An occupational hazard of being a firefighter was a tendency to over-prepare for that event in one's home, but Alex had made sure to impress upon his son the importance of having an escape plan. 'This is like that,' he said, and he nodded in the direction of the two men. 'Those men, they're the flames, right? They catch hold of us, we get burned. You understand?'

'So we can't run out the front,' said George, catching on. 'We have to go a different way. Out the back.'

'Yeah.' The garden behind the house ended in a fence, and beyond it an unkempt common turned into scrub and woodland. It would be pitch dark and, if they could make it, on the far side of the woods there was a main road where there might be traffic, people and hopefully *safety.*

'Can't we go next door?' George hissed the question.

'The flames will follow us,' said Alex, after a moment. 'We can't let them spread to someone else's house, can we?'

He thought about their neighbours on either side – the Singhs, with their newborn girl who'd only just started sleeping through the night, and Judy and Thomas, the young couple with a friendly beagle named Chips. The idea of bringing these callous, violent men to their doors made his gut twist.

His eyes wide with fear, George pointed his finger in the direction of the kitchen and the door that led out into the rear garden.

Alex nodded slowly to make sure his son understood. 'When you hear me shout out "fire", you run, right? You run for the woods and you don't look back.'

'I'm not g-going on my own.' George blinked back tears, wiping his hand under his nose.

'I'll be right behind you,' began Alex, but he choked off the rest of the sentence when he realised the man with the greying hair was standing in the doorway, watching them intently.

'What are you whispering about?' He folded his arms over his chest, eyeing the pair of them.

'My boy's hungry,' Alex said coldly. 'We haven't had our dinner, have we?'

The grey-haired man studied Alex for a moment, then touched his own face in the same place where he had struck Alex. 'How is the wound?'

Alex had been able to staunch the bleeding with a wad of kitchen paper and a sticky plaster, but the pain was still there and his cheek felt thick and swollen. 'I'll live,' he said.

'Only if you behave,' came the reply.

George's small hands tightened into fists. 'Why don't you j-just go away?' His voice crackled with emotion as the boy poured all the defiance he could muster into his words. 'We don't have anything you want – leave us alone!'

The youngster's outburst drew a chuckle from the thuggish man out in the hallway, but a stern look from his colleague ended that quickly.

'George does not realise what is going on.' The man with the grey hair pulled a face, looking away toward Alex. 'Mr Walker, what you and your son have or want is irrelevant. All that matters is what Katherine Hood wants.' He moved his hands, revealing the long silver handgun once more. 'If she wants you to live, you will. If she does not care to do as she is told, you will not.'

'Katie, c'mon! Be reasonable.' Breeze banged her fist on the secure door once again, one-two-three in a fast staccato. 'Talk to me. Tell me why you're doing this.'

Ray watched the American lean her head on the door, attempting to listen through the armoured layers. 'Anything?'

'I hear her moving around . . .' Breeze said quietly, lowering her voice. 'Shit. I can't tell.'

'Did you find anything useful in the emergency kit?' Finn stood in the vestibule, arms folded across his chest, throwing the question at the co-pilot.

'This, maybe?' Ray offered him a short, thick plastic rod coloured in the same international orange as the kit bag. 'It's a marker flare. Not the kind that shoots off . . .' He made an arcing motion with one hand. 'It just burns. But the tip is white phosphorus; it burns incredibly hot. If you put it up against the metal door hinges, it might, I don't know, *melt* them?'

From behind him, Ray heard the prisoner give an incredulous snort. 'You will kill us all . . .'

'I gotta agree,' Breeze sighed, 'it's a fucking dumb idea. What about the smoke, huh? You think wc could open a window?'

'Well, bollocks to it, then.' Irritated, Ray jammed the inert flare back into the kit and closed it up again. 'We'll sit here with our thumbs up our arses and wait for divine intervention!'

He was angry at the situation, angry at that snarky cow up in the cockpit and the sarcastic Yank, but mostly Ray was angry at himself for being duped into allowing the mid-air takeover to happen.

If he had stopped to *think* for a moment before he'd let himself react to a non-existent danger, he never would have left the flight deck and allowed her to lock herself in. The blame for this whole sorry chain of events rested on his ill-considered decision, and the co-pilot's churning frustration had nowhere to go.

But then he found somewhere to aim it. Ray dropped into the seat across from Yusuf al-Amal and jabbed a finger at him. 'You set this up, didn't you? Your people did something to Price, I bet. You have Hood on your payroll. And we bloody well walked right into it, didn't we?'

Yusuf sat stiffly in his chair, tracks of dried tears visible on his sunken cheeks as he tried to maintain an even tone. 'Price . . . Hood . . . Those names mean nothing to me.'

'I'm supposed to believe anything you say?' Ray snorted with derision. 'You wouldn't be cuffed up and on your way to the back of beyond if you weren't some sort of terrorist enabler! Only dangerous people end up sitting where you are.'

'You truly think so?' Yusuf met Ray's gaze. 'You think America and Britain and the other countries like them won't make a victim out of an innocent man, if they can benefit from it? Do you believe your government is always right in everything it does?'

'We're not Russia,' insisted Ray. 'We're not North Korea. We have rules.'

'From where I am sitting, it does not seem that way.' Yusuf gave a bitter, nervous laugh, pulling at the restraints around his wrists. Then he rocked forward in his chair and, for the first time, the man showed something like anger. 'You kidnapped me off the street and you are taking me to a gulag! Tell me how that is different to the deeds of criminals and dictators!'

Finn grunted, moving closer. 'He does make a good point.'

'Should've kept him bound and gagged,' muttered Breeze from the far edge of the conversation.

Ray didn't take his eyes off the prisoner. If anything, berating Yusuf stoked his annoyance instead of bleeding it off. 'Admit it,' he demanded. 'You're part of al-Sakakin and your jihadi mates are behind this whole thing. You say you're nobody, but that's a load of crap. They want you back, so that means you are *someone*.'

'No.' Yusuf took a long breath, and the colour in his face from his momentary outburst ebbed. 'I am as ignorant of the situation as you,' he said firmly. 'I have no control over what is going on with this aircraft.'

'He's not lying,' offered Finn, and the off-hand tone in the other agent's comment made Ray glance up at him.

'What makes you so sure of that?' Ray didn't like the smugness underlying Finn's words. It grated on him. The other man knew something he wasn't sharing with the rest of them, that was a given, but it didn't sit well with the co-pilot.

Finn studied the captive. 'I'm a good judge of character.'

'It does not matter if you believe me.' Yusuf let out a breath and looked away, staring blankly out of the cabin window. 'We are all someone's prisoners now,' he said.

The ringing of the telephone was meant to be a distinctive but agreeable sound, not jarring or unpleasant, but it still made Alex and his son jump with fright when it began to sound from the floor above them, echoing down the landing and into the hallway.

The thug was instantly in the room, a menacing snarl on his lips. 'What is that?'

'Phone,' said Alex. 'There's a landline. Upstairs, in the bedroom.'

'Another one?' The grey-haired man with the gun stood out near the threshold of the kitchen. 'You neglected to mention it.'

'I didn't . . .' began Alex, but the man ignored him. He gave his colleague a terse command in their shared language and the thug grimaced, setting off at a run. Alex heard his heavy tread stomp up the stairs and across the landing floorboards overhead.

The thug had made sure to rip out the cables for the handsets in the kitchen and the living room but he clearly hadn't made a thorough enough check to spot the third one in the master bedroom. He didn't reach it in time, and Alex heard the faint click of the answering machine kick in and the low burble of the automated message apologising for the lack of a pick-up.

The grey-haired gunman walked to the bottom of the stairs and Alex watched him stare up into the dimness. He was tense, wound tight and hyper-focused on the unexpected interruption.

A nerve in Alex's leg twitched. *Is this it? Is this our chance?* His body stiffened, and he felt George's hand on his arm.

'Dad?' The boy's whisper was barely a breath. 'Now?'

Alex rose silently, careful to keep out of sight of the man in the hallway. George came up with him, mirroring his movements. He placed a hand on his son's chest, holding him where he stood.

The entrance to the kitchen was less than a metre from where they were standing. It would take only seconds to get to it, then a few more to make it to the back door. But would they have enough time? How quick was the man with his pistol?

Fast enough to drill a bullet through Alex's back? Fast enough to shoot George before he could get outside?

Then there was a woman's voice he didn't recognise, carrying down to them from the bedroom upstairs, coming from the other phone. *'Hello, this is Constable Isla Grace with the Kent County Police Service. I'd like to speak with a Mr Alex Walker, if you're there?'*

She paused, waiting for someone to pick up. George squeezed his dad's hand and Alex knew what he was thinking. Had someone seen the men barging into their house and called the cops?

He hesitated, the fight or flight reflex in him pulling Alex in two different directions at once. Part of him wanted to drop back and let it play out. Maybe the police were already on the way, maybe they would deal with these men and this nightmare would come to an end. Or maybe that would be the worst thing that could happen. Police officers banging on the door and the man with the gun making a violent choice in the heat of the moment.

Alex gave a shake of the head. *We can't wait,* he told himself, *this chance might not come again. They're distracted. We have to go now.*

'Luka!' The gunman snarled the thug's name, clearly annoyed at him for not cutting off the call.

'If you get this message,' the woman on the phone was saying, *'can you ring back immediately, please?'*

'Fire!' Alex made his choice and gave George a shove, propelling him toward the kitchen. *'Fire!'*

George exploded into motion, speeding down the hall as fast as a scalded cat, racing toward the kitchen. Alex came storming out after him, his fists already swinging, turning to waylay the gunman.

He grabbed the first thing within arm's reach – a particularly ugly vase that Kate liked but he hated – and hurled it at the man at the bottom of the stairs.

With a crash, the heavy vase shattered across the man's gun arm. Caught wrong-footed by Alex's shout and unexpected attack, he lost his grip on the long silver pistol and it thudded to the rug at his feet.

Alex followed up with a heavy left cross that put his fist right in the gunman's temple. He staggered back and Alex hit him again, but by then the other man had caught up and he was going on the offensive.

The firefighter had the edge in size, but his foe was faster and harder, his wound-tight energy coming out in a sudden release, a flurry of blows against which Alex could only raise his guard and let them land.

Somewhere behind him, glass smashed and the door creaked open. Alex heard George's scrambling footsteps on the stones of the patio and knew the boy was out. He staggered back, trying to deflect more punches and failing.

The heavy tread upstairs thudded across the floorboards and the other thug – the one called Luka – yelled out his colleague's name like a question. 'Matvey? Matvey! *Chto sluchilos?*'

That broke the concentration of the man with the grey hair, giving Alex a shot. He put a pile-driver blow into his opponent's solar plexus with enough force to knock him back. The other man, Matvey, caught his boot on the edge of the rug and stumbled, going down on one knee.

He and Alex both spotted the pistol where it had fallen and the grey-haired man dove toward it, even as his big friend came thundering down the stairs to join in the melee.

Alex pushed himself off the staircase banisters for a burst of speed and he ran hard, into the kitchen, desperately racing for the back door.

He dreaded the thought of a searing spear of agony hitting him in the spine, of a silenced bullet from that silver pistol bursting out of his chest in a gush of blood; then he was at the door, through it, slamming it closed behind him.

When the shot came, he barely heard the metallic chug of the gun. It turned the double-glazed glass in the door into a spider web of fractures, and Alex jerked away.

'Dad!' George dithered at the fence where a section of the wooden lapped panels had been kicked through from the other side. 'Over here!'

'I told you to run!' Alex snapped, pointing the way. 'Go, go!' He kicked over garden chairs as he ran, following the boy into the puddle of darkness, past which the glow from the houses did not reach.

Alex's trainers squelched on damp grass and uneven ground, and he caught sight of George ahead of him, the gangly form of his son a collection of shadows skating over the murky common.

He risked a look over his shoulder. Through the hole in the fence he saw the two men boil out into the garden, grey-haired Matvey leading with his gun, the wolfish Luka casting around and spotting the direction they had taken.

George had slowed again, and Alex almost knocked him down as they ran into one another. Skidding to a halt, he crouched and pulled the boy to him. Together, they left the open common and the clear paths running across it, making for the cover of the long grass and the trees.

'They can't see in the dark,' whispered George, to himself. 'They can't.'

'No,' Alex promised, 'but they might hear us. So you have to do exactly what I tell you, right?'

'OK.' George's reply was uneven, like a whimper.

'Listen to me.' Alex's grip tightened on the boy's arm. 'You need to be tough tonight, you understand? No crying. No whining.' *Or we'll end up dead*. He didn't say the last few words, but he didn't need to.

In the darkness, George's head bobbed woodenly and he sniffed. 'I'm scared.'

'Yeah, me too.' Alex put his hand between his son's shoulders and guided him forward, past the tree line and into the thicket.

Behind them, the sounds of the two men talking came up on the wind. He didn't know what they were saying, but the cadence and the hard tones were enough to carry the meaning.

They were angry, and they were hunting them.

FOURTEEN

The blackphone in her jacket gave off a hard pulse of vibration and Breeze immediately felt another surge of dismay wash over her.

'What the hell now?' She asked the question to nobody in particular as she fished the device from her pocket, pushing away from the door to the Hawker's cockpit and down the length of the cabin.

'What is it?' asked Finn, craning his neck to look at the screen as she passed him.

Breeze deliberately ignored the Brit's question and walked to the back of the jet, fumbling for the wired earpiece and microphone spool she habitually kept to hand. Jacking it into the device, she sat heavily against the rear bulkhead where she had a view of the cabin and everyone in it, and answered the call. 'Talk to me.'

'*You got company?*' As usual, Knox dispensed with the niceties.

She watched Finn, the co-pilot and the asset. 'Just the two of us,' she confirmed. Breeze was far enough away from them, and the ambient noise from the engines meant she wouldn't be overheard.

'*The situation down here has changed.*'

160

Knox's dry, argumentative tone carried a bleaker note than usual, and Breeze picked up on it instantly. 'On a scale of one to ten, how fucked is it?'

'*Off the dial.*' She heard him moving around, and in the background there were echoing, indistinct voices. '*The pilot you were supposed to get, the guy MI6 used before . . .*'

'Price?' She recalled the man's face from a file Marty had shown her.

'*I had the local cops here. He's dead. Car accident. Happened no more than an hour before we arrived at the airfield.*'

The hairs on the back of Breeze's neck stood up. 'That can't be a coincidence.'

'*Gets worse,*' said Knox. '*Long story short, I had to lean on the locals. Their senior cop knew the drill, gave us the whole thing. Turns out the pilot's wife and daughter were stabbed to death tonight. They're saying it's a probable murder-suicide, but—*'

'That's bullshit.' Breeze cut him off and put her head in her hands. 'Fuck, fuck, fucking *fuck!*'

The whole horrible mechanics of the situation spun out around her. Breeze pictured it in her mind's eye like one of those crazy 'conspiracy walls' so beloved of cop shows, where chains of events were visualised with photos tacked to a cork board, connected by threads of crimson twine.

Somebody on the other side had got to Price, either to push him into doing something he didn't want to, or to take him off the board, and by design or accident, the poor bastard and his loved ones wound up dead. It was a crude and messy play, but an effective one.

More than once, Breeze had seen the same kind of set-up used against the Agency's operations in other mission theatres – insurgents working under the radar in

Afghanistan against American-friendly sources, or Russian hitters targeting drivers and pilots under CIA control to screw with US covert actions. But doing something so blatant inside the United Kingdom, on the home turf of a major NATO partner and a nation from the Five Eyes intelligence coalition? That was troubling.

Her mind immediately went to the Russians. This kind of thing was their stock-in-trade, and they had form, as the Brits liked to say. Assassins from the Federal Security Service of the Russian Federation had terminated dissident citizens and ex-spies from their side on the streets of British cities more than once, and done it brazenly. The FSB had grown out of the corpse of its notorious Cold War progenitor, the KGB, but it lacked the subtlety of the old Soviet-era espionage machine. Today's Russian agents were more like mafia hitmen, swaggering and vicious, unconcerned about hiding their activities in the shadows.

But how does that connect up with al-Sakakin? She shot a look at her prisoner. The terrorist group had no more love for Russia than it did for any Western nation, but then there was that old, oft-proven adage about war making strange bedfellows. There were plenty of ex-Soviet private contractors outside the axis of government willing to do murder pay-for-play, regardless of where the fee came from. Breeze put that fact aside for later consideration. Here and now, she had more immediate concerns.

'*The pilot you have up there, Hood,*' said Knox. '*She's obviously been compromised by the same actors.*'

Despite herself, Breeze snorted with derision. 'Gee, I hadn't noticed. I figured she was taking us to Disneyland.'

'*You're not reading me, Lillian.*' Knox's unexpected use of her first name brought Breeze up short. '*Whoever got to Price, they*'

*got to Hood as well. And to do that, to be that quick off the blocks,
they have to have a source* inside *the circle. You copy that?'*

'I copy.' Breeze's senses abruptly became hyper-acute. She
felt the rumble of the jet's engines through her bones, felt
the pressure and the chilly dryness of the processed air inside
the cabin. She studied Finn, Ray and Yusuf, the three men
becoming three questions she didn't have the answers for.

Knox was on to something, his blunt evaluation crystalising
the nagging disquiet that had been pulling at Breeze's
thoughts from the get-go. This hijack, this whole situation, it
was predicated on having insider knowledge, and more than
the raw data that some hacker might have been able to skim
off a secure computer server.

She thought about her own people, considering the pressure
points that somebody might try to use against them. Marty
Chester had been part of Breeze's line-up for a while, and he
was far too afraid of her to bite the hand that fed him. Knox,
well, that nasty son of a bitch was too damned ornery to be
capable of this kind of backstab, and not subtle enough to try
and double bluff. Maybe someone further outside her team
could have been coerced, perhaps some desk jockey back at
Langley ... but Breeze had deliberately kept the circle tight
on this operation to avoid exactly that occurrence.

Which meant that the leak had to be at the British end
of the op. It made no sense that the co-pilot would be the
insider, because if the enemy had Ray in their pocket, why the
hell would they have to deal with Teller's aircrew? It would
have been Ray bolting himself in behind that security door,
not Hood.

She glanced at Finn. He looked right at her, that slightly
sleepy gaze of his holding Breeze's eye line, his free hand

running over his perfectly manicured beard. She ran back every word the MI6 agent had said to her tonight, mentally reviewing them, searching for some sign or some inflection that might have been missed in the moment.

But in the end, he saved her the trouble.

'It's a funny thing,' said Finn, pitching up his voice so Breeze could hear him. 'I always thought Americans had good poker faces.' His other hand came out from behind his jacket with a stubby black pistol in it, a small-frame Glock G26 subcompact that vanished into the man's long fingers.

Whatever tell had shown on Breeze's face in that second, as she put two and two together, it was like the guy had been waiting for it from the start. Finn seemed pleased that the penny had finally dropped.

Yusuf shrank back, physically recoiling from the sight of the weapon. Across the table from the captive, Ray's eyes widened in confusion and surprise. The co-pilot didn't get it, not straight off. He wasn't sure what he was seeing, not until Finn waved the gun in Breeze's direction and motioned for her to end her telephone conversation with a throat-cutting gesture.

With exaggerated slowness, Breeze pulled out the phone's ear bud and let the wire drop away, but she didn't kill the call. 'Thought you didn't want to use that in here,' she said, nodding at the gun.

'Please, give me some credit,' he replied. 'I prepared for this eventuality. It's loaded with low-density frangible rounds. They'll make a nasty mess of a person but they break up on impact with hard surfaces. Won't go through the fuselage.'

'I know what they do,' said Breeze. 'Wow, you really are smarter than you look. Who would've known it?'

'Finn, what's going on?' Ray half rose out of his seat, but Finn waved him back.

'She's played us,' he replied. 'This diversion is her doing.' Finn shook his head, not quite pointing the Glock at Breeze. 'I imagine not even her people at the CIA know what she's up to.'

'*I'm* playing *you*?' She snorted. 'That's the way you're going with this? I take it back, you're not that smart after all.' Breeze looked straight at Ray. 'Let me ask you. How well do you know this guy?' She pointed at Finn. 'You ever work with him before today? No? Let me guess. You were pulled into this op at the last second, no prior notice, right?'

The co-pilot didn't reply, but he didn't need to. Breeze saw her answer on the other man's face and watched the doubt creep into Ray's expression.

'Let me tell you something about Lillian Breeze,' said Finn, drawing himself up as if about to give a lecture. 'She's a burnout waiting to happen. She has few friends at Langley, and many more people who would quite happily see the back of her. And why? It's because she can't leave well enough alone. Lillian here has been on a personal crusade against al-Sakakin for years, and do you want to know the reason?' He looked her way. 'What was the name of the double agent you sent into the lion's den? The asset that you personally turned, Lillian. Your friend. Sophie, or something like that, wasn't it?'

Breeze became very still. The woman's name was Sophia Betel, and she had been a civilian aid worker with a Spanish NGO in the Middle East. Smart, capable and one of the few people Breeze had ever met who could keep up with her.

She had never been honest with Sophia; never told her that she would be working for the CIA by passing on the snatches of information she came across in al-Sakakin's backyard. On dark nights, lying awake at three in the morning, Breeze would torment herself by wondering what was more damning: that Sophia might have gone to her death never knowing that she'd been lied to, or that her murderers had revealed Breeze's lie of omission, right before they beheaded her and filmed it for their propaganda reels.

Sophia hadn't been the first asset that Breeze had recruited and then lost in the line of duty – but she had been the last. The death of the gentle, bright young woman had broken something inside her that could not be mended. It had pushed Lillian Breeze beyond a point of no return.

The memory of a smiling, little-sister face the CIA agent kept buried with her other secrets threatened to break out and fill her thoughts, but she stamped it down without mercy, refusing to let Finn weaponise that pain against her. Instead, Breeze refocused on him, homing in on the mistake he had just made.

'You shouldn't know about that. Those details weren't passed on to the British Security Services.'

Finn covered a momentary flash of dismay with a false grin. 'Are you sure? Your reputation *does* precede you.'

'Oh yeah,' she replied. 'See, if there's one thing the Agency hates, it's having its fuck ups paraded in front of foreigners, even if they are our allies. Believe me, I've made enough of them.'

Ray raised his hands, trying to play peacemaker, as he rose from his seat again. 'Finn, listen,' he began, 'you might be jumping the gun here—'

The mask of disinterest on the other man's face dissolved, just for a split-second, but long enough that Breeze caught the contemptuous expression before it was gone again, as Finn made his choice.

'I'm really not,' he said, and he shot Ray point blank in the chest.

The gun crashed, the sound of the discharge harsh and metallic. Yusuf cried out in shock as Ray fell back into his seat, clutching at the ugly wound. The co-pilot's face caught not in pain, but in stunned disbelief.

Breeze threw herself off the bulkhead in the same instant, scrambling to grab the microphone cord where it lay hanging. *If Knox had kept the line open, if he had heard the shot* . . . She snatched it up and shouted into the tiny pickup. 'Finn's been turned!'

The pistol shouted again, and a heavy, burning-hot impact slammed into Breeze's belly. A wave of absolute agony bloomed out from her right side, stopping the breath in her lungs and sending jagged, twitching shocks up her nerves.

Her legs turned to water and she crumpled to the floor of the cabin, wheezing for air, briefly losing contact with her body as the pain washed in and out with tidal force. Then she became aware of exactly where the frangible bullet had entered her torso, and she had to tear her gaze away from the wet rosette of red-black growing over her stomach. She could feel every last one of the bullet head's splintered fragments, the hot needles of ceramic caught in her flesh.

Adrenaline pulsed through her and Breeze trembled with shock, hovering on the edge of passing out. She forced her way back and held on, panting hard.

It hurt like hell, but she wasn't dead. Not yet. Breeze held on to that notion, gulping down air, each new ragged breath filling with blades. She rewarded Finn with a snarled curse heavy with every ounce of her agony.

'You . . . mother . . . *fucker.*'

Yusuf shook his head but Finn ignored him completely, coldly evaluating Ray's pain as the man lay slumped in his seat, quivering with the effort of staying alive.

There was no emotion on his face as Finn leaned in, placing the slide of the Glock against the co-pilot's throat. He put his other hand over Ray's nose and mouth, and methodically stifled the panicked breath from the wounded man. He let him scratch and claw and flail until Ray's movements weakened, became feeble, then finally ceased.

Finn gave Yusuf a sideways look. 'One pilot is enough.' Then he stepped back into the aisle and came for Breeze.

She had her own weapon, of course, a little Taurus Curve pocket pistol more for comfort than for fighting, but the blazing pain in her side and the numbness in her fingers made it impossible to reach for. And, unlike Finn, Breeze hadn't thought to load non-standard ammo, so even if she could have shot the bastard, the round would have carried on right through him and punctured the thin metal skin of the Hawker.

But, despite that, Breeze still struggled to pull it when Finn's shadow fell over her. He batted her hand away and plucked the gun out of her jacket pocket.

'This isn't how I hoped it would go,' he told her, with a frown.

She waited for him to kill her too, but he made no move to finish her off as he had with the luckless co-pilot. 'Sorry to . . . piss on your parade.' Breeze forced out the words, the rusty smell of her own blood catching in her nostrils.

'That's quite bad,' he said, considering her injury. 'Survivable?' Finn gave a shrug. 'I give you five-to-one odds, if I'm being generous.'

'I'll take that bet.' She couldn't figure out why he didn't put her out of her misery, but every second she was still breathing meant there still might be a way to come through this.

Am I lying to myself now? She fought past the question and gritted her teeth.

'You know what'll happen next, huh?' Struggling to maintain her focus, Breeze watched him stoop to gather up her encrypted blackphone from where it had fallen. 'You really screwed the pooch, hipster.'

'They'll try to shoot us down, I imagine.' He blew out a breath. 'Have to do something about that.' Finn put the satellite phone aside and produced one of his own, a chunky all-weather model. He thumbed the redial and Breeze heard the chiming as it made its connection.

He walked away and she strained to pick up Finn's end of the conversation, delivered in clipped phrases of Russian. 'Matvey. It is me.'

Breeze held on to the first word, repeating it to herself: *Matvey.* A man's name. It was of Eastern European origin. That and the language shift made her previous suspicions snap into place.

Finn listened to the burble of a voice on the other end of the line, then cut off the reply with his own. 'I'm sorry to hear that but I'm afraid I have problems of my own.' The Brit's tone became caustic. 'Tell the pilot there's been a change of plan.'

FIFTEEN

Kate heard the sound of the first gunshot through her headphones and pulled them away with a start, twisting back in the pilot's seat to look toward the secure door.

Her first thought was to wonder if Breeze had been foolish enough to actually try shooting through the locking mechanism, but she couldn't believe that. The American's manner was irritating but she didn't seem like an idiot.

Kate gripped the flight yoke firmly with one hand, quickly double-checking the oxygen mask and rig stowed by her seat, ready for the warning signals that would sound off if the Hawker's cabin pressure suddenly began to drop. A bullet through the fuselage would cause rapid decompression, putting everyone on board at risk of going out cold as the thin air robbed them of consciousness, but with the mask on, Kate would still be able to fly them down to a lower, safer altitude.

In those dark minutes after she had locked herself in on the flight deck, Kate had thought hard about deliberately depressurising the plane herself. In theory, she might have been able to do it, overriding the activation of the emergency masks in the cabin so as to put Breeze and the others out in a minute or so. Then, with only the pilot still conscious, she

170

would be free to turn the jet around and make a fast run for the airport at Gibraltar.

But doing something so dangerous carried huge risks, not the least of which was the possibility she might accidentally kill four people through oxygen starvation.

And then there was the threat from the man on the phone. *We will know. There will be consequences for disobedience.*

He could be bluffing but Kate couldn't bring herself to chance it. Not while Alex and George's lives were hanging in the balance. Putting herself in danger was one thing, but endangering them? She couldn't do it.

Kate started to wonder if she had been mistaken about the sound when a second shot rang out, but then she was certain. It was definitely the report of a small calibre pistol, but further away.

'They're not shooting at me.' She voiced the thought aloud and it brought a torrent of horrible possibilities with it. Her shirt was damp with sweat from fear and effort, and she shivered as she pulled at the collar, waiting for what would come next.

Her phone began to ring. Kate took a deep breath to steady herself and re-engaged the autopilot before removing the handset. The caller ID on the screen read ALEX WALKER, but she knew the voice she would hear on the end of the line would not be his.

Kate pressed the tab and raised the phone to her ear. 'I'm here.'

'*Open the door.*' The man's words had taken on a different timbre. Before he had been metered and controlled, but now he was irritable and out of breath. There was a flatness to the ambient background sounds as well, and Kate guessed that the speaker was outside, in the open air.

'You told me to—'

'*Plans have changed,*' he snapped, cutting her off. '*You will open the door. You will do it now!*'

'I heard shots in the cabin.'

'*A man will make himself known to you,*' said the voice, his annoyance rising, paying no attention to her comment. '*Do what he tells you or the boy and your lover will suffer.*'

Kate swallowed hard. 'I'm not doing anything else for you until I talk to Alex.' She forced herself to make the demand, barely keeping the fear from her tone.

'*Suka!*' She didn't know the literal meaning of the curse but Kate could make a good guess based on the venom and inflection. '*Open the fucking door or I gut the boy like a pig, understand? You have one minute!*'

The line went dead and left her there in the company of her own terrors. Then there came a careful knock on the cabin door, polite in its restraint.

Checking the autopilot once again, Kate climbed out of her seat, still holding the phone. Once again, she had no choice but to obey.

She moved to the security latches and released them one by one, until the door slid back and she found herself looking at the bearded, shaven-headed man who had quizzed her before take-off. There was a new coldness to his manner that made her skin crawl.

'Ms Hood,' he said, by way of greeting. 'I'll take that.' The man pulled the cell phone out of her hand and pocketed it before she could protest. 'My name is Finn; I don't think we were properly introduced before. I want you to know I appreciate your compliance with my colleagues. Keep it up and we won't have any problems.'

172

'I don't—' She started to speak but the words caught in her throat as she smelled the faint odour of gunpowder in the cabin's air. And something else. *Blood.*

Kate's gaze fell on Ray, finding the lifeless body of the co-pilot slumped against the inside curve of the cabin wall. His slack face lay against one of the Hawker's windows, his eyes blank and sightless. 'Oh no ...' Her hand flew to her mouth in horror.

'He shot him.' In the seat across from the dead man, Breeze's prisoner offered the explanation with blank clarity, nodding in Finn's direction. 'Killed him.'

'Regrettably,' agreed the bearded man. 'Which means we are now fully reliant on you, Ms Hood, to get us to our destination. I hope you realise the import of that.'

'Tell him to kiss your ass.' With visible effort, Breeze called out from the back of the cabin, and Kate's shock deepened when she caught sight of the mess of red across the American woman's blouse.

'He shot her too,' said the prisoner. 'But she has value. She won't die yet.'

'Joke's on you, shithead.' Breeze forced the retort with a wet gasp. 'I'll bleed to death before you know it. Then you won't have dick!'

The co-pilot was beyond help but Breeze was another matter. Kate's training kicked in and she shoved her way past Finn, ignoring his protests, pulling the Hawker's emergency medical kit from a locker on the floor. She knelt by the other woman's side, the kit open on the deck.

'Oh, Katie,' said Breeze, managing a crooked smile. 'My hero. You got any morphine in there, honey? Cos this hurts more than my last divorce.'

'Sorry,' said Kate. Peeling back the sticky layers of Breeze's blood-soaked jacket and blouse, she found the entry wound and swallowed her instinctive revulsion at the sight of the gory injury. In the RAF they had given Kate basic medical instruction as part of a survival skills program for front-line pilots, and she drew on that, putting her own concerns on hold for the sake of the other woman.

She worked fast, her fingers becoming sticky with fluids as she cleaned the site of the bullet hit, before tearing open a packet of blood-clotting haemostatic granules. Breeze let out a long, low groan of agony as Kate poured the yellowy powder into her wound. The granules and an adhesive bandage patch would slow down the blood loss, but it was clear to even Kate's untrained eye exactly how bad Breeze's wound was. Unless she could get the American to a hospital, internal bleeding and the bullet fragments lodged in her gut would condemn the woman to a slow death.

Kate looked up and found the American watching her. 'You're here, so who's flying the goddamn plane?' Breeze blinked, groggy with pain.

'It'll be all right.' Kate offered the platitude without thinking.

'Really?' The American gave a hollow chuckle. 'Honestly, we're both screwed.'

Miles stood with his back to the hangar's exterior and peered up at the thick, gloomy blanket of clouds overhead. He felt a faint pinprick of rain on his face but there was no renewed deluge, at least not for the moment. The air was cold with the chill from the evening's earlier downpour, and puddles glistened here and there on the black asphalt of the aircraft apron.

He badly wanted a smoke to warm him up a little but the multiple signs warning about volatile aviation fuel storage and the like made Miles hesitate to light up. Instead, he walked in circles, hands buried in the belly pocket of his hoodie as he tried to keep them warm and stave off his nicotine craving.

He caught sight of one of the PMCs standing sentinel near the grassy median across the way. The man held a submachine gun out of sight beneath his jacket, and he scanned the cold night with a fixed, robotic manner, waiting for a threat to materialise.

Miles had been ringside to watch the CIA guy Knox giving the mercenaries an ear bashing after those two local plods had wandered on to the airfield unhindered. Both of the constables had since been sent away, the pair of them sufficiently cowed by not only the presence of guns and serious-looking men, but by the way their commanding officer had immediately ordered them to give up all they knew about the death of John Price.

That's enough to put the frighteners on anyone, he thought. Once upon a time, Miles had been on their side, living in the 'white' side of things where most people went about their daily lives, instead of the clandestine realm of the 'black' world where MI6, CIA and all the other intelligence agencies operated.

He felt sorry for the coppers. They were out of their league, having stumbled right into something that rose far above their pay grades. If they were smart, they'd keep their traps shut, their heads down and do their jobs.

The information they had unknowingly brought to the team at the airfield blasted a hole in the middle of the operation, sending shockwaves back through the British and American intelligence services. Miles had no doubt that phones were ringing in offices all over Whitehall and Washington DC, as people scrambled to catch up with the unfolding clusterfuck that the al-Amal rendition had become.

More than anything, he needed someone out of Six, someone senior to him, to step in and take over. But so far that hadn't happened, and he remained the man on the spot, the only British intelligence officer in the midst of this mess. It was a responsibility he did not want.

Sooner or later, someone would catch up to the fact that Miles was only a driver, a low-tier field officer, and kick him aside. But that hadn't happened yet, and part of him wondered if it was deliberate. If tonight's work ended badly, a nobody like him would be the perfect person to pin the blame on.

That bleak thought dissipated as he heard fast, heavy footsteps coming up behind him. Miles twisted to see Knox coming his way with his pistol drawn and a face like thunder.

'You!' The American aimed the gun at Miles's chest. 'Show me your hands, do it now!'

'What?' He took a step back but did what he was told, slow and steady. Behind him, the PMC who had been on guard reacted by raising his own weapon, covering Miles from another angle. 'OK, hang on a sec—'

Knox came at him, and with fingers like iron talons, he grabbed Miles by the shoulder and pulled him back toward the SUV. 'What the fuck are you limey assholes doing?'

Miles shook his head, bewildered. 'I have no idea what you're on about mate!' The PMC stood right behind him, eyes darting nervously left and right.

'You got some explaining to do,' said Knox, who gave him an artless shove toward the open door of the mobile operations unit.

Inside, Miles saw the CIA's tech working at a laptop, the screen before him filled with sonic waveforms. He looked up and warily met the other man's gaze. 'There's been a development on the flight.'

'Run it for him.' Knox gestured with the pistol.

Chester nodded, tapping a key, and a speaker inside the SUV played a snatch of crackling audio. Miles heard muffled voices, one of which definitely sounded like Finn's, but he couldn't pick out the words. Then there was a clutter of echoing noise and a flat crack, like a piece of glass snapping in two.

'That's a weapon discharge,' said Chester. 'Acoustic signature matches a nine-millimetre round, subsonic, close range.'

Miles shook his head, a denial forming on his lips even as Chester let the playback roll on.

The next thing Miles heard was Breeze shouting out a desperate warning. *'Finn's been turned!'* Then another glass-crack report, then dead silence.

He met Knox's hard gaze. The CIA operative had his pistol aimed at a spot on the ground between them, but Miles knew if he so much as twitched, the black muzzle would be right in his face.

Chester played Breeze's cry of alarm again and again, until Miles waved him off. 'All right, all right, I heard it!'

'Two shots fired,' Knox said darkly, 'the aircraft under the control of a rogue pilot, your man Finn called out by one of ours. And we just lost the tracker signal from Breeze's blackphone. You want to tell me what the actual fuck MI6 is doing up there, son?'

Miles swallowed hard. His mouth was desert dry. 'This . . . I don't know anything about this. I'm the bloody driver! Mission mobility, urban operations, that's my gig. Finn pulled me off the transport rota to drive tonight, so I drove! If he's up to some shit, I know nothing about it, swear down!'

Knox glared at him like he was staring right into Miles's soul, before finally turning his head to spit. 'Sounds like your guy is a fucking traitor.'

'You don't know that . . .' Miles started to argue, but the words came out weakly and he couldn't finish the sentence.

He dredged up what little he knew about Thomas Finn. It was barely anything with depth; a few comments from some of the other ground-level team members about the bloke. He was considered competent, if regarded as something of a twat, but given the character of many of the privately schooled chinless wonders who populated much of MI6's mid-tiers and higher ranks, that wasn't uncommon.

But was Finn the kind of man who could cold-bloodedly betray his country and its allies? It galled Miles that he really didn't know enough about him to be certain.

The full import of what he had heard on the audio recording landed hard and Miles stiffened. 'I have to call this in to Control.' He reached for his own cell phone, but off a nod from Knox, the PMC jabbed him in the back with his weapon and took the device from him.

'You're not gonna talk to anyone unless I say so,' said the American. 'This is a CIA operation now. You Brits have zero credibility from now on, you read me? Count yourself lucky I don't bag and tag you just to be on the safe side.'

'You can't do that!' Miles stepped forward, but the mercenary prodded him again.

'It's done,' snapped Knox, turning his back on the other man. He gestured to Chester. 'I need a direct feed to the SAC. We gotta make a Third Option call, right now.'

'No!' Miles raised a hand, a crawling chill running up the back of his spine. *SAC* meant the *Special Activities Center*, the division of the Central Intelligence Agency responsible for what were euphemistically described as 'kinetic' operations. These were the so-called Third Option that Knox referred to. By any other name, that meant blowing things up and killing people. 'Look, we need to take a breath here, not immediately go for the cowboy shit, yeah?'

Knox didn't bother to reply, or even look in Miles's direction. He addressed his next words to the mercenary. 'Keep him out of my way.'

'Move back.' The PMC prodded Miles a third time, and he jerked away from him.

'All right, back off big man!' Miles snarled at the merc and retreated a few steps from the SUV, but not so far that he couldn't watch Chester working at his screen.

The tech gave a nod and Knox picked up a headset. Pressing it to his ear, he listened intently for long moments before speaking again. 'Copy that. Be advised, I am requesting green light authorisation for an airborne intercept. Location, western Mediterranean Sea. Expedite immediate.'

'That's enough,' said Finn. 'Get back to work.' He waved his pistol in the direction of the Hawker's cockpit, but Kate only rose to her feet, standing her ground.

'Or what?' She jutted her chin at the gun. 'You'll shoot me too?'

He sighed theatrically. 'Must you be so difficult? You know it's not you who'll suffer if you cause problems.'

Kate stiffened. 'I want to talk to Alex. I want to know he's all right.'

'Who?' Finn frowned, then caught up quickly. 'Oh. The boyfriend, yes? Well, no. I'm not at liberty to provide that. We're going to keep communications with the outside world to a minimum for now.'

He nodded toward the table, where the broken remains of Breeze's satellite phone and Kate's more ordinary handset lay in a pathetic pile of glass and plastic fragments. Finn had methodically destroyed both devices, smashing them with the butt of his semi-automatic until they were broken and useless.

'Speaking of which ...' Finn reached into his pocket and removed his own sat phone, waking it with a press of the thumb. He laid the device down on the table in front of Yusuf, who eyed it warily.

'What is this?'

'I'm doing what I was paid to do,' Finn told the prisoner. 'I was told a detainee would be transferred tonight. I made certain I was in charge of the detail. I picked the team. I set this up.' He indicated the phone, then produced a lock knife and used it to cut the ties securing Yusuf's wrists. 'My employer expressed a desire to speak with you. Just give it a minute.'

'You never contacted MI6 about Price, did you?' said Breeze.

'No. That was an unexpected hiccup, I'll admit, but it's been managed. I imagine there are a lot of people at Vauxhall Cross running around like headless chickens right now.' He smirked. 'Shame to miss it, really.'

Breeze hauled herself up to a sitting position and wiped a film of sweat from her brow. 'Don't keep us in suspense, hipster. Tell Katie here why you decided to betray your oath to King and country.' She panted out a shallow breath, delivering a weak but pointed addendum. 'You lousy dickwad.'

Finn's eyes narrowed. 'I haven't killed you outright because you might actually be worth slightly more alive than dead,' he snapped. 'But don't tempt me.'

Breeze snorted and glanced at Kate. 'You get it, don't you? You know what he is.'

Kate gave a slow nod, looking back at Finn, seeing the facts of the man with clarity for the first time. 'You're not some believer. Not doing this for a cause. You're a hireling.' She sneered at him. 'You sold out for money.'

A nerve twitched in Finn's jaw and Kate knew she was on the mark. He gave a shrug. 'In fairness, it is an extremely good payday. Much better than the pittance I was getting from the penny-pinchers in the Ministry. And ideology is such an outdated concept.'

'Do you even know why you're doing this?' Kate pushed harder.

'I didn't ask,' said Finn, 'because I genuinely don't care.' He indicated Yusuf. 'I don't know if this man is somebody or nobody. I don't know if the men paying me want to rescue him or slit his throat. I don't care.' He smiled, finding his stride. 'I've had enough of working for a bunch of feckless, self-serving idiots. I'm cashing out with a decent jackpot.' As he spoke, the phone on the table began to vibrate, moving across the surface in little jerks of motion. 'Here we go. Right on time.'

Yusuf stared at the device, rubbing his wrists where the ties had cut into his skin, and at length he reached out and put a finger on the phone. The answer tab lit up, and a voice emerged from the speaker grille.

'*I want to speak to my brother.*' It was a man, his timbre deep and rich, with a Middle-Eastern inflection to his words. '*Are you there? Do you hear me? This is Nasir. Will you speak to me, Hamid?*'

181

'I thought you said his name was Yusuf,' said Kate, struggling to keep up.

'Hamid.' From behind her, Breeze said the word like it was the darkest, foulest curse the woman could ever have uttered. 'You sneaky fucking bastard!'

The man seated at the table gave Kate a sideways glance, and it was as if he had instantly become a different person. The mask of panic he'd worn from the first moment she saw him dissolved, and in its place rose an icy, affectless expression. Absent of malice, absent of fear, absent of anything.

'Brother,' he said, picking up the phone. '*As-salamu alaikum.*'

SIXTEEN

As it had been with every turning point in Hamid's life, the circumstances he now found himself in sprang from a violent death.

He could measure the arc of his existence with grave markers, one after another, stretching back along the horizon line of his life. Hamid came into the world on death's hands, his mother perishing in childbirth after terrible complications and an under-equipped hospital collaborated to leave him with a father who would always resent the boy. His older brother Nasir was the only light throughout his younger years, the two of them growing up as an inseparable pair amid poverty and dust, each a bulwark for the other against an indifferent, uncaring world.

Life was hard for them in Saddam City, one of the poorest districts on the edges of Baghdad despite the grand name bestowed by their country's bellicose president. The crushing, day-to-day grind of living in that milieu took their father soon enough, the man run down by a speeding army truck that did not stop after the fact. Rootless and orphaned, Hamid and Nasir found another family among other lost youths. The firebrand imam who took them in, preaching rage and fury, became their new father figure.

Hamid killed his first man at the age of sixteen, a junior officer in the People's Army extorting protection money from one of the mosques. He committed the act with a butcher knife – more with anger than accuracy – and he did it telling himself that the officer had been the driver of the truck those years before, as if his need for revenge made the deed permissible.

But on reflection, Hamid found he didn't really *need* that justification, not for that murder, or the next, or the next, or any of those that followed.

His whole life justified it. Sentenced by circumstance to live a stunted existence in neglected, crumbling ruins, while the ruling caste enjoyed their lavish lifestyles and their casual cruelty, he had hate enough to fuel him. The officer, and every man like him, they were an affront to God. The imam let Hamid find his way to that realisation, that *permission*, until he walked the bloody path he had been destined to follow.

Hamid was born to be an equaliser, a force to balance the injustice of the world. At first, his targets were the Ba'athists in power and their lackeys. In time, the scope of his work grew wider, expanding beyond the borders of Iraq, spilling over the nations of the Middle East and growing to encompass the West. He mined a rich seam of hatred for all of them, finding like-minded others who needed righteous warriors with that kind of fire in their hearts.

But even that new brethren paled at the ruthlessness of Hamid's actions. He had no qualms about spilling the blood of women and children, or killing believers in numbers equal to infidels, if that was what was required.

It was the first lesson life had taught him, and he saw it as his duty to teach it again and again to those who required instruction. Only death gave life meaning, and if the world had to drown in a sea of crimson for its balance to be restored, so be it.

He heeded Nasir's voice burbling away from the sat phone in his hand, muttering platitudes and making promises. Hamid listened with half an ear, staring into the sightless eyes of the corpse slumped across from him, against the wall of the jet's cabin. The dead man had seen Hamid's truth in the last, fearful seconds of his life. He had *understood*.

And as much as Hamid could care for his older brother, he knew Nasir did *not* understand. He wasn't capable of it. He lacked the vision, which was why the younger sibling had risen to eclipse the older back when they were still teenagers. The closeness they had once shared slowly dissolved and Hamid's brother gradually become a stranger, meaning little more to him than the other fighters in their organisation.

Nasir could plot and he could scheme with the best of them. He saw the warp and weft of connections between people, and he knew how to exploit them. But compared to cunning, savage Hamid, he was inert.

Hamid led from the front. He got his hands bloody. Rather than hide in caves and make plans, sending other men to do the work, he steeped himself in the game of it. Hamid took on cover identities for months at a time so he could get close enough to a target to end them in a single, pitiless instant.

This was how al-Sakakin, *the knives*, had come to be. Playing the pliant, complacent soldier to the hilt, Hamid had waited for the right moment to murder his superior and forge his own group of warriors for the long war of jihad. That man – the old imam – had been a brute, but he was artless and short-sighted with it. And ultimately, too great a coward to dare antagonise the powers of the foreign nations who constantly meddled in the affairs of their people.

His mother bled to death. His father crushed into the highway. The officer stabbed a dozen times. The imam's skull burst by a bullet. Each one a marker among countless others on Hamid's lengthy path, joined only days ago by Yusuf ibn Saleh ibn Kalb al-Amal.

He looked at his hands, paying no attention to Nasir's words, remembering the weight of the heavy glass ornament he had used to stove in the honey-seller's skull. Hamid was here because of Yusuf's foolishness and ineptitude – and perhaps, if he was willing to admit it, because of his own desire to make a point. There had always been a plan to kill Yusuf, right from the start of their association. That was inevitable, given the honey-seller's weakness of character and obvious shortcomings. Al-Sakakin had not decided on when that time would come, instead using the man for his business connections and the cover of his international dealings in Europe. But with plans under way to commit a strike against the United States, he was becoming a liability.

Hamid felt the moment was close. That was why he had travelled to Amsterdam on a fake Qatari passport, meeting secretly with Yusuf to gauge exactly how much usefulness the man still had for the organisation.

They met late in the evening at Yusuf's townhouse in Nieuwmarkt, a well-appointed building filled with dark wood interiors warmed by an open fireplace. Hamid's host was pleasant enough, for a timid fool. Outwardly, the two of them were alike in many ways, similar in build and features, enough that someone might mistake the men for siblings. But any likeness ended at the surface.

As Hamid gently interrogated Yusuf, he found his faint-heartedness repellent. The other man lived with his head buried in the sand, willing to let al-Sakakin use his network for their ends but too content with his wealth and comfort to risk more. Yusuf lied to himself, pretending he was a good man, untouched by blood. He desperately wanted to remain an innocent, but he could not see that no such thing existed. No one was innocent, not even the newborn who had ended his mother's life coming into the world.

Hamid recollected the cold, ghost-weight of the glass ornament as his fingers closed around it, pulling it off the shelf above the desk in Yusuf's study.

'*It is an award*,' the other man had said, delight in his eyes. '*For my business acumen.*' He was so pleased with it, proud like Hamid imagined a parent might be.

His smile crumbled when Hamid questioned him about the security of his communications. Yusuf had been given an anonymous burner phone for his use, along with an array of SIM cards that could be activated once and then disposed of. But Nasir suspected Yusuf had become lax, inviting the attentions of those who wanted their organisation wiped out. It would only take a single intercepted message for MI6, the CIA, Mossad or any one of their insidious enemies to set about tracking them down. One weak link could doom them all.

Yusuf assured Hamid that he had been using the burner as instructed, but the lie was poorly masked. Yusuf's reluctance to hand over the phone confirmed it, and Hamid had to compel him with a back-handed slap.

As he examined the device, as Yusuf attempted to laugh off the whole exchange, Hamid's blood ran cold. There in the memory was evidence of multiple messages sent without swapping the SIM, the most recent of which had occurred only twenty minutes before Hamid arrived at the townhouse.

He stepped to the window and his suspicious gaze quickly picked out a courier van parked near the bridge over the nearby canal. It faced in a different direction from the other vehicles, set up so that it could move off at speed. Exactly the positioning Hamid would have chosen if he were conducting surveillance on Yusuf's house.

As he watched, a blink of light briefly illuminated the hard, pitiless faces of two white men sitting in the courier's cab, both of them clad in the dark blue tactical jackets of the Dutch counter-terrorist unit, their so-called Special Intervention Service.

The rush to action swept over him. If the Dutch were outside, an interception could be only moments away. To survive what was coming, Hamid had to act with speed and efficiency. He couldn't rely on his fake passport, and its falseness would quickly become apparent to anyone who gave it a thorough checking. But there was another option.

Hamid studied Yusuf, gaining a quizzical look from the honey seller. He didn't understand why Hamid asked him to take off his jacket, empty his pockets and open his safe, but he did it out of fear. And when his back was turned, Hamid cracked open his skull with a blow from the glass ornament.

Yusuf was still alive, mewling in pain as Hamid dragged the man to the middle of the room. Then, with the sharp end of the ornament, he finished him off. Hamid took care to destroy Yusuf's face, mashing at it until it was an unrecognisable pulp of gore.

Hamid took the dead man's jacket, his wallet and his papers from the safe, dropping his own coat into the fireplace along with the Qatari passport, the burner phone and the envelope of unused SIMs. Risking a look out of the window once more, to Hamid's alarm he saw the shadows of the men moving at the back of the courier van. It would not be long now.

He moved quietly to the ground-floor kitchen below, locating an aerosol can of oven cleaner in a cupboard under the sink, and amid the pipes hidden from view there, his hands traced over a gas line. It took effort, but he ripped it out of the wall and broke the tubing. The rotting reek of natural gas hissed into the air and he covered his mouth with a dishcloth as he loaded the can of cleaner into the maw of a microwave oven. Setting it for ninety seconds at full power, Hamid sprinted to the front door – and then exited on to the street at a steady but regular pace. He willed himself to be just another unimportant person out in the evening. A cipher. *A nobody.*

He walked unhurriedly along the pavement of the Raamgracht, heading east in the direction of the Rembrandt Corner across the canal, where the Golden Age painter's home still stood. Hamid did not look back as he heard boots on brick, and he did not slow down when someone called out for him to stop.

Their accent was English, he noted, something that would count for much more in the days ahead. But in the moment, he ignored the voice.

Then events happened on top of one another, a ripple effect he later recalled more as vague impressions rather than full and complete instances.

A hand grabbed his shoulder, dragging him to a halt.

In Yusuf's kitchen, the can in the microwave reached the point of combustion and exploded.

That ignition blossomed into a room filled with gas, supercharging the fireball into a roaring burst that blasted out the windows of the townhouse and set it ablaze.

Hamid was knocked off his feet with the shock, as was the man who had tried to waylay him. But he had been ready for it, and Hamid was back up and running, counting on the distraction to give him the time he needed.

Except that it didn't.

He was sprinting for the mouth of an alleyway when a shotgun-propelled taser dart hit him in the small of the back and poured its full electric charge into his spine.

He crashed back down on to the brick weave and lay there, shuddering violently, unable to rise again, the stench of fire and burning wood choking him.

'You have been missing for two months, brother,' said Nasir. *'To say we have been troubled by your absence is a grave understatement.'*

Hamid's sibling switched to Arabic but still he picked up the phone on the table and pressed it to his ear for some semblance of privacy. He was well aware that both the turncoat MI6 agent and the American woman Breeze could understand the language. As for the other woman, the British pilot, he could not be certain, but for the moment she had left the cabin to attend to the aircraft.

'Your concern for my health warms my heart,' said Hamid, without weight. 'I take it I have you to thank for this liberation?'

He glanced up at the bearded man, who hovered nearby, watching him with renewed interest. Just like the American, the turncoat could not hide his shock at the revelation of his prisoner's true identity.

'*It has not been without its challenges, nor are we beyond them yet. It became necessary to engage outside contractors to handle the work. But we could not leave you wherever the infidels took you.*'

Hamid sensed the shape of an unanswered question lurking in his brother's pauses. 'You are aware of who took me in Amsterdam? The British working with the Dutch, their leashes held by the CIA, as usual.'

'*Indeed.*' He could almost hear Nasir nodding. '*At first we thought you were dead. The gas explosion in the house – a body was found in the rubble but it was too badly burned for certainty. And then our sources told us Yusuf had been arrested.*'

'He was, in a way. I became him,' said Hamid. 'I wore his identity like a cloak. A stroke of good fortune I chose to exploit to the fullest. Had they known who I was from the beginning, we would not be having this conversation.'

'*They took you to England, then? You were interrogated.*' There was challenge in Nasir's tone, faint but obvious to one who knew him well.

'They interrogated *Yusuf*,' said Hamid, with scorn. 'Thanks to the care I have taken in the past, the infidels had no idea what *Hamid* looks like.'

'*They learned nothing from you, of course,*' Nasir replied, the statement hovering on the verge of being an accusation.

'Of course.'

There was another long pause and Hamid listened carefully to the silence on the other end of the line. Wherever he was, his brother was not alone. Hamid wondered if the others were there – perhaps taciturn Malik, Nasir's unsmiling attack dog, forever on the verge of a violent outburst, and most likely the venerable Zameer, the eldest of their cadre held over from the old days, who was treated by the younger men as the voice of wisdom.

What have they been saying in my absence, wondered Hamid? *What is being kept from me?*

He cleared his throat, reaching for a way to reassume control of the narrative. 'This pilot, the British woman. You have her under control.'

'*You need not be concerned,*' said Nasir. '*It is in hand. The contractor is dealing with that aspect of things, and you and I will be reunited in due time. I know you understand that circumstances have changed since . . .*' He paused, reframing his words. '*We had to react to the unexpected consequences of your capture, yes?*'

Hamid's tone hardened. 'Your meaning escapes me.' Now he was certain his brother and the others were hiding something.

'*It is of no concern,*' repeated Nasir. '*I must conclude this conversation for the moment; there are preparations to be made.*' There was a wan smile in his voice as he ended the call. '*Have faith, my brother. All will be well.*'

Sitting crookedly in the pilot's position, Kate used a half dozen wet wipes to clean her hands, staining the damp fibre of the tissues a ruddy pink with the blood from Breeze's wound. She rubbed them hard over her skin, feeling the sting of the chemical cleaner. The odour of it brought up unpleasant memories for her, recollections that threatened to drag Kate back into the past she had boxed up and buried.

She tried to put herself beyond it – staring over the Hawker's control panel and out of the canopy – but there was only black sky out there, and rather than absorb her fears, it reflected them back at her.

Movement behind her broke through Kate's gloomy reverie and she pivoted as the man in the prison jumpsuit, the one Breeze had called Hamid, entered the flight deck.

He was different in every way to the man he had been when Breeze's team had dragged him aboard the jet. He stood taller, a new confidence stiffening his back, his head raised instead of his eyes averted. He surveyed the confines of the jet's cockpit, his gaze finally falling on her.

'All your tears and panic, that was for show,' she said. 'You're exactly what Breeze said you were.'

'I am much more than that.' The accent Hamid had been using before dropped away. 'From this point forward, you will take your orders from me.'

Despite the flatness of his tone, Kate's frustration triggered into a hard jolt of real anger. 'And who the hell are you?' She nodded toward Finn. 'They told me to listen to him.'

'*They?*' Hamid was irritated by that. 'My brother?' When she didn't reply, he carried on. 'In answer to your question, I am the person standing between you and death.'

'Is that so?' She met his gaze, refusing to look away. 'Well, how about I put this thing into a steep dive and crash it into the Med, and we'll see who ends up dead. Because from where I'm sitting, it seems like *I* am the person keeping *you* alive.'

Fury flashed in his dark glance, and Kate thought he might lash out and hit her, but then Hamid came forward and climbed into the vacant co-pilot's chair, settling in so he could meet her eye to eye on the same level.

'What was the transaction?' He cocked his head. 'The bargain made so you would do this?'

She thought of Alex and George, and her gut twisted. 'You know.'

'I do not,' he admitted. 'But I can guess. You are not a mercenary, not like him.' Hamid indicated Finn with a tilt of the chin. 'You have been coerced. The men my brother employed have someone you care for.' He read the certainty in her expression, as much as Kate tried to hide it. 'At least that part has clarity.' He leaned forward and examined the moving map display on one of the cockpit's screens.

Kate's jaw hardened. She was tired of these men pulling her around like a dog on a chain, forcing her to go where they wanted. 'Whatever you think is going to happen, wherever you think you are going, we'll never make it there.'

'Why?' Hamid raised an eyebrow. 'Because you will fly us into the ocean in some grandiose display of self-destruction?'

'No.' She shook her head. 'Because the people who put you in cuffs – Breeze's people, the CIA or whoever – you have to know they won't let you run.'

He studied her again, and Hamid's piercing gaze made her skin crawl. 'I think you were once a military aviator. You have the manner about you, and I know that the West thinks nothing of putting its women into battle. Am I correct?'

'How does that matter?'

'You were Royal Air Force?' He sounded out the words and, again, he didn't wait for her to acknowledge it. 'I wonder how many combat sorties you have flown. How many bombs you have dropped.' Kate's throat turned dry as Hamid's tone darkened. 'I wonder how many of my kindred killed by those weapons could be attributed to you.'

'That's rich, coming from a terrorist,' she said, pushing back. 'I've seen what you're responsible for. You're a mass murderer. There are a lot more ghosts following you than me.'

Kate thought that would anger him but instead Hamid smiled coldly. 'Yes. You are right. And I will add more without regret or hesitation if you fail. Those you love will join the count if anything happens to me. So it is in everyone's best interest that you keep me safe.'

Her attention shifted suddenly as a flicker of light over Hamid's shoulder drew it away, and Kate stared out into the dark sky. Through a break in the heavy clouds, a shaft of grey-white moon glow caught on long, narrow wings off the Hawker's starboard side.

There was another aircraft out there, thin and insect-like, half hidden in shadow.

'What do you see?' Hamid whipped around, following her line of sight.

'I warned you,' she told him. 'They've sent a Reaper.'

SEVENTEEN

In ground training at flight school, Kate had excelled in observation tests. She had a sharp memory for it, being able to parse the blacked-out silhouette of an unknown aircraft in seconds, quickly spooling off details of identity, nationality, armament and capability. She could catch a glimpse of something streaking past at Mach 2 and know exactly what kind of plane it was.

And so there was absolutely no doubt in her mind as to the nature of the craft paralleling the Hawker's flight. She pulled a pair of compact binoculars from the storage bin beside her seat and held them up to her face, steadying the optics with both hands.

A slate-coloured form came into view through the lenses, drifting lazily through the night air. Long and gangly, the drone's prow began with a blind, windowless nose that looked more like something sea-bound than a combat aircraft. Narrow wings resembling straight razors emerged from either side of the skinny grey fuselage, and the shape ended in a Y-form triad of stabilisers and the blurred blades of a fast-spinning pusher turboprop.

She looked for and found the faint signature of a star in a barred roundel, rendered in low visibility paint on the closest wingtip. The drone belonged to the US Air Force, and its official designation was an MQ-9 Reaper Unmanned Combat Aerial Vehicle, or UCAV. It was doubtless being piloted remotely by some console cowboy sitting thousands of miles away in an air-conditioned container unit inside the wire of an American military base.

The Reaper pulled into echelon position, alongside and just ahead of the Hawker's nose, and Kate saw moonlight reflect off a glassy panel in the hemispherical turret beneath the prow of the drone. The sensor head pivoted around to take a good look at the jet, and Hamid saw it too, instinctively retreating out of its line of sight.

Kate remained where she was, looking the thing right in the eye as the cyclopean scanning pod turned slowly to track along the length of the Hawker. She knew the Reaper's intelligence capabilities from her time in the RAF, having become grudgingly familiar with the British-flown variants of the MQ-9 during her last deployment. It handled a live video feed with infrared and image-intensifying systems, a laser rangefinder, a multi-modal radar and more. A lot was packed into that slim frame, but what drew her eye were the stubby objects hanging off the armament rails beneath its wings. Even in the half darkness, Kate could recognise the distinctive shape of an AGM-114 Hellfire missile.

'It's armed,' she said carefully. 'And they want us to know it.'

'They won't fire on a civilian aircraft.' Finn stood in the vestibule, drawn by Kate's warning. His features were tight with disdain. 'It's a bluff, nothing more.'

She shot him a hard look. 'Are you willing to take that chance?' He didn't reply, and she let the binoculars drop.

With the moonlight framing the Reaper's dark, cruciform profile, Kate saw the drone aircraft rock its wings with deliberate, measured pace, before settling back to a stable attitude. Then, the UCAV's navigation lights flashed on-off, on-off.

'Why is it doing that?' Finn came forward, crowding into the cramped cabin with Hamid, peering through the side of the canopy. 'What does it mean?'

'It means I have to respond.' Kate reached forward to reactivate the radio, but the bearded man snarled at her before she could do so.

'No! I told you before, no communications.'

She let out a grunt of annoyance. 'Listen to me! The wing-rocking and the blinking lights? That's pilot shorthand, right? Whoever's controlling that drone is telling us we've been intercepted by the military. We have to either acknowledge that fact by radio call or make the same moves, and then follow them to a landing site of their choosing. If we do anything else—'

'They will attack.' Hamid gave a terse nod, then glared at Finn. 'Did you not account for such an eventuality when you planned this operation? Or were you hoping to trust in providence?'

'I had limited time to prepare.' Finn became defensive. 'A situation made worse by the loss of the original pilot. But we're talking about the shooting down of a British-registered civilian jet in the middle of a commercial air corridor!' He snorted in contempt. 'Whitehall will not allow it to go that far! And once we enter Algerian airspace, they won't dare follow us.'

'You stupid, arrogant tosser.' Kate shook her head. 'That's an American drone. Who do you reckon is calling the shots back home? I'll bet you it's not anyone who gives a damn about what flag is painted on our tail.'

'Despite her coarseness, I must concur with the pilot.' Hamid locked eyes with Finn and the other man visibly shrank under his steely glare. 'The time has come for full disclosure. You will tell me precisely what my brother is planning and how that plan will be executed.'

'No, that wasn't the agreement,' said Finn, backing off a step. 'I was told to secure and deliver a passenger. Until we land, I'm in charge here.' He drew himself up again, trying to assert whatever brittle authority he could muster. 'We just have to keep our nerve.'

'Yeah, well, sod that.' Kate pulled her radio headset up from around her neck, but before she could slip it over her ears and position the mike at her lips, Finn was right behind her.

'I said *no*,' he spat, and with a savage jerk he tore the headset away and tossed it into the back of the flight deck. The cable whipped by Kate's face, the metal audio jack stinging her cheek as it went.

'You idiot!' She shouted back at him. 'You're going to get us killed!'

Hamid folded his arms. 'How long until we reach Algerian territorial waters?'

'Not soon enough,' Kate growled, biting out each syllable.

Knox leaned in, close enough to smell the odour of the acrid sweat gathering around the rim of Marty Chester's collar. 'What's the word?'

Marty blinked, pressing one cup of a set of headphones to his ear. Knox could faintly hear the crackle and burble of military communications leaking from the other earpiece, the live signal feeding back to the MOU via satellite from the USAF's active network. 'No joy,' said the technician, after a long moment. 'No response on radio, no reaction from the jet.'

'Shit.' Knox stared at the ground, feeling the metaphorical walls closing in around him. Every one of his limited options was slamming shut, narrowing the possibilities for his response with each passing second.

The asset could not be allowed to make it into unfriendly territory. And with the currently foul political status between the United States of America and the People's Democratic Republic of Algeria, the latter certainly counted as enemy turf as far as he was concerned. If the jet crossed the border, it would mean the immediate involvement of men far above the CIA operative's pay grade. Drawing their attention was the last thing he wanted.

Knox had no confirmation either way of Lillian Breeze's status, alive or dead, and no idea if the pilot and co-pilot were still in the equation. He tried to put himself in the position of the limey who'd turned traitor.

If I was jacking the jet, how would I do it?

Breeze would have to be neutralised first, of course. Then maybe waste one of the aircrew, to thin the numbers. Plus, there was the unavoidable fact that Finn had already co-opted the pilot. The turncoat held all the cards.

'He's gambling that we won't burn them out of the sky,' Knox muttered, voicing his thought with a shake of the head. 'Wrong play.'

'What's going on up there?' The other Brit, the pale chump in the hoodie, called out from a few metres away, where one of the PMCs kept him under guard. 'Come on, mate, you have to tell me.'

'I don't gotta do shit for you.' Knox deliberately turned his back on the MI6 operative and fixed his attention on Marty. 'What about visuals on the plane?'

Marty blinked again and let out a breath. 'The UCAV pilot reported they saw lights and movement inside the cabin. Whoever's running the show up there, they know the drone's on them. They're ignoring it.'

'Calling our bluff.' Knox gave a slow nod and made the inevitable choice. There would be hard questions to answer, he knew, after the dust settled. And as much as Breeze could be a colossal pain in the ass, the woman was gutsy, and he respected that. She deserved better.

But Knox was firm in his conviction. *Breeze would do the same thing if she was here and I was there.* 'All right,' he said. 'Tell the drone jockey to splash the jet.'

'Uh . . .' Marty's watery eyes widened and he hesitated.

'Did I stutter?'

'No.' The technician licked his dry lips. 'It's just . . . well, the weapons payload it's carrying, it's not configured for air-to-air. I mean, we had to take what was already up there and inside intercept range, right? It's mounting a Hellfire. It's not optimal.'

'It'll have to do,' insisted Knox. 'Give the word.'

'OK.' The other man spoke into the radio mike again. 'Yard Dog, Yard Dog, this is Authority, over. How copy?'

Yard Dog was the call sign for the Reaper, a unit attached to the USAF's 52nd Operations Group, and *Authority* represented exactly that – the liberty granted by the CIA's operations command to exert lethal force in the national interest. Killing a member of al-Sakakin certainly fell right in the middle of that, even if it would come with a steep collateral price tag.

Knox heard a mutter of acknowledgement over the radio and then Chester gave the fatal order in a dull, blank-eyed monotone. 'Weapons free. Yard Dog will commit, over. Release one, repeat, one on designated target.'

'*Copy weapons free.*' In the moment of silence that fell after the command, the faint voice of the drone pilot rang over the open channel. Then in the next second, he repeated the brevity code for the launch of a Hellfire missile: '*Rifle.*'

'Where is it going?' Finn called out, and the tone of his voice made Kate's gut flood with ice. 'The drone, it's leaving.'

She shook her head and shot a look at Hamid, who remained at the rear of the flight deck, his hands kneading the headrest of the co-pilot's chair. 'It's not leaving.'

'It's dropping back to firing position, yes?'

'You two, go strap yourselves in,' she replied. 'If we want to survive the next few minutes, I'm going to have chuck us around a bit. You get me?'

'This is an executive jet, not a fighter aircraft,' said Hamid. 'We have no countermeasures on board. What exactly do you intend to do, Ms Hood?'

'Not die,' she shot back. 'Get back there and belt up, man! And make sure everyone else is secured.'

Hamid hesitated at the door as Finn pushed past, back into the main cabin. 'Do not fail.'

'I'm not doing any of this for you,' Kate retorted, then shouted so her voice would carry back to the cabin. 'Finn! Go to the window! Can you still see the Reaper?'

'Off the starboard wing now,' he called. 'Extending away.'

'Watch for a missile launch,' she told him. 'You'll know it when you see it.'

Kate gripped the Hawker's flight yoke and disengaged the autopilot. Her free hand dropped to the throttles and she eased them forward, increasing speed. For a moment, she blotted out everything else and concentrated on her tactical options, as they had taught her in air combat training.

She visualised the space around the Hawker in her mind's eye – the sky above, the sea below, the spindly drone riding the wind as its chin turret turned to aim a targeting laser at the jet. The invisible spot from the beam would act as a homing beacon for the sensor head in the missile, following it right in to impact on the fuselage.

The moment she saw the Reaper, the pilot had been terrified that the drone would be armed with AIM-9 air-to-air weapons, the notorious Sidewinder missiles that Kate had carried herself on the Strike Tornado she flew for the RAF.

A Sidewinder was built to kill a combat jet with brutal efficiency, and an unarmed plane with no electronic defence systems – one like the civilian Hawker 800 – would be no match for it.

But the Hellfire was a different story. While no less lethal than the AIM-9 in the hands of an experienced warfighter, the AGM-114 wasn't designed to shoot down other aircraft. It was an anti-armour weapon, used against slower-moving targets like tanks, ships and ground vehicles, or static objectives like buildings and bunkers. It needed a laser beam constantly 'painting' its intended target in order to hit home, but holding a glowing dot on the side of a speeding jet was a difficult proposition, even with computer assistance.

Kate's gut tightened. That fact – that the drone was using the wrong weapon for an aerial intercept – granted her the slimmest of chances to avoid the Hellfire's strike. But it wasn't a prospect she welcomed.

There was a story Kate had heard, a half-remembered pilot-lounge tale about an Israeli combat helicopter taking out a rogue prop plane with a Hellfire, successfully using the air-to-ground weapon in an air-to-air engagement. She had no desire for tonight's flight to become another example that validated that possibility.

Her eyes dropped to the map screen. Algerian airspace was near, but not near enough to matter, and she imagined it unlikely that Hamid's terrorist cohorts had the influence to get any local MiG interceptors sent out to escort them in.

'We're on our own,' she said aloud, just as Finn cried out from the cabin.

'I see a flash of light! A burst of smoke!'

Here we go, Kate told herself, and she rammed the yoke down hard, putting the Hawker in a sudden, brutal dive toward the glittering ocean.

The thick rod of the Hellfire spiralled out through the night air, the rocket motor in the casing propelling the missile after the Hawker as fast as a hunting dog gaining on a running fox.

The sensors in the clear dome on the tip of the missile scanned the world around it for the particular light frequency of the Reaper's laser designator. It found it in a dazzling flash of reflected glow – invisible to human eyes – that flickered over the white flanks of the executive jet. Above and behind, the cruising drone's targeting system spotlighted the Hawker, its remote pilot framing the plane in a set of digital crosshairs.

But then the jet fell like a stone, plunging toward the surface of the Med, picking up speed as it dropped. For an instant, the laser lost purchase on the Hawker and the missile reacted, hesitating, the hunting dog briefly losing the scent.

But only for a moment. The drone pilot compensated, retargeting and reacquiring the target, the laser finding the jet once more. The Hellfire continued its supersonic approach, the tiny fins jutting from its sides shifting to adjust its flight path.

The unfolding sea beneath was a shimmering expanse ranging away in all directions, low waves rolling as the falling howl of the Hawker's engines echoed across them. At the last possible second, Kate pulled back on the flight yoke and flattened out the jet's trajectory. The Hawker skimmed the waves barely metres from the cold embrace of the ocean.

Another pilot, someone less skilled, someone less willing to risk it, might have flown the jet straight into the drink, but Kate's luck held as she pitched the aircraft over, raising the starboard wing to begin a shallow climbing turn.

The Hawker shuddered and complained under the unexpected G-forces; it was built for gentle, easy flights and careful landings, not to be dragged around the sky under enemy fire. But still, it was nimble enough to make the drone pilot's work harder.

Glaring into his monitor screen, the faraway attacker was being forced to constantly recompute his firing solution and find the jet again and again, as Kate zigged and zagged it through the air. Framed against the surface of the sea, the targeting laser's return became choppy and intermittent.

Confused by conflicting inputs from its targeting sensor, the leading Hellfire dipped low, barely adjusting its heading to avoid smacking into a whitecap. The missile made the turn after the Hawker and continued on toward the glowing patch of laser light shimming unseen over its wing root.

Aboard a combat aircraft there would have been threat systems and sensors to warn those on board that a weapon had locked on to it. There would be a banshee howl alert preceding an incoming missile, the split-second caution to the pilot telling them to dump sunburst flares or radar-fogging chaff, telling them to jink their aircraft and break the lock.

The civilian Hawker had nothing like that. The first and only warning Kate and the others on board would get would be the millisecond of brilliant light as the Hellfire's high-explosive payload detonated, before it tore open the fuselage and killed them.

The missile entered its terminal phase, burning in at near Mach 1 as it closed the distance, and in the Hawker's cockpit, Kate saw a flicker of rocket exhaust from the corner of her eye as the jet turned, still running less than a hundred metres above the water.

She instantly threw the yoke in the opposite direction, slamming the jet hard to port and applying as much thrust as the Hawker's engines could provide. Against every screaming instinct in her body, Kate turned the aircraft into the missile's flight path, dragging it nose-high so the speeding Hellfire would roar past beneath them.

Weapon and target crossed over one another with less than a few metres between them, and the missile clipped the surface of the sea as it tried vainly to adjust its attitude.

The warhead exploded, sending a spray of white-hot shrapnel into the belly of the fleeing jet.

EIGHTEEN

The hipster wasn't as smart as he thought.

After Breeze had ground him down, complaining long enough to convince him to let her have the first-aid kit, she'd dry-swallowed a handful of the painkillers she found inside and palmed the little pair of medical scissors when he walked up to the cockpit. Of course, the scissors were inadequate as an improvised weapon – some blunt-tipped bullshit she couldn't use to stab the fucker – but the cutting edge of the blade was still sharp, so maybe she could still slice him if the opportunity arose.

But her plan – and how it was to laugh at giving it so grandiose a name – went to hell when Finn started yelling about a goddamned drone on their tail.

Lillian Breeze wasn't into the idea of karma and that kind of crap, but she had to wonder if this was some sort of cosmic balancing of the scales. How many times had it been her at the end of a command chain, giving the go order to some guy sat in a comfy chair with his hands on a glorified X-Box controller who was flying a Predator or a Reaper to drop warheads on foreheads?

She'd seen enough of that grainy, black-and-white drone camera footage to last a lifetime. The silent plumes of grey light blossoming out of some jihadi asshole's hideaway as the missile struck it. The laconic pilot voice over the tactical net saying two familiar words in a mundane litany of death: '*Good kill.*'

Was that going to be the last thing anyone said about her when this jet blew apart over the Med? Lillian Breeze's legacy – just a bad reputation, a good kill and bunch of oily wreckage washing up on a beach somewhere.

The fire in her belly was so fierce that she half-welcomed the idea of oblivion, if only to make the pain go away. Hood's work with the field dressing kept Breeze from leaking out all over the cabin, but the wound from the glazer bullet burned and burned. The meds were doing nothing to help.

She used that to keep herself awake and tried to concentrate. She panted like an animal, blinking sweat out of her eyes as Finn came striding back into the cabin. He ignored her and moved to the window, pressing his face to the plastic oval.

Breeze thought about stabbing him in the back with the scissors, but then she remembered she couldn't do that. She blinked again. It was hard to stay in the moment when the agony of the wound did all it could to eat every last bit of her focus.

When she looked up again, the asset was there as well, belting himself into the chair on the far side of the cramped compartment. He ignored her, his expression unreadable.

Then the jet dropped unexpectedly, and Breeze's head bounced off the wall of the cabin. She clung on to the arms of the seat as the aircraft shuddered through a power dive.

Breeze thought that they might have already taken a hit, that they were crashing. The idea of that was worse than getting instantly cooked in an explosive fireball. Who wanted to know to count off the seconds before auguring into the sea, knowing it was inevitable?

Then the jet changed attitude and G-forces pressed her back, a heavy, woolly pressure crushing her body into the leather cushioning of her seat. The invisible giant's hand tightened around Breeze's torso and, impossibly, the pain from the bullet wound became worse. She teetered on the brink of passing out and Breeze dug her nails into the padded armrests, forcing herself to stay present. Each sluggish gulp of air she took felt like blades against the inside of her ribcage.

It was less than seconds but it felt like forever before the aircraft's descent levelled out and, mercifully, the pressure on her eased. Her level of distress dropped from *infernal* to just *terrible*, and she sucked in as deep a breath as she dared.

Finn was close, standing in the aisle between the rows of seats, bracing himself against the low curved ceiling as he peered past her and out of the window on Breeze's side of the cabin. 'Is that it?' He asked the question but she wasn't sure if it was for her. 'I don't see it any more!'

See what? The thought processed through Breeze's mind with glacial slowness. *Is he talking about a missile?*

The jet shuddered violently, the metal tube around them complaining as the stresses resonated down the length of it, and once again the aircraft lurched to one side. The floor tilted sharply, unexpectedly, and Finn lost his footing.

He fell against Breeze's chair and, all of a sudden, he was within her reach. She had no sense of conscious choice about what came next, it just happened from out of nowhere. Her body reacted on her animal instinct to do some harm to the man who had shot her. Breeze grabbed a clump of the hipster's thick, lustrous beard and yanked his chin down, bringing his face to meet her balled fist coming up.

Finn's nose broke beneath her knuckles with a damp, satisfying crackle. She kept on pounding him in the face with one blow after another, but what energy Breeze could muster had been spent in the first hit. She could feel herself quickly ebbing, the follow-up punches becoming weak and ineffectual.

Still, he couldn't extract himself immediately, pinned against her by the force of the jet's turn. Breeze maintained her death-grip on his facial hair and fumbled for the scissors she had stolen. *I'll slit his throat*, she vowed.

A sphere of smoky yellow light flashed outside the aircraft and the jet's rear end kicked up at a ten-degree angle. Explosion noise vibrated through the curved hull near Breeze's head and she lost her momentum, fearing that the next thing she'd see would be the wall unzipping and the black sky beyond reaching out for her.

She lost her grip and Finn fell away, collapsing to the deck, clutching at his face and newly crooked, blood-streaming nose. But the asset took his place, the neutral expression on his face replaced with a mask of taut fury.

'No,' he told her, the single word warning her that her clumsy attempt to fight back would not be tolerated. 'No.'

Hamid deliberately applied hard pressure on Breeze's bandages and a new wave of searing fire washed over her. It hurt so bad that she couldn't even scream, her mouth locking open to emit a strangled rasp, tears streaming from her eyes. She lost her grip on the scissors and they tumbled away from her nerveless fingers.

One instant of that would have been enough to make his point, but the man kept on going, past the point of punishment and into brutal, deliberate torture. He glared at her and Breeze was lost in the dark fire of his gaze, left with no other choice but to hang on until, at last, he relented.

As she gulped for air, he rocked back and wiped his hand on his prison jumpsuit. 'That is only a taste of what you feed to my kind in your black sites.' He looked like he was about to spit in her face.

Breeze had to work to find her voice again. 'Eat shit, Hamid.' She shook her head, dizzy with it. 'Hamid. Not Yusuf. You were never Yusuf, yeah? He died in that house in Amsterdam. I should have fuckin' known. But I was right about one thing.' She stared at him. 'Knew you were lying to me from the start.'

'What did that gain you?' Hamid cocked his head. 'No victory. Only a grave loss.' He considered that for a moment. 'You should have had them execute me. Your people will never get such an opportunity again.'

Behind him, Finn was back on his feet, and he let out a low moan as he used the heels of both hands to reset his broken nose. He sat heavily on the edge of an empty seat and fixed Breeze with a baleful glare, sniffing back blood-pinked snot and spittle.

'Bitch,' he managed.

'Wanker,' she retorted, deliberately choosing the British insult.

The aircraft trembled again, and Breeze caught up to the notion that their flight had suddenly become a lot less smooth. As if she were reading her mind, Kate called out from the flight deck, her voice carrying down the aisle to them.

'Good news, we're still alive.'

'Bravo.' Breeze bowed her head forward, sagging in her seat.

'Hold your applause,' continued the pilot. 'They missed us, but barely. We've taken damage from the detonation.' She let the statement hang.

'Can you maintain altitude?' Hamid took a few steps toward the front of the cabin.

'For now,' Kate called back. 'I'm keeping us down on the deck. And, for what it's worth, we've crossed into Algerian territory. We'll be over the coastline of North Africa in about five minutes.'

'They won't come after us now,' insisted Finn.

'They should not have come after us *at all*,' said Hamid. 'The pilot turned off the transponders. How did they track this aircraft?'

'I don't know.' Finn eyed Breeze coldly. 'I destroyed her sat phone.'

She tried to keep a poker face but the pain wasn't going to let that happen. Finn saw something in her eyes and stormed back towards her, his hands tightening into fists.

The secondary tracker, her back-up, wasn't much bigger than a small coin, and Breeze had been able to secrete the little thing in a pocket when Finn had first searched her. Now she grabbed it and cupped it in her hand, intending to swallow the plastic-coated disc as an additional 'fuck you' to the hijacker, but fatigue made her slow and Finn was on her before she could do it.

He pried open her fingers and took the tracker, then smashed the device into fragments with the butt of his pistol.

'Well, shit on this,' muttered Breeze, and with a hollow sigh she finally passed out, slipping into unconsciousness.

The hatchet-faced Sikh with the submachine gun was a menacing presence around Miles, never letting him move more than a few steps around the hangar before leaning in to make it clear how little freedom he really had.

The MI6 operative cast around, eyeing up the other black-jacketed mercenaries orbiting at the edges of the building. The patchy rain, making itself known again, rattled harshly off the metallic roof overhead.

The noise made it hard for Miles to pick up what was being said over by the CIA's mobile unit. He tried again to slip in that direction, but the merc saw him and shook his head.

'Don't muck about,' warned the Sikh, one hand resting on his gun.

'Who you with, bruv?' Miles studied the other man. 'Hawkeshead? Aleph? Rapid Line?' He searched his memory for the names of the ask-no-questions private military contractors known to be favoured in certain quarters of the intelligence community. 'They paying you good?'

'Better than government wages,' said the mercenary.

That reply spoke volumes, and Miles seized on it. 'The way you said that – I reckon you served, didn't you?' Only someone who had been an underappreciated servant of the Crown could be that salty about being paid what they were worth. 'Before this, what was it? Army?'

'Piss off.'

'Royal Marines then.' Miles had guessed Marines right away, but he deliberately threw in the Army suggestion to get a reaction to confirm his theory. 'You like fetching and carrying for the Yanks?'

'A client is a client.'

Miles gave a nod. 'I get it. No code, just cash, innit? Dollars tucked in your G-string.'

The mercenary's eyes narrowed. 'You don't know when to keep quiet, do you?'

'It's been said.' Miles pressed his point. 'You think you're actually gonna get paid when it turns out matey boy over there shot down a plane with a civvie and two British agents on board?' He jutted his chin in Knox's direction. 'You really want to let me call this in, man. Let me contact Vauxhall Cross. If not for this, then at least to warn those poor coppers you sent off.'

'Why would I want to do that?'

'Because you and your pals aren't the only dogs out and about tonight, are you? Someone else has people roaming around, up to no good, and those plods are walking right into it.' Miles held up three fingers, one for John Price, his wife and his child. 'Three murders tonight so far. You wouldn't want someone thinking that was your crew's work.'

'Shut your gob.' The mercenary retorted, his expression becoming a frown. He reached for the radio mike handset clipped to his lapel, and Miles knew he had planted a seed of doubt, enough to split the man's attention. 'You stand there, you don't move.'

The mercenary walked away to get some privacy and spoke quietly into his radio, something about ordering a check-in. When his back was turned, Miles used the opportunity to draw closer to the CIA vehicle. Careful to stay out of sight, he focused his attention to catch wind of the conversation going on inside through the half-open tailgate.

'That's confirmed,' the technician was saying. 'Secondary tracer has gone dark.'

'So that's it?' Knox demanded. 'The jet's down?'

Miles stiffened at the question. If the Hawker had been destroyed, that meant Finn and Ray were definitely fish food – and he would be the only operative from Six on this job still breathing. If the CIA decided to roll up the loose ends connected to tonight's misfortune, there was nothing stopping Knox from making Miles disappear as well.

But then the tech's reply gave him a ray of hope. 'That's a negative. Yard Dog could not confirm a kill on the target. They had to turn back the drone before it crossed the line of demarcation.'

'Damn it!' Knox spat out the curse and Miles heard a dull thud as the American punched something in frustration. 'You know how many favours I had to call in for that hit, and it still didn't work?'

'What now?' Breeze's guy sounded beaten down by the whole sorry enterprise. 'I mean, we lost the tracer and they're not on radar.'

'We reconfigure,' said Knox. 'I need a best guess to where they're headed.' The vehicle lurched as the American shifted inside it, moving to the half-open door. His momentary burst of anger was gone and he was stone-cold again. 'Contact signature interpretation in Langley, give 'em the jet's last-known position, speed and heading. They may know something.'

Knox climbed out of the vehicle and came face-to-face with Miles, catching on quickly that the MI6 agent had likely heard every word he'd just said.

'That pilot up there has the luck of the devil,' he said, after a moment.

Miles met the man's gaze and shook his head. 'Trust me, bruv. No one is feeling lucky tonight.'

The hunters were good at this game.

At first, Alex chose to take the direct route, the faster path as the crow flies, across the common behind the houses and through the woodlands. Keeping his son close to him, he guided George into the overgrowth, across a fallen tree and down along the lines of muddy ditches. They stayed in the deepest parts of the darkness, going as quickly as they dared.

Alex started to hope that maybe they were going to succeed, even as the mercurial rain came back and chilled the air. The path they were on led them right to the edge of a B-road pointing toward a local village, and once there he planned for the pair of them to seek sanctuary in the pub and call the police.

George saw the hunters before his father did. The boy froze and grabbed his dad's hand, squeezing it tightly. Alex skidded to a halt a few metres from the edge of the tree line and dropped into a crouch. 'What's up?'

George didn't speak, he just pointed.

Alex blinked. His eyes had become dark-adapted as they moved through the woods, but now, short of the well-lit road, he'd momentarily lost some depth perception. Looking carefully, what he'd thought were shadows cast by a huge, overhanging oak tree were actually the shape of a parked car, its engine off, its lights out.

He recognised the vehicle. A black BMW, the same one that had been parked out across the street from the house when the man called Matvey had come knocking on the door with his story.

Alex felt foolish. He'd been so caught up with the adrenaline rush of escaping, convincing himself he'd done the right thing, he hadn't stopped to consider how cunning these men might actually be.

As he watched, a tiny red ember of light – the tip of a lit cigarette – moved around inside the car like a trapped firefly. Then he heard footsteps, the scrape of boots, emerging out of the background mutter of the rain. The sound was close, on their side of the road.

He felt George push in on his side and Alex tried to make himself smaller – to make the two of them nothing more than a blob of indistinct, unremarkable shadow. Through the wet grass, he saw the man called Luka walking slowly up the roadside, his head turning left and right as he scanned the woods for movement.

There was a moment when Luka stopped and looked right at them, and Alex swore that the thug could see them clear as day, but then the man moved on, continuing his patrol.

They knew, Alex thought. *We fled, but they knew where we were going to go.*

It was obvious now that he thought about it. If he had been able to figure out the path of least resistance, the hunters coming after him could figure it out too and get there first.

Alex glanced back over his shoulder in the direction they had come. He could make out the gardens of the houses on the far side of the mile or so of woods and common, and he wondered if they could turn around and slip away. Double back to the house and phone for help? Would they have left someone there, lying in wait?

There were three of them, at least. Alex pictured their faces. The one who seemed like he was in charge, Matvey. Luka, the one up there on the road, with a feral, rat-like face. And the third who hadn't spoken, the one Matvey sent back to the car. Could there have been a fourth in the BMW? Or maybe another car entirely?

Alex sucked in a breath and forced his train of thought to slow before it ran away from him. They had no way of knowing exactly what they were up against. All Alex Walker could be sure of was that these people were willing to employ violence and coercion to get whatever they wanted.

His gaze drifted up to the islands of dark cloud and the night sky that cut around them. He thought about Kate and his chest tightened.

He knew she had secrets in her past that had left deep scars on her. He'd never once pushed her to reveal them. Alex had told Kate that he would listen to anything she had to tell him, that he would give her all the time she needed to find her way. But now he was afraid, not just for his son and himself, but for Kate and whatever this mess was about. Matvey and his thugs wanted to hurt them to make Kate do what they told her, and as long as Alex and George were in jeopardy, she was trapped as much as they were.

He closed his eyes, wishing he could gather them both into an embrace and carry them away, far from the danger.

'What are we going to do?' George whispered the question into his dad's ear.

Alex didn't have an answer. On a shout, with a raging fire right in front of him, he would know exactly what to do. But here and now, he had no solid plan of action.

'We need help.' He cast around, suddenly disoriented, grasping for a solution. 'Down by the main road, the junction. If we go that way, we might be able to flag someone down.' Alex started moving, but George dragged on his arm.

'Dad, no.' The boy pulled him in the other direction. 'It's this way.'

'What?'

George pointed up at the sky. 'You were going east and we need go west. That's where the junction is.'

Alex looked up again and saw the bright glow of the North Star his son had pointed out only hours ago. 'Right. Polaris.' In his rush to act, he'd almost sent them the wrong way. He gave a rueful smile and a trace of hope returned to him. *We might still get through this yet,* he thought.

NINETEEN

The Hawker spoke back to Kate through the controls, the warning lights and the quivers through the flight yoke, and what it said was 'I am wounded'.

She was still trying to get her head around the notion that the Hellfire that had come snapping after their tail *hadn't* blown the jet into scrap metal. There was nothing like being shot at to concentrate a pilot's mind wonderfully but it wouldn't gain her anything to question whatever thin streak of luck was keeping the bird airborne.

As the dark ocean beneath the wings gave way to the rocky Algerian coastline, Kate went around the board double-checking the jet's systems. Electrical power and batteries appeared nominal, as did the ailerons and the control surfaces. The Hawker's two engines remained in the green but her fuel was markedly lower than expected – likely an accelerated burn due to the unexpectedly violent manoeuvres the pilot had employed to shake off the missile attack.

What worried her were the intermittent warning lights from the Hawker's hydraulics. The jet's sluggish response on her gentle pedal turns was troubling. If the conduits carrying vital fluid to the flaps, the air brakes and undercarriage had been holed by fragments from the Hellfire's detonation, it would put them in serious jeopardy when it came time to land.

If the fluid leaked away, if the flaps seized up or she couldn't get the landing gear down and locked, Kate would be looking at something every pilot dreaded. A controlled crash. And unlike the Tornado from her combat flying days, Kate didn't have the option of banging out of the cockpit in an ejector seat.

She heard movement behind her and half-turned to see the man in the prison fatigues walk back on to the flight deck. *Yusuf,* she thought. *But no, that wasn't his name, was it? His name is Hamid.*

Was he really one of the men responsible for multiple atrocities throughout Europe and Asia? Was it him who had given the word to bomb the military base at Akrotiri?

He handed back her headphones, sat down in the co-pilot's chair, then slipped on the other headset hanging off the arm so that they could speak privately over the cockpit intercom. 'Where are we now?'

Kate gestured at one of the video screens on the control panel. 'We're close.'

Hamid leaned forward and scrutinised the display, tapping at the digital terrain shown until it zoomed out to present a narrow slice of the coastline. There was an indicator on the map, programmed in from the coordinates Kate had been sent by the men holding Alex and George hostage. 'This is our destination?'

She nodded. 'You recognise it?' Kate had little or no idea what would be waiting for them on the edge of the wilderness.

'I know of it,' Hamid allowed. 'It was once an outpost belonging to the Algerian Air Force. It fell into disuse and we claimed it.' He paused. 'It is remote. Finn told you to land there?'

'No, the men threatening to kill my loved ones did that.' She made no attempt to hide the bitterness in her tone.

'The runway is short,' he continued, ignoring her comment. 'You will need to take care.' Then Hamid smiled thinly, the change in his expression fleeting. 'I have confidence you will manage it. Your skill in avoiding the drone was impressive.'

She shot him a look. 'If you want to thank me, tell your friends to let Alex and George go.'

'Alex and George.' He rolled their names around. 'A husband and a son?' Hamid glanced at her hand. 'Or not. You wear no wedding ring.' He sniffed disdainfully. 'You live with a man and a boy but you are unmarried. It is unseemly.'

'I don't give a toss what you think about who I'm shacked up with,' she retorted. 'I want them to be left alone!'

Hamid looked away. 'I have no control over that.'

'Bullshit!'

He glared at her. 'If you were my wife, you would lose your tongue for such foul language.'

'You're squeamish about a woman swearing at you but you're happy to let innocent people be hurt or killed? Your moral compass is fucked up.'

Hamid gestured angrily. 'All this, everything that has happened since we took off? I am afraid I am just along for the ride, like you!'

Kate had the immediate sense that he had let something slip in his annoyance, and she concentrated on that, struggling to put aside her fears for the safety of Alex and his son. 'You know what? I believe you. You're as much in the dark as I am. You didn't even know where we were going until a moment ago.'

She watched him bite down on a reply and swallow it. *It's not just getting shot down that worries him,* she thought.

He genuinely doesn't know what will be waiting for him on the ground.

As if he sensed her thoughts, Hamid tapped the map screen. 'Is it possible to divert this aircraft again, to another airstrip?'

'I'm not doing that,' she told him. 'Not for you. And where would we even go? If we don't show up on time where they told me . . .' Kate shook her head, unwilling to finish the thought. 'Like you say, if you're not in charge, I'm not listening to you.'

Hamid's lips thinned and he muttered a curse under his breath. 'It is likely you will be executed after we arrive, you realise that? They will have no more use for you.'

'I'm past caring about myself,' said Kate, and saying those words aloud opened up a bleak, hollow space inside. But that knowledge let something free in her as well. If she was going to follow this all the way to the bitter end, then she had to find some edge, something she could use against Hamid, Finn and the others. Once before in her life, Kate Hood had given up on a future she wanted, and she vowed never to let that happen again.

'I will not be able to help you once we land,' he said.

'Are you helping me now?' Kate straightened. 'I'm pretty sure *I* have been helping *you* from the start.' She studied his frown in the reflection of the canopy. 'You're in trouble with your pals, and you know it. You're telling me I'll catch a bullet when we land. Well, maybe *you* will too.' Hamid's expression turned stony and she pressed her point. 'Yeah, I'm right, aren't I? How long were you out of circulation? I bet your pals think you talked. That's why they're meeting us in the middle of nowhere, isn't it?'

'I did not talk.' Hamid growled the denial back at her. 'Despite everything your government and the Americans did to me, I said nothing. For all they knew, I was Yusuf al-Amal. And he knew nothing!'

'I'm not the one you need to convince,' Kate told him. 'How are you going to prove you didn't sing like a bloody canary?' She shrugged. 'I mean, everyone breaks eventually, don't they? They taught me that in survival training. No one can hold out against interrogation forever.'

Hamid snorted. 'Only the weak and the faithless believe that.'

'Maybe,' she offered. 'But if the situation was reversed, and you were the one down there on that airstrip waiting for this plane, what would *you* do with the bloke stupid enough to get captured?' Hamid's silence was all the answer she needed. 'Yeah, that's what I thought.'

Kate sensed movement behind her and turned to see Finn standing in the doorway. He held his encrypted satellite phone in one hand, the 'burner' that he had been using to communicate with the rest of his co-conspirators. 'I have received new orders from Nasir,' he began, and glanced at the pilot. 'Switch the radio back on.' He read off a frequency from the phone's screen. 'There'll be someone on that channel to guide you into the airstrip.'

Kate looked out over the dark landscape of hills and plains. She caught sight of a glimmer of white lights flickering to life in the distance, a line of them laid out along a wide valley floor to the east. Reluctantly, she turned the Hawker's nose to track the approach to the airstrip and began the pre-landing checklist.

Finn followed Hamid back into the main cabin, throwing a last look back over his shoulder at the pilot. 'What were you talking to her about?'

'It is not your concern,' said Hamid firmly, making it clear he would answer no more questions about the matter.

'As you wish.' Finn dropped into his seat and secured the safety belt over his lap.

Turning the sat phone over in his hand, he glanced at the American woman on the opposite side of the cabin. She sat heavily against the cabin wall, her head back against the panel. Her moon face was pallid and sweaty, her eyes closed. If it hadn't been for the stuttering movements of Breeze's chest with each intake of breath, Finn might have thought she was already dead. On some level he admired her tenacity, but he knew there had to be a limit to it. If she could be kept alive long enough for an al-Sakakin executioner to finish her off on camera, there might be a bonus in it for the turncoat and his colleagues, but her time was over.

Finn checked his watch, still set on Greenwich Mean Time, and dialled Matvey's number. It was time to start tying up the remaining loose ends.

The Russian picked up on the first ring, and when he spoke he sounded breathless and distracted. *'This is not a good time.'*

'You mistake me for someone who gives a shit,' Finn retorted. 'Have you regained control back there?' On a previous call, Matvey had made oblique references to some problems with the hostages, but Finn had been too busy dealing with the situation aboard the plane. Now, as the operation moved into its final phase, he needed to be sure that there would be no last-minute surprises.

'We are ... working on it.' In the background, Finn could hear road noise. The Russian was in a vehicle, on the move.

'We're almost done with this,' he told the other man. 'I don't want any more complications. What is going on?'

'*I told you, we are handling it,*' insisted Matvey. '*That is what we are paid for.*'

Finn hesitated, then decided not to press the point. He had enough to be dealing with himself. As soon as the jet touched down at the rendezvous point and the asset was handed over, al-Sakakin's payment to Finn's ghost account in the Cayman Islands would be deposited. With that money secured, he would be free to buy himself a brand-new identity and disappear to somewhere warm and remote, far beyond the reach of MI6. The fates of Matvey and his men were a long way down his list of priorities. They would get their payment and he would never see or hear from them again.

'Begin the clean-up,' he told the other man. 'You know the exfiltration plan. Your pick-up will be waiting for you at the arranged location. Make sure there are no witnesses, no traces left behind. Stick to that, and in a few hours you'll be out of the country.' With those words, any promises that had been made to Kate Hood crumbled, but then the plan had always been to kill the hostages when their usefulness was at an end.

'*I will need an insurance policy,*' said Matvey. '*Some leverage of my own.*'

Finn sighed. 'Fine. Kill the father. Keep the boy. You can dump him later, after you're clear, yes?'

'*That is acceptable.*'

'*Just get it done,*' said the Englishman from the other end of the line. '*And by tomorrow morning, your money will paid in full.*'

The other man cut the call and Matvey pocketed the burner phone, his expression turning grim.

'You didn't tell him,' said Stepan, sitting across in the BMW's driving seat. 'You let him think we still have the hostages.'

'If I had told him they fled, what would happen?' Matvey grimaced. 'We want to end this night's work with our pay in our hands. That will not happen if he believes we have failed.'

'What he does not know will not concern him,' offered Luka, from the back seat. 'We will get them back.'

'He is a snake of a man,' said Matvey. 'The Englishman will surrender us in a heartbeat if it will be to his benefit.' He took a breath and ran a hand through his hair. 'We need to find the boy and his father. They were on foot! They could not have gone far!' He glared out of the car's window, scanning the dark roadside as they circled the area. Matvey's frustration and anger were simmering close to the surface, and he pulled the silenced pistol from inside his jacket, checking over the loaded weapon. He vowed that when they found Walker and his son, he would punish them both for their defiance.

'They did not cross the road behind the woods,' said Stepan. 'Which means this is the only other route they could have taken.' He nodded at the road ahead.

Matvey nodded, his mind racing as he thought through his options. If they could not find the escaped hostages soon, they would have to abandon them entirely. But leaving the boy and his father alive dramatically increased the risk. Matvey, Luka and Stepan had shown their faces. A live witness would be able to identify them.

'There!' Luka pointed, interrupting Matvey's thoughts as he caught sight of something. 'I see them! Moving away from us, they don't know we are here.'

'Slow down,' ordered Matvey, and Stepan obeyed, the car's progress dropping to a crawl. He followed Luka's line of sight and saw what the other man had spotted.

Sure enough, he saw the shadows of two figures framed against a wall of bushes, both of them moving quickly along the roadside path, one a stocky adult, the other a skinny youth. They were heading toward a turning off from the main road, a lay-by where cars could pull in, where a mobile food van sat to ply its trade. The van was shuttered up and dark, and parked a few metres beyond it was another vehicle, long and boxy with a high-visibility strip along the side and a light bar on the roof. Even from a distance, the uniformed figures seated inside were visible.

'Police,' said Stepan.

'*Chort!*' Matvey ground out the swearword.

Luka sighed. 'That complicates things.'

'No,' said Matvey, with finality, 'it does not.' He weighed the pistol in his hand and made the cold calculation as to how he would proceed. Gesturing to Stepan, he reached for the door handle. 'Keep the engine running. This will not take long.'

When they arrived at the address given as Kate Hood's residence, Isla Grace had known right away that tonight was going from bad to worse.

The house didn't look right; a few lights on inside but no answer at the front door and no pick-up when Harris tried again on the home phone. The two police officers shared a wary look and a silent communication: this was the same circumstances as the Price house earlier that night, and both of them dreaded the prospect of discovering the same horrors inside.

But what they found was more questions. A missing doorbell unit. A cheap fence panel around the back that had been kicked in to gain access to the garden. What could only be a bullet hole in the glass of a double-glazed door. And a mess of footprints in the damp earth, including one that looked a lot like the military boot Grace had spotted at the crash site a few hours ago.

'Someone's done a runner,' said Harris, waving a hand to take in the common land and the nearby woods. 'Could be anywhere.'

They moved back to the car and circled the area, eyes open for anything that set off their suspicions, and finally Harris made the decision to park up and put in a call back to base. There was too much going on for a pair of regular coppers to deal with on their own. It was the middle of the night, they were long into overtime and they needed the dog section or the helicopter unit out here. Grace couldn't fault his logic.

They didn't talk about it but they were both disturbed by the encounter with the armed men at Ridley Hill, and the ramifications of what had come next. Detective Inspector Khan hadn't hesitated for one second to give those people what they wanted, and Grace felt horribly out of her depth. It was one thing to roll around the Kent countryside enforcing the law of the land. It was quite another to find oneself in the middle of something out of a spy movie. Khan had warned them in no uncertain terms to do their jobs and keep their mouths shut, but all either of them wanted to do was clock off and leave this behind.

Grace was ready to hang up her stab vest and let the night's events fade away like a bad memory, but Harris had barely picked up the radio mike before someone came running up to the car, banging on the windows – a bloke in a rain-soaked jacket with a thin kid hanging on his arm – and both of them looking as fearful as anything.

Grace immediately got out of the Volvo, one hand held up, the other one close to the handle of her ASP baton in case the situation turned ugly. 'What's all this?'

'Please,' implored the man, 'you have to help us! These blokes forced their way into our house, they were threating my lad and me . . .'

'One of them had a g-gun,' stuttered the boy, his eyes darting around.

'All right, take it easy,' said Grace. The call-in forgotten for the moment, Harris had climbed out too, and he cast around, keeping a watch on their surroundings. She exchanged a wary look with him, then focused her attention on the man. 'What's your name, sir?'

'Alex. Alex Walker. This is George, he's my son.'

'Walker?' Harris stopped short. 'You live in a semi down on Luna Road?'

'That . . . that's right.'

'We've been looking for you,' said Grace. 'Your partner is a woman named Katherine Hood, yes?'

Walker hesitated, a flash of recognition in his eyes. 'You were the one who called the house. You left a message . . .'

'But you didn't pick up,' said Harris, 'so we came to have look around.' He trailed off.

'They broke the phones,' said the boy, with a morose sniff.

But the other police officer's attention was elsewhere, as something further down the roadway caught his attention. 'Who's this now?'

Grace heard a strange noise, a metallic rattle crossed with a strangled cough, and Harris jerked backwards like he had been kicked. His gloved hands came up to clutch at a ragged, bleeding gash in the side of his throat, and Walker's son cried out in shock as Grace's partner collapsed in the lay-by, blood fountaining from a fatal wound.

Her ASP baton was in her hand as she saw a man coming up the road, a long weapon in his hand, the muzzle of it tracking her way.

Then the noise sounded again, and a burning impact struck her in the chest, the sudden force of it slamming Grace against the side of the police car.

TWENTY

Fear turned to relief, then to confusion, and finally shock.

When Alex spotted the patrol car idling in the lay-by, his first thought was that they would finally be safe. He and George could be free of this nightmare, if he could get the police to believe them.

But like everything else that had happened tonight, it wasn't that straightforward. Something about the female police officer's voice rang a distant bell in his mind, and it wasn't until her partner told him they'd been trying to find them that he remembered the phone call back at the house.

This is Constable Isla Grace with the Kent County Police Service. I was hoping to speak with a Mr Alex Walker.

He was still processing details when a low, wasp-buzz noise cut through the damp air and Grace's partner spun away, his throat torn ragged, blood spattering over the window of the car. George let out a cry of pure animal terror and shrank back from the grisly sight. Alex pulled him away, instinctively trying to put himself between his young son and any source of danger.

Grace's arm jerked and her collapsible baton shot out to its full length, but before she could do more, the buzzing noise sounded again and the woman grunted in pain, stumbling back against the side of the vehicle.

They've found us.

The bleak realisation unfolded in Alex's mind as he caught sight of the man with the greying hair who had come to his door, the one called Matvey. He advanced, each step slow and considered, leading with the elongated shape of the silenced silver pistol.

Alex backed away, pushing George down and out of sight along the flank of the police car.

'This is your fault, Alex,' called Matvey, sniffing at the air. 'If you had stayed in the house. If you had obeyed me, it would not have been necessary to do this. Now there will be consequences.'

'Dad.' George clutched at him, wide-eyed. 'Did he kill that policeman?'

Alex had seen the other copper go down, collapsing into a trembling heap. He had seen the awful wound that opened the man's neck. In the moment of quiet that followed, both of them heard the choking noises coming from the other side of the lay-by. He had seen enough injuries in his time to know that Grace's partner wouldn't survive his.

'Buh. Bastard.' The female police officer lay slumped nearby, wheezing with each agonising exhale she made. Grace tried to right herself but her pain had to be excruciating. Matvey's second shot had hit her in the chest, the round slowing as it passed through the layers of her stab vest. But the vest wasn't armour plate – it was good against knives but not bulletproof. Alex saw a dark, wet patch growing on Grace's undershirt, her pupils darkening as shock set in.

'Dad, we have to run!' George pulled on Alex's arm. 'The fire, Dad! The fire's coming!'

It was as if the last desperate hours fleeing through the rain and the mud hadn't even happened. They were back at the start of everything, desperately trying to figure out what to do next. It was happening again – the same horrible choice replaying. Alex wanted to tell his son to flee, but the moment George moved, Matvey would see him. And he would use that gun on Alex's boy.

'Quiet,' he hissed, pressing a finger to his lips. George blinked, but he did as he was told and held his tongue.

Against the ticking of the rain, the only other sound was Harris, the poor sod breathing wetly as blood filled his mouth. Matvey's footsteps grew louder as the man with the gun walked up to the opposite side of the police car, until he stood a few metres from the wounded policeman.

Alex risked a look, raising his head to see through the window of the driver-side door still hanging open. Dull moonlight glittered off the length of Matvey's pistol as he raised it and fired again. Two more shots clattered through the night as the gunman finished Harris off with clinical precision.

'I do not wish to leave behind a mess,' said the Russian. 'But I have little option. Come now.' He turned, walking slowly toward the rear of the long Volvo. 'Do not hide like cowards. Face me. Show some courage.'

Grace grunted as she dragged herself off her knees and looked toward Alex. 'Get out of here.' With a monumental effort, she used one hand on the patrol car's flank to pull her body back to a kneeling position, still gripping the baton in the other.

Alex hesitated, and Matvey called out, seeing the movement. 'There you are,' he said. 'No more running.'

Not bloody likely. The same choice was laid out before them, as it had been back at the house. The simple equation remained unchanged – for George to escape, someone had to get in the way, to give Matvey something else to deal with while the boy ran for his life. Before, Alex had been determined not to let his son go through this alone, but now he realised the cost of his choice might make that impossible.

'Run, George!' He called out to the boy. 'Don't wait for me, run!'

'Dad . . .'

'Run from the fire!' Alex shoved his son hard in the back, propelling the skinny boy away from the police car, and his shout had the desired effect. George stumbled into a wild, scampering sprint across the road, feet splashing through puddles as he broke away from cover.

Matvey saw him and came racing around the rear of the car, but Grace was already up and lurching toward the gunman, swinging her baton at him. Alex tore his gaze away from his son and rushed up behind her. He briefly dared to hope that together, the two of them would be able to put this creep down and stop him for good.

The grey-haired man took a step back and did not hesitate. He pulled the pistol's trigger, releasing a fan of shots that emptied the weapon in less than a second. Alex saw white pulses of discharge flash from the silencer, he heard the heavy double thud as Grace was hit twice more by rounds at close range, her vest soaking up the sizzling hits.

As she fell back against him, the near-miss of a bullet droned wide of Alex's head and he flinched. But then another followed, a savage, burning bolt of agony that struck him in the bicep. His body resonated with the aftershock and he fell against the police car's bonnet.

I've been shot.

The realisation came over him in a searing wave, his nerves catching alight. It was like no pain he had ever experienced before, as if a piece of his arm had literally been ripped from him.

'*Chort.*' Matvey swore, standing his ground as he worked the slide of his gun. He ejected the now-empty magazine and scowled at it, then reluctantly pocketed the pistol.

Alex fought down the waves of pain from his wounded bicep, dragging Grace as best he could toward the front of the police car and out of Matvey's line of sight, pulling her into the white blaze cast by the Volvo's headlights by the collar of her stab vest. He could smell the reek of burnt plastic curling up from the impact holes in Grace's body armour, where the hot rounds from the gun had lodged themselves in the material. Grace was still alive but she trembled with pain, and a foam of pinkish spittle drooled from the corner of her mouth.

She locked eyes with him and he saw her fear. Grace tried to speak, but she could only let out stuttering gasps.

Then a shadow fell across them both, and Alex looked up. Matvey had the ASP in his hand, and he used the police officer's baton to strike Alex across the head, sending him reeling.

Alex crashed down on to the wet ground, lights and fire pin-wheeling around inside his skull. His body wanted to shut down but he held on, reaching into a well of stamina.

Whenever his crew were called out to fight a blaze that went beyond all expectation, Alex had to dig deep for that energy, and he dragged it up now. He refused to submit. Every second he could keep going was a second more for George to get away. Nothing else mattered.

He shifted position, hands pressed flat against the road, struggling to push himself up. Matvey hit Alex again before he could rise, and the blow echoed through him. Ignoring the pale, semi-conscious policewoman, the Russian came in with kicks then, landing one after another in Alex's torso.

'This *sranyy* country,' growled the Russian, in between blows. 'I am sick of it and sick of all of you. Nothing but problems.'

And then, through the ringing in his ears, Alex heard the high-pitched scream of a child and his blood turned to ice. It took all his effort to roll over and look in the direction of the sound.

The black BMW was on the far side of the road, windscreen wipers flashing back and forth, a pennant of fumes coiling from the exhaust pipe. He saw the man called Luka dragging his son by his throat, hauling the boy toward the car's open door.

'No!' Alex tried to shout. 'You animals! Let him go!'

'Dad!' George managed a cry for help before Luka backhanded him hard enough to make the boy go limp. The thug forced Alex's son into the back of the car and climbed in after him.

The grey-haired man looming over Alex spun the police baton around and hit him again, this time hard enough that he blacked out for a moment.

'Just. Die.' Matvey snarled with each strike. Panting, he took a last moment to spit on the road before striding away from where Alex lay in a heap, towards the waiting BMW.

Enraged and bloody, Alex was so racked with pain that he couldn't move, his body hurting in dozens of places. Dimly, he heard the BMW's driver shout something in Russian, and Matvey climbed inside the vehicle. They were taking his son and leaving him for dead along with the two police officers.

With a skirl of tyres, the black car shot away and roared off into the rain.

The Hawker juddered as Kate put the jet into the turn for the final approach to the desert airstrip. It moved sluggishly, taking twice as long to do whatever she told it, and she had to compensate to keep on her line.

As Finn had promised, a terse and thickly accented man on the radio had granted her landing clearance, setting her up on the single runway, warning her not to deviate from his orders.

The pilot ignored him. She didn't need help to put the aircraft down – all she wanted to do was make sure that it would be able to get back in the air if the moment came. Out through the canopy she could see a skeletal control tower, a pair of decrepit hangars with curved metal roofs, a block of concrete buildings and what looked like a cluster of jeeps and technical trucks gathered around a set of portable floodlights. Beyond the airstrip perimeter was nothing but dust and darkness. The place was worryingly remote. Anything could happen out here and the rest of the world would be none the wiser.

Not much difference to where I was taking Hamid, she thought. *A black site by another name. But this time, it's me who won't be leaving.*

Kate shook off that bleak thought. Despite everything that had happened to Kate in her past, she had vowed that she wouldn't die on some nameless patch of dirt, and the pilot had no intention of reneging on that promise to herself. She toggled on the 'Fasten seatbelts' sign in the main cabin as a matter of course and calculated the vector for landing.

The runway was shorter than she would have liked, but the Hawker would be able to handle it. The markings on the ground were dulled with age to the point they were barely readable, so she used the flickering approach lights to gauge the distance.

Placing the dull strip directly off the nose of the Hawker, Kate set the ailerons to landing configuration and put down the undercarriage. Her fear that the hydraulics had been too badly damaged for the landing gear to deploy proved unfounded, and the wheels locked into place with three green indicators. Compensating for a slight cross-wind over the valley floor, she let the jet sink on to the glide path.

All thoughts of where she was and what would happen next went away. For the next few moments, Kate was only a pilot, existing second to second as she guided the Hawker back to earth.

'*Three hundred.*' A recorded announcement from the jet's automated reporting system counted off the descent. '*Two hundred. Hundred above. One hundred.*'

Kate dropped the flaps and drew back on the throttles, catching a glimpse of two pick-up truck technicals off to the right as they jerked into motion, to race along parallel with the airstrip. From the corner of her eye she could see the long lances of heavy-calibre machine guns bolted to the flatbeds of the trucks, the weapons turning to train on them as the Hawker descended.

'*Fifty. Forty. Thirty. Minimum.*' The call from the auto-voice told Kate she was at the jet's decision height. From here, she could only commit to landing or put power back to the engines and climb away again.

Her knuckles whitened around the throttles and she considered putting the Hawker into a power ascent, leaving Hamid's people in the dust. *Would they open fire on us if I tried?* Kate couldn't risk it.

The jet sank into the embrace of gravity and the wheels smacked the sand-scarred runway with a hard crunch, the nose coming down smartly a heartbeat later. Kate automatically chopped the throttles and opened the air brakes, the aircraft rocking as she reversed thrust as firmly as she dared, slowing it down before it rolled off the end of the short strip.

Normally a rough-and-ready, hard-jerk touchdown like this one would have thrown her usual kind of passengers around the cabin, spilling whatever caviar and Champagne they might have been consuming, earning Kate an earful of reprimand from Brian Teller after the fact. Here and now, though, she didn't give a damn.

The Hawker slowed to a crawl and she angled the jet around in a lazy one-eighty. The technicals came racing up to flank them as the nose shifted back to aim past the hangars and the clump of low buildings. Hand-held flashlights flickered down the side of the fuselage, briefly flooding the cockpit with yellowy illumination.

'Park it,' said a voice, and Kate looked back to see Finn standing by the open security door.

'Please remain seated until the aircraft has come to a complete stop,' she replied, mimicking the tone of an in-flight announcement on some commercial airliner. Worryingly, crimson warnings were blooming again on the control panel, and Kate grimaced as she checked the systems. It wasn't just the hydraulics now; there were problems with the oil pressure and possibly the fuel pumps. Whatever fragmentation damage the Hawker had taken from the missile's near-hit, it was starting to make itself obvious.

'Are you listening to me?' Finn's temper snapped. 'Shut it off, now!'

'Roger that,' she said, with deliberate insolence, setting to the task of closing down the engines and the fuel lines. As the whine of the Hawker's twin engines ebbed, Kate became aware of the shouts from the armed men outside.

An open-topped jeep raced up from the hangars and slewed around in front of the aircraft. She caught sight of a man in the passenger seat sporting classical leonine features and a heavy beard. His broad shoulders were lost in the volume of a grubby, sky blue thawb – the traditional Arabic male long robe – and his hair was grey, shoulder-length and wild. She saw the family resemblance to Hamid immediately. The man dropped out of the jeep before it had stopped moving and he strode over to the jet with a commander's confidence.

Behind her, Finn watched the new arrival. He leaned in, lowering his voice. 'Some advice, Ms Hood? Keep your mouth shut from now on, and you might live a little longer.'

'I was going to say the same thing to you.'

He glared at her. 'The plane is on the ground. Your usefulness as a pilot is now spent. You'd best concentrate on convincing these men you still have some value.'

TWENTY ONE

Hamid didn't wait for the others to come to him. He cranked the lever that released the jet's passenger door and let it drop open, allowing the dry night air to meet him as he stepped down.

He took a deep breath as his bare feet slapped the black runway, the surface beneath his soles still holding some of the heat of the day. It should have tasted like freedom but instead it was arid and stifling, no better than the metallic, processed atmosphere inside the airplane.

'Little brother.' Nasir flashed a smile that did not reach quite to his eyes and drew Hamid into a firm embrace. 'I thought you might never return.'

'We will not perish easily,' he replied, and this time Nasir's smile became true and real.

The response was something from their past, something the old imam had told the two orphan youths soon after taking them into his stewardship. *You will not perish easily*. He had seen it in them, even at that young age: the lion hearts that beat in the breasts of a pair of ragged street urchins. The shared will between them to survive against the odds, and to make their enemies pay ten times over for every harm inflicted upon them.

His brother looked him up and down. 'What did they do to you?' Nasir guided him away from the aircraft, searching his face. 'Torture? Or worse?'

Hamid's lip curled. 'They might have done worse, had they known my real name.' He shook his head. 'I will not lie. A part of me always dreaded capture at the hands of the Westerners. But now I have experienced it ...' His derision grew. 'They are idiots. They had me and they never even knew! Their monumental arrogance makes them slow. I told them I was Yusuf and they believed it.'

'The lion masqueraded as the lamb, eh?' Nasir let his arm drop from Hamid's shoulder and something about the action rang a wrong note. 'You have always known the right lies to tell, in the right moment.'

Hamid was unsure how to respond to that, but before he could say more, Nasir's attention returned to the jet as his men removed the people on board. The Englishman complained loudly, and Hamid made a terse gesture, telling the soldiers to let Finn have his freedom. The traitor had made good, after all, and it appeared that whatever deal he had forged with Nasir in return for rescuing Hamid would be respected.

Next off came a stocky man with a shouldered rifle, dragging the body of the dead co-pilot down the steps. The corpse, shrouded in a blanket, was dumped unceremoniously in the back of one of the technical pick-ups and then ignored. Last, the two women deplaned, the sharp-faced pilot helping the wounded American as she laboured her way off the aircraft.

Pale and sweating, the CIA agent grimaced with each movement she made, but she still had enough defiance in her to throw Hamid a brittle smirk. 'I distinctly recalled requesting the limousine service. What kind of resort are you people running here?'

The pilot turned toward Finn, indicating Hamid with a nod. 'He's here. He's safe. I did what you wanted. Now you keep your end of the bargain.' She jabbed a finger at the turncoat MI6 agent. 'Make the bloody phone call! Tell them to let—'

Finn cut her off with a shake of the head. 'Later.'

'No!' The pilot's voice rose to a shriek. 'Not later, *now*, you bastard!'

The Englishman gave an exasperated sigh and spread his hands, as if to say, 'She doesn't get it.'

'Keep them both quiet!' Nasir spat the order at one of his riflemen, and the younger man strode up to point an assault rifle at the pilot's head. The English woman fell silent, but her eyes were full of rage.

With savage shouts, the rifleman forced the women into the back of the other pick-up, and the vehicle grumbled away toward the concrete buildings.

'The American is an intelligence agent,' Hamid told his brother, watching the truck go. 'The other one is British. A former military aviator.'

'A blood value for both, then.' Nasir considered that. 'Have no doubt, Zameer will find a good use for them.'

'Zameer.' Hamid repeated the name of the absent man. 'Since when are you allowing that old goat to take the lead?' He chuckled dryly. 'How long was I absent?'

'Long enough.' Nasir's expression turned stony. 'And you should show him some respect. He was a fighter when you were still an itch in Father's balls.'

Hamid's smile faded. 'Oh, I remember. I've heard him say such things a thousand times, just like the other war stories he loves to fill the hours with. But respect must be earned.'

Despite Zameer's record as a fighter of repute, his tales were long on personal heroics and short on specifics. Hamid suspected the old man of padding his part, but he had always let it pass.

There were few real veterans in their calling. Zameer's age made him a representative of the old ways, a touchstone for al-Sakakin to be noted, but not emulated. He played a valuable role in the group, and he could be entertaining in his own manner, even capable of the occasional insight. But he was not meant to command.

Age did not make one superior, something Hamid had proven time and again, the young lion's bold actions eclipsing those of his elder brother and the long-toothed grey beards. Zameer frequently made clear his displeasure at that, but only when he believed he was beyond Hamid's earshot.

'You are speaking,' said Hamid, 'but I hear the old goat's words in your mouth.'

'Zameer is wiser than you give him credit for.'

'Is he? Or does he just say what others like to hear?'

An unpleasant possibility began to form in Hamid's mind. He knew that Zameer wanted to reconnect with their old allies, to make alliances with the same cadres they had broken away from. Of course, if they did that, in those places a revered old veteran's words would carry far more authority than those of a younger lion.

Had the elder used Hamid's capture and absence to drive that agenda forward? He studied Nasir's face. There had always been friction between the brothers. It was human nature that siblings fought one another as much as they loved their kindred, but now Hamid pondered on what seed of resentment Nasir might have been nurturing against him. A seed that Zameer could have given ample water in his absence.

He looked back at the airstrip buildings, seeing the red flicker of the technical's tail lights, and the pilot's warning words came back to him in a rush. *You're in trouble with your pals, and you know it.*

When Nasir spoke again, his brother's aloof manner made it clear how much had changed while Hamid had been in captivity. 'The British and the Americans will be searching for you,' he began. 'It would be best if you remained somewhere safe for the time being. You can gather your wits and rest after this ordeal at the hands of our enemies.' He glanced down at Hamid's bare feet and prison garb. 'I will have fresh clothing brought for you.'

'I do not need to rest,' Hamid was saying, but Nasir spoke over him.

'Zameer is coming. He will be here before sunrise, and then we will talk.'

'I have been questioned *enough*,' growled Hamid.

'We will find clarity together.' There was a finality in Nasir's words that made Hamid's gut tighten. He was suddenly aware that the armed men surrounding them looked not to him for authority, as they once had, but to his older brother.

Hamid leaned in, lowering his voice. 'What do you think I did, Nasir? You know me better than any man alive. Do you honestly think I would give anything to our most hated foes?'

'It does not matter what I *think*,' Nasir replied quietly. 'It only matters what men *believe*.' He stepped back and gestured to another of the riflemen to come and escort Hamid away.

'Be patient, little brother,' he said, loudly enough for the whole group to hear. 'If you remained strong in the clutches of the enemy, then you have nothing to fear.'

Fighting his way back through the pain, Alex made it to his feet. He fashioned a dressing around the stinging wound in his bicep before dragging the injured woman to the kerb to set her against a grassy bank.

'Jake.' The police officer pushed the name out. 'Where ... where's Jake?' She blinked, her gaze unfocused.

Alex felt the colour drain from his face. He didn't know how to tell her the grim truth.

The other copper lay on his back a few metres away. Sprawled over the asphalt, he had been ruined by the execution-style shots the Russian had put through his skull.

'Hard to breathe.' She was panting like a cat, mouth open, the air coming in gulps.

'Help's on the way,' he said. 'I used your radio. An ambulance will be here soon, don't worry.'

Suspicion creased her expression. 'How'd you do that?'

'I'm Fire and Rescue,' he said, tapping his chest. Part of Alex's firefighter training included a working knowledge of Airwave radio systems, and while the fire brigade operated on different protocols to the cops, he'd been able to call in the location of the shooting and alert the policewoman's colleagues. 'What was your name again?' he added, trying to engage her and keep her alert.

'Isla. Grace.' She stifled a painful cough. 'Everyone calls me Gracey.'

Alex squeezed her hand. 'Gracey, I'm going to ask you for a favour.'

'Oh?' She turned her head slightly. 'Is Jake here?'

'I have to go,' he told her. 'I'm sorry, but I can't stay with you. You have to hold on for a bit on your own, all right, love?'

A ripple of fear crossed the woman's face. 'Jake's dead, isn't he?' She blinked back tears. 'Did that bloke shoot him? He shot me.'

Alex gave a slow nod, and his voice caught in his throat. 'He took my son.'

'Where?'

'I don't know.' He gestured in the direction the black BMW had gone. 'East, away from the city. My boy, he's all I've got.'

'I get it.' Grace nodded stiffly, clinging to consciousness. 'You . . . you need the car. Keys still in . . . the ignition.' She chuckled and it pained her to do it. 'Can't let you do that . . .'

'You're in no shape to stop me.' He gave a pained smile.

Grace grunted. 'Arrest you for that, mate,' she slurred, 'if I wasn't half-concussed.'

On the breeze, Alex heard the distant whoop of an approaching siren, and he looked up. Blue lights strobed in the distance, off the bottom of the low clouds. 'The ambulance is coming, Grace. Not long now. Just hold on. Will you do that for me?'

'Yeah.' The police officer's head lolled forward. 'Wait. Give you something.' She fumbled at her waist and pulled a pistol-shaped device from a holster on her stab vest. 'Here.'

She pressed the thing into his hands. Made of bright yellow plastic, it looked like one of George's toys. Alex had never held a taser before, but he'd seen enough movies and TV shows to guess at how it worked.

'Get your kid,' said Grace. 'Give that Russian wanker a shot from me.' Then she slumped against the bank, the effort of talking pushing her into unconsciousness.

'OK,' he agreed, stuffing the taser in his jacket. 'I'm sorry.' Alex gave the injured woman one last look, then limped as quickly as he could to the police car.

Just as Grace had promised, the keys were in the Volvo's ignition, the engine still idling. Alex snapped his seatbelt tab into the lock and jammed the vehicle into gear. With a hiss of rain-heavy tyres, the car lurched out of the lay-by and bit into the road.

The vehicle revved as he put his foot down. It had a powerful engine under the bonnet and it was tempting to floor it. Alex's fingers found the controls of the police car's lights and sirens – the blues and twos as they were known – but he held back from firing them up. The vehicle was conspicuous enough, ice white in colour with a neon yellow and bright blue checkerboard livery down the flanks. Alex didn't want to think of what Matvey would do to George if he spotted a pursuer.

He put aside his guilt at leaving Grace alone in the drizzle and concentrated on the road ahead of him.

'*Think*, man,' Alex said aloud, guiding the car along the road down which the BMW had disappeared, searching the distance ahead for any sign of the fleeing vehicle. 'Where would they go?'

The men with rifles forced Kate along at gunpoint, and she did as best she could to help Breeze stagger over the crumbling flagstones and into the airport's run-down buildings.

They put the pair of them in a space that looked like it had once been a storage room. It had been stripped out at some point and populated with a few reeking old army surplus camp beds and, incongruously, the same kind of cheap plastic injection-moulded lawn furniture that Alex kept in the garden shed back home.

Breeze let herself be planted on the least smelly of the beds and dragged herself up until she was propped against a wall. The guards grudgingly provided canteens of stale water and a cardboard box containing what turned out to be decades-old packets of army rations.

'Red Army issue,' said Kate, examining the Cyrillic script and Soviet-era crimson star on the packaging. 'Pre-Gorbachev.'

'Huh.' She handed one to the American and Breeze scrutinised the writing. 'More like pre-Brezhnev.' With effort, she peeled off the wrapping with her teeth and sniffed at the contents. 'Ugh. Stinks like bad feet. That's enough to kill my appetite ...' Breeze trailed off. The effort of speaking was wearing her out.

But the bad odour wasn't just coming from the spoiled Russian rat-packs. Neither woman had said anything about it, but Breeze's belly wound was giving off an unhealthy smell that did not bode well. Kate marched to the door and banged on the frame to attract the attention of the man outside. The door was heavy, a plate of steel with a thick bolt, and she realised that was why they had put them in this particular room.

The metal door opened a crack and a wolfish face glared back at her. 'We need a medical kit,' said Kate, enunciating each word carefully. 'You understand? Medicine. Bandages. For her.' She pointed in Breeze's direction.

'No.' The guard began to close the door, but Kate jammed her foot in the gap.

'*Yes,*' she insisted. 'You want her to die? No medical kit, she dies. Your fault!' Kate pointed at the man. 'Hamid will be very angry with you!'

Invoking Hamid's name seemed to do the trick and, at length, the guard gave a sullen nod and backed away. 'I get,' he allowed.

The door clicked shut with the rattle of a lock, and in the moment of silence that followed, Kate heard Breeze's laboured breathing.

'Girl,' she managed, 'you oughta run. Right this fuckin' second, I mean. While he's distracted. While Hamid and his brother are still figuring shit out.'

Kate looked toward her. 'What, and leave you behind?'

'Yup.' Breeze waved in the direction of a dirt-smeared window on the far side of the room. 'You're skinny, your ass might fit through there.' She coughed wetly. 'They taught you escape and evasion in the RAF, didn't they? Time to use it.'

'They'll kill you,' said Kate, finally letting out the dark thought.

'That's pretty much gonna happen no matter what.' Breeze nodded to herself. 'Always swore I wasn't gonna tap out in some rat-infested hole. Just kept deluding myself I'd die peacefully in my sleep.'

'Neither of us are dead yet,' Kate said firmly.

'Well, the night is young,' sighed Breeze. 'Sorry you and yours were dragged into this. This is my mess and now you got it on you.'

'Alex is strong,' Kate said, more to herself than to Breeze. 'He'd never let anything happen to George.'

'No doubt, no doubt.' Breeze looked away.

'You think they're already dead, don't you?' Kate felt cold, the words coming from a dark and terrible place buried down deep.

'These men put no value on life. Not theirs, not ours. They only see blood as something they can spill to prove a point.'

Kate tried to find a reply but her voice caught in her throat. She was afraid that, if she spoke, all that would emerge would be a cry.

Behind her, the guard opened the door to let Hamid enter. He had cleaned himself up, washing off the dirt and sweat, dressing in a new robe and sandals. He carried himself with wary poise, stalking into the room.

'Well, look who it is,' muttered Breeze.

'You wanted this.' He had a threadbare medical pack in his hand, and Hamid threw it at Kate like he was passing her a ball. She caught it awkwardly and returned a grimace. 'For all the good it will do,' he added.

'Gimme.' Breeze made grabbing motions at the air as Kate came over with the pack. Before she could stop her, the American snatched it from Kate's grip and poured the contents out over the tiled floor. 'C'mon, c'mon,' said Breeze, pawing through the bandages and yellowing packets, 'Momma wants her candy.'

She found a disposable syringe loaded with a morphine-derivative solution and Breeze jabbed it into the meat of her thigh. She shuddered as the potent painkiller flooded her system, and Kate realised how much agony the woman had to be enduring.

'Better?'

Breeze nodded woodenly. 'Better.' As Kate started to gather what she needed to dress the American's wounds with fresh bandages, Breeze turned to stare at Hamid.

'She needs a doctor,' said Kate.

'She has you,' he replied. 'Make do.'

Kate set to work on the dressings and Breeze made a spitting noise. 'Don't ask him for nothin',' she told her. 'He has no juice any more. Knew it back there at the plane. Funny.'

'What are you talking about?' said Kate.

'Hamid.' Breeze pointed at him, and as she did the guard at the door pushed it closed, slamming the bolt back with a decisive thud of noise. 'I know a lame dog when I see it. Big bro reckons little bro might be broke.' She gave a guttural snort of amusement.

Confusion on his face, Hamid moved back to the door and banged on the steel panel, his voice rising to a shout. He bellowed the name of his brother, but the lock remained firmly shut.

At length he swung round, and in his eyes Kate saw fury. For the first time, an echo of that faked terror he had shown as Yusuf. *But real now*, she thought.

TWENTY TWO

'*Before we get started,*' said the man on the screen, '*I want to establish a few details.*' He peered out of the monitor fitted to the inside of the mobile operations unit, as if it were a window he was looking through. His expression resembled that of a visitor to a particularly disappointing zoo enclosure. '*Who am I talking to?*'

And we're the animals in the cage. Marty Chester entertained that depressing thought, keeping his expression neutral, crossing his fingers that the man on the screen wouldn't look his way.

At his side, Knox removed his baseball cap and drew himself up. 'Harlan Knox, sir. Ground Branch.'

'Martin Chester, tech ops.' He kept his gaze downturned.

'*Who currently has operational control at your location?*'

'I do,' said Knox.

The man nodded. Dark skinned and full-faced, he had small eyes and an unsmiling mouth, his hair trimmed like a politician's, atop a grey suit, white shirt and a blood-red tie.

'*I'm not going to ask you if you know who I am,*' he went on, '*because if you don't know the answer to that question ...*' he flashed a humourless smile, '*you'd have to be morons. And I would really like to believe you are not.*'

254

Chester had to admit, he didn't actually know the man's name. But he didn't need to. He knew his reputation, and that was more than enough.

Red Tie was a figure from the rarefied heights of the upper floors back at Langley; one of those men who had no particular portfolio but a ton of power and the freedom to wield it with impunity. Up until tonight, Chester had tried very hard to carry on his career at the Central Intelligence Agency without ever drawing the attention of men like this one, but now that hope had gone away.

'*Dear Lord, why is it when I hear the name Lillian Breeze, I know I'm going to have to reach for my antacids?*' Red Tie did the smile again, and this time he added a brittle chuckle. '*Well, gentlemen, she took enough rope to hang herself this time, don't you agree?*' He paused, waiting for one of them to offer a supportive answer, but he didn't get it.

The man sat at one end of a conference table, and with terse flicks of his fingers, he paged through a file lying in front of him. '*This is quite the mess you've delivered, Knox. My wife owns an elderly, incontinent Labradoodle that cleans up after itself better than you have.*' He closed the cover of the file with a slow, deliberate motion. '*I would like to know how a simple rendition operation has turned into something so utterly and completely botched.*'

'Sir, there were a number of variables we couldn't account for.' Knox's tone was straightforward. 'The Brits had a penetration in their team. The enemy had a man inside the mission before we even got off the ground.'

Chester glanced across at the window in the side of the SUV, catching sight of Miles, the British intelligence officer, standing alone on the far side of the hangar. He wondered what was going through the other man's mind. *He's as screwed as we are.*

'*That's something I will have a less-than-cordial chat about with my MI6 counterpart after we're done.*' Red Tie paused to chew his lower lip. '*Believe me when I tell you, there'll be copious amounts of blame to spread around on this one. But let's try and salvage something from this comedy of errors, shall we?*'

Knox leaned forward. 'We can sanitise this location and withdraw to a safe house on your order, sir.'

Chester frowned at what the word *sanitise* might encompass but said nothing.

Red Tie shook his head. '*Oh, you're not going anywhere. Movement draws attention and we really,* really *do not want that right now.*'

Knox shot Chester a sideways look. 'Very well,' he allowed.

'*This is what is going to happen.*' Red Tie drew himself up and signalled to someone out of range of the video pick-up. Another folder slid across the table to him and he studied the contents. '*That call of yours to the Interpretation team, Chester? Good thought. It turns out the probable flight vector the jet was on before it went dark correlates with a known location of interest. We've had a disused airfield in that part of Algeria under satellite surveillance for some time, suspected as a possible al-Sakakin outpost. Training camp? Whatever.*' He shrugged. '*We'll have solid confirmation if the plane is there soon. But that's not the good news. Would you like to know what is?*'

'Very much, yes.' Chester answered without thinking.

'*We have PRISM signal captures from a phone associated with a known al-Sakakin driver. It's coded but we got the gist of it . . .'* Red Tie's smile flicked on and off again. *'A senior faction member is en route to the airfield. A top man.'*

Kate finished up applying the new dressings to Breeze's injuries as best she could. 'That's as good as it gets,' she said quietly.

'Appreciate it,' said the American, with a breathy sigh. She chuckled to herself. 'I see it now.'

'See what?'

Breeze shook her head. 'Never shoulda been a combat pilot, Katie.' She prodded the other woman with a thick finger. 'You don't have the killer instinct. You like people too much.'

'Not *all* people.' Kate looked away, finding Hamid where he stood by the locked door. The man's arms were crossed over his chest, his expression was thunderous.

He caught her eye and spared her a mordant glance. 'You have something you wish to say? Spit it out.'

'You never intended to keep your word, did you?' Kate stood up, refusing to be cowed by the snarl in his tone. 'To me, or anyone else.'

'I made no bargain with you.' Hamid cocked his head. 'Why do infidels always assume there are rules we will follow? Rules that you set, that favour only you?' His lips thinned. 'You bombed civilians when you were in the RAF. Why should I do any different?'

'I engaged military targets and enemy combatants.' Kate glared at him. 'I never targeted innocents!'

'A lie you tell yourself,' Hamid retorted. 'None of you are blameless. Your nations, your governments, your legacy of colonisation and corruption. It tarnishes all of you. And so to end that dominion, it is necessary that there are *no* rules.

No lines that cannot be crossed. Surely you understand that by now?'

'Waste of time,' said Breeze, 'trying to debate this son of a bitch. Folks like us, we're less than animals to him. Ain't that so?'

Hamid turned away, finding a camp bed where he could sit and ignore them.

'I know these bastards,' said Breeze. 'See, I've been tracking them for years. Warned my bosses about them when Hamid here was getting up to speed, not that anyone would listen.' She paused, struggling for a breath. 'I told them. Said, "Watch out for his name, put a face to it, find him and run him down before it's too late." Didn't listen to me. *He's gonna be the next Bin Laden*, that's what I said. No one wanted to hear it.'

'Bin Laden made the mistake of letting you know his identity,' said Hamid. 'I never did.'

'You know what he's done, right?' Breeze met Kate's gaze. 'How many deaths he's responsible for?'

Kate nodded, grim-faced. 'I've seen the news. Military bases and hospitals blown up with vehicle bombs. And secondary attacks, designed to kill first responders coming in to help after the initial blast.'

'Callous fucker, am I right?' Breeze stifled a cough. 'But that shit is just what the TV covers. Al-Sakakin has done other stuff that don't make it to CNN; the kinda thing that would give you nightmares. Whole villages full of people butchered because someone didn't wanna hide one of his jihadis in a barn. Blood-cost deals cut with criminal gangs and people traffickers. Dealing in drugs and slaves. I mean, how do you think they pay for bullets and bricks of C-4?'

'For the righteous man in the pursuit of victory, in time of war any deed will be tolerated.' Hamid offered the thought without looking up.

Breeze levelled a finger at him. 'There you go. *Righteous*. He believes that. It gives him permission to be the nastiest son of a bitch alive.'

'Only God can judge me,' he said with a sniff. 'He has already found you wanting.'

Breeze's gaze turned stony. 'One day, I made a vow to myself, y'know? I promised I would find the man called Hamid and take his organisation apart, stone by stone if I had to. And he's been my crusade ever since.'

'But you never knew his face,' said Kate, glancing back at the man. 'You stood right next to him and you thought he was someone else. Yusuf.'

'He's clever, I'll give him that.' Breeze nodded.

'Why?' Kate sat down next to the American. She sensed there was more beneath the surface, something dark and terrible that Breeze could barely conceal. 'Why did you make this personal?'

Breeze exhaled, a slow breath that shuddered as it left her. 'Sophia Betel. She was my source, a civilian I recruited to work as a CIA asset. She knew what buddy-boy here and his playmates were doing out in the Levant. They had no idea she was feeding details on their movements back to me.'

'I remember her,' Hamid said distantly. 'Pretty, for a foreigner. At least, she was to begin with.'

'Sophia wasn't an agent, you get it? I didn't want to put her in, but I had no other options.' Breeze rubbed the heel of her hand at the corner of her eye. Kate realised she was seeing the woman's real self for a brief instant. 'She was smart, brave as all get-out! And funny! I liked her.'

'Is that why you lied to her?' Hamid offered the question to the air. 'Is that why you let her die?' He made a tutting sound. 'Are you capable of guilt? After that, you should be drowning in it.'

'It was . . . complex. Her cover was blown.' Breeze stared at the floor. 'I couldn't get her out in time. They killed her.'

Kate's blood chilled at the awful certainty of it.

'Eventually.' Hamid took over the thread of the conversation. 'First, I allowed some of the men to take a payment from her. As a lesson to others, yes?' His tone turned flat, without even expending the effort to be cruel. 'And when that was done, she was made to kneel upon a sheet of plastic, and I had one of the new recruits record her last moments on camera. Her execution has played out thousands of times since then, on the internet channels we use to recruit, and the videos played to stir the martial fire of our warriors.'

'They . . . took her head.' Breeze made a weak gesture at her throat.

'No, no.' Hamid held up a finger. 'Not *they*. It was *I*. The hand holding the blade? It was mine. You never knew this?' His lip curled. 'I gave the witch a far better death than she deserved.'

Breeze stiffened, colouring as anger shot through her. 'You're a coward and a piece of shit,' she spat.

Hamid rose in a swift movement and came striding toward them. Kate was on her feet, immediately putting herself between the wounded American and the hard-eyed killer. 'Stay back!'

Hamid ignored her, his gaze boring into Breeze. 'Before, when we were aboard the aircraft. You asked me a question, do you recall? You asked me what I wanted Allah to see.'

'I remember,' said the other woman, in a dead voice.

'I did not respond at the time because I was hiding my truth from you. But now we see each other for what we really are, I can respond with honesty.' He glanced at Kate, as if daring her to try to stop him. 'I want him to see you die.'

The moment stretched to a breaking point but Kate stood her ground. If Hamid attacked her, she wouldn't falter. But then he broke away and wandered back to the camp bed, his hooded gaze returning to the locked door keeping the three of them prisoner.

'There's a meeting out there,' said Knox, putting together the variables. 'With the asset?'

Red Tie shrugged again, his voice tinny through the speakers inside the mobile unit. *'You know, for all her bluster, Lillian Breeze may have been right about one thing. The asset, whoever he is, has more value than we initially assumed.'*

Chester frowned. It was the second time the man back at Langley had talked about Breeze in the past tense, assuming she was already dead. He found himself speaking before he could stop. 'We don't have confirmation of her status.'

'We can safely assume so at this point,' said Red Tie, his manner cooling. *'Given the lack of evidence to the contrary.'* He schooled his expression into something shaped vaguely like regret. *'We'll put a star for her up on the memorial wall. That is if we don't bury this whole sorry episode entirely after the fact.'*

'Sir, what outcome are we looking for here?' Knox spoke up, effectively halting anything else Chester had to say. 'And how do we fit into it?'

'I want you monitoring remotely from that location,' came the reply. Red Tie made a motion with his hand. *'In the event of*

any additional complications. But as to outcome . . . we're going to use this opportunity to deploy against a gathering of high-value targets. Then at least I'll have something of worth to show the Director when the smoke clears.'

Chester baulked at the finality of that last sentence. 'Sir, if I may. When you say deploy—'

Red Tie's weary sigh cut off Chester's words. *'The USS Clancy is at sea in the Mediterranean and she's currently under way to a location off the Algerian coast.'* He glanced at the flashy gold watch on his wrist. *'Should be on station in the next hour.'*

'The *Clancy's* an *Arleigh Burke* class ship,' said Knox, reeling off the details by reflex. 'A missile cruiser out of the Sixth Fleet, Task Force 60.'

'Exactly,' said Red Tie. *'And when the moment comes, her captain will wipe that airfield off the map with a couple of precision-targeted Tomahawks.'* He mimed cleaning his palms. *'Problem solved.'*

'Sir . . .' Chester straightened in his chair. 'With all due respect, the purpose of this operation is to gain intel, not kills. I don't have to remind you that al-Sakakin has been planning a hit on US soil for months now. We need details—'

'Correct,' Red Tie snapped. *'You* don't *have to remind me. And if Breeze had not exceeded her operational mandate with this this half-assed mission, maybe we would have gotten that. But we're playing the hand we've been dealt.'* He tapped the file in front of him. *'This is actionable intelligence on the whereabouts of one, if not more, HVTs. If we can't get information on where these bastards are planning to hit us, we do the next best thing. We hit them first and we hit them hard.'* He gave that a moment to sink in. *'We've seen what they did in Europe and Asia. This is our*

chance to make sure the same thing doesn't happen in an American city. We cut off the head of the snake.'

'You're going to fire two cruise missiles into Algerian sovereign territory without its government's knowledge or permission?' Chester didn't keep the thought to himself. He couldn't stay silent; couldn't let this escalate further without saying something. 'Launching an attack that will also kill American and British citizens?'

Red Tie gave Knox an incredulous look, as if he couldn't believe Chester's naivety. *'Someone needs to look up the words "collateral damage", am I right?'* he said, with a sniff. *'Seriously, how has this man worked for the agency for this long and not developed an appreciation of that?'* He went on, without waiting for a reply. *'We'll tell the Algerians after it's done. They'll keep their mouths shut when we remind them they're giving safe harbour to terrorists, and America has a lot more Tomahawks to burn.'* Then he leaned in, his face growing to fill the screen. *'And, quite frankly, I find it disingenuous that you're becoming squeamish about this option, considering it was your team who ordered an air-to-air drone attack a short time ago.'*

'Didn't agree with that, either,' muttered Chester, turning away from the screen.

Red Tie's eyes narrowed. *'What was that?'*

'Understood, sir,' said Knox, covering for him. 'We will remain on site and monitor comms, as ordered.'

Red Tie looked as if he was going to say more, but then he shook his head and sat back in the chair. *'Gentlemen, by tomorrow morning, this will be behind us and I will have forgotten both your names. It's in your best interests to make sure that outcome doesn't alter, yes?'*

'Understood,' Knox repeated, but the screen had already gone dark, the video call ended from the other end.

Chester took a breath and opened his mouth, a half-formed thought on his lips, but the other man glared at him, strangling the moment.

'You shut the hell up,' Knox told him, pulling his cap back over his head, 'and you do your job.' He kicked open the MOU's door and stalked away, out into the cold of the night.

TWENTY THREE

The police car gripped the rain-slicked road, holding the turns as Alex guided it from the narrow back lanes and on to the junction, going as fast as he dared. The Volvo ate up the distance, steering around the late-night traffic.

Below, the wide asphalt strips of the M2 motorway spooled away in either direction, occasional clusters of crimson lights flowing one way, and white headlights going in the other.

The burning pain in his torso, his legs and along Alex's arm were a constant ache, but he didn't dare stop to check his bandages for fear he might not go on. There wasn't any time. He circled the interchange, searching the road signs on each turn-off as he passed them, as if they might provide the answers he desperately needed.

What would the men who took his boy do? Would it be smarter to stay on the less-travelled roads and keep away from built-up areas? Or had they made a different choice, trading risk for expedience?

Heading westward, in the direction of London, might let them get lost in the city's outskirts, but police surveillance was thicker there and the chance of getting stopped increased exponentially. Going east in the direction of Canterbury would send the black BMW deeper into the Kent countryside and, taken to its eventual conclusion, they would hit the coast and run out of road.

Perhaps Matvey and his men had already doubled back. Perhaps Alex had been going the wrong way all along, and with every mile that passed, he was getting further and further away from his son.

An icy claw of dread tightened around Alex's stomach, with the needle of his emotions flicking between abject panic and unfettered fury. He smacked the centre of the Volvo's steering wheel with the heel of his hand and let out a wordless bellow of frustration.

'I don't know where to go!' He shouted at nothing, his roar rebounding around the confines of the car. Alex stamped on the brakes and the Volvo lurched to a halt on the middle of an overpass bridge. Before he knew it, he was outside and standing at the edge, looking down at the sparse traffic. He gripped the cold metal barrier before him. Any one of those lights could be the BMW, and despair filled him at the hopelessness of the moment.

Through the open door of the patrol car, a woman's voice, tinny and shot through with static, issued out of the radio on the dash. *'Paramedics are on site at incident on Caister Lane. Reporting one officer wounded, one officer fatality, over.'*

The name caught his attention – Caister Lane was where the lay-by sat, where he had left Grace and her unlucky partner to wait for an ambulance. Alex veered back toward the vehicle, realising that he was listening to one half of a conversation between the police dispatcher and another unit.

'We have confirmation, police vehicle is missing from site.' The radio voice read off the car's call-sign code, identical to the

letters and numbers on the ID plate bolted to the Volvo's dashboard.

Alex felt a surge of relief, taking some comfort that the injured police officer was in safe hands, but it faded quickly when he realised he was on borrowed time. Every copper in the county would soon be on the lookout for the people who had killed one of their own, and Alex would be right in the middle of that with the stolen car in his possession.

But there wasn't time to stop and explain. George's life hung in the balance, and Alex had gone too far to stop now, to surrender and hope the cops could sort it out.

Then the radio crackled again, and the voice threw Alex the lifeline he so desperately needed. '*Member of the public reports speeding driver heading east on the M2, black BMW G30. Location, junction 5. Any units in the vicinity? Repeat, do we have police units in the vicinity?*'

He looked up, finding the nearest road sign. The number '4' designated the junction he was standing at. The BMW had been sighted a few miles away.

He was close.

Alex rushed back to the driving seat and slammed the Volvo into gear, reversing back along the overpass, hauling round the steering wheel to aim the car toward the slip road. This time he didn't hesitate on the accelerator, pressing the pedal into the floor, kicking up rainwater as the car shot down the ramp and on to the motorway.

When the door clanged open again, Kate rose to her feet, convinced that this was going to be the fatal moment.

But the armed man filling the doorway only gave the two women a cursory glance, then focused on Hamid, beckoning

him sharply. He said something tersely in Arabic, and with a
wary look on his face, the other man followed him out of the
room.

The door locked shut behind him, leaving Kate and Breeze
alone. 'What the hell is going on out there?' The American
asked the question with a sigh. 'Nothing good,' she added,
supplying her own reply.

Kate moved to the barred window and looked out into
the night through the dust-caked glass, but it was hard to
see anything clearly. 'We're never getting out of here,' she
muttered.

'Nope.' Breeze shook her head. 'Probably not. So you better
pick how you wanna go out, if you get my drift.'

'What's that supposed to mean?'

Breeze looked her way. 'Here's what they told me at the
Agency. If you're a woman and you ever get captured by these
fuckers, if the clock runs down, don't go quiet. Make 'em angry.
Pick a fight with the nastiest-looking one of the lot. Get him
to shoot you.'

Kate's throat turned arid. 'Why?'

'Because a bullet is quick, and then you're dead. Then they
don't get to soak you in gasoline, lock you in a cage and toss in
a match. Or feed you to their dogs. Or cut off your—'

'I get the picture,' Kate broke in. 'Shit.'

'Yes, *shit* indeed.' Breeze nodded solemnly. 'So, any last
words, thoughts and prayers? Now's the time.'

Kate thought about Alex and George, remembering the
cold air in the darkened garden and the starry sky overhead.
She'd been happy in that instant, truly happy for the first time
in a long while. It had only been hours ago but it felt like
those moments belonged to a different person and another

lifetime. Now she had no way of knowing if Alex and his son were even alive, and grim uncertainty as to when her own end would come.

How could so much that was good in her world be ripped apart in so short a time? How was it fair that life could be this fragile? She took a shuddering breath.

It wasn't the first time fate had taught her this hard lesson, but Kate had survived that ordeal. Perhaps, subconsciously, she believed enduring that would immunise her from further hurt. *I'm an idiot to believe it.*

'What really happened to you in the Air Force?' Kate looked back and found Breeze watching her carefully, as if watching the play of her thoughts on her face. 'Why'd you quit?'

'You said you read my file from the MoD,' Kate replied. 'You know the reason.'

'Wasn't clear,' Breeze noted. 'Vague references about an accident during a training exercise. People died. And then a lot of bureaucrat bullshit-ese about "operational suitability" and "unit incompatibility".' She shrugged. 'But I can read between the lines. I know a frame job when I see one. Let me make a guess, someone wanted you out of the cockpit, someone with pull, but you turned in your papers before they could make it a dishonourable discharge. Am I on the mark?'

'You really are one of the most annoying people I've ever met,' Kate growled. The American was unpleasantly perceptive. She cut closer to the facts than the pilot wanted to admit.

'Guilty as charged.' Breeze stifled a wet cough into her hand. 'C'mon, talk to me. Tell me who fucked you over. What do you have to lose?'

Kate put her head in her hands and let out a low exhale. She'd never told anyone the whole sorry story, not even Alex.

But now it was pushing at her to spill out. And, at length, she let it go.

'There was a collision. A mid-air.' When she closed her eyes, Kate experienced the moment again, the thunderous crack of metal on metal shaking the airframe around her, the flash of crimson emergency lights and the skirling cry of a master alarm. 'We were on an exercise, flying Hawks – two-seater jet trainers. Me and my back-seater, Jeff Ward. Called him Wardy.'

She remembered him shouting in fear as the impact from below shunted him up, his flight helmet banging against the inside of the canopy. In her hands, Kate held the ghost of the Hawk's control stick, recalling how it shook so much that she could barely keep a grip on it.

Outside the cockpit, a winged shadow spewing orange fire had briefly blotted out the sun, as the other trainer spiralled into a death-dive, almost striking Kate's Hawk a second time. A black contrail and a shower of metal fragments coiled away, reeled in by gravity. The other jet fell until it hit the hills below without an explosion, disappearing into a plume of smoke and displaced earth.

Kate believed she was going to die, and her mind bifurcated, part of her drowning in utter panic, part of her cut off from fear and emotion. Now, looking back, it was the terrified Kate that she recalled, the one who screamed silently. But it was the other part of her that guided the wounded Hawk back to the ground, the part that made it down in one piece and brought Wardy home.

'Jeff didn't fly again,' she explained, tapping her neck in the spot where the man had suffered his life-changing injury. 'He's in a wheelchair now. Spinal damage.'

'But it wasn't your fault,' prompted Breeze. 'The collision, I mean.'

'I was to blame,' she corrected. 'Just not in the way you might think.'

The name of the pilot in the other Hawk was Piers Bolton. It was his jet that destroyed itself on impact, killing him instantly along with his back-seater, a father of two girls, a nice guy the rest of the flight had nicknamed Snowball, on account of his prematurely whitening hair. Bolton was a cocky bundle of a man with a winning smile and the physique of an Olympic swimmer. He had a tendency to overestimate his skillset – like his ability to seduce women, although it had definitely worked on Kate – and his tolerance for stimulants. But one talent he did have was hiding things.

There had been a point, some time prior to the mid-air, when Kate had found out that Piers used chemical help to maintain his edge, and right then and there she should have cut off their relationship and turned him in. But he made 'plain and simple' Kate feel bright and special, and desired in a way she never had before. The illicit thrill of their secret trysts was its own kind of high for her. He promised he would quit, any day now, and she believed him because she wanted to.

Looking back on it now, it was hard to understand how she could have been that naive. At the time, Kate would have called it love, but only because she had never really had something better to compare it to.

That fateful day, Bolton had been wired and she let it go. It was her responsibility to tell someone, but she let it go because she trusted him.

'The exercise was a simulated two-ship intercept on a third Hawk, piloted by an instructor and a trainee,' Kate explained.

'Piers pulled in, way too close. His judgment was impaired. His reactions were slow. Whatever the reason, we bumped.'

'And two men died,' said Breeze.

Kate gave a nod. 'Because I covered for the man I was having an affair with.'

'He was married?'

'Not only that, Piers Bolton was the son of a politician high up in the British government. Someone with – how did you put it? – pull. And they didn't want the family name dragged through the mud after the fact.'

Breeze made a spitting noise. 'So they pinned the blame on you.'

'They were going to.' Kate's cheeks coloured, old shame reaching out of the past to claw at her. 'I got out before that could happen. Gave up my career in fast jets. It was that or nothing.' She sighed. 'But I couldn't escape becoming a pariah. All that's left are the rumours, but the truth is worse. If it came out, nobody would ever want to fly with me again. People won't put their lives in the hands of a pilot they can't trust.'

'You really fucked up, Katie,' said Breeze. 'And those shit heels made you carry the can for them.' Then, out of nowhere, she gave a dry chuckle. 'Y'know, in the Hall of Fame for Bad Choices, you and me could practically be twinsies.' She waggled a finger at her. 'I knew I liked something about you.'

'Forgive me if I say that that's not a big help.' Kate had hoped unloading the weight of her confession would make her feel better, but it didn't. If anything, it made the mistakes of her past even heavier.

'Oh, I know,' admitted Breeze. 'Folks who say confession is good for the soul are talking out of their asses. Only thing it *is* good for is facing your mistakes head-on. Then if you're smart, you don't make them again.' She paused, catching her breath from the effort of speaking. 'You and me are here because of *my* mistakes,' she went on, then looked up to meet Kate's gaze. 'Wanna help me try to walk some of that back?'

Kate folded her arms across her chest. 'A moment ago, you were telling me we don't have a cat in hell's chance.'

'No,' Breeze corrected, 'I said we need to pick a fight.'

The guard led Hamid to a room elsewhere in the building, and along the way the younger man refused to meet his gaze, ashamed to be holding him at gunpoint.

The door opened to reveal a towering figure filling the entrance. Malik, his brother's brutish second-in-command, was a bear of a man, heavy-set with huge hands that could crack a skull if the need arose. And it often did. Prone to sudden outbursts of anger, Malik's ever-present threat made other men tread carefully around him.

Hamid had never warmed to the big man. It was one thing to use brutality when needed, but quite another to do so without control or forethought.

Malik sized him up with a thin smile, then dismissed the guard with a cut of the hand. He stood aside, mocking Hamid with a welcoming gesture, bowing theatrically as he beckoned him into the room.

Hamid ignored the false humility and strode in, finding his brother seated by a low table, upon which lay a pewter pot and a pair of blue-hued glasses. Nasir looked up at him but did not rise. 'Will you share tea with me, brother?'

A grimace pulled at Hamid's face. 'Is this your idea of a joke? You rescue me from the Americans, then you accuse me of

273

cowardice and imprison me. Now you offer me a refreshment as if we are enjoying a quiet afternoon together.'

'Sit.' Nasir nodded at the chair across from him. 'We can talk here, where no one else will intrude.'

Hamid shot a look at Malik. 'No one?'

'*Sit*,' repeated Nasir, and this time it was an order.

Malik came over and pressed one of his heavy palms on to Hamid's shoulder, pushing him inexorably toward the chair. Hamid shook him off with an angry jerk of motion, but he took the seat, sliding it back so he could keep both men in his field of view.

Nasir poured a brew of rich, dark tea for both of them, and in a tiny but deliberate breach of good manners, Hamid took up his cup and drank from it without thanking his brother.

'No sugar?' asked Nasir, nodding at a metal container. 'You've always liked the bitterness.'

The hot tea seared Hamid's throat, giving him fuel for his ire. 'What is the point of this? You and I have often disagreed, brother, but you know me. You know I am not a traitor to our cause.'

'It's not treachery that threatens us,' replied Nasir. 'It is hubris. You've grown too arrogant, little brother. You believe that Hamid's way is the only way. And look what that got you. You let the enemy take you alive because you were too prideful to see the trap you were walking into.'

Hamid's jaw stiffened. 'I dealt with Yusuf in person because you would not. You lacked the courage to kill him with your own hands.'

'We have men to do such deeds for us,' Nasir countered.

'The moment we become afraid to get blood on our hands is the moment we are no longer worthy of the cause.' Hamid's voice dropped to a low snarl. 'You cannot expect to lead while hiding in a cave. You cannot ask a fighter to give his life if you will not face death beside him.'

Nasir shook his head, pouring more tea. 'Ever since Father perished, I have waited for you to grow up, Hamid. But you never did. You are still the angry young boy, convinced his rage makes him invincible, unkillable. For too long you have done whatever you wished, and I cleaned up after you.' He grunted. 'No longer. Your grave error in Amsterdam broke the spell of your charisma over the men. They now see you for what you are – flawed and overconfident.'

Hamid held down his annoyance with an iron will and refilled his own cup. 'Did Zameer help them to that understanding I wonder? Or did you?'

'Circumstances have changed,' said Malik, breaking his silence for the first time. When he spoke, it sounded like the snapping of twigs. 'Your reckless actions exposed our network in Europe to our enemies. We lost many men, material and support after your capture. All because you had to flatter your own ego. So now it is decided that the little brother no longer leads.'

'It is rare to find a dog that speaks like a man.' Hamid noted.

His eyes alight, Malik took a warning step toward him, but Nasir waved the big man back. 'While you were gone, we came to a new understanding. A reconnection to the older, better ways. Zameer's voice lit the way for us.'

Hamid snorted. 'He dragged you back into his dogma, you mean?'

Nasir carried on as if he had not spoken. 'Zameer reminded us of what the long war is really about. It is not one man's jihad. It belongs to all of us.' He sipped his tea.

'He will be here soon. And then, with his learned counsel, a decision will be made as to the fates of the infidel women. And to yours.'

'You would let that toothless old goat call for my death?' Hamid's fingers tightened around the cup in his hand. 'Do you nurture such enmity for me?'

'I only want what is best.' A momentary conflict coloured Nasir's expression. 'A harsh judgment can be avoided, if he believes you show repentance. If *I* believe that you do.' Nasir blinked. 'Please, little brother. Find that within yourself.'

Hamid hung his head and fell silent. 'I understand,' he said, at length, becoming contrite. 'My capture was my mistake, so I must make amends. Perhaps, it will be enough if I bend the knee to you? If I accept your superiority?'

For a moment, Nasir seemed credulous enough to accept this show of humility from his younger sibling. But Hamid couldn't hold on to the lie and his anger burned through it.

With a feral shout, Hamid threw the hot tea in Nasir's face, then spun about to pitch the heavy glass at Malik's head. The big man recoiled from the blow and Hamid was back on his feet, fists cocked as he glared at his older brother.

'You worm!' he spat, his rage bursting its banks. 'I made you what you are! I made al-Sakakin! Not you, not Zameer! You should kneel to me!'

Hamid's tirade was cut short as Malik struck him with a brutal, crushing impact, hard enough to knock him down to the floor on his hands and knees.

'I gave him a chance. The fool used it.' Bells ringing and lights flashing in his skull, Hamid heard his brother's voice from far away. 'Put him back with the women, where he belongs.'

He held on to consciousness by a thread, half aware of the corridors passing him by as powerful hands dragged him back through the dimness.

Then Hamid was lying on a tiled floor, the blurry shape before him slowly resolving into the form of the British woman, the pilot.

'Hood?'

She nodded. 'You look worse for wear.'

'Is he still breathin'? More's the pity,' the American called out from close by.

Hamid rolled over and spat out blood. 'It is already decided. They will kill all of us,' he said, with grim certainty. When he looked up again, the pilot was watching him coldly.

'So what are we going to do about it?' she said.

TWENTY FOUR

Alex warred with himself, the hot-headed and heedless part of him wanting to charge in at full speed; the careful and thoughtful part struggling to rein in the impulse to find his son and do whatever it took to protect him.

The seams in the roadbed thudded against the police car's tyres as he approached the next motorway junction. He kept to the outermost lane, driving with the lights off. Alex gripped the steering wheel tightly, staring fixedly through the windscreen, searching the other lanes for any sign of the black BMW. But there was nothing.

Where are they? Am I too late?

At this time of night, the only traffic on the M2 was the occasional articulated lorry, mostly high-siders or refrigerated trucks bound for 24/7 distribution hubs. The only other cars he saw were going in the opposite direction, blurs that sped past, barely registering.

He forced himself to stay in the moment, but it was hard to hold on. In Alex's mind, the scene of George being struck down and bundled into the back of the BMW kept playing over and over, cutting him like knives.

When Alex had split up with his wife – or more correctly, when Laura had walked out on them – he had quietly vowed that he wouldn't let his boy drift off and become isolated, like some children did when divorce tore through a family. It was a duty, and the guilt of it weighed him down with his failure to keep George safe.

Alex was a firefighter, a lifesaver by choice, and he risked himself every day to keep strangers from harm. To admit that he couldn't do the same thing for his son was galling for him, and it stirred up a mess of emotions that were hard to keep a lid on.

I wish Kate was here. She'd know the right thing to say.

Thinking of her made the knife in his chest twist even more. Whatever this night's madness was about, Kate was caught up in it as much as Alex and his son. The notion that both of them might be taken away from him made him curse out loud.

Alex shook off the bleak thought, took a long, shuddering breath and fought down the turmoil in his thoughts. 'Enough,' he said aloud. 'You panic, it's over.'

He glanced at the Airwave radio set on the Volvo's dashboard. He'd touched nothing since hearing the police dispatcher call out a sighting of the kidnappers' car, but the voice had not returned. Aside from occasional pops and clicks of static, the radio remained ominously silent.

A worrying thought occurred to him. Were the Kent Police tracking the patrol car he had stolen? He knew that the fire engines his rescue unit drove were fitted with GPS trackers so their movements could be coordinated from home base, so it stood to reason a police vehicle would be similarly equipped.

'If the cops know where I am, then they're on another radio channel.' Alex voiced the thought. 'Where I can't hear them.' On impulse, he reached over and turned the radio off entirely.

They would be coming after him, and Alex had no way of knowing how close the police were. He had to find George before they caught up with him.

And then up ahead he saw a glitter of sodium bright light reflect off the shiny, beetle-black curves of the BMW. The car was overtaking a bulk tanker truck, changing lanes and slowing.

Reacting quickly, Alex put the police car into the tanker's blind spot and drifted into its slipstream. Gently he eased out of its shadow, enough so he could keep the BMW's tail lights in view.

His heart hammered in his chest. *That's them.* He was certain of it. The black car moved quickly but steadily, and Alex hoped that meant they were unaware of him following on behind.

But now he had them in his sights, what could he do? He thought about making a run at the car, maybe trying to rear-end it and force them off the road, but there was too much danger in something so reckless. He pictured the black car spinning end over end into a fatal crash, and felt sick.

As the next junction came into view, Matvey and his men made the decision for Alex. The BMW dropped away, off the motorway and on to a slip road that would take them toward the Medway coast and the Thames Estuary. Alex slowed as much as he dared. As the other vehicle vanished into the turn-off, he slewed the police car's steering wheel and bolted for the exit. Tyres screeched as he veered over thankfully empty lanes, briefly mounting the safety strip before bouncing back.

He passed beneath a tall pole topped with a cluster of traffic cameras and winced. If someone was monitoring them, they would know exactly where he was going.

'Don't think about that,' he told himself. 'Just keep driving.'

The broad span of the motorway immediately narrowed down to a tight country road, just wide enough for two cars to pass one another. On either side, a flat, shadowy expanse of farmland vanished into the horizon, and Alex felt cold sweat on his neck as he tried to keep pace with the BMW, while still driving with the police car blacked-out.

The other car turned north and the road tightened even more, the footpaths on either side vanishing into thick hedges that flickered at the edges of Alex's vision. The BMW picked up speed, charging through villages and past clusters of cottages clinging to the side of the lanes.

He had the sense that whoever was driving knew exactly where they were going. Speeding over a railway bridge and past a rustic pub, Alex caught sight of a sign bearing the names Seasalter and Whitstable. He recognised them vaguely as sleepy coastal towns that were home to caravan parks and long stretches of pebbled beach.

Then, without warning, the red flare of the BMW's tail-lights dissolved into the blackness and Alex reflexively stamped on the brakes. The patrol car hissed to a jarring halt, and he held his breath, uncertain if the driver of the other car had spotted him and stopped, made a blind turn, or done something else unexpected.

Alex dropped the side window and leaned out into the cold night air, straining to listen. He could hear the distant rush of tidal breakers and the mumble of a car engine. In the near distance, white light flashed over a low sea wall and a line of static homes as the BMW passed by and disappeared behind them. It had left the road, halting at the edge of the beach.

Jamming the police car into reverse, Alex guided it into the driveway of a shuttered building off the coast road and left it out of sight. His dark jacket blended him into the gloom as he scrambled awkwardly up a wet, boggy rise toward the caravan park and the shoreline beyond it.

In the summer months, the place would be busy with holidaymakers from the city on a seaside getaway, but now all but a couple of the weather-beaten prefabricated buildings were silent and unoccupied, most of them buttoned up for the off-season with heavy wooden shutters.

The static homes stood on short, thick stilts raising them up off the ground – high enough to keep them safe from any surge tides – and the shadows beneath had the added bonus of giving Alex somewhere to conceal himself as he crept forward.

A bitter wind off the estuary carried to him and he heard voices he recognised. Seeking the source sound, he soon spotted Matvey and one of his mates. They stood on the beach close to the car, where a long concrete quay extended out into the water. Moored out at the far end was the squat, slump-shouldered shape of a fishing boat, lit by a yellowy glow inside its wheelhouse.

Breathing hard, Alex watched the trawler rise and fall in the swell. In the back of his mind, he'd been expecting these men to make a break for Dover and the ferries across to the continent. It had not occurred to him that they might have another exit route already in place. Under cover of night, a smaller boat like this would easily be able to slip across the English Channel to France or Belgium.

The other thug, the one called Luka, was busy at the back of the car, and when he rose into view, Alex physically recoiled.

The man carried George over his shoulder, the boy hanging limp and unmoving.

Alex's breath caught in his throat. Had they drugged his son? Or done worse? George didn't utter a sound or show any sign of life as Luka brought him up to the quay, his arms swaying from side to side.

Luka tried to get Matvey's attention, but the grey-haired ringleader waved him away irritably. Matvey talked into a mobile phone – the chunky, heavyweight sort with a thick antenna rod that bounced signals off satellites rather than any regular cellular network. Whomever he was speaking with, he didn't appear happy to be having the conversation.

Alex bottled up his anger and made it his fuel. He gauged the distance from his hiding place beneath the static home to the BMW. He could make it in a few seconds, but he would be seen the moment he left his cover. Alex had not forgotten the burning pain in his shoulder from Matvey's glancing bullet and he had no desire to get shot at a second time.

Wait, he told himself, fighting down the urge to rush out, to attack. *For George's sake, watch and wait.*

Breeze's gaze was hooded, and she laboured through her words – but none of that blunted the edge in her tone as she glared up at Kate. 'Do you have, like, an undiagnosed head injury I don't know about? That's the only excuse I can come up with for you suggesting something this idiotic.' She leaned back against the wall and made a snorting noise.

'You and I can't get out of here on our own, that's a given. But we might make it, if Hamid helps us. And right now, he's up shit creek like we are. We'll hang separately or we'll hang together – at this point it makes little bloody difference.' Kate could barely countenance the words coming out of her own mouth, but she knew they were past the point of anything else. She took a different tack. 'I thought the CIA did this kind of thing all the time, making deals with terrorists and sundry other rat-bags.'

'Yeah, Katie, we do.' Breeze's eyes flashed. 'I've done it hundreds of times. Getting into bed with people who make my skin crawl for the greater good. I would pucker up and kiss the bright red ass of the devil himself if I thought it could save lives. But *that* man?' She pointed a trembling finger at Hamid, who stood across the room, listening at the locked door. 'He has no motive to trust. He hates us like fire, don't you get it? He will absolutely back-stab you at the first opportunity.'

Kate let her run out of steam, then went on. 'Can you honestly tell me you're pushing back on this because you believe it, or because of what he did to your friend Sophia?'

'Both,' spat the other woman. 'I've sold out and been sold out enough times to know how it works, and forgive me for noting you have no goddamn idea about it. This is a lose-lose proposition.'

'We are wasting time,' said Hamid, looking through a thin gap between the door and its frame. He threw a glance in Kate's direction. 'Forget the American. She will only slow us down.'

Breeze gave her a look that said *See, I'm right*, but Kate ignored it. 'No. We all go or no one goes. That's the deal.' She gestured at the door. 'There are two guards out there with assault rifles and itchy trigger fingers. Good luck dealing with both of them on your own.'

Hamid said something under his breath that Kate guessed was a swearword, but at length he gave a reluctant nod. 'I have little choice but to agree.'

Kate grabbed the medical kit and brought it back over to Breeze. The other woman shook her head. 'This is the pinnacle of bad ideas,' she told her. 'The Mount Everest of clusterfucks. We both know it.'

'Then, by all means, give me something else. You're the expert.' Kate rooted through the kit and found what she was looking for.

'Piss off,' Breeze retorted. 'You know I've got nothing.'

'You want to die here? What happened to Team Belligerent?' Kate's temper broke and she barked the questions. 'Do you want to go out being a snarky bitch, or do you want to keep kicking and screaming right up to the bloody, bitter end? I know what choice I'm making.'

Breeze said nothing, then snatched the kit from her. 'Give me that thing, stupid. If we're doing this, then at least follow my lead.'

Uzal found it hard to talk to Yuba.

Yuba was a newer addition to the ranks of al-Sakakin's foot soldiers; a gaunt young man with the features of someone ten years older, lacking the rangy build that characterised Uzal. Yuba did not smile, he did not laugh, and when he did speak, he wasn't interested in anything but parroting scripture or whatever epistle the old man Zameer had most recently posted on social media.

Yuba thought that everything was *haram* – disrespectful, foreign and against the will of God – and while Uzal certainly considered himself a true believer, he found the other man's endlessly grinding, bitter piety wearing, to the point that the two guards stood their posts side by side, but rarely spoke.

But tonight was different. Uzal adjusted the rifle on his shoulder and caught Yuba's eye. 'What?' said Yuba.

Uzal couldn't keep quiet about what bothered him. The arrival of the aircraft and everything that had happened after played on his mind.

He jerked his head at the locked door. 'The man in there, that is Hamid! Hamid the warrior!'

Yuba didn't seem convinced. 'How do you know? Have you ever met him?'

'Well, no, but …' Uzal stumbled over his answer. Hamid was a legend to the lower ranks; the ghost who moved unseen through the halls of the infidels, putting them to the sword and leaving no trace. I mean, I heard talk—'

'You are like the old women in a village square,' Yuba turned away, his lip curling, 'with their gossip and their stories. But you have no facts.'

'Hamid is a hero.' Uzal reframed his thoughts. 'He should not be treated like a prisoner and made to share a room with foreigners.'

'Zameer says we are all heroes, unless we weaken and become traitors.' Yuba sniffed, as if he smelled something foul, and patted his weapon. 'Only a traitor would be caged and guarded.'

Uzal searched for a reply but, before he could form one, he heard movement on the other side of the door. Someone banged a fist on the metal panel.

'Hey! Hey, you outside!' Uzal knew enough English to understand the woman's words. 'The American's not breathing! I can't wake her up!'

Yuba frowned. 'What is the female saying?'

Uzal translated for him. 'If the American dies, Nasir will not be happy.'

'This is a ruse.' Yuba let his rifle drop into his hands, as the woman continued to bang on the door, becoming more agitated by the second. 'Ignore her.'

Uzal readied his own weapon, shaking his head. 'Do you want to be the one to say we stood by and did nothing?' Nasir had promised Uzal that he would be on the execution detail when the time came to kill the infidels. It was an honour to be selected for that, and one he didn't want to lose. 'What will Zameer say when he arrives and learns the American perished before she could taste justice?'

That gave Yuba pause, and he nodded. 'Very well. Open the door.'

'We come in!' Uzal shouted, in broken English. 'You back, back!' He released the heavy industrial padlock and slid aside the bolt, kicking open the door.

Yuba rushed in first, his rifle raised to his shoulder, and he turned it to aim at Hamid's chest. Hamid slowly raised his hands and kept his gaze averted as Uzal followed the other guard into the room.

The two women were in the far corner of the room, the American ashen-faced and unmoving where she lay on a sleeping pallet beside the contents of a medical pack, the British pilot hovering over her.

'Back!' Uzal shouted in English. He pointed his weapon at the pilot, and she nodded, retreating meekly into the corner of the room. Cautiously, he approached the woman on the pallet and gave her a kick. When she didn't respond, he shot a look at Yuba.

He frowned. 'Is she dead?'

'I don't know,' Uzal replied. Now they were inside the room, he was unsure how to proceed.

'You need to be sure, Uzal,' offered Hamid, catching him off-guard.

'You know my name?' Uzal blinked, suddenly uncertain.

'Be silent, collaborator,' snarled Yuba.

'Watch him.' Uzal shook off his moment of doubt and leaned down, shifting his rifle with one hand so he could reach down and put his fingers against the American's neck, to check for a pulse.

When he touched her skin, it was as if he had pressed a switch on a dormant machine. The woman's eyes snapped open and, before he could react, her arm came up between his legs and agony exploded there. She rammed a blade of blunted metal, part of a pair of medical scissors, as hard as possible into the meat of Uzal's inner thigh.

He screamed, the cry thin and reedy, as the woman twisted the blade through the thin cotton of his robe, gouging into flesh. The pain was breathtaking, and blood gushed from the wound as he fell backwards, unable to remain standing.

The taller of the two guards fell down, howling in agony, and his cry caught the other gunman's attention, distracting him for a split second.

As Kate kicked off the wall and came forward, Hamid brought his hands down and knocked the other man's rifle, forcing the muzzle of the weapon away from his torso.

'Get him!' shouted Breeze, rolling her weight away from the man she had stabbed, putting the effort she could into driving her makeshift dagger even deeper.

Kate snatched at the arm of one of the plastic lawn chairs and it came up in her hand. Lightweight and flimsy, it rattled as she swung it at Hamid's opponent, breaking across his back. The chair splintered into pieces, knocking the guard forward.

Hamid snatched at the exposed stamped-metal workings of the rifle, jamming his fingers against the cocking handle so it could not fire, even as the other guard mashed the trigger. They stumbled against one another, fighting for control of the gun.

Kate grabbed the man from behind, both hands clamping round his head, fingertips digging into his cheeks and his eyes. He cried out as she tried to wrench him away, letting go of the rifle with one hand, fist flailing as he swung blindly, trying to connect with a wild punch.

It was the opening Hamid needed, and he kicked hard against the younger man's shin, breaking bone. The guard sank, and Hamid twisted the rifle from his grip, following his opponent down with a blow from the wooden butt of the weapon.

Then, without a second of hesitation, Hamid flipped the rifle along its length and jammed the muzzle into the fallen man's chest. Kate opened her mouth to call out, but he had already pulled the trigger.

A rifle round punched through the guard's sternum and blasted blood and lung matter over the dusty floor, the shot as loud as thunder in the quiet of the night.

For an instant, Kate thought the next bullet would be for her, but Hamid sighted past her shoulder and fired again. His second bullet drilled a black hole in the back of the other guard's head, sending him sprawling down to the ground in spreading mess of wet crimson.

The rifle's muzzle pivoted in Breeze's direction, and without thinking, Kate stepped in front of it. 'No,' she told Hamid. 'We all go or no one goes.'

He glared at her before letting the weapon drop away. Behind Kate, Breeze sat back on her pallet, her hands bloody against her pale skin. The American scrambled to gather up the dead man's weapon, while Hamid surveyed his work with a cold expression.

'You had no need to interfere,' he told Kate. 'I was dealing with it.'

'You killed both of them.' Kate felt bile build in her throat and swallowed it down. 'You knew those men.'

'Does it matter? Nothing will be accomplished without bloodshed. Better theirs than mine.' He moved to the door, risking a quick look outside. 'Time to go. The others will have heard the shots.'

'He must piss ice water,' muttered Breeze, as Kate went to her to help her up. She tossed away the red-stained scissors and used the rifle as a prop. 'This is getting messy.'

'Yes.' Kate breathed through her mouth, the sickening mix of spent gunpowder and blood thick in her nostrils. 'I've got you, come on.' She pulled the other woman's arm over her shoulder to take her weight.

Breeze stifled a groan of pain as they moved, and she pressed the dead man's rifle into Kate's hands. 'Here. You have it. It's taking all I got to walk upright. Can't shoot as well.'

'Right.' Kate shouldered the weapon by its strap to hang it at her hip, one hand clasping the pistol grip, aiming it ahead of them as they lurched toward the open doorway and the corridor beyond. 'Put one foot in front of the other,' she added. 'Let me deal with anything else.'

'Sure.' Breeze slurred her words. 'Walk in the park.'

TWENTY FIVE

'Do not be late,' Matvey growled into the sat phone, making sure his contact in Belgium knew he was serious. 'If I need to come looking for you, you will regret it.'

'*I'll be there*,' came the reply. '*You make sure the Coast Guard doesn't follow you.*' The call cut and Matvey collapsed the phone's thick antenna, jamming the chunky device into the folds of his jacket.

He took a deep breath of the damp, briny air, listening to the rush of the waves on the rattling beach. He didn't like working with the Albanians. Matvey found their manners crude and bellicose, while they considered the Russians to be uneducated idiots, but he couldn't deny their ample skills in illegal trafficking across the Low Countries. For better or worse, he needed them to get Luka, Stepan and himself as far from Britain as possible. Matvey did not want to remain on this rainy, dreary island another second longer than he had to.

The plan was to make a fast run to Ostend, putting in the trawler at a wharf where a car would be ready to pick them up. From there, a short drive to Antwerp and the three of them would go their separate ways, secure in the knowledge that the money they were owed for this night's work would be safe in their bank accounts. But until he stood on Belgian soil,

Matvey would not be able to relax. The police would know that murderers were at large, and they would be combing the countryside for any trace of them.

Stepan approached him. He was hunched forward, hands rammed deep into his pockets. The light jacket he wore wasn't cutting the cold wind in off the water, and he was grumpy about it. 'Luka put the kid in the cabin,' he began, nodding at the trawler at the far end of the concrete quay. 'He says he is ready to go when you are.'

Matvey eyed the boat. 'You are sure he can handle that thing? Do we trust him not to sail us into the side of a car ferry?'

'He is from St Petersburg,' said Stepan, with a shrug, 'his family were *koryushka* fishermen.'

'I am from the Urals,' Matvey retorted. 'That does not mean I know anything about growing potatoes.'

'He told me he crewed boats when he was young. You want to find someone else to do it? It was enough trouble getting the trawler here, never mind a crew!'

Matvey made a negative noise and blew out a breath. 'No. We do not want any more eyes on us.' He started walking, but Stepan hesitated. 'Something else?'

The other man shifted from foot to foot. 'Do we really need to take the kid with us?'

Matvey eyed him. 'Do not go soft on me now, Stepan.'

'I am not!' he retorted hotly. 'I do not see the point, that is all.'

'You are right, there will be no use for a hostage after we cross the water.' Matvey considered it. 'When we are under way, find a weight, a rope or something. Then when we are in deeper water, we send him to the bottom, yes?' Stepan didn't reply, looking past Matvey's shoulder at the line of clapboard houses along the beach. 'You hear me?' Matvey prodded him.

'I hear you.' Stepan hugged himself against the cold, staring into the gloom as if he had seen something troublesome.

'What is it?' Matvey followed his line of sight, but he saw only shadows and darkened buildings. 'Someone there?'

'No,' said Stepan, after a moment. 'It was nothing.'

'Then cast us off,' ordered Matvey, striding away toward the waiting boat. 'It is time to be gone.'

As Kate and Breeze made their way down the corridor, a shout of automatic fire sounded and all the lights in the building went out, plunging them into darkness.

Kate smelled smoke and burned oil, turning to find Hamid striding out of a machine room across the way. Behind him she could see the sparking remains of a large petrol generator, the outpost's power source now rendered useless. 'This will give us an advantage,' he said, reloading his weapon. 'Keep moving.'

Advancing with his stolen rifle at his shoulder, he moved ahead of them, kicking in doors along the way, swinging the weapon's muzzle left and right with quick jerks of motion.

Up ahead, another door banged open and two men in grubby fatigues came racing through. Hamid met them with a burst of fire that threw them off their feet and down into a jumble of limbs. Without hesitation, he moved up and put single rounds through their heads to be sure they would not rise again.

'Cover me,' he called, bending to search the dead for ammunition.

'If we make it outside,' puffed Breeze, leaning close, 'what's the plan?' Her breath was hot against Kate's bare neck, and it had an unhealthy, metallic reek.

'Get to the plane and get away.' In her mind's eye, the pilot visualised the Hawker where they had left it behind. As long as Nasir's men hadn't messed around with anything, she'd be able to taxi it on to the runway and put the jet back in the sky. Past that point, she was still hazy on the details. *One step at a time*, she told herself.

In the air, even running the risk of another drone, another missile attack, it would be better odds than waiting around on the ground for sun-up and certain death.

'Two more behind!' Breeze yelled suddenly, as Kate heard another door crash back in the direction they had come. The American lurched away, off Kate's shoulder as she spun in place and blind-fired the rifle at the source of the sound.

A dagger of yellow cordite fire leapt from the muzzle of the weapon and brass casings streamed from the ejector port, pinging off the wall. The gun's report was horribly loud, and Kate had no idea if she hit the men trying to flank them, but in the aftermath there was no movement in the shadows.

'Move!' Hamid shouted from the other end of the corridor. 'Follow me!'

Taking Breeze with her, Kate marched after him as quickly as they both could manage, over the cooling corpses of the dead men and out through creaking double doors.

They emerged inside one of the airstrip's wide, high-ceilinged hangars, a broad arc of corrugated metal patched with rust. In the middle of the gloomy, shadow-filled space sat the sorry remains of a Russian-made Mi-8 transport helicopter, an aircraft Kate immediately recognised as a 'Hip', using its NATO codename. The Hip was a gutted shell of its former self – engine gone, panels missing, rotor blades gathered on the ground beside it like warped planks of wood. Crates and oil drums sat around it in clumps. The whole scene had the air of a job that had been abandoned mid-way.

'That ain't gonna fly,' muttered Breeze.

One whole side of the enclosure opened to the runway, and off at the closer end of the apron, Kate caught sight of the Hawker's ghostly silhouette. The navigation lights on its wings were still blinking steadily, and it appeared intact, but Nasir's men hadn't moved the thing. It seemed miles distant.

Metal clanked against metal somewhere on the other side of the abandoned helicopter's fuselage, and Kate saw bits of shadow break apart. Figures were moving towards them. She pulled the rifle's trigger, barely aiming the weapon in their vague direction, and another braying howl of fire leapt from the muzzle. Ricochets punched through the thin hull of the Hip and sparked off the oil-stained concrete floor, scattering the would-be attackers.

Hamid was already behind the cover of a heavy tool rack, picking his moments to pop up and lay down kill-shots. He emptied another sickle-shaped magazine in short order and let it fall, seamlessly jamming a fresh one into his rifle's frame. Three-round bursts lanced through the hangar's dusty, unmoving air, drawing fire from the men who had failed to ambush them. Gunpowder flares lit the hangar in yellow strobes.

Grateful for the distraction, Kate let Breeze slip down to relative safety behind a crate, then pushed herself over to the side of four oil drums clustered on a wooden pallet.

She pulled out her rifle's magazine and weighed it in her hand before reinserting it. *Half left*, she estimated. Kate's marksmanship training in the Air Force leaned toward pistol shooting with a Browning semi-automatic, and even then she had been average at best. With the assault rifle, she knew she was out of her depth.

A fresh salvo of rounds clanked into the oil drums at her back, and Kate flinched, drawing in to make herself as small a target as possible.

This was the worst possible situation to find themselves in. If they couldn't keep moving – if the three escapees remained here, pinned down – every man Nasir had on the base would eventually surround them, and that would be the end of it.

The shrieking chorus of gunfire was never-ending, but then someone shouted a command in Arabic and the shooting abated. Kate thought the voice was a familiar one, and when it came again, the words were in English. 'You can't get away, you must know that!'

'Hipster?' Breeze coughed. 'That dickweed can go short-stroke a rhino.'

She heard the traitorous MI6 agent snort with derision. 'I won't waste time talking to anyone else. Kate Hood, I know you can hear me. Surrender. Toss out your weapon and stand up. Hamid and Breeze, they're the ones with value, not you. You are going to die, but I can make it quick and clean. That's more than the others will get, believe me.'

'Tempting offer, Finn,' Kate yelled back, her words bouncing off the tin roof. 'You go first.' She sounded more defiant than she felt.

'Why would I do that? I'm not the one with something to lose, like you.' Finn's voice had an echoing quality that made it hard for her to be sure where it came from.

Hamid gave a dull whistle, attracting Kate's attention. 'Ignore him, he is trying to distract you.' He checked his weapon, then looked in her direction. 'I need more ammunition. Your rifle, throw it to me.'

'Sod off,' she replied, ducking low as she crabbed her way to another piece of cover.

'Do not listen to him!' hissed Hamid. 'Give me the rifle!'

'No.' Kate moved out of Hamid's line of sight, staying in the depths of the shadows.

'If I can interject,' Finn was saying, 'I have a phone here, with a man on speed-dial quite capable of committing cold-blooded murder on my say-so.' Kate's gut twisted with fear as she anticipated what would come next. 'I'm going to call him up. I'll tell him to wring little George's neck, and I'll put it on speaker so we can listen in. Is that what you want, Kate? Do you want that poor lad's screams to be the last thing you hear?'

'You are scum.' Kate said the words into her chest, clutching the rifle to her. She hid behind a gear locker, crouching low behind it.

'The boyfriend, what's his name? Alex, isn't it? He's dead already, most likely.' Finn continued. He sounded closer now, and Kate raised her weapon, aiming down its iron sights into the jumping shadows. 'That's because of you, Hood. Give up now and at least the kid will survive.'

'Kate!' Breeze rasped, fighting for breath. 'He's right there!'

'I am.' Finn's voice came from directly behind her, and too late Kate realised he had been working his way round the helicopter wreck, closing in on her position.

The hard edges of a pistol barrel pressed against the back of Kate's head, and she heard – as much as felt – the resonant click as he thumbed back the hammer.

'Offer expired,' he whispered. 'Lose the rifle. I won't say it again.'

Kate threw the weapon away, letting it skid across the floor and into the darkness.

Alex waited until Matvey and the other thug were on board the trawler before he bolted from the shadows that were keeping him concealed. He dashed to the back of the BMW, pausing to catch a breath, then slinked forward, staying as low as he could.

There had been another moment earlier when the other man had looked directly at him, and Alex froze, convinced that the Russian was staring him in the face. But then he turned away, and Alex knew that the darkness had shrouded him.

He didn't have that advantage any more. All it would take was someone catching sight of his movement and he'd be done.

The fishing boat's engine grumbled and caught, the chug of it bringing a gust of diesel fumes over the quay as Alex drew closer. He could see the lanky one, Luka, moving around inside the wheelhouse, the man's attention on the trawler's controls. Matvey had gone inside the vessel and the third man moved around the bow, pulling ropes off the mooring cleats. Any second now, the boat would be floating untethered and free to move off.

I have to chance it. Alex broke into a full-tilt run, covering the last few metres to the stern. Just as the sea behind the boat began to churn as the propellers bit into the briny water, he threw himself over the widening gap between the end of the concrete pier and the trawler.

He landed badly, one foot clipping a guard rail, throwing him face-down on the wet and oily deck. Chewing on the shock of the fall, he hoped that the noise of the engines had covered the sound of him boarding. Alex rolled over on to his back as the trawler kicked out through the shallow waves, heading into the estuary. The pain in his chest and his arm seethed.

Boots clanked on the deck plates, and he realised that his 'run and jump' hadn't gone unnoticed after all. The third man – the once called Stepan – came his way, advancing along the line of the guard rail with a heavy wooden oar in his hands, searching for the source of the noise.

There was little light around the boat's stern, so the thug had to be close to see Alex where he lay, but Alex had nowhere he could go, backed up against the arching gantries where nets would be deployed overboard on the trawler's usual voyages.

Then he remembered the blocky lump of plastic inside his jacket – the extra edge that Grace had given him back in the lay-by. Alex fumbled for the police-issue taser as Stepan came into view, looming over him with the brutal mass of the oar.

The thug swore and swung up the wooden paddle, intending to bring it down like an axe blade on Alex's head.

Alex pulled the taser's trigger and a light blinked on the front of the plastic pistol. With a metallic crackle, two darts trailing wires leapt into Stepan's chest, and the powerful voltage from the gun's battery pack flowed into him.

The man's body locked up, the muscles in his body going into spasm. He trembled and shook, powerless to move, and Alex kept the trigger pressed down, suddenly unsure what to do next.

The shallow pitch and roll of the trawler's deck decided for him. Unable to let go of the heavy oar, the weight of it cost Stepan his balance, and he teetered backward over the guard rail, pulling the taser out of Alex's grip as he went.

The thug slipped into the water with barely a splash, and Alex didn't see him come up again, briefly catching sight of the oar bobbing in the trawler's foamy wake before it too was lost.

He hesitated, straining to hear over the chugging engine, listening for any sign of alarm. Nothing.

Alex took a deep, shaky breath and started forward.

Kate slowly raised her hands as the steely mass of Finn's gun pressed against her skull.

From across the hangar, the rattle and bang of weapons continued unabated as Hamid waged his one-man battle against his former comrades, but for Kate the melee had contracted down to the distance between the pull of Finn's trigger and the fall of his pistol's hammer.

She felt a colossal pressure building inside her head, like the mother of all migraines, as if the catastrophic power of the bullet in the pistol was struggling to burst out and turn her face into red mist.

'You've been a pain in my balls from minute one,' Finn told her, punctuating each word with a blunt nudge from the pistol barrel. 'If that idiot Price had done as he was told, none of this would have happened. I had a plan, a simple plan. You messed it up.'

'Sorry not sorry,' she managed.

He grabbed her by the shoulder and spun her round, glancing left and right into the shadows. 'Where's Breeze?'

'Slipped away,' she lied. 'So you won't get your bonus, will you? That's if you ever would have seen any money. Nasir strikes me as the type who would rather deal in lead instead of silver.'

A flicker of doubt crossed Finn's expression, but then it vanished under a crushing scowl. 'Doesn't matter. I'm finished with you.'

He pulled the pistol's trigger and Kate flinched, ready for the world to explode, but the semi-automatic gave out an oily click as the mechanism jammed solid. Finn swore and pulled at the gun's slide.

Kate remembered back on the plane – when Finn had used his gun like a hammer to smash their phones and the tracking device Breeze had secreted on herself – and she recalled something else, a truism that her firing instructor had drilled into his trainees back in the day.

Use your sidearm for making the other bloke fall down and nothing else. You bang it about like some pillock and, I promise you, it'll let you down right when you need it the most.

She kicked Finn as hard as she could in the crotch, her foot connecting with his bollocks with a satisfyingly solid impact. As he recoiled, Kate burst into motion to flee across the hangar.

Finn finally unjammed the gun and hobbled after her, firing as he moved. Bullets zipped past her head and Kate swore in fright.

Then, ahead of her, a stocky figure slumped beside a crate raised the rifle she had tossed away moments before and let off the rest of the clip.

Kate ducked as Breeze fired past her, cutting down Finn in mid-run. The bearded man spun and crashed into a pile of oily tarpaulins. He didn't move again.

The echo of the rifle discharge faded and the hangar sizzled with spent gunpowder and the moans of the wounded. But for the moment Kate forgot that and rushed to the woman who had saved her life.

'That asshole.' Breeze coughed wetly. 'Did I ever tell you? I *hate* hipsters.' Breeze let the weapon drop. 'All that artisanal, organic bullshit they love. I just want a cheeseburger.' She gave a weak sob. 'Oh man, I *really* want a cheeseburger before I die. How dumb is that?'

Kate helped her up, to sit atop the crate. 'You're not done yet.'

'Optimist,' she managed. 'Shoulda had that knocked out of you by now.'

'Oh, you know me, I'm a ray of bloody sunshine,' Kate retorted. 'Wait here.'

She returned to Finn's corpse and rolled him over, grimacing as she searched his pockets. Hamid emerged from the shadows, still clutching at his rifle, and his wolf-like gaze found her. 'I killed the others. We cannot delay. More are coming.'

Kate couldn't hold his gaze for more than a second. He was somehow transformed by the act of the kill, and it was chilling. Aboard the plane, before they left Ridley Hill, the man called Yusuf had appeared to be a weak, fragile soul. Someone terrified of their own shadow.

And then he had changed right in front of her, dropping that persona like a snake shedding its skin, becoming Hamid, the cold-eyed and clinical terrorist.

Now she saw something new, perhaps the final layer that hid beneath that version of himself. Kate saw a murderer in his element, splashed with blood, teeth bared. 'What are you doing?' he demanded.

'Re-arming,' she told him. Kate recovered Finn's pistol, working the slide to make sure it was fully clear, then helped herself to the dead man's spare ammunition. Unseen by Hamid, she found and concealed the sat phone Finn had brandished earlier.

'We have to get to the aircraft,' said Hamid. 'I need you to fly it, but not her.' Once again, he aimed the rifle at Breeze.

'I won't leave her here,' insisted Kate. 'Non-negotiable.'

Hamid spat angrily on the ground and strode away, without waiting to see if they followed.

Kate put Breeze back on her feet again, and they supported one another, limping out into the cool, dry night. Off toward the main block of buildings, Kate heard men shouting and saw flashlights moving against the dark. Nasir's men had been caught unawares but they were not fools. They would quickly figure out that there was only one place the escapees could be going.

The American's head lolled against the pilot's shoulder, and she whispered in her ear. 'Hamid has nothing to lose. Don't lose sight of that.'

'I know.'

Breeze looked at her through watery, distant eyes. 'Can you kill a man in cold blood, Katie?'

TWENTY SIX

The trawler's name was the *Margaret III*, according to a weather-worn wooden plaque on the hull, and she motored along at a steady clip, staying out from the shore but following the line of it, rolling every few moments as a low wave brushed her hull.

Alex moved up from the stern, planting each foot carefully, well aware that his cheap off-brand trainers didn't have a good grip to them, and one wrong move might cause him to slip on the wet deck.

Above, the vault of a cold, dark night ranged from horizon to horizon, dotted with the bright pinpricks of stars. Alex looked and found Polaris, getting his bearings. The boat was sailing east across Tankerton Bay, in the direction of the yawning black void that marked the beginning of the English Channel. Behind them and to the northwest, he could see the retreating lights of Southend-on-Sea, and to the south along the coast was the seaside edge of Whitstable town. Across the water, the distances were hard to judge.

He kept his eyes fixed on the wheelhouse in front of him. Raised up on a platform in front of the trawler's main cabin, the little flying bridge was no larger than a garden shed, glassed in on all sides with grimy windows. Luka, the man at the wheel, stood hunched forward, scanning the black horizon intently. If he decided to abruptly take a look over his shoulder, he would see Alex immediately. There was no real cover on the open deck, just a few yellow plastic barrels and rusting metal lockers.

Alex could see a marine band radio up in the wheelhouse mounted on the control panel. If he could reach it, he could use it to contact the Coast Guard and help would come quickly. But to do that, he would need to deal with Luka first, and the only weapon he'd had on him – Constable Grace's borrowed taser – now lay at the bottom of the bay.

He sucked in a breath of damp air and stiffened. His son George was somewhere on the boat, and every instinct in him told Alex to abandon everything rational and go charging in after the boy. But what would that get him?

Stop the boat first, he told himself. Step by measured step, Alex closed the distance to the wheelhouse, running through every possible approach he could make. It was a few metres away now, past the cabin, up a wide step.

He would have to act quickly to catch the man at the helm by surprise. Anything else would be doomed to failure. And if it came to it, how far would he have to go?

He thought about Stepan, the man who had gone overboard without a sound. Was he dead? Would he wash up somewhere on the Medway coast in a few days? Try as he might, Alex couldn't find any compassion for the man. Matvey and his men had proven they were willing to kill without compunction. Alex wasn't afraid of violence, but could he deliberately, intentionally take a life in order to save his son's?

Yes. It was alarming how easily that decision came to him. But thinking it and doing it were two different things.

That thought still burned in his mind when, without warning, the metal door at the rear of the trawler's cabin compartment swung open.

Alex found himself looking Matvey right in the eye, a look of shock scarring the grey-haired man's face.

In his hands, the Russian held two tin cups full of black tea, steam curling upwards from the hot fluid. His moment of utter surprise shattered like glass, and Matvey let the cups drop to the deck, one hand darting into the back of his jacket where his pistol was holstered.

Alex could only do one thing – he lowered his shoulder and rushed at the other man, slipping on the deck as he charged bodily into the killer.

Matvey's gun had cleared leather as the two of them collided, but not enough to bring the long, silenced muzzle around to bear. Alex grabbed at Matvey's arm and tried to force him down, as Matvey swore and put his effort into resisting. The gun trembled between them, the black barrel dancing in the air, wavering back and forth.

Alex had mass and momentum, but Matvey was stronger in his muscle and sinew, and inexorably the gun began to drift the wrong way, closer and closer to its intended target.

Risking it, Alex shifted the position of his fingers, surrendering some of his impetus in exchange for a better grip on the weapon. He tried to jam his thumb into the gap behind the pistol's trigger, and Matvey pressed hard, firing a shot. A bullet whistled past Alex's head. He flinched but kept holding on as tightly as he could.

The two of them turned on the deck, caught in a violent pirouette, and Alex felt his footing drift again as his heel skipped over a greasy patch on the metal.

'Ha.' Matvey grunted in triumph and pressed his advantage, pushing the gun nearer to Alex's face. Another shot cut past him, the wake of it so close that Alex thought it had parted his hair. A few centimetres more and the muzzle would be pressing on his temple.

'No,' Alex retorted, clutching at the trigger, surprising Matvey for the second time that night. Deliberately squeezing with all his strength, Alex forced the Russian to pull the trigger again and again, trying to make him empty the gun before he could bring it to bear.

Matvey struggled to disengage without success and swore again as bullets arced away, ricochets keening as they sparked off the deck. He yelled and tried one last time to force the pistol into Alex's face, but the weapon's slide locked open as the final round in the magazine was discharged.

Behind them, glass pealed as random rounds shattered the wheelhouse's windows. Alex caught a glimpse of Luka jerking backward from the trawler's controls, hands clutching at an ugly red bloom that had appeared on his chest. The man fell out of sight and away from the helm, and the fishing boat listed sharply as the next wave caught it.

The bow bounced over the whitecap, and without Luka's hands on the wheel to guide it, the trawler lurched wildly off-course.

Alex was still reacting to the sudden motion when Matvey kicked forward and used the frame of the spent pistol as a cudgel, cracking him across the bridge of the nose.

Agony exploded across Alex's face as the reek of blood filled his nostrils. He struck back in blind, flailing rage, and landed a lucky hit, punching Matvey in the throat. Choking, the Russian staggered, losing his grip on the gun. The spent weapon fell to the canting deck and slid away into the shadows.

Alex didn't wait, following up with a front-footed kick that put his heel hard in the man's belly. Matvey slipped on the greasy spot and fell badly.

The trawler pitched to port, throwing Alex against the side of the cabin with an impact that blew the air out of his lungs, before rocking back the other way. Across the bow he could see the lights of the shoreline growing nearer as the out-of-control vessel motored at full speed toward the pebbled beach, boosted by the waves of the incoming tide.

Grabbing at a metal rail, Alex held on as the fishing boat rolled level again, finding himself pressed up against a grubby porthole in the side of the cabin compartment.

Inside, under a wash of dirty orange light, he could see a tiny crew space with a table and bench bolted to the floor. In one corner was his boy, knees drawn up to his chin, arms hugging himself tightly, his brown eyes wide and his face pale with terror.

'George!' Alex banged on the porthole, at once elated and petrified that he had found his son in the middle of this madness. 'I'm out here!'

He sensed movement behind him and jerked away, as another breaker clipped the boat and rocked it. Matvey was coming right at him, the blur in his hand a billhook – a curved talon of rusted iron.

Razor-sharp, the tip of the hook slashed through the air and caught Alex's jacket in passing. It tore through the material and the lining, through the layers below, just kissing the skin of his chest. A line of fire cut over Alex's breast and he howled. A little closer and the billhook would have opened him down to the bone.

He had no idea where the Russian had found the wicked thing, but it didn't matter. All Alex could do was hang on as the trawler raced on through the worsening swell, the deck bucking under his feet like the floor of a fairground crazy house. They were dangerously close to the shore now, caught in the turbulence of the beach-break.

The Russian didn't notice; his expression of gritted teeth showing his only interest was in killing Alex. Slashing the billhook high and low in wild diagonal strokes, Matvey came stomping up the boat towards him. Alex ducked, trading places with his attacker, trying to stay beyond his reach, but it was impossible in the narrow confines of the gangway. He stumbled against one of the yellow barrel floats and barely kept on his feet as the boat tilted again. Blood streamed down his chest from the new cut, and more soaked his arm from the aching bullet graze in his bicep. In the cold and wet, his energy was leaking out as well, dripping off him on to the deck.

Matvey snorted and tossed the weighty billhook from one hand to the other. 'I will make sure your corpse is the last thing your little brat sees before I toss him over the side.'

Alex couldn't make out the other man's features any more. He was a shadow wreathed in the vapours of his exhaled breath, with a massive claw for one hand, back-lit by the sodium glow of shore-side streetlights and the neon jumble on the fronts of the arcades along the coastal road. Alex had nowhere to go, trapped between the cabin wall and the barrels. Matvey would bury the hook in him with his next blow.

And then the bow of the *Margaret III* ran into a sandbar hidden under the surface of the waves, striking it with enough force to send a rolling shock down the length of the trawler from bow to stern. The deck flicked Alex up and he bounced off the side of the cabin before pitching into the rack of hollow barrels.

Standing in the open with nothing to support him, Matvey went tumbling, losing his footing with a strangled yell. The back of his skull, at the spot where it connected to the top of his spine, slammed hard into the starboard guide rail and bone shattered.

Alex scrambled back to his feet, the deck vibrating as the trawler's diesel motor roared uselessly. Matvey lay sprawled in front of him, eyes open and staring at the sky, his neck twisted at an unnatural angle. He made a long, drawn-out wheezing sound.

Matvey gave a last choke and fell silent. Still, Alex gave the Russian a kick, just to be sure.

'Dad!'

Alex was in a dozen different kinds of pain, lacerated, bruised and bleeding badly; wet and freezing, shaky with adrenaline, but still the sound of his son's voice made him break out in a big, goofy grin. 'All right, kiddo?'

George came off the bench and across the cramped cabin like a gangly rocket, lanky arms wrapping round his father as he hugged him for dear life. Alex couldn't stifle a moan of discomfort, and the boy let go, blanching as he saw his father's bloodstained jacket and shirt.

'Oh shit,' he said, and under the circumstances Alex decided he could allow the swearword to go unmentioned. 'What did they do to you?'

'Rough night for both of us,' he managed. 'You up for a paddle? We have to get off this thing.'

'OK.' George didn't hesitate, reaching back to gather up his hoodie from where it had fallen.

As he moved, the boy's foot clipped something on the deck. There was a mess of tin mugs, papers and other debris there, thrown down when the trawler ran aground, but George had disturbed the blocky shape of the satellite phone that Matvey had been using back on the beach.

On an impulse, Alex grabbed it, weighing the thing in his hands. These men had come after him and his son, and they'd done it to get to Kate. Would she be on the other end of this? Could he use it to reach her?

'Dad?' George pulled on his sleeve. 'I'm ready.'

'Me too,' he lied, and Alex jammed the sat phone in his pocket. Leading them back out into the night, he moved to the edge of the trawler's deck and looked down at the sea. The beach didn't seem too far away, but the water would be icy and turbulent. 'Hold on tight, yeah? This is not going to be fun.'

'You think?' He might have barely been old enough to call himself a teenager, but despite his ordeal tonight, George still retained the capacity to be sarcastic to a parent. 'Because we've had a *lovely* evening so far.'

Alex caught George's gaze drifting toward the gangway where Matvey's body lay, and he squeezed his son's hand to distract him from the grisly sight. 'Here we go!'

They leapt off and struck the water with a crash. It was deep enough at the sandbar to reach Alex's chest and swallow George whole, so he waded forward, pulling the boy to him. George came up coughing and spluttering, cursing a little more, and again Alex gave him a pass.

Harsh waves and salt spray buffeted them, but soon they had the shifting masses of stones beneath their feet. Stride by exhausting stride, the two of them climbed out of the breakers and on to the beach proper.

Shivering with the chill, Alex looked up and saw faces staring down at them from the other side of the low sea wall, locals who had been roused by the sound of the *Margaret III* catastrophically grounding itself.

'All, er, right?' Alex called out, his teeth chattering madly as he waved at the onlookers. He wanted to say more, but past the numbness in his extremities, the pain in his chest and the pressure in his head, Alex realised that a heavy, droning wind was blowing around him, loud enough that he could feel it in his bones.

Pure white – brighter than a supernova – drenched the pair of them in illumination as the beam of a night-sun searchlight snapped on overhead. The droning became a helicopter's clattering, thunderous rattle. Behind the white blaze, Alex saw strobing flashes of blue up on the coast road. The police had found them.

'*Stay where you are.*' A voice boomed from an amplified speaker out in the black sky. '*Do not move.*'

'You.'

Miles almost dropped the cigarette in his hand as the gruff American called out. He turned as Knox marched toward him, his eyes flint-hard and pitiless. *Oh bloody hell,* he thought, *what now?*

For hours, the Americans and their pet mercs had effectively kept Miles under armed guard at the airfield, and all the MI6 officer had to go on were snatches of conversation he wasn't supposed to have heard. He nursed the nasty suspicion that they had only held him here so they

312

would have someone from the British end of tonight's fuck-ups to hold responsible.

With that in mind, and precious little else he could do, Miles had finally given up on passing the night without a smoke, choosing to ignore the warning signs around the hangar, finding a spot out of the wind where he could sneak a ciggie. Now he took a quick draw to give him a little courage and stood his ground as the bigger man loomed over him.

'What?' Miles folded his arms. 'How much longer do I have stay here holding my cock and doing nothing?'

'Give me one of those.' Knox jabbed a finger at the cigarette. 'I thought you had a vape.'

'Threw the goddamn thing in the trash,' he replied. 'Was trying to cut down, maybe quit, but screw it.'

'Yeah, not a good night for that.' Miles proffered his half-empty packet of Silk Cut and a disposable lighter, which Knox snatched from his hand. The American lit up and greedily pulled on the cigarette, filling his lungs with nicotine smoke before tossing them back.

'This'll be over soon.' Knox volunteered, in a tone that was almost apologetic. If anything, the unprompted change in the man's attitude was more worrying to Miles than any of his previous behaviour had been. 'Just sit tight.'

'Yeah, nah.' Miles shook his head. 'I've been doing that for hours. Why don't you tell me what's really going on?'

'National security, need to know.' Knox automatically gave the rote reply.

'Piss off, mate!' Emboldened by his simmering annoyance, Miles took a step towards the other man. 'I've had enough of the silent treatment. I heard what you said on the call with that geezer with the tie. Something about a ship?'

Knox sighed and looked at the bulky, over-engineered mil-spec watch on his wrist. 'In less than thirty mikes, that aircraft, the asset, the tangos who interdicted them? They'll be gone. Thunder's coming, courtesy of the US Navy. This time, we won't miss.'

Miles blinked, parsing the operator's reply into something jargon-free. *The Yanks are going to blow up the plane and everyone in it.* 'There's gotta be another way!'

'You know as well as any of us, there ain't.' Knox drew on the cigarette again. 'We have to contain this. Control the narrative moving forward.'

'What's that supposed to mean?' Miles tensed, wondering if this was the moment the CIA were going to hang him out to dry.

'My people and yours, we have to follow the story. The jet was hijacked, we lost our agents on board, the civilian pilot too. Aircraft was tracked to a terrorist training camp, missile strike destroyed said camp. File closed.'

'Except that's bullshit,' Miles replied, half-distracted. He could hear a noise on the wind, a distant thudding coming closer. 'We don't know who's alive and who's dead.'

'That's already been decided,' said Knox. The sound became clearer, resolving into the beat of rotor blades.

The American looked up and Miles followed his line of sight. The boxy shape of a police helicopter in midnight blue and yellow passed over the runway, circling around as the pilot picked a spot to land.

'My boss has talked to your boss,' Knox said, pitching up his voice. 'It's already done. You and me, we just gotta toe the line.'

'What's this?' Miles countered, gesturing at the helicopter as it settled on to the asphalt.

'Civilians,' replied Knox, 'the pilot's boyfriend and his kid. Your local flatfoots did good and secured them for us.' He shook his head. 'We'll have to manage them. They were exposed to the contractors working with Finn. I need you to work with me. Make sure they see it the right way, understand?'

Miles didn't answer, jogging over to the helicopter as the rotors spun down and the rear compartment opened. Inside, one of the aircraft crew worked on an injured man with a blood-darkened shirt. Sitting close to him was a boy who couldn't have been much older than Miles's kid sister Juliet. They were both wrapped up in foil blankets, their faces weary with survivor's fatigue.

Another of the helicopter's crew dropped out on to the apron, and Miles saw she had the rank tabs of a police officer. She stepped into his path. 'Are you in charge here? Is someone going to tell me why the hell I had to bring this man here instead of straight to a hospital?'

'National security. Need to know.' Miles echoed Knox's earlier words, brandishing his Security Services identity card in the woman's face as he stepped round her. He swallowed his own doubts and spoke directly to the injured man. 'Sir. Are you the partner of Katherine Hood?'

'Yes. My name's Alex Walker. This is my son, George.' He nodded at the boy. 'Is Kate here?'

'I'm afraid not.' Miles was aware of Knox coming up behind him, with a trio of PMCs at his back. 'We're trying to determine Kate's situation. Are you aware of anything that could help us?'

'I'm not sure.' Alex looked away. 'The men on the boat, they kidnapped George, they said they wanted something from Kate ...'

'What men?' Knox interjected.

'There was an incident on the Medway coast,' said the woman, apparently unmoved by Miles's attempts to silence her. 'A boat ran aground. Bodies on board, both Russian nationals. It's a mess.' She pointed at Alex Walker, her ire rising. 'And that man is required for questioning about a murder investigation, the assault on a police officer and the death of another!'

'Understood,' Knox told the woman. 'We'll take it from here.'

'No, I don't think you will!' she shot back, kicking off an argument that Miles tried to blot out.

'Mr Walker,' he said, leaning closer. 'Kate and the people with her are in grave danger, if there's *anything* you can—'

'Dad, the phone!' The boy came forward, grabbing his father's arm. 'They were using it all the time!'

Alex nodded, pulling the blocky shape of a satellite telephone from his jacket pocket. He offered it warily to Miles. 'I took this from them.'

Miles flicked it open. The device was still charged and it had a single number encoded in its memory. But who would be on the other end of the line?

That rat Finn? Or someone else? Before he could second-guess himself, Miles extended the sat phone's antenna and hit the redial button.

'I'm gonna need that,' said Knox, coming in to grab the phone from him.

'Nah, mate.' Miles ducked out of Knox's reach, making his choice. 'Not this time.'

TWENTY SEVEN

They found a decrepit Toyota pick-up parked in a shadowed alley between the two hangars, and Kate walked Breeze to the flat bed, helping her up to slump against a pile of old sacks.

Even in the starlit darkness, Kate could see the other woman was fading fast. Breeze's florid complexion had drained, turned pasty from her exertion and injuries. The way she favoured her side told the pilot that her wound was worse than she wanted to admit.

Despite the temperature of the desert air, Breeze shivered constantly. Kate tried to stave it off, draping her flight jacket around the woman's shoulders.

'We'll be airborne soon,' she told her, compelled to offer some kind of hope. 'I'll get you to a doctor.'

'Sure,' said the American, coughing weakly.

Kate couldn't look her in the eye. She stepped away, back toward the front of the pick-up. The vehicle was missing its driver's door, and Hamid sat behind the wheel, fiddling with the ignition system. In lieu of a key, the starter had a screwdriver jammed in it, which he used to coax the engine into life.

'Is it going to work?'

Hamid didn't look up. 'It must. If we try to reach the plane on foot, they'll cut us down before we get ten metres.'

She couldn't argue with that stark evaluation of their chances. Out on the darkened airstrip, men with guns were sweeping down the runway in a ragged skirmish line, some of them holding flashlights as well as firearms. They were passing the turning apron, getting closer. It wouldn't be long until they came across the bodies of Finn and the others in the main hangar. Then Kate, Breeze and Hamid would have nowhere left to go.

Among the calls of the gunmen, Kate heard one gruff voice bellowing over the others. Hamid hesitated briefly as he caught it too, then went back to work.

She eyed him. 'You know who that is doing the shouting?'

He nodded. 'His name is Zameer. He gave the order to kill me.'

Hamid broke off as the lights across the desolate airfield buzzed back into life, throwing stark pools of white across the hangars, the weed-choked runway and the other buildings.

'Guess they had a back-up genny, huh?' Breeze offered the observation to the air. 'No rush, though. Take your time.'

Kate raised her pistol to the ready. With the lights on once more, they no longer had the benefit of long shadows to conceal them and the Toyota. The first gunman who came into line of sight would see exactly where they were hiding.

Hamid twisted the screwdriver and the pick-up's starter motor gave a weak buzz, but didn't catch. He hissed and pulled at a mess of wires dangling from beneath the steering column.

She watched him struggle with it. The irony was acidic, that her life and Breeze's were now in the hands of a man who had nothing but hatred for both of them. A man who, in other circumstances, would be sharpening the blade to cut their throats.

In the distance, a loud snap of static sounded and then the gruff voice sounded, now amplified over a loudspeaker. The unseen man – Zameer – spoke in rough phrases of Arabic, delivered with a smoker's grunt and a curled lip. Kate heard Hamid's name mentioned and, while she didn't understand the words, the older man's condescending tone was unmistakable.

'What's he saying?'

From the flat bed, Kate heard Breeze give a pained chuckle. 'That guy is *pissed*. Talking about Hamid here like he's the little kid who shit the bed.'

'Zameer is a senile old fool with a big mouth,' grated Hamid. 'He demands that I surrender to him.'

The voice droned on, and Breeze stifled a hollow cough before translating more. 'He wants to know why you can't be more like your brother. Damn, this guy thinks he's your dad!'

Hamid stopped for a moment, moderating his rage before he spoke again. 'All he knows how to do is talk and talk. Zameer and his kind are poison to my cause.' He pushed out of the pick-up's cab, shoving Kate aside as he moved to the front of the vehicle and raised the bonnet. 'Ignore him,' he spat, as he pulled at connections inside the engine, 'and be ready to move!'

Kate grimaced and climbed back into the flat bed, resting her stolen pistol on the roof of the Toyota's dented cab. She felt a tug on her ankle and looked down at Breeze slumping beneath her.

'Katie,' breathed the American. 'Hear that?' She fumbled at the jacket Kate had put around her shoulders, looking for something.

A blocky shape fell out of a pocket, buzzing quietly. Finn's sat phone.

Breeze picked it up and snapped it open before Kate could stop her, putting the device on speaker mode. 'Hostages R Us,' she said, with a feeble smirk, 'how may I direct your call?'

'*Who's this?*' Through static, Kate heard a man with a distinct Londoner's drawl on the other end of the line, and she felt a pang of hope. The man who had made threats and forced her to do their bidding had been a Russian. '*Identify yourself.*'

'Lillian Breeze, C-I-*goddamn*-A. Who the hell are you?'

'*Breeze? She's still alive!*' The comment was directed away, toward someone else.

'Not for long,' muttered the American.

The other voice returned. '*My name's Miles Todd,*' came the reply, '*I'm with the British Security Services. Where's Thomas Finn?*'

'Your pal sold us out. He's deader than disco, Miles.' The effort of speaking was hard on Breeze, and she cradled the phone close to her face. 'And we're up shit creek. Unless you wanna come get us?'

Kate faintly heard someone else in the background of the call, another male voice, but she couldn't pick out their words. Below her, Hamid eased the pick-up's bonnet back down, then glanced up. 'What are you doing? Who are you talking to?'

On impulse, Kate reached out and snatched the sat phone from Breeze's hand. 'This is Kate Hood, I'm the pilot,' she spoke quickly into the device, her words coming fast and breathless. 'My partner Alex Walker and his son, the men working with Finn abducted them!'

All she cared about was Alex and George – all she wanted in that moment was to hear them and to know they were alive – and a wave of relief engulfed her when Miles broke in.

'*They're here with us,*' he said. '*A bit beat up, but safe.*'

Hamid came to the back of the vehicle, pointing his rifle at her. 'End the call!'

'*Listen to me,*' said Miles, his tone becoming urgent. '*We know where you are. There's a missile strike inbound on your location, do you understand? Get out if you can, go now!*'

Hamid heard the words and his rifle dropped. He scowled. 'Of course. If the West cannot win a battle through guile, they scorch the earth!'

'*That's enough, gimme that,*' said the other voice, and the sat phone crackled as someone tore it out of the British agent's hands. '*Lillian? You there?*' When they spoke again, Kate recognised the hard growl of the rough-faced man Breeze had left behind at Ridley Hill.

'First names again, Harlan?' Breeze coughed. 'Must be serious. That Brit – is he on the level?'

'*Yeah.*' There was a pause. '*Sorry. But you know how the game is played.*'

'Prick.' Breeze shot back the insult, but it didn't matter. The line had already been cut.

'Can you start this thing or not?' Kate threw the demand at Hamid.

'It will run,' he replied.

'Then drive!' Kate felt a surge of renewed energy course through her, and she banged on the cab.

Alex and George were alive. She could see them again. This could be over.

If I can survive.

Hamid muttered a prayer under his breath before twisting the screwdriver once again. This time he was blessed with the rattle and thud of the pick-up's engine turning over.

Jamming the stick shift into gear with a crunch of metal on metal, he floored the accelerator and the ageing Toyota bounced forward with a roar of noise, kicking up dirt. Cloying black smoke vomited out of the broken exhaust and the vehicle came racing out of the alley and on to the cracked concrete apron in front of the hangars.

Immediately, a chorus of shouting and yelling kicked off from the northern end of the base, where Zameer's search party had assembled. Hamid had his assault rifle lying across his lap, and a notion crossed his mind to scatter them with a burst of gunfire, but he decided to conserve his meagre supply of ammunition for when they reached the aircraft.

He could see the executive jet, still standing where the pilot had left it hours before. The shadow of the Hawker was a series of hard angles, lit from within by blobs of light through the cabin windows. To get to it in a straight line meant crossing the overgrown median strip between the turning apron and the runway, and Hamid did not want to chance forcing the pick-up through the knots of dry scrub and over uneven ground. A single unseen pothole or a chunk of debris would be enough to stop them dead.

The Toyota complained as he pulled the steering round, the rear of the vehicle fishtailing into a juddering skid. There was barely any tread on the tyres and the engine stuttered and over-revved. The truck was one of dozens that al-Sakakin's fighters cannibalised to build what the Western military called 'technicals', turning the work-horse pick-ups into mobile platforms for heavy machine guns or troop carriers. This one had been left aside, and now Hamid understood why. The steering was mushy, the brakes barely worked and, from the odours it gave off, the truck was leaking as much oil as it burned.

But it didn't need to cross the desert for him. All Hamid needed was to get to the jet before the missile strike arrived.

He risked a look up into the night sky, as if he might see them coming, then chided himself. The American rockets would remain unseen until the last moments of their run, coming in low and swift over the terrain before leaping high to arc down and make their terminal attack.

Hamid had seen the aftermath left by a cruise missile once before – a blackened crater of fused sand and unidentifiable fragments of metal where a fighter outpost had once stood. Of the men who had been on that spot when the weapon hit, nothing remained, not even their ashes.

Such machines are an oppressor's tool, so the old imam had said, when Hamid and Nasir were still boys. *Only infidels would dare to field a weapon that mimics the wrath of God.*

A bullet shrieked off the pick-up's frame, shocking him out of the memory. Hamid turned the steering wheel, zig-zagging away down the apron as Zameer's men bracketed the vehicle with gunfire. For long seconds, he made it appear as if he was fleeing heedlessly toward the far end of the compound and away from the attackers, and then Hamid brought the truck around in a jerky skid, across an adjoining access route and on to the airstrip.

Behind him, the American woman complained loudly, but he paid her no heed. Quite how she was still alive was a mystery to him. Had it been his choice, Hamid would have helped Breeze to her inevitable end. But the pilot wanted her with them, and for now Hamid needed the pilot.

He heard pistol shots ring out from the flat bed as the British woman fired at the men running after them. She had little chance of hitting anything, but the same went for the gunmen. Sprays of red-orange muzzle flare flashed, and rounds clipped at the asphalt speeding beneath them. A hot ricochet keened off the cab roof and Hamid hunched forward against the wheel, as if he could *will* the vehicle to go faster.

They came up quickly on the jet, racing to meet it head-on. Hamid saw two men with rifles dithering at the open hatch near the front of the aircraft. One sprinted down the wing to get a better angle with his weapon, as the second man ducked under the fuselage for cover.

Hamid wanted to shoot but he did not dare risk it, for fear that a random shot might strike the jet and damage something vital. Timing his actions to the instant, he twisted the wheel so the pick-up veered off the faded white line bisecting the runway, and into another skidding turn.

The gunman near the wing saw the vehicle coming and realised too late what Hamid intended. The man tried to get out of the way but he wasn't quick enough to avoid being rammed by the Toyota's cracked grille. Broken by the massive impact, his body spun away into the weeds alongside the airstrip.

Hamid stamped on the brakes and snatched up his gun, storming out of the cab and into a jog while the vehicle slowed to a halt. Rifle up at his shoulder, aiming down its vertical iron sights, he swept around the jet's conical nose, searching for the next man to kill.

Kate's stomach twisted at the crunch of bone on steel as Hamid ran the first guard down, and she lost her handhold as the pick-up staggered to a halt alongside the Hawker.

She picked herself up from the flat bed, aware of Hamid leaving the cab with his rifle at the ready. The pistol she had liberated was empty and reluctantly she tossed it away.

'Breeze, come on,' she said, reaching for the American. 'We're here. All aboard.'

Breeze's breaths came in faint pops of air and her eyes were hazy. 'Right . . . behind us,' she managed.

Breeze was correct. The men chasing them were coming their way at a run, only slowing to fire shots in their direction.

'I know!' Kate grabbed her arm. 'So move your arse!'

'Nope. Won't. *Can't.*' Trembling, Breeze pulled open the jacket Kate had put around her, revealing the sticky, reeking, coppery mess it concealed. Dark, glistening crimson-black covered Breeze's side, her clothes saturated up to her chest and down her thigh. Bleed-out through the bandages over her belly wound pooled on the flat bed, soaking into the rough hessian of the empty sacks she lay on. 'There's more of me outside than in,' she coughed again, blood gathering at the corner of her mouth.

Kate tried to speak, but nothing came. All along she had been moving too fast to stop and consider that Lillian Breeze might not actually be able to make it to the plane. Now the reality of that reached out and sucked the pace from her.

'I've chased that monster for years,' said Breeze, her gaze slipping out of focus. 'For all the things he did, all the lives he took. Got away – every fuckin' time.' Breeze gripped Kate's hand tightly. 'He can't disappear again.'

'I—' Kate's voice dried up as Breeze let go, and the rise and fall of her chest stuttered to a halt.

Gunshots crackled on the other side of the aircraft and she heard a man scream, then a body fall. Hamid reappeared at the front of the jet and called out to her. 'What are you doing? Get in there!'

'Breeze—'

'Is dead, yes?' Hamid grabbed Kate by the arm and dragged her off the flat bed. 'I have no wish to join her, do you?' He raised the rifle and fired bursts across the back of the pick-up, in a vain attempt to slow their pursuers.

Kate climbed the steps on the hatch, half in a daze, half by instinct. She was aware of Hamid coming in behind her, still firing, picking off any attacker who came close, but it seemed to be happening at a great distance.

She sucked in a dry breath and shook off the hazy grip of shock, forging forward into the cockpit. The gunfire outside subsided and Kate wondered if, after everything that had happened, Zameer and his cohorts still wanted Hamid alive.

The pilot pushed that thought aside, taking her seat at the controls. The Hawker's systems were still in standby mode, and enough charge remained in the aircraft's batteries to bring it back to life.

The power unit whined as lights blinked on across the control panel, not all of them favourable. The damage the Hawker had suffered before would make take-off and flight difficult, but not impossible. Turbine blades began to spin, and the jet rocked forward, slowly picking up speed. The abandoned pick-up, with Breeze's body still aboard, disappeared from Kate's view. She gave the other woman a silent farewell.

The pilot heard Zameer's amplified voice shouting out, his tone turning furious, and Hamid answered back with the final rounds in his rifle. 'That is all,' he called from the vestibule, as he pulled the hatch shut. 'Now we live or die on your skill.'

'No pressure,' muttered Kate, dropping her hand to the throttle. Dull metal thuds sounded through the fuselage and she realised that the gunmen had given up on capturing them. Now they were firing at the jet.

She had no time to taxi to the end of the runway and set up for a full controlled roll-out and take-off. This would be a combat departure with the throttle all the way to the detent, in an aircraft that wasn't designed for such a thing. Kate double-checked the harness securing her to the seat and pushed power to the engines.

The Hawker's twin turbofans screamed in the thin desert air and the jet surged, wind buffeting the wings as it ate up the short runway. As their speed increased, she held tightly on the Y-shaped control yoke, willing the aircraft's nose to rise, praying silently for lift.

Then she saw them. Off in the middle distance but closing fast, two dark rods on flares of white fire coming in from the west, one leading the other.

Tomahawks.

TWENTY EIGHT

Nasir rocked in the back of the jeep as Zameer's driver raced the old man's vehicle over the cracked, pot-holed asphalt, almost running down their men in his haste to catch the jet before it could escape.

But the aircraft was already rolling down the runway, gathering speed as it crossed in front of them. His errant brother's transgressions were now complete and total: he had abandoned them.

'They are escaping!' Zameer stood up in his seat, bellowing in rage, the length of his grey-white beard whipping in the wind. 'Kill them! *Kill them!*' The old man glared down at Nasir, with eyes afire. 'You allowed this to happen! You let your bonds of family blind you to his offences!'

Zameer's hot breath reeked of stale tobacco and Nasir scowled back at him. 'I did no such thing—'

'Liar!' Zameer's rage was out of control, and he smacked Nasir around the head, like a teacher disciplining a troublesome student. 'You have always been irresolute where Hamid was concerned!' He jabbed a finger at him. 'You should have let Malik break his neck! You shame me, you shame al-Sakakin, and you shame God himself with your faults!'

But Nasir was no longer listening to the older man's spittle-flecked ranting. His gaze was caught by a blaze of smoky white light in the air above and the echo of strange thunder off the distant sides of the valley.

The first of the cruise missiles hurtled by in a blur, the crackling rocket motor passing over the Hawker as the rolling jet reached the mid-point of the airstrip.

Kate fought the impulse to turn her head and watch the weapon hit, but still the impact lit up the night like a brief flicker of daybreak.

Guided in by coordinates drawn from satellite imagery, the lead missile roared over the heads of their pursers and struck the airfield's central buildings, the stubby control tower, the barracks and the block where Kate and the others had been held captive. Its penetrator warhead drilled into the foundations before it detonated, fire bursting up from beneath the structures like a volcanic eruption.

The shockwave threw up debris and fractured concrete, briefly compacting the air into an expanding ring of white vapour that swept over the airfield, knocking down anyone on their feet and slamming on to the fleeing jet with the force of a charging rhino.

Kate felt the Hawker jerk sideways, and she fought it, putting all she had into raising the nose. The juddering undercarriage left the ground as the second Tomahawk made its death-dive through the blossoming dust cloud created by the first.

The trailing missile dove into the far end of the runway, where the satellites had pegged the location of the parked jet. The Hawker wasn't there any more, but Zameer, Nasir and the men with them were. They perished without time to scream as the missile tore open asphalt, earth and sandstone.

The second shockwave hit the jet with enough force to whip Kate's head back and forwards against the seatback, sending a bolt of livid agony down her neck. The Hawker's nose dipped alarmingly, but she countered by forcing it into a sharp, climbing turn, fighting it every last degree with more power from the engines.

'Fly, you bugger!' she shouted, *'Fly!'*

Green indicators on the control board answered back by flicking to amber and bright red. The jet's yoke vibrated under her hands and every dial Kate looked at had something bad to tell her.

Twitchy with adrenaline, she fumbled at the navigation panel, forcing herself to keep her fingers steady as she stabbed out commands on the illuminated keypad. As the plane banked, she caught sight of the glow of fires on the ground through the canopy's side window.

From the inky darkness of the night sky, it was hard to pick out detail, but it was clear that the airfield had been ruined, scoured from the face of the world in a brief and terrible hell storm.

Kate forced herself to look away and not dwell on Lillian Breeze, on the co-pilot Ray and the dead men they were leaving behind. The Hawker was up, and they were flying. But how long that would last was a question she didn't have the answer for. The jet was losing fuel and hydraulic fluid at an alarming rate, something that could only have been caused by multiple bullet punctures through the fuselage.

She straightened out the turn as best she could, finding the jet on a swift northerly heading toward the Algerian coastline and the Alboran Sea beyond. Kate frowned as she tried to calculate their fuel consumption, hearing movement back in the rear cabin.

'We live,' said Hamid, as he made his way on to the flight deck. 'Once more, you prove your worth.'

'Yeah, well, you can take your praise and shove it,' she replied coldly. 'I should have kicked you off and left you behind to cook with the rest of your shit-bag mates.'

Hamid chuckled, entertained by her resentment. 'But you did not, because you are not capable of that act.' He climbed into the co-pilot's seat once again, scowling at the warning lights. 'I know your kind, Hood. You can kill when it is as easy as pushing a button to drop a bomb on a faceless target. But when you have to look your enemy in the eye? Your will is lacking.'

She couldn't find a response – on some level Kate knew he was right. Tonight she had used a gun in anger. She had shot at men who wanted her dead, but it was still at a remove. It was impersonal and distanced. And, after all of that, she still hadn't been able to save Breeze's life.

Hamid leaned forward, studying the map screen. 'We must leave this area as quickly as possible, before the Americans come to check on their handiwork.' He smiled slightly. 'In a way, they have done me a service. They have disposed of the dead wood.'

'Your brother was down there.'

He shrugged. 'Nasir made his choice. And he has paid for it.'

Kate expected nothing more. If Hamid was true to anything, it was only his ruthless sense of self-preservation.

She turned back to the controls, studying the flickering digital map, thinking aloud. 'The nearest airport we can approach is to the west, at Nador-Al Aaroui across the Moroccan border.' She looked in that direction. 'They have a long runway there; I can declare an emergency.'

'And deliver me into the hands of the very enemies I sought to escape?' Hamid shook his head. 'No. You will maintain this heading across the water.' He fiddled with the map display, shifting the image, and Kate sensed he was piecing together a plan of action as it came to him. 'There is an airfield in southern Spain, in the Sierra de Tejeda range. I have contacts in that region.'

Kate considered telling Hamid that it was unlikely the Hawker would make it that far, or that the Spanish Air Force would scramble its F/A-18 Hornet interceptors to shoot them down if they appeared on radar – all probable fates for the wounded jet. Instead, she asked the more pertinent question: 'Why the hell would I do anything you say?'

Hamid cocked his head, watching the thin line of the coast as it passed beneath the Hawker's wings. 'Because those you care for are not safe from me. Al-Sakakin could find them before, and I will have them found again. Let us say you take us to Morocco, say that I am arrested and incarcerated once more. Do you think that will make you safe from me? The equation has not changed. Your lover and his son will die screaming if you do not take me to safety. That is the bargain that was struck tonight, yes?'

He delivered his ultimatum with cool arrogance. Beside Kate sat a man who lived a life soaked in violence, willing to do anything and everything to justify his twisted, odious impulses. In that moment, she saw right through – finally – to who Hamid *really* was.

'You do what you do and you say it's about a God and a religion,' she told him, 'but it isn't. That's a mask you wear, the same way you wore Yusuf's identity. That man Zameer knew it, didn't he? That's why he wanted you gone. You use that lie to justify the horrible actions you commit; the murders and the bombings. You do it because, deep down, you're not really a believer. You're just a stunted little fucker with a black heart full of hatred.'

Anger flashed in Hamid's eyes, but then he looked away. 'Perhaps so. But I am still the one in control here.'

Breeze's last words echoed in Kate's mind. *He can't disappear again.*

She fell silent, the moment stretching as they flew on into the darkness over the sea. Kate knew Hamid *would* disappear, if by some miracle they made it to landfall in Spain. He would kill her the moment they touched down. He would vanish into the shadows, gather those still loyal to him and resurface in a few months at the head of another terrorist atrocity. And Kate would have allowed it to happen.

'No,' she said, at length. 'You're not in control. *I am.*'

Her right arm shot out and she punched Hamid in the head with as much force as she could muster, slamming his face against the control panel. Then, before he could recover from the blow, Kate rammed the flight yoke all the way forward.

The Hawker's engines shrieked as the nose dipped sharply, and the jet fell into a terminal dive toward the wave-tops rolling beneath them.

Hamid reeled back in the co-pilot's chair, his face a mask of red from a free-flowing gash across his forehead. The G-force of the jet's full-speed descent pressed both of them into the backs of their seats, but still he tried to clutch at her, clawing wildly at Kate's arm as he cursed and yelled.

Starlight glittered over the surface of the water, giving it the look of a sheet of beaten silver, and Kate focused her attention on sending the Hawker into its embrace. She remembered the off-hand threat she'd made earlier, to crash the jet into the sea and end this whole damned nightmare of a flight. Now that promise would consume her.

With a cry of effort, Hamid pitched across the flight deck's centre console and grabbed her, landing a powerful punch in Kate's stomach and pulling at the yoke. As she reacted, the Hawker's nose came up, but it was too late to stop the inevitable.

Even with its terminal trajectory flattening, it was impossible to pull away in time. The jet's damaged underside struck the wave-tops with a stunning crash of splitting metals. For one dizzying second, the Hawker skipped over the sea, and then a line of fracture from the collision opened a jagged rent in the starboard wing root. Conduits, cables, framework and skin peeled back and the wing tore off, flicking up and away.

Still moving forward as it slowed against the resistance of the waves, the Hawker's fuselage rolled over, its portside wing coming up like the sail of a racing yacht. On the flight deck, Kate twisted upwards, held in her seat by the safety restraint belts. Hamid had no such protection, dragged away from her by gravity to fall downward against the starboard panels.

Shock made her shiver, and she swallowed back vomit. Kate's chest, arms and joints seethed with pain from the force of the impact. She tasted blood in her mouth and let out a ragged cough.

The stricken jet listed in the swell as the last of its forward velocity bled away. Then it tilted sharply backwards, the tail falling and the nose rising, as the heavy engines clustered at the rear of the Hawker pulled it down.

Behind her, Kate heard the percussive gush of seawater flowing into the passenger cabin, punching its way through the damage done by the lost wing. As the cabin flooded, the jet's weight increased. It would quickly be dragged under the waves and, if it didn't break apart, all the way to the bottom of the Mediterranean shallows.

Hamid rolled off the panels and skidded to the back of the flight deck, still alive and still mobile despite Kate's hopes to the contrary. He growled in pain, clutching at a broken wrist, but the sound shifted abruptly. The terrorist laughed at her.

'Incredible,' he snorted, wiping blood from his face. 'I have taught my lessons well. You learned, Hood! You learned from me! Finally you are willing to kill your enemy, even if you lose your life in the act.'

Is he right? The question burned like the pain across her body. *This mad, suicidal gesture. It is what he would do!*

Kate twisted, working the release on the safety restraints as the jet's nose rose slowly toward the vertical, the lights on the control panel flickering and dying.

He can still get out, she realised. The escape hatch over the wing was awash, but the main boarding door was above the waterline. *He can reach it and slip away. He can still disappear.*

'It will not be enough,' Hamid told her, as if intuiting her thoughts. 'I have not come this far to be ended by the likes of you. Be assured – when I am safe and this is over, I will make sure those you love pay for your defiance.' Then, without giving her another moment of consideration, he scrambled down the steepening incline of the deck and into the vestibule, clutching at handholds.

Looking back – looking down at him now – Kate could make out Hamid's shadowed form as he worked at the boarding hatch's emergency release mechanism. Beneath him, briny water churned and frothed as it continued to fill the cabin.

In that second, Kate had never hated anyone as much as she hated Hamid. Not those martinets who had shredded her dreams of flying fast jets, not the man who had told her he loved her and lied to her face, not the people who had used her and threatened her with the mistakes of her past.

Hamid was all that stood between Kate and peace. He was too lethal to be let back out into the world. Not just to her, or to Alex and George, but to anyone unlucky enough to be caught in the firing line of his rage.

Kate rolled off the back of her seat and dropped down the flight deck, the floor and the ceiling now the walls, the rear bulkhead now beneath her feet. She clipped the frame of the safety door as she fell, scoring a nasty wound on her shin, but the pain was a brief flash of sensation as she passed through the gap and slammed full tilt into Hamid.

The force of the impact tore him away from the half-opened boarding hatch and both of them crashed into the stinging, night-cold water filling the back of the cabin.

Coiling about one another, Kate and Hamid went under, trading sluggish blows and kicks, the flood around them choked with floating debris. Strange pulses of colour illuminated the water, blood-shade crimson glowing from the remaining navigation light and white flashes from the anti-collision strobe.

Hamid loomed over her and bellowed, air frothing out of his mouth in a foam of bubbles and furious sound. He punched at her torso and Kate felt the knife-stab of a rib cracking.

She knew that if she ran out of air, if she had to go back up to the surface, he would win this fight. Her only allies were speed and violence.

He doesn't think you're capable of fighting back, said a voice in her head, a voice that sounded like Lillian Breeze's sarcastic drawl. *Prove him wrong.*

Ignoring the burning in her lungs, Kate clawed at Hamid's face, jabbing her thumbs into his eyes. Then she grabbed his shoulders and forced him down deeper into the cold seawater, putting her full weight on him as he flailed madly.

In the flashes of light, Kate saw a line of nylon cargo netting adrift around them, floating up from where it was tethered to the deck.

She snatched the closest handful of net and pulled it across, bunching it up, wrapping it around Hamid's thrashing arm. He tried to jerk free, but it had the opposite effect, stirring the water and dragging up more of the nylon webbing. He saw what she was trying to do and landed another brutal blow in her belly. She lost her breath in a rush of air bubbles and fought down the urge to flee.

Kate pushed hard against the cabin wall and heaved the cargo net over Hamid's head. Every fibre in her body screamed for breath, begging her to swim away. She twisted the line around Hamid's neck and kicked him in the head, shooting upward with the force of impact.

He grabbed at her ankle and tried to pull her back down, but Hamid was caught between trying to save himself and taking Kate with him. For an instant, she feared he would let himself die just to make her pay for fighting back, but then her foot cracked him across the nose and he let go, struggling frantically to free himself as the Hawker sank deeper.

Kate's head and shoulders burst out of the water. The flooding had risen to the level of the vestibule, with another torrent streaming now in through the half-open boarding hatch. As a last act, she grabbed the day-glow yellow mass of a life vest floating nearby and put her shoulder into the hatch, screaming with effort as she forced it open wide enough to drag herself through.

The pull of a wave caught her, shoving her away from the sinking wreck. She managed to tug the vest over her head and secure it. Pulling the inflation toggle, compressed air filled the yellow bladder around her neck and torso, automatically righting her to a head-up position.

She could only float in the peak and trough of the shallow waves and watch as the Hawker submerged. The crumpled pinnacle of the jet's nose cone retreated into a slick of oil and loose debris floating on the surface. With a last outgassing of air, like a sad exhalation of breath, it went under.

Kate stared fixedly at the spot where the plane sank as the cold of the sea crept through her clothes and her flesh, pushing its way into her bones. Her numbed, shaking hands found a shard of broken aluminium fuselage floating among the wreckage and she held it tightly, barely registering the sharp edges against her palm.

She waited for what seemed like forever; waited for the water to froth and eject a furious Hamid back into the air. Ready to bury her makeshift dagger in his throat. Ready to look him in the eye and kill him, if that was what it would take.

But that moment never came, and slowly Kate allowed herself to accept that her ordeal might be over. She let go of the metal shard and it drifted away.

Triggered by immersion in the water, the flotation vest's automatic emergency light and locator beacon blinked into action, broadcasting a signal that would be picked up by any ships in the area. If someone had seen the Hawker go down – if a vessel was close enough to get to her in the next couple of hours – she might still win the race before hypothermia set in. *But if not . . .*

Kate pushed that dark thought away, into the depths. She sank back, her aching neck pressed against the vest's thick collar, and looked up at the cloudless night filling the sky above her, from horizon to horizon.

Stars shone diamond-bright up there, and she let out a gasp. The hot streaks of tears lined Kate's face over her pale, cold cheeks, and finally she found the brightest glow above; the resolute light of Polaris.

Smiling, as she thought of Alex's warm touch on her hands and the sound of George's laughter, Kate closed her eyes and waited for the dawn.

Acknowledgments

Writing a book can often feel like flying a plane – working to get air under the wings and keeping things at altitude to go the distance – but while the author is the pilot, there's always a big crew of people who help to keep everything airborne with provision in personal and professional capacities.

With that in mind, my eternal thanks go to Mandy Mills, Pauline Swallow and all my friends for their ceaseless moral and emotional support. Thanks to Robert Kirby, Kate Walsh and all at United Agents. Thanks to Jon Elek, James Horobin, Jennifer Edgecombe and everybody on the team at Welbeck and Headline. And thank you to Ben Aaronovitch, Rowland White, Mike Sutton, Trevor Paglen, Jim Risher and James Ilecr for vital technical back-up and research materials (any errors in this book are either artistic licence or mine to shoulder!)

Lastly, thanks also to Biggin Hill Airport, *Business Jet Traveller*, Embraer, Flight Frames Aviation, Flightstore, Guardian Jet, *The Intercept*, Privaira, Private Jet Coach, Skybridge Space, SkyService, South and Down Under, and Textron Aviation for their invaluable resources.

About the Author

James Swallow is a *New York Times, Sunday Times* and Amazon no. 1 bestselling author, and a BAFTA-nominated scriptwriter. He is a former journalist and the award-winning writer of over sixty books, including *Airside* and the critically acclaimed Marc Dane thrillers, *Tom Clancy's Splinter Cell* and many more, along with numerous scripts for radio, television and games.

He lives in London and is currently working on his next novel. Find him online at jswallow.com.